About the Author

Michelle Betham is a media technician turned author of contemporary romance, with a kick!

Addicted to binge-watching TV dramas she struggles to think of a life before Netflix, loves rock music, tattoos, spicy food, and Keanu Reeves - a crush that's lasted over twenty years, and one she blames entirely on 'Point Break'.

Her dream is to ride a Harley. And visit Las Vegas. And be able to eat any amount of chocolate without putting on weight...

She lives in County Durham, north-east England, with her husband and West Highland Terrier, where she can be found most days drinking tea and making up stories.

D0491039

Shirley Valentine Goes to Vegas

MICHELLE BETHAM

All rights reserved. No part of this publication may be reproduced, stored in a retrieval system, or transmitted, in any form or by any means, electronic, mechanical, photocopying, recording or otherwise, without the prior permission of the publishers.

Harper*Impulse* an imprint of
HarperCollins*Publishers* Ltd
1 London Bridge Street
London SE1 9GF

www.harpercollins.co.uk

A Paperback Original 2015

First published in Great Britain in ebook format by Harper*Impulse* 2015

Copyright © Michelle Betham 2015

Cover images © Shutterstock.com

Michelle Betham asserts the moral right
to be identified as the author of this work

A catalogue record for this book is
available from the British Library

ISBN: 9780008119447

This novel is entirely a work of fiction.
The names, characters and incidents portrayed in it are
the work of the author's imagination. Any resemblance to
actual persons, living or dead, events or localities is
entirely coincidental.

Automatically produced by Atomik ePublisher from Easypress

Printed and bound in Great Britain

LANCASHIRE COUNTY LIBRARY	
3011813303614 9	
Askews & Holts	14-Dec-2015
AF GEN	£8.99
ECL	

For everyone who believes in a little bit of fate...

And to Helen at Indigo Rose, thank you, for giving me the tattoo of my dreams.

Prologue

Dragging the suitcase down from the top of the wardrobe I threw it onto the bed, standing back as it hit the mattress with a resounding thud. For a couple of seconds I just looked at it as if, all of a sudden, I'd temporarily forgotten just what the hell it was I was doing. Was that deliberate? Was that actually my own subconscious giving me a little bit more time to think about everything? To make sure this really was the right thing to do?

Leaning back against the wall, I closed my eyes, breathing in deeply. My heart was still beatingfast, pounding away inside my chest as I tried to shut out the noise drifting up from the party going on downstairs: a party I should be getting back to. But I couldn't. Not now.

'… *this is just something she needs to get out of her system…*'

His words were playing over and over in my head like some never-ending record I couldn't switch off.

'*She loves me, and she knows I need her to do certain things if this is going to work a second time…*'

Yeah. I loved him. But did I love him enough? Enough to strip myself of everything I'd fought so hard to become?

I slowly opened my eyes, taking another deep breath, my gaze falling back on the empty suitcase.

'Lana?'

I swung around so quickly I almost lost my balance, my breath catching in my throat as I saw him standing there.

'What's going on?'

'I'm leaving, Adam.' I'd thought my resolve would weaken the second I saw him, but I was obviously stronger than I thought I was. 'And this time, I'm not coming back.'

1

My brother, Finn, slid something a rather startling shade of orange towards me.

'What's that?' I asked, eyeing the drink warily.

'A cocktail.'

I threw him a withering look. 'Yeah. I can see that. It's what's in it that's bothering me. What *is* in it?'

He shrugged. 'No idea. Just thought you might like one, you know, you being a woman and all that.'

My withering look turned into a wide-eyed stare. 'Seriously?'

He shrugged, a look of mock innocence on his face.

'When have you ever known me to drink cocktails, Finn? When?'

'Just get it down you. Might help you loosen up a bit.'

I loved Finn. I loved him a lot, despite his knack of being able to wind me up at a moment's notice. But he'd always been able to do that, right from when we'd been kids and he'd realised how easily I could be sucked in.

At thirty-five years old Finn was four years younger than me. And with his short, dark, messed-up hair, a multitude of tattoos that adorned his entire body, and a black and red Ducati Multistrada that I was extremely jealous of, he was handsome in that rough, edgy, rock-star kind of way – a bit of a cross between a younger version of Aerosmith's Steven Tyler and The Foo Fighters' Dave Grohl – which meant he was never short of female attention. And the fact he was also one of the most reputable tattoo artists in the north-east of England didn't do him any harm, either. His studio – Black Ink – saw people travel to Newcastle-upon-Tyne from as far afield as Cumbria, north Yorkshire, and even Scotland, to be 'inked' by my brother. I was incredibly proud of him. Even more so after everything he'd done for me over the past twelve months. He'd been my rock. The best friend I could have asked for. Because the past twelve months had seen my life change in a way I could never have anticipated. A year ago I'd walked out on my husband, and left behind the only life I'd known for almost two decades; a decision that hadn't been an easy one to make, because Adam was a good man. We'd been together almost twenty years, and been married for eighteen of those. I'd thought I'd found my soul mate. But sometimes, even when – or should that be *especially* when – you've been together for as long as we had, people can grow apart. They lose each other. And when neither of them really make that effort to find their way back, well, it stops working. There's no point any more if the fight has gone.

We'd started wanting different things – or, in my case, things I'd always dreamed of, but thought I could never have. Those things I'd put to the back of my mind whilst I'd concentrated on doing what everybody else wanted me to do, instead of doing things that actually made me happy. I guess I'd just wanted an easy life. But now I considered 'easy' to be dull. Now I wanted a bit more excitement. Was that selfish of me? Maybe. But when you know you're not the person you really want to be, there comes a point when you either accept that this is the way things are always going to be or you realise the stone-cold reality that you only get one life, and you've got to go out and live it. That's exactly what I'd done. I'd moved in with Finn, got to know my brother again, and gradually started putting my life back together. By changing it completely.

'Can I just have a beer?' I asked, still warily eyeing the cocktail. 'I mean, do I look like the kind of woman who'd drink something that colour?'

'Lana, there were nights when you'd drink anything of any colour, remember? As long as it got the end result you were looking for.'

I couldn't argue with that. There'd been times when I could have quite easily reached for the mouthwash, but I was past all of that now.

As kids, I'd always been slightly jealous of Finn, of the way he just seemed to know exactly what he wanted to do. His fascination with tattoos had started as a teenager, and after he'd got his first one on his eighteenth birthday that had sealed the deal for him – he knew where his life was going. I'd always been less decisive, finally letting my love of the theatre guide me in the direction of a BTEC in performing arts and an eventual job as a deputy stage manager in a theatre in Newcastle. A job I'd walked out on the same day I'd walked out on Adam. I didn't do things by halves, that was for sure. But I'd had to cut those ties, leave behind the old so I could start the new. Any remnants of the past would have only held me back.

I'd started hanging out at Black Ink, watching Finn and the guys work, soaking up the atmosphere that I'd never really paid that much attention to before, because I'd never really seen all that much of Finn after I'd married Adam. We'd moved out of Newcastle and settled in north Northumberland, but it wasn't just distance that had seen me lose touch with my brother. Our worlds became very different, and we'd inevitably drifted apart, coming together only for the obligatory family weddings, birthdays and Christmases. But the more I hung out at Black Ink, the more I began to realise that Finn's world was where I really felt comfortable. It was the kind of world I wanted to be a part of – a world where people didn't judge. A world where it was okay to be different. It was the world I'd always dreamt of. I just hadn't realised it, until now.

So, just a few days after walking out on my marriage, I began putting the wheels of my brand-new life in motion by doing something the old Lana would never have done – I got "inked". By Finn. Twice. A beautiful tribal design in deep black that covered the underside of my left forearm, and a deep-red rose emerging from a mass of tangled thorns on my upper right arm. Finn had been a little unsure, at first, about being the one to permanently tattoo his once rather straight-laced and conservative sister, but he understood I'd needed to do something drastic to kick-start my new journey. To give my life the complete turnaround it needed. But, looking back, I suppose it had been a bit of a shock for him to see the speed at which I'd turned from wife of one of the region's top businessmen to tattooed biker chick. It had unnerved *me* for a day or two, but just two weeks after getting those new tattoos, changing my hair, acquiring a whole new set of friends and an attitude I hadn't even known I'd had, I'd made another decision. I was truly fascinated by the work my brother and the guys at Black Ink did, but I wanted to play a bigger part than just observing. I needed a new career, something to aim for, and, after talking to Finn and going over the options, the decision was made – Finn was going to take me on as his apprentice. I was going to train to become a tattoo artist. It meant I could stay close to my brother and stay inside that world I'd fallen in love with.

I'd spend hours at the studio watching, in complete awe, as Finn created intricate and beautiful designs on a wide variety of clients, each tattoo different and personal. From deep blacks to colours so vivid they almost jumped off the skin, there was so much beauty in body art, which was why that tattoo Finn had given me on my upper right arm had now turned into a sleeve, covering the skin from the wrist, stretching all the way up over my shoulder. It was the most beautiful thing I'd ever seen – from the multitude of colours that ranged from bright oranges and aqua blues and the rich, dark red of bloodied roses, to the way it snaked across my skin, the designs merging, fading in and out of one another; intertwining, blending. In my eyes, every single inch of it signalled a move forward from a life that had once stifled me, into one that was slowly setting me free. As I'd watched it take shape, felt that needle dig into my skin, it really had felt as though that tattoo was wiping away the past and ushering in my new future. It had taken weeks to complete, but just watching Finn work on it had been an almost cathartic experience.

It was going to take a couple of years before I became a fully qualified tattooist myself, but I woke up every day now just itching to get to work. And I hadn't felt like that in a long time. The people who came into Black Ink, the heavy rock music that blasted out of speakers placed all around the two floors of the studio; the whole atmosphere of the place – it really did feel as though, somehow, I'd found my spiritual home. It was somewhere I'd always wanted to be but had never had the confidence to seek out before because I'd spent most of my life "settling". Whilst Adam had been quite happy to let our lives "tick along", the thought of that going on for years to come had, in the end, terrified me. I hadn't wanted my life to "tick along" anymore – I wanted to live it and, with Finn's help, I was getting there.

Even though this weekend in Las Vegas – at one of the biggest tattoo conventions in the world – was something of a busman's holiday for me, Finn and the rest of the guys from Black Ink, after the year I'd had I was hoping it was going to give me a chance to kick back, cut loose for a little while, even if it was only for a couple of days. The past few months had been exhausting, and though I barely recognised the woman I'd used to be, I still felt as though there was a tiny bit more shaking off to be done. And this weekend, I intended to do a lot of shaking. Right now, I wasn't totally feeling the Vegas vibe, but I was probably just tired. We'd not long arrived at the hotel, it was late, and it had been a long day.

'Here. Is this more your kind of thing?' Finn handed me a bottle of Budweiser.

I smiled at him. 'Thank you.'

'You're welcome. Now drink your beer, beautiful.'

He always called me beautiful, and I loved him for that, even if he was probably just saying it because I was his sister. I'd just never felt all that comfortable blowing my own trumpet, that was all, so I'd never really thought of myself as beautiful, though Adam had often told me I was. And I suppose I *could* scrub up pretty well when I put the effort in. I'd managed to keep my long blonde hair in pretty good condition, despite the amount of styling products it had seen over the years, and a good few inches of it, from the bottom up, had been dyed black now, which I loved. My eyes were a bit more grey than blue, but I'd never seen that as a negative. And my body wasn't looking too bad for a woman hurtling towards middle-age, and by that I mean I could still rock a bikini on holiday as long as I laid off the doughnuts for a couple of weeks beforehand. Or have a complete mid-life meltdown, leave my husband and throw my old life away to head off into the unknown. Both had much the same effect as far as weight loss was concerned.

'And start enjoying yourself,' Finn went on. 'We're in Vegas, remember?'

I picked up my beer and took a large, probably slightly unla-dylike, swig.

'I *am* enjoying myself,' I protested, throwing him a look.

He threw one right back. 'You might want to try telling your face that, then.'

I ignored him, taking another swig of beer. 'I might have an early night,' I sighed, running my finger up and down the ice-cold bottle, watching as it left a trail of condensation in its wake.

Finn almost choked on his own drink. 'Early night? Do you know where we are?'

I blinked a few times as I looked at him. 'I'm well aware of where we are, thank you. You keep reminding me every five minutes.'

Finn's eyes widened as he stared at me. 'And?'

I frowned. 'And what?'

'Where *are* we?'

'How many beers have you had?'

'We're in Las Vegas,' Finn went on, completely ignoring my question.

'Yes, I know we are. I was on that plane this morning, too.'

'So, people come to Vegas to party.'

'Do they? *All* of them?'

'You're giving me a headache now.'

'That's my job.' I took another long drink of beer, looking around the busy bar. The music was loud, the atmosphere everything I loved. I just knew I'd love it a whole lot more when I didn't feel so tired. I was such a lightweight sometimes. I turned back to face my brother. 'I'm just a bit tired, okay? It's been a really long day. I'm sure I'll be much more my usual self after a good night's sleep.'

'You're really having an early night?' Finn asked, his expression verging on disbelief.

I ran a hand along the back of my neck as I took another look around me. I'd noticed a small group of bikers come in earlier, and they were still there, hanging out in the corner of the bar, dressed in leather and denim with their messed-up hair and unkempt beards. Sexy as hell in my eyes. The fact I found that kind of man sexy now was weird, because my husband had been a clean-shaven businessman who loathed tattoos, hated facial hair and didn't really trust bikers. Which was why he and Finn had never really been that close. Their two worlds were so far apart it had been hard for them to find any common ground. Another reason why my brother and I had drifted apart.

Secretly, though, I'd always found the idea of a hot, tattooed, bearded, rough-looking bloke on a motorbike incredibly attractive. Even more so since I'd started hanging out with Finn and working at Black Ink. It was just that now I didn't have to make a secret out of it. And I couldn't help smiling to myself as I realised that.

'What's distracting *you*?' Finn asked, frowning slightly as he noticed my expression change.

'Nothing.' I quickly tried to lose the smirk, but I wasn't quick enough.

Finn turned around, looking over at the bikers in the corner, a slow grin spreading across his face. 'Oh, I get it. Still after that biker boyfriend, huh?'

I didn't reply. Just took one last drink of beer.

'I've told you, kiddo. Bobby could fix you up with any number of our mates from the club. They all love a hot, inked woman. Have a word with him. I'm sure once we're home he'll sort you out.'

I wrinkled my nose up at the thought of Bobby – Finn's number two at Black Ink – and his biker friends. Lovely guys, but not really the hot-and-handsome type. Their bikes were pretty sexy, though, but that's where the attraction ended. 'You've somehow managed to make all of that sound slightly sleazy.' I slid down from my stool and kissed Finn quickly on the cheek. 'I'm off to bed.'

'Alone?'

'You're hilarious.'

'Well, you've got to pass 'Sons of Anarchy' over there on your way out. Who knows what might happen between here and your hotel room.'

'I'll see you in the morning,' I said, acknowledging him only by raising my hand, without looking back. I was too busy concentrating on where I was going as I headed for the door, passing the group of bikers on the way. I was aware of a low whistle coming from their direction as I passed them, and although I didn't have the nerve to look back and check, I was going to hope it was aimed at me. I'd worked hard to cultivate this biker-babe image. It'd be nice to get some appreciation from the men who mattered. But as I finally headed out of the bar, I felt the hairs on the back of my neck suddenly stand on end, the weirdest feeling washing over me.

I wasn't sure where that had come from, or why it had happened, but as the loud music and the party atmosphere still emanating from the bar surrounded me, I suddenly began to feel the Vegas vibe kick in. Big time. And I smiled to myself again. Yeah. I was going to be so ready for this weekend after a good night's sleep. I mean, this was Vegas! And I might only be here for a couple of days, but who knew what could happen in that time? I just had no idea that what was about to happen was going to shake my life up even more – in ways I couldn't begin to imagine...

2

'This place is crazy!' I gasped, turning right around on the heels of my Harley Davidson biker boots, taking in the huge space filled with people sporting all manner of tattoos, every colour of the rainbow, every shade of black and grey adorning bodies both male and female. There were booths and stalls set out all around the vast area given over to this convention; I could even see places where you could get a brand-new tattoo right there and then, and I was tempted. Wildly oversized TV screens were also everywhere you looked, all of them show-casing the very best the world of ink had to offer. I felt like I'd come home. And, as expected, the Vegas vibe was really kicking in now. A good night's sleep had seen to that.

'I still can't believe you and Adam never came here. To Vegas.' Finn stuck his hands into the pockets of his skinny black jeans as he followed me further into the room. 'You seem to have been everywhere else on the planet.'

'He was never that keen,' I said, still trying to take in everything that was going on around me. 'And when you're married you tend to compromise on things like holidays. Not that you'd know anything about that.' I threw my brother a half-smile. He just pulled a face.

'Why would I want to get married, huh? And disappoint the female population of the north-east of England?'

'Yeah. You keep telling yourself that.'

He winked at me. I just rolled my eyes. 'Anyway, sis, if you're talking compromise, then surely he could've suffered Vegas for a couple of days? For you?'

'Not seeing Vegas was a sacrifice I was willing to make, Finn. Because Adam and me, we visited so many other amazing places together. Just, not *this* amazing place.' I let my mind briefly jump back in time, to those holidays Adam and I had shared, before things had started to go stale. Stagnate. Before we'd started to drift apart, and a little piece of me felt sad that we hadn't been able to cling onto those times, because we'd been so happy. Once.

'Why did you marry him, Lana?'

I turned to face my brother, cocking my head and frowning slightly. That was a question I hadn't been expecting. 'I loved him, Finn. And things weren't always as bad as they ended up being.'

'I never really took to him,' Finn sniffed, sliding his arm across my shoulders as we ventured further into the room. 'I mean, he's like Mister Straight-Laced businessman, all clean-shaven and well-spoken. And then there's you.'

I stood still, folding my arms and fixing Finn with a look that almost dared him to say something he might regret. But I couldn't help smiling, so the stern edge had been slightly lost there. And what he was saying was largely true anyway – Adam *was* a bit straight-laced, always smartly dressed, and *always* clean-shaven, even at weekends. And his accent *was* a touch milder than mine, with him hailing from rural Northumberland rather than the heart of Newcastle. But it wasn't like he'd been brought up in Downtown bloody Abbey.

'Then there's you…' Finn carried on, grinning just a touch too widely for my liking, '… with your black-dipped blonde hair and all those tattoos.'

I didn't say anything to that, my gaze suddenly dropping to the floor.

Finn tilted my chin up so I was looking at him. 'What's wrong?'

'The divorce. It came through, just before we flew out here.'

Finn ran a hand through his hair, throwing his head back and sighing heavily. 'Jesus, Lana, I'm sorry. I didn't know.'

I shrugged. 'I didn't really want to talk about it. Anyway, it's over now. Time to put it completely behind me, once and for all.' I slipped my hand into his, smiling again as I stood up on tiptoes to kiss him quickly. 'And anyway, before I started hanging out with you I was Miss Ordinary, remember? This hair and these tattoos, they were non-existent until my marriage started to break down. Until I finally threw off those shackles of normality and joined the freak show that is your world.'

He smiled at me, slipping his arm back around my shoulders and squeezing them tight. 'Yeah. And now there's no escaping the dark side.'

'I quite like the dark side.' I hugged his waist, leaning in against him as we walked. 'Daylight scares me.'

'Weirdo.'

'I learned from the best.'

'Yeah. And don't ever forget that. Come on.' He took my hand, pulling me towards a stand that was manned by one of his heroes – a legendary Vegas-based tattoo artist from whom Finn had gained a lot of inspiration due to his edgy designs and use of colour. Finn's tattoo studio back home had a bit of a reputation for cutting-edge ink itself, and it was something he prided himself on, which was why so many people made that special journey to be "inked" by Finn Black and why I was so excited to be serving my apprenticeship under him. He was an incredible teacher. An amazing tattooist. The best brother I could have asked for, at a time when I really needed one.

'Do they do drinks in here?' I gasped, out of breath at trying to keep up with Finn's brisk pace.

'And she's back.' Finn pulled a few dollars from the back pocket of his jeans. 'The bar's just out there. Get me a beer, will you?'

'What did your last slave die of?'

He threw me a wink. 'I don't have slaves, kiddo. I have willing participants.'

I couldn't help smiling at him, rolling my eyes again before I turned and made my way across the crowded space in search of the bar. Catching sight of it, I pushed my way through the maze of people, almost throwing myself against the counter with relief as I ordered a couple of beers.

'That's not a local accent.'

I heard the voice coming from right beside me, but I didn't know whether that comment had been aimed at me or not, so I kept my attention focused on the barman, watching as he flipped the lids off the beer, setting the bottles down on the counter in front of me.

'Newcastle-upon-Tyne, north-east England. Am I right?'

I paid for the drinks and slowly turned to face the person to whom the voice belonged. And that's when the same strange feeling I'd experienced last night as I'd left the bar hit me again, causing my breath to catch in my throat. I was rendered speechless for a second or two, which was quite unlike me. But I just couldn't take my eyes off the man standing beside me. And I wasn't entirely sure *how* I could describe him, because he wasn't exactly handsome in the conventional sense of the word – he was no clean-shaven pretty boy, that's for sure. Quite the opposite. But he was attractive on a whole other level. A sexy-as-hell, rough-edged kind of way. He had the most beautiful, dark, almost black, eyes. I knew that much. Eyes that seemed to verge on dangerous, which for some reason just made him even hotter. His hair was a dark brown, but greying slightly at the roots, so that gave me some indication as to his age, as did the colour of his goatee beard and moustache – a lighter brown streaked with grey. I was guessing mid- to late-forties. But he looked good on it. He looked *really* good. And he was tall. That was always a bonus. Then I suddenly realised I was quite obviously staring and immediately

15

looked down at the ground, feeling a touch embarrassed. I didn't normally do that kind of thing. Ever. I'd just had the weirdest feeling that I'd seen him somewhere before. But, surely, if I had, I'd have remembered him?

Swallowing down my surprise – and my slight embarrassment – I slowly raised my gaze, giving him what I hoped was a friendly smile. 'You're right.' I was managing to keep my voice quite steady, considering. 'And, if I'm not mistaken, *that's* not a local accent, either. Scottish, huh?'

He returned my smile; a rather nice smile, actually. No, make that a *really* nice smile. 'Glasgow. Place called Newbank, just north of the Clyde.'

'Okay… Well, it's good to meet another Brit.'

'Aye. It certainly is.' Those dark eyes were fixed on mine, making it hard for me to look away, but I did so only briefly, taking in his battered jeans, his heavy boots and what looked like an extremely worn leather biker's jacket. I couldn't find any negatives so far. 'You have a name, darlin'?'

I let the corner of my mouth curl up into a smile. 'Have *you*?'

He laughed, a low, almost rasping, laugh. Jesus! That was hot! *So* hot! 'I'm Eddie,' he said, throwing me that smile again. 'Eddie Fletcher.'

I felt my stomach give a huge, almost three-sixty-degree somer-sault as my eyes once more locked with his; something that, quite literally, took my breath away. It was a crazy feeling, but I was quite liking crazy. Crazy felt *good!*

'Lana,' I said quietly, my voice suddenly refusing to rise above a whisper. 'Lana Saunders.'

'Lana…' he repeated, his eyes still fixed on mine as he spoke my name, all slow and sexy. 'That's a beautiful name.'

I was still running with crazy, but, seriously, I'd only gone to the bar for a couple of beers. I hadn't expected to bump into a drop-dead-gorgeous biker dressed in leather and denim with a smile that seemed to have the ability to floor me within seconds.

'You here on your own?' he continued, and I looked back up at him, unaware I'd actually broken the stare, but I must have done at some point. 'I'm here with friends. We work in a tattoo studio back home in the UK.' There really was something about this stranger that made me feel as if I'd known him for years. Or that I'd, at least, seen him somewhere before. And I just couldn't shake that feeling.

He leant back against the counter beside me, folding his arms as he looked out ahead of him, and I followed his gaze, watching the crowds as they flitted from stand to stand, doing whatever it was people did at events like this, because I really had no idea. This was all still quite new to me. It had a good vibe, though, I knew that much.

'So, you're here for the convention, then?' he asked.

I nodded, then remembered he wasn't actually looking at me, so he wouldn't have been able to see my response. 'Yeah. Yeah, we are.'

He turned to face me. 'You in Vegas for long, Lana?'

Oh, dear God! The way he said my name! How did he *do* that? 'A couple of days.'

My fingers tightened around the beer bottles I'd suddenly realised I was still holding, as his eyes once more met mine.

'You're not hanging around, then.' It was more of a statement than a question.

'No. No, we're not.'

I finally broke the stare, looking down at my boots.

'Okay, so, if you're not gonna be around for long… How do you fancy a night to remember, sweetheart?'

I almost dropped the beers, my head shooting straight back up. 'I'm sorry?'

'Come out with me. Tonight. What d'you say, darlin'?'

3

That had thrown me. Somewhat. 'I… I don't know…' *Why* didn't I know?

Just say yes, Lana. Just say yes!

'I know we've only just met, but…' He shrugged. 'Does that really matter?' He raised an eyebrow, his mouth twisting up into a slight smirk. How could *anybody* manage to make that look so incredibly sexy? And even though there was a part of me that wanted to scream, *Do you know what? We might have only just met, but what the hell! Yes, I'll go out with you!* there was another part of me – remnants of the old, more reserved and cautious Lana, maybe – that was holding back. A part of me that was slightly wary of accepting his invitation.

'No. It doesn't really matter, but…' That cautious part had won. 'Look, I… I really should go and find my friends…'

He pushed a hand through his hair, and I watched as his expression changed, his eyes dipping briefly before he looked back at me. 'I'm sorry. I really didn't want to make you feel uncomfortable, in any way, it's just that, when I saw you last night…'

'You saw me last night?' My voice appeared to have gone up an octave, and I gave a little cough in the hope it would return to

18

normal next time I opened my mouth. 'Where?' Thankfully, it had.

'In the bar, downstairs. You staying here?'

I nodded, and then I suddenly realised where I'd seen him before – or, at least, where I *thought* I'd seen him before. 'Were you with a group of bikers?'

He smiled, and I kind of liked the way his eyes crinkled up at the edges when he did that. 'You saw us?'

'Yeah. Yeah, I saw you.'

'You were with a tall, tattooed guy,' Eddie went on. 'Boyfriend?'

'Brother,' I corrected, pleased my voice appeared to be behaving itself now.

'Do you *have* a boyfriend?'

My eyes were fixed on his as I spoke, my voice still steady as a rock, despite my insides misbehaving in a way they hadn't done in a long, long time. 'Is that any of your business?'

He laughed quietly, raking a hand through his hair. 'There's something about you, Lana.'

I continued to stare at him, right at him. That weird feeling I'd experienced last night, as I'd left the bar – was that down to him?

'You stood out, from everybody else in that room last night.I don't know why, I just… My eyes, they went straight to you, the second I walked in. And that incredible sleeve tattoo you've got, that might've had something to do with it. That's some pretty eye-catching ink there, darlin'.'

I looked at my arm, absentmindedly running my hand up and down it.

'You seem like the kind of woman I…' He trailed off, his eyes dropping to the floor. 'Anyway, seeing you here…'He raised his gaze, looking straight at me. 'Do you believe in fate?'

I narrowed my eyes slightly. 'About as much as I believe in the tooth fairy.' I wasn't sure I'd meant that to sound quite as cynical as it had come out.

He raised that eyebrow again, and I was beginning to wish he'd stop doing that because it was really messing with my head.

'You've never believed in the tooth fairy?'

I shrugged. 'I was a cynical child.'

'And…are you *still* cynical?'

I couldn't stop myself from smiling. He kind of made me want to smile. 'Not as much.'

He smiled too, and I found myself relaxing that little bit more, a strange yet comforting warmth flooding through me. I was actually starting to enjoy myself now.

'That's a shame. Because you don't look like a cynical woman to me.'

'And what does a cynical woman look like, exactly?'

His head dropped again, and I couldn't help noticing the way his hair fell forward; the way he quickly pushed it back off his face as he turned to look at me again. 'About tonight…'

His eyes almost burned into mine, my skin breaking out in goose bumps as a warm shiver ran right up my back. And for a few seconds – a few glorious, almost unreal, seconds – it was like we were the only two people in the room. 'I… Eddie, I can't. I can't.' Reality – and my over-cautious side – returned. And the moment was gone.

'Okay.' He shrugged, sticking his hands in his pockets. 'I can't say I'm not disappointed, but… You take care now, darlin', you hear?'

I nodded, giving him one more smile before I turned and started to walk away, bumping straight into Finn, who was quite obviously on his way to find me.

'Where the hell have you been?' he asked, taking a beer from me. 'Thought you were brewing the stuff yourself… What?'

I took a quick glance behind me, and Finn's gaze followed mine.

'What am I supposed to be looking at?'

My eyes were still on Eddie as he disappeared back into the mass of people. 'That guy over there. The one in the black-leather biker jacket… He's pushing a hand through his hair now, look! Him.'

Finn frowned. 'Yeah? What about him?'

I took a second or two to let that totally unexpected encounter sink in a little more before I spoke again. 'He just asked me out.'

'Fuck off!' Finn laughed, his expression changing only when he saw mine. 'Really?'

'Yes, really.'

'And what did you say?'

'I said I couldn't.' I closed my eyes and threw back my head, letting out the longest groan. 'Why did I say that?'

'Beats me, kiddo.'

I looked at him. 'You're no help.'

'What do you want me to do? I can go check him out for you, if you like. You know, do the brotherly thing, find out if he's got any dark secrets...'

I threw Finn a look. 'I just got a shock, you know? It was a bit of a surprise, that's all. I mean, it's not like it's been an everyday occurrence for me, has it? Men asking me out.'

'Only because you've shied away from any attention of that kind, Lana. Believe me, sis, there's a queue of people back home all gagging to ask you out, but that look you give sometimes... it kind of warns them off. You do know you're doing that, don't you? It's like a fucking death stare...'

'I'd just walked out on Adam.'

'That was a year ago, Lana.'

'I'd just walked out on my life, and I'm still trying to get used to a new one. Relationships have been the last thing on my mind.'

'And now?'

'My divorce has just come through, Finn.'

'And your point is?'

I threw him yet another of my withering looks. 'I turned him down, okay? Conversation over.'

'Why –did you turn him down, I mean?'

'*Why*?'

'Yes. Why?'

It was a question I'd probably be asking myself for days to come, if

I was honest. 'Look, the ink isn't even dry on my divorce papers...'

'What's that got to do with anything? Listen, Lana, it really is time to start living again. I know this year's been tough on youand I know you've tried to move on, but you haven't really made all that much progress, have you?'

I stared at him with wide eyes, indicating my tattoos, my black-tipped hair; my skinny jeans and biker boots. '*This* isn't progress?'

'That's all wrapping paper, kiddo. I'm talking about what's going on inside.'

'You're very perceptive, all of a sudden.'

He pulled a face, downing another mouthful of beer. 'Why not take a chance now and again? That's all I'm saying.'

I looked back out into the crowd, even though I knew Eddie would be long gone and the slight pang of regret I'd felt since he'd walked away intensified. Why couldn't I just have said yes? There'd been something about that manand not just the way he looked, all edgy and rough and, quite frankly, hotashell. There'd just been something about him... the way he'd looked at me. There was a connection there and I'd just severed it, dead. 'Should I have accepted?' I asked quietly, still staring out into the crowd, as though willing Eddie to reappear. Eddie Fletcher – the kind of Prince Charming who wouldn't so much ride up on a white stal-lion, he'd be more likely to cruise up on a Harley, and I'd turned him down!

Oh God! I'd said no! How could I have said no?! Lana, you idiot!

Finn shrugged, his voice pulling me back to reality. 'All I'm saying is, you're trying to build this new life for yourself, right? And I can only do so much, you know? I mean, I've given you one hell of a kick-start...'

I playfully nudged his arm. 'Don't sell yourself short or anything.'

'I really am being serious now, Lana. Sometimes in life you've just got to take a risk. And this could have been one of those times.'

I sighed. 'I'm not looking for any kind of relationship, Finn, you know that.'

'He asked you out, sis. He didn't propose.'

He put his arm around my shoulders again and I hugged his waist tight as we walked. 'It just all feels a bit... I dunno. Odd. Surreal.'

'Truthfully, did even the tiniest part of you want to say yes to him?' Finn asked.

'Yeah. It did. It really did.'

'Then you should have gone with your gut, girl.'

'I know,' I sighed, because regret was kicking in big-time now.

'I mean, what happened to that fun-loving, kick-ass woman you told me you were gonna become? I thought you were someone who was determined to take life by the balls and live it.'

'I am. It's just... it's still hard for me, sometimes, to get my head around the fact that this is me now. You know what I was like before, and this – this is so different.'

Finn flashed me a huge grin. 'Yeah, but just remember how boring your life was before you started hanging out with me again.'

I smiled at him, knowing he was kind of right. But my life hadn't been *that* bad before. It just hadn't been the life I'd wanted in the end. 'Even if I *was* looking to start all that dating crap again, Finn, I'm not sure... Look, all of this is pointless. I said no, he's gone, it's over.'

Finn gave my hand a little squeeze. 'You've still got me.'

'Yeah. I've still got you.' I leant over to kiss his cheek. 'And I've still got this weekend in Vegas.'

But what kind of weekend *could* it have been? The chance to find out was gone now. I'd blown it. Whoever Eddie Fletcher was, I'd probably never see him again. And that was nobody's fault but my own.

Pulling the hem of my dress, which I still thought was a little too short, down over my thighs, I quickly looked around as I waited for the elevator to arrive. Black, strapless, and just about skimming my arse, I couldn't deny I loved the way it made me feel, despite its slightly daring length. I'd teamed it with knee-high, black, spike-heeled boots, which made my legs look pretty much incredible, even if I did say so myself, and with my long blonde-and-black hair hanging in large, loose curls down my back, my make-up all dark eyes and pale lips, those tattoos I was so proud of all on show, I felt every inch the wannabe biker chick I'd always dreamt of becoming. I was slowly getting used to the fact that I could scrub up pretty well for a woman about to hit forty. I still had it, and I was damn well going to make sure I flaunted it, while I still could.

Taking a quick peek in the full-length mirror on the wall beside the elevator, I studied my reflection carefully. The woman staring back at me was one I still wasn't all that familiar with, but I was getting a little more used to her as each day passed. And a lot of that was down to Finn. He'd made me realise it wasn't a crime to change, if that was what you needed to do. He'd given me a strength and a confidence I'd never had before, and I loved him so much for that. So much. Because, without him, I wasn't sure I'd be where I was right now.

As the elevator doors slowly slid open I pulled the hem of my dress down again, wiggling my hips slightly to help it on its way.

'Whoa!'

That voice, accompanied by a long, low whistle, made my head shoot up and I could have died of embarrassment as I saw him standing there, leaning back against the handrail. Eddie Fletcher. Bold as brass and twice as hot as I remembered him being a few hours ago. Shit! I wasn't prepared for this. I mean, it was like all my prayers were being answered now, bumping into him again after I'd spent the entire afternoon berating myself for letting him go. But a little bit of warning would have been nice.

'Looking good there, darlin'.'

Jesus! That accent! I'd never found a Glaswegian accent sexy before. Never. But on this guy it was like honey dripping off a hot crumpet…

24

What the hell was I talking about?

I quickly brushed down my dress, shook out my hair, and walked into the elevator, displaying what I hoped was an air of confidence, which was more difficult than it should have been thanks to boots I wasn't quite used to walking in yet.

Leaning back against the rail beside him, I watched as the doors slid shut, neither of us saying anything for a second or two. But I was more than aware of my heart picking up a rhythm that was faster than I'd have liked it to be.

'Where're you heading?' he asked, taking his hand out of his pocket and hovering his finger over the buttons on the wall to his left.

'Ground floor.' It was taking every ounce of strength I had to keep my voice steady. I hadn't expected to see this man again, and yet, here we were, sharing an elevator. Just the two of us. Was I going to mess up a second time? I wasn't planning on it.

He pulled his hand away, shoving it back in his pocket. 'Me too.'

I took a sneaky sideways look at him. He wasn't dressed all that differently to how he had been when I'd seen him earlier, still wearing those battered jeans and biker's jacket, and those heavy black boots I found strangely sexy.

As he took his left hand out of his pocket again, raking it through his hair, I tried to see if he was wearing a wedding ring, and then quickly turned away as I realised I was probably staring. Again.

'I've never been married,' he said, as though reading my mind, which made me squirm slightly. Was I that transparent? Still, at least that was one question answered. 'Never felt the need.'

I turned my head to look at him again, and he was smiling at me, a smile I really liked because it reached his eyes – those beautiful, dark eyes… I really had to get a grip here. I was in Las Vegas. This place didn't exactly epitomise reality, and what was happening here, this wasn't real. And even if the invitation to go out with him was still open, which I had yet to find out, in a few days' time he'd be heading back to wherever he came from, and

I'd be on my way back to England. That was the reality of the situation. So was it even worth me telling him I'd changed my mind? That I would, after all, like to go out with him? And what if he'd already found a woman more willing to take him up on his offer? It wouldn't surprise me if he had.

'What about you?' he asked, his voice pulling me back to the here and now. 'You never did answer my question earlier. When I asked if you had a boyfriend.'

I dropped my gaze, his question making Adam and my past life come rushing back to the forefront of my mind – a place I'd wanted to try and keep both well away from.

'I'm divorced,' I replied, the words falling from my mouth before I could stop them, my eyes back on his. 'Finalised a few days ago.' He hadn't really needed to know that. And I had no idea why I'd told him.

It was his turn to lower his gaze, his hair falling down over his eyes as he dropped his head. Once more I felt the strangest feeling flood through me, something I couldn't really explain, it just felt – I don't know – like there was some invisible spark between us that kept firing off little shots of, well, it was like a heady mixture of excitement tinged with fear and… I was confusing myself now. It just felt – it felt nice. Really nice. Different.

'I'm sorry.' He looked back up, pushing his hair away from his face. 'I didn't mean to make you feel uncomfortable, I just… I guess I let my mouth run away with me, huh?'

I smiled. I couldn't help it. Once more he was just making me feel like smiling, and I wasn't fighting that. 'It's okay. We'd been separated for a while and…' I stopped talking, because this really was information he didn't need to know. And I really didn't want to talk about it.

He returned my smile, his eyes looking right into mine, and all I wanted now was a drink. Something to calm the sudden nerves that had taken over, caused by the close proximity of this darkly attractive man. A man I wanted to get to know better, and I wasn't going to lose this opportunity a second time.

So when the elevator reached the ground floor, shuddering to a halt with a light thud, I almost willed him to ask me again; the same question he'd asked me this morning, because this time my answer would be yes. A huge, enthusiastic yes. Looking briefly down at my boots I waited for the doors to open, longing for him to ask that question, and wondering whether I should just make the first move myself before it was too late.

But I didn't get the chance, because all of a sudden the elevator started moving again…

4

My head shot back up and I stared at him. Mainly because I couldn't quite work out what was happening.

'Sorry, darlin', but I'm not giving up without a fight.'

I continued to stare at him. 'Not giving up *what*?' Feisty Lana was starting to emerge now. Which was good. I had a feeling I was going to need her.

'You.'

The way he said that, with that accent of his and that mean and moody look on his face, it was so sexy I actually felt my knees give the tiniest of wobbles. Or that could've been because I hadn't eaten all that much since breakfast, which in a place like Vegas, with its wall-to-wall mega-buffets and endless restaurants, was quite a feat. But I preferred to believe it was because of Eddie.

I gripped the rail behind me tightly as the elevator started to rise again. 'Where are we going?' Not that I cared. Not really. Anywhere would be good. I was just relieved I hadn't messed up again, because there was something about Eddie Fletcher that was drawing me to him, more and more, with each second we spent together.

'There's a bar at the top of this hotel,' he replied, his hands in his pockets, his eyes focused on the elevator doors as we continued to ascend. 'You get an amazing view of Vegas from up there. And I think we could both do with a drink, don't you?'

He'd got *that* right. Those nerves still needed steadying.

I looked down at my boots again, raising one leg up, resting my foot against the glass wall behind me. 'I could call this kidnapping, you know.' I slowly raised my head, my eyes meeting his, a slight smirk on my face.

'You want to call security?' He raised that eyebrow again, causing me to grip the rail even tighter, but at least I was managing to hold his gaze. Good. Feisty Lana was holding her own here.

I shook my head, a slow smile starting to spread across my face. 'No. You're alright. I kind of trust you.'

'Kind of?' He still had that eyebrow arched.

'Well, I still don't *know* you, do I?'

He smiled again. But thankfully he'd lowered the eyebrow now. 'Stick around for a couple of hours, sweetheart, and you'll know enough.'

I wasn't quite sure what he meant by that, but just trying to get my head around this whole scenario was exhausting enough without asking any more questions. I'd decided to just go with it now. See where the night took us.

The elevator doors finally slid open and he held out his hand. And, like an idiot, I just stared at it, not really sure if I should take it. But that's obviously what he wanted me to do, right?

'I won't bite,' he said, that smile still there on his really quite handsome face, if you went for the rough, weathered, bearded look, which I did. Oh, I really, *really* did.

I paused for just a second longer before tentatively slipping my hand into his, his fingers tightening around mine, and I took a small but deep breath as my stomach fluttered. 'You okay there, darlin'?'

I looked up at him, my eyes once more meeting his. No. This definitely wasn't a dream. He was very, very real. The fact he was squeezing my hand was telling me just how real he was.

'I'm fine. I'm just… It's been a while, that's all. Since I've done this.'

'Done what? Embarked on a night out with a stranger?' He'd raised that eyebrow. Again. And my stomach acted accordingly.

'How do I know you don't make a habit of this?' I asked, not realising I'd just voiced my thoughts out loud until I heard the words. Still, I couldn't take them back now, could I? 'I mean, you could pick up different women on a regular basis for all I know.' I figured I might as well get it all off my chest, because it *was* something I'd been wondering.

He threw me another smile. 'Come on. Let's get that drink.' He didn't even attempt to answer my question, but what the hell. I wasn't going to push it.

I clung onto his hand as he led me through some wide double doors into the busy bar, a space that seemed to go on forever – but the view! He hadn't been wrong about that. The walls surrounding a huge, circular counter in the centre of the room seemed to be made of nothing but pure glass, meaning that everywhere you looked you could see the lights of Las Vegas down below, the city spread out like a colourful blanket. I gasped as I tried to take it all in. What a view! It was utterly mesmerising.

'Beautiful, isn't it?' He turned to look at me. 'Just like you, Lana.'

Jesus Christ! I wanted him to say my name over and over again, just keep saying it, because he was making it sound like the sexiest thing in the world right now.

'Beer!' It was a statement rather than a question, as if he'd known me for ever.

Okay. One word and the mood could change in an instant, but… Did he know me that well already? All that stuff about fate – maybe he was right. 'Yes. Please.' I was grateful for the lovely, comfy couch behind me to sink into as his hand slowly slipped out of mine.

'I'll be right back,' he said, his expression suddenly turning serious. 'Don't go anywhere. Okay?'

As if! But all I could do was nod. And stare after him as he walked over to the bar, even though there were servers hovering around all over the place. But I was glad he'd gone over there himself. It gave me a chance to do two things – watch him walk, because he had a swagger I'd never seen on a man before and I was finding it incredibly sexy, and quickly text Finn to let him know what was happening. I didn't want him sending out a search party.

Less than two seconds after pressing send on that text my phone rang. I quickly answered it. 'You decided to take that chance, then,' Finn said.

I looked over at the bar. Eddie was talking to the bartender, smiling and laughing, pushing a hand back through his hair and I watched as it fell forward again almost immediately. 'Yeah. What the hell, huh?'

'That's my girl. Just be yourself, beautiful. Okay? And try and enjoy the night.'

I sighed quietly, my eyes still on Eddie. 'He knew what to get me from the bar without even asking.'

'Nothing a ridiculous shade of orange, then?' Finn deadpanned.

I finally pulled my gaze away from Eddie. I didn't want to be caught staring again. 'No. Nothing a ridiculous shade of orange… He's coming back! I'll call you later.'

'If you need us…'

'I'll be fine.' I ended the call, quickly throwing my phone back into my bag.

Eddie sat down on the chair to my left, handing me a bottle of beer. 'I didn't get you a glass. Do you want one?'

'Do I look like the kind of woman who needs a glass?'

He smiled. I was fast becoming addicted to that smile of his. There was something safe about it, almost. Something warm and comforting, which was a little bit at odds with the way he looked – that rough-around-the-edges exterior he displayed with the messed-up hair and beard; those dark, almost dangerous eyes.

'You sure you're okay?'

'I'm fine,' I replied, taking a quick drink of beer, thankful for the small but significant hit it gave me.

He leant forward, resting his elbows on his slightly open knees. 'So, shall we start getting to know one another?'

All those nerves had gone now. In fact, I was feeling more relaxed than I had in a long time. 'You look like a bit of a bad boy to me.' Possibly too relaxed, because I wasn't entirely sure I'd meant to say that out loud. But he did have that aura about him; the way he looked, the way he dressed. Even the way he spoke.

He laughed quietly. 'I think "boy" might be pushing it a bit, darlin', but... Does that put you off?'

Quite the opposite, actually, but I wasn't going to tell *him* that. And at almost forty years old I should probably be past the whole "bad boy" thing but, hey, I'd lived with a good guy for way too long. Was it so wrong to fancy a change? 'Would it matter if it did?'

He narrowed those beautiful dark eyes of his as he looked straight at me. 'My name's Eddie Fletcher, I'm forty-seven years old and I own a motorcycle shop in downtown Las Vegas. I live not far from the Strip in a place called Rancho Oakey, own two Harleys, ride regularly, hang out at biker bars and my MC clubhouse. I like beer and Mexican food, and can't stand jazz music. And lastly, I'm still hanging around this hotel, instead of just going home, because I was hoping to see *you*.'

I blinked a few times, trying to take it all in; where I was, everything that was happening. But none of it was easy. I still felt as though I'd suddenly stepped into some kind of weird and unfamiliar parallel world that I wasn't altogether sure I should be a part of.

'You don't *have* to tell me anything about yourself,' Eddie went on, his voice shaking me back to the here and now. 'But, you know, I'd quite like to find out a little bit more about you.'

I stared down at my beer, closing my eyes for a second before I looked back up at him, fixing a smile on my face. 'Let's just say

I've left a lot behind, and I'm starting again.'

He looked at me – right at me – for a few, long seconds. Long enough for my heart to start knocking out a fast and heavy rhythm, pounding away inside me like some pulsating drum. If I'd been standing up I might well have felt faint, but as I was sitting down I just felt a little light-headed.

'There really is something about you, Lana…' The smile he gave me seemed to send a wave of calm washing over me. Like I'd just had a shot of something warm and relaxing, and I found my confidence returning.

Putting my beer down on the table in front of us I curled my legs up underneath me, resting my elbow on the arm of the couch as I looked at him. 'You live here in Vegas?'

He nodded. 'Have done for over fifteen years now.'

That explained the slight hint of US twang in his accent. I hadn't really noticed it earlier today, but tonight it was coming through a little more.

'Came over for a bikers' convention, and I never went home.'

He didn't seem in a hurry to offer up any more information, and I wasn't going to push it. I'd hardly been forthcoming with mine.

'You said something, this morning, about fate,' I said, staring straight at him. 'Do you really believe in all that?'

He shrugged, taking another drink. '*You* obviously don't.'

'We're not talking about me. And I told you, I'm cynical.'

His eyes were still locked with mine and for a few seconds nobody said anything. But it didn't feel like one of those awkward silences, and that was weird, in a way, given how long we'd known each other. Which was all of five minutes.

'Maybe fate's the wrong word,' he said quietly. 'Coincidence… is that a better one?'

My eyes refused to leave his, which was fine because, in all honesty, I could have sat staring at him all night. 'So, were you really gonna hang around the hotel tonight on the offchance you'd bump into me again?'

33

'I told you, that's exactly what I was planning to do.'

'Okay, well, you've found me, so… what else did you have planned?'

He laughed quietly, his eyes dipping briefly before meeting mine again. 'I hadn't really thought that far ahead, darlin', if I'm being honest. But, you know, a few drinks, a club, then… maybe, back to my place…'

I broke the stare, those final few words killing the moment. 'I'd better go.' I swung my legs down from the couch, grabbing my bag as I stood up.

'Lana, wait! Please. Just, wait.'

Oh, God, why did he have to say my name like that? Why?

I turned around, standing completely still as he walked over to me.

'I'm sorry. That was really…' He bowed his head, running a hand along the back of his neck before he raised his gaze. 'It was inappropriate. But you… you're… Jesus, Lana, you're hot, you know?'

I couldn't stop myself from smiling. 'Thanks.'

He laughed, the mood suddenly lightening. 'Come on.' He took hold of my hand, and my fingers automatically curled around his, clinging on tightly as he led the way out of the bar, beating a steady pace to the elevator, his long legs taking the kind of strides my slightly shorter ones weren't capable of in the dress and boots I was wearing. 'I know a great club not far from here.' He stopped for a second, smiling that smile again, his hand still holding tightly onto mine. 'You're gonna like this place. I promise.'

It was a bit early to be making me any kind of promises, but his eyes – I trusted him, I really did. As much as you could trust anyone you'd known for less than an hour, anyway.

Neither of us said anything else until we were back in the elevator, winging our way down to the ground floor.

'I'm gonna give you the night of your life, Lana Saunders.' He winked at me before slipping on a pair of dark glasses, his hand still holding mine. And it was a nice feeling, holding his hand, his thumb running gently over my knuckles. 'I won't hurt you, I promise,' he said quietly, a slow, sexy smirk spreading across his roughly handsome face. 'Not unless you want me to.'

I couldn't stop a full-on smile from appearing. 'I'll get back to you on that one, okay?'

'Okay.' He squeezed my hand, and I felt the most insane sensation shoot through me. I had no idea what it was, or where it had come from, but it both scared and excited me. 'Let's play it by ear, huh?'

I was happy to go with that. I'd come *this* far…

He squeezed my hand again, pulling me closer to him, and I felt a tiny shiver run through me as my hip nudged his. I'm not saying sparks were flying or anything like that, but I definitely felt that hint of a shiver, and my fingers curled tighter around his, almost as if I really did believe this was nothing but a dream and if I let go of him – well, then he'd disappear. And I didn't want him to disappear. Not yet.

The elevator doors slowly slid open and he looked at me, his expression a touch more serious than it had been before. 'If you don't want to do this, Lana…' I took a second to let the way he said my name wash over me, bringing with it the return of that tiny shiver, before I interrupted him.

'You just promised me the night of my life, Eddie Fletcher. I want to see if you can live up to your promises.'

He grinned, and if I hadn't been holding onto him I swear my legs would've buckled underneath me. 'You got it, sweetheart. Let's get out of here.'

He continued that rapid pace he seemed to favour as we exited the hotel and headed out onto the Strip, its bright lights and noise giving everything an unreal, almost fairytale, atmosphere. It was as if I'd, somehow, stumbled into someone else's life and I was just looking in from the sidelines. But the excitement that was bubbling away in the pit of my stomach, I couldn't ignore that. I didn't want to. I was in a place I'd always wanted to visit, with the kind of man I'd always dreamt of. So I was grabbing this experience with both hands and not letting go. Not until I had to.

'Okay, sweetheart, here we are.' We'd stopped outside a building not far from the hotel; an unassuming place with a small entrance way and stairs that seemed to descend forever down into darkness. 'It's a hidden secret, this is. One of the best clubs in Vegas. I come here all the time; it's my kind of hang-out. And I'm guessing it might be yours, too.'

'You think you know me that well, huh?'

He turned to face me, smiling slightly. 'I think I'm getting there.'

I shook my head, but I was also laughing. It was crazy, to be this comfortable in the company of a man I'd only just met, but that's how I felt. 'Well, let's see if you're right, hmm?'

He laughed too, letting go of my hand and sliding his arm across my shoulders. Overly familiar maybe but, hey, I wasn't complaining. This was Vegas and whatever happened here, it stayed here, apparently. Not that anything was *going* to happen. And even if it did…

I slid my arm around his waist, leaning into him as his thumb slowly stroked the back of my neck, turning that tiny shiver I'd felt earlier into a long, languid tingle running slowly up and down my spine. Okay, so maybe this *was* crazy. A little unreal. But I was going with it. You only got one life, and I'd promised Finn – I'd promised *myself* – I was going to start living mine. Even if this hadn't really been the start I'd planned. Or expected.

We headed into the building, making our way down the stairs, the sound of heavy rock music coming from somewhere below, my fingers gripping the material of Eddie's t-shirt for dear life because the stairs were so steep, and not that easy to navigate in my choice of footwear. It was only when we were about halfway down that I loosened my grip, although I didn't let go of him completely. I was enjoying being this close to him. Adam and I, we'd never really been the hand-holding, waist-hugging type of couple. And now I realised what I'd been missing, that comforting feeling of closeness. It was nice. I liked it.

'You holding up okay there, darlin'?' Eddie asked, letting his thumb wander over the back of my neck again. God, that felt *so good*!

I nodded, once more concentrating on those stairs. We seemed to be descending more than I could count now, until we finally came to a long, black-walled corridor, a corridor that, thankfully, seemed to be leading us to the entrance of the club. Once there Eddie had a word with a tall, well-built man at the door who seemed to know him rather well, and after a lot of laughter and genial back-slapping – during which he never once let go of me – we eventually headed inside.

The club itself had a dark, almost dangerous, atmosphere, yet, I didn't *feel* in any danger. Nothing felt threatening, and that was probably because I'd been to clubs like this before, with Finn and our friends. They'd taken me to so many places I'd never had the chance to experience before, from biker bars, like this one, to rock gigs, pub lock-ins and house parties that ranged from wild all-nighters to chilled-out evenings spent listening to Pink Floyd and eating great food with good friends. So this world, it wasn't completely alien to me. It was still quite new, but not completely alien.

Loud, thumping rock music pulsated from what I could only imagine were concealed speakers, because I couldn't see any anywhere, filling the space with a vibe I couldn't describe, but I liked it. I craved it. Because this was a place where nobody seemed to care what anyone else thought. The people here were dressed in everything from denim to leather, skinny jeans to short skirts, and tattoos certainly seemed to be something favoured by the clientele, which suited me just fine. The walls, like the corridor outside, were mostly dark, the prominent colours being a deep, almost blood-red and black, all of them decorated with images of rock stars, reapers and huge swirling snakes wrapped around bloodied thorns. I felt like Alice walking into my very own warped kind of wonderland.

'I knew you'd like it here,' Eddie murmured, his mouth so close to my ear I could feel his breath on my neck. And that shiver returned. It was growing stronger with every visit.

I gripped his waist tightly again as we walked over to a booth at the side of the room, my head turning this way and that as I tried to take it all in. He let go of me as we sat down, and I continued to stare out ahead of me, watching everything with a slight sense of awe. It was like another world; one I was quite happy to frequent.

'I've ordered beers. That okay with you?'

I turned my head to look at him. 'Yeah. Yeah, that's fine. I'm not really a champagne kind of woman.'

He slid his arm along the back of the couch, finally taking off his dark glasses and slipping them into his jacket pocket.

'Are you always this perceptive when it vomes to women?' I asked, shuffling my body around slightly, pulling my legs up underneath me, tucking them in, resting my elbow on the back of the couch, our arms touching, just a brief second of contact but enough to cause goose bumps to form.

He smiled, pushing a hand through his hair, although it was refusing to stay back off his face tonight. But I quite liked that just-got-out-of-bed look that he was managing to pull off quite magnificently.

'I've always thought I was rather good at reading people, if that's what you mean.'

I could have listened to him talk all night. Constantly. I'm sure if he was to sit there reading a take-out menu to me I'd still find it incredibly sexy. He had a way of rolling his tongue that was just so hot! 'So, do you think you can read *me*?' I asked, trying desperately to stop imagining what else he could do with that tongue.

'I know you're looking for something.'

I smiled at the pretty, dark-haired waitress as she set our drinks down on the table in front of us before I let my eyes meet his, and all I could do was stare at him. Again. Because I didn't really know what to say to that.

'I'm sorry,' he said, breaking the stare and bowing his head. 'I'm pushing too much.' He slowly raised his gaze, our eyes locking once more. 'None of this matters tonight.'

'No,' I whispered. 'None of it matters.' Did any of it matter at all? But maybe he was right about tonight. It was too early, too soon – it was pointless getting into any kind of deep conversation about our pasts and who was looking for what when this was nothing more than some chance encounter I really should just be making the most of, while it lasted.

I felt his fingers slide between mine, and I looked at our joined hands, blinking a few times as I tried to force feisty Lana back out of hiding. I needed her right now, because I had a feeling that, tonight, I was either going to do something I could end up regretting for a very long time, or something I might actually enjoy. If I let myself. I just wasn't sure which it was going to be. Either way, it was going to be something completely out of character – for the old me, which was why I needed feisty Lana back.

'And in answer to one of your earlier questions,' he went on, reaching out with his other hand to push my hair back off my shoulder, '... I don't do this on a regular basis. Pick up random women, I mean. I'm not gonna pretend I'm some kind of monk either, but... You're different, Lana. I know you are. I can *feel* it.'

The way he put the emphasis on the word *feel*, with that low, sexy voice and eyes that seemed to be so sincere, it did something to my insides I hadn't felt happen before. And they'd been experiencing a lot of new activity over the course of the day.

His hand moved up to my neck, resting gently against it, his thumb lightly stroking my cheek. 'Are you okay with this, darlin'?'

I felt my eyes slowly close, his thumb still stroking my cheek, an action that was almost hypnotic, and all I could do was nod, aware that he was moving closer now.

'Good,' he whispered. 'Because this is something I have wanted to do ever since I saw you this morning.'

I laid my hand over his, our fingers intertwining as his mouth touched mine, and I swear I had never felt anything like it before. I'd never experienced a kiss like that in my entire life, because for most of my life I'd only ever kissed one person. So how could I possibly have known *this* kind of kiss existed? His lips moved ever-so-slowly against mine, opening just a touch, his tongue hesitating only slightly before pushing its way into my mouth, and I accepted it immediately. I let his hand slip lower, onto my hip, stroking it gently as he continued to kiss the hell out of me. And I was in no hurry for him to stop. Whatever the rights or wrongs of this situation; however weird or unreal it could yet turn out to be, right now I didn't care. I just didn't. I might be acting like some teenager out on a Saturday night, but I really didn't care. Being with Adam from such a young age, I'd missed out on so much. Was it *that* wrong of me to want to have some fun now?

Eddie pulled away, but only slightly, his forehead resting against mine, his hand back on my neck, his thumb stroking my cheek again. 'Should I be saying sorry?' But he was smiling, and I returned it, shaking my head.

'No.'

'Lana, I…' He pulled away a touch more, so he could look at me properly, dropping his hand from my cheek, pushing it back through his hair. 'I promised you the night of your life, right?' Our eyes locked, both of us unable to keep the grins off our faces.

'Yeah, you did. I guess it's time to see if you can deliver, then, biker boy.'

5

'Down in one, darlin'. Down in one,' Eddie shouted, slamming his empty shot glass down onto the table.

Picking up my drink I knocked the clear liquid back in a single mouthful, quickly sucking on the lime in my other hand, which made me choke slightly as the juice mingled with the tequila in my throat, causing Eddie to laugh out loud.

'Bastard!' The fact I was laughing too only caused me to cough even more. 'Still got it down, though.'

He threw me an appreciative look, taking a sip of his beer. 'You can hold your own, sweetheart, I'll give you that.'

I sat back, closing my eyes briefly to let the alcohol hit take hold. I was verging on tipsy, but nowhere near drunk. I was determined to keep as clear a head as I could tonight, because I had a feeling I was going to want to remember this. When it was all over.

'Come on,' he said, draining the last of his beer and grabbing my hand, pulling me up off the couch. 'It's time to hit the casinos.'

This night was turning out to be a fast-paced, whirlwind of an affair, with my feet hardly having time to hit the ground as we almost ran from bar to bar, all of them favourites of Eddie's, grabbing a drink, meeting all the people Eddie knew – a wonderfully eclectic mix ranging from musicians to artists to fellow bikers. People that reminded me a bit of the new friends I'd made back home. And because of the speed at which everything seemed to be moving, I'd almost forgotten that I was doing it all in a dress that was probably way too short and boots that were a little too high. I was just having the best time. It was the most exhilarated I'd felt since my college days and the weekly Friday-night pub crawl. But this – this was on a whole different level.

Despite the pace at which Eddie was playing this night, I had no urge to fall into bed just yet. This was a twenty-four-hour town, and I was going to make the most of every single one of those hours. As far as casinos went, well, this was Vegas! And you had to hit at least *one* casino when you were in Vegas, right?

Back out on the Strip, the blast of fresh air was more than welcome and I took a few seconds to catch my breath, once more marvelling at the bright lights and vibrant atmosphere this town was so good at creating. I'd fallen head-first in love with the place.

'What time is it?' I asked, snaking my arm around his waist, sliding my hand up under his t-shirt, biting down on my lip as it touched his skin.

'No clue, darlin'. Could be eight in the morning for all I care.'

All of a sudden he stopped in his tracks, taking me by surprise as he pushed me gently back against the nearest wall, his fingers winding in my hair as he kissed me slowly. So slowly I felt my whole body relax, bit by bit, with every touch of his lips against mine.

'Still want to check out those slot machines?' His mouth was twitching at the corners, his eyes trying to stay deadly serious and I couldn't stop a fit of the giggles from taking over.

'Where did you come from?' I whispered, pulling him closer by his jacket collar, running my fingers over his beard, my eyes following their every move.

'I don't know, baby,' he murmured, his mouth gently brushing that soft space just below my ear, causing the most delicious sensation to course right through me. 'But wherever it is, I'm in

42

no hurry to go back there.'

I rested my hand against his cheek, turning his face to look at me, leaning forward to kiss him again, sighing quietly as his mouth opened slightly, our tongues touching as he pulled me closer. The second our bodies connected I felt a heat the like of which I hadn't known could exist just from touching another human being; it was like a series of minute electric shocks were being fired into me, one after the other. 'I think we should probably go check out that casino now, don't you?' I whispered, my mouth resting against his as I spoke. I could almost feel him breathing into me – breathing *life* into me. A new life. The life I'd always been looking for?

His face broke into a smile, his thumb stroking my cheek before he pulled back slightly. 'This night ain't anywhere near over, darlin'. You got that?'

I threw my arms up above my head, stretching out, my eyes still locked with his. He had my answer.

Cocking his head just a touch, he raised that eyebrow again, a slow smirk forming. 'Am I doing okay here, kid?'

'You're doing just fine,' I breathed. 'But you've still got some work to do to make this the night of my life.'

'You throwing me a challenge there?'

'Call it whatever you like, biker boy. I just can't wait to see what you do with it.'

All of a sudden he lunged at me, grabbing me around the waist and nuzzling my neck, causing me to shriek out loud and laugh even louder as he tickled me, pushing my body up against his in the process. I just fell into his arms, letting him kiss me again, over and over, every time we came up for air the kisses growing longer and slower. Sexy, soulful kisses. If there was a heaven out there, I hoped to God it was something like this.

'Oh, you are really playing for points now, aren't you?' I smiled, gently stroking the hair at the back of his neck, running my fingers through it.

'Well, I've got something to prove, haven't I? I'm a man who keeps my promises, sweetheart.'

It was me who pulled away first, shaking my hair out and composing myself before I took his hand. 'Casino. Come on. I'm feeling lucky tonight.'

It hadn't been intentional, to end up back outside the hotel I was staying in, but we seemed to have found ourselves there.

Eddie looked at me, his hand giving mine a little squeeze. 'We can go somewhere else, if you'd prefer.'

'Why would I want to do that? We're only going to play some roulette, maybe a little blackjack. Aren't we?'

He grinned and that only made him twice as handsome, doubly hot. Oh boy, was I loving this night? 'Whatever you say, kid.'

'Let's start small, huh?' I winked, leading the way inside.

'Small?' he questioned, his grip on my hand tightening.

I glanced at him over my shoulder. 'Slot machines. I want to ease myself into things gently, okay?'

He grinned again, swinging me around so I fell back into his arms. 'You're one hell of a woman, Lana Saunders. I kind of need you to know that, darlin'.'

I reached out to touch his face, letting my thumb run lightly over his cheek. 'Yeah, well, you're proving to be a bit of a surprise to me, too, Eddie Fletcher.' Grabbing his hand I started pulling him towards the sound of a barrage of slot machines coming from the hotel casino. 'Come on. We're wasting valuable gambling time here.'

Clutching a fistful of money, I sat myself down at a random machine, Eddie behind me, the closeness of his body something I was used to now. It kind of felt odd if he wasn't there.

'I'll go get us a drink,' he said quietly, leaning over so his mouth was practically touching my ear. It was an action that sent a lovely sensation coursing through my body. 'You get started, okay?'

I turned my head to smile at him, my mouth catching his in a quick but still unbelievably hot kiss. And I couldn't help but let out another of those unfamiliar, tiny gasps as I watched him walk over to the bar, that sexy swagger meaning mine wasn't the only head that was turning.

Back off, bitches, he's mine!

Smiling to myself, I turned back to face the machine, carefully sliding a note into it, watching as that first attempt at a win failed. But so what? I had a feeling I'd already won the best prize of the night. Hitting the jackpot here would be nothing but a bonus.

'Any luck?' Eddie asked, handing me a beer.

I shook my head, concentrating on my next attempt. Which also failed.

'Here.' He leant over me again, his body touching mine from behind as he reached out to take a note from my hand, sliding it into the machine. I could feel his breath on my cheek, his beard rough against my skin, and I had a sudden urge to just pull him down and kiss him until our mouths ached. But I took a drink of beer instead, my head spinning slightly, telling me I was probably on the edge of being drunk now.

His luck was no better than mine, as far as the slot machines were concerned, and I smiled as he swore quietly, making no attempt to pull away from his position behind me. 'Lady Luck ain't smiling on us tonight, darlin', he sighed, his fingers trailing lazily along the back of my neck.

Flip!

I wasn't sure if he was aware of exactly what he was doing to me, but I could feel myself heading in a direction I still wasn't sure I should be heading in. I needed a bit more time to think about this.

Grabbing my beer and stuffing the money down the front of my dress, I took his hand, dragging him over to the roulette wheel.

'Oh, we're going bigger now, are we?' He smirked, and I threw back a slow smile.

'You have no idea how big I intend to go tonight.'

'Feel like giving me a clue?'

I shook my head, digging out a handful of chips from my bag. 'Stick these on red.'

He looked at me. 'Any particular reason why?'

I shrugged. 'I like red.'

'Good enough,' he said, turning to place the chips on the table. I slid my arms around him from behind, resting my head against his shoulder, breathing in the smell of leather and cigarettes as the wheel turned, round and round, faster and faster, until it inevitably slowed down, that tiny white ball jumping in and out of the red and black compartments. It was actually quite strange, the level of excitement that small ball could create, but as it finally settled in red even I couldn't stop myself from giving a shriek of delight and high-fiving Eddie. This was fun!

'Red again. Or do *you* want to choose this time?' I asked, my excitement reaching child-like proportions now.

'No. What the lady wants, the lady gets.' Eddie smiled, his eyes meeting mine for a brief and surprisingly intense second. Enough time for me to know, for sure, that I was done with the alcohol for tonight. I really needed to keep my head as clear as possible. I could cope with slightly woozy, but any more than that and I knew I was going to forget too much of tonight. And I didn't want to forget any of it.

'Stick it on red then, handsome,' I whispered, lightly kissing the back of his neck.

'You're killing me here, darlin',' he murmured, reaching behind him to rub my bottom. *Oh yes!* No way did I want to forget this night!

I felt his hand slide into mine as the ball once more bounced into the red, and I let out another tiny squeal of excitement, squeezing Eddie's hand probably a touch too hard.

He let go of me, leaning forward to retrieve our winning chips, scooping them up and dropping them into his pocket.

'Come on, kid. We're quitting while we're ahead.'

'We are?'

I let him take my hand again as we headed out of the casino. And it wasn't until we were back outside in the hotel's sprawling foyer that he stopped, swinging me around to face him, reaching out to cup my cheek in his hand. 'You ready to call it a night yet, darlin'?'

I stared up at him, those dark eyes of his boring into mine, that intensity I'd sensed before coming back with a vengeance now. 'I'm not sure,' I said slowly, and then inwardly shook myself, taking a very quick, very deep, breath. 'Tell you what… Let's go grab a whisky or something. Outside.' I didn't really fancy another drink, but I didn't feel much like letting him go just yet, either. And this was the only compromise I could come up with on the spurofthemoment.

'Suits me.' He shrugged, letting me lead the way out to the pool bar. But the second we were outside he stopped, pulling me back into his arms. 'What are you scared of, Lana?' His mouth was already closing in on mine, and I felt my heart start to beat faster. Harder. Louder.

'I'm not scared of anything,' I breathed, grabbing onto his jacket collar to steady myself as my knees started weakening again. I was still putting that down to Eddie. To this. To everything that was happening. Was *that* what I was scared of? *This*?

'I think you are,' he whispered, his hand in the small of my back, pressing me against him.

'I thought we were getting a drink?' And I wasn't entirely sure why I was almost pulling back from this, because it felt good, being this close to him. It was everything I wanted. Everything this night had inevitably been leading up to.

'In a minute.' His voice had a beautiful, gravelly tone to it now, probably due to the cigarettes and alcohol he'd been indulging in tonight. It was so sexy I almost moaned out loud. 'I'm not finished here yet.'

I closed my eyes, letting my hand fall loosely around his neck as his mouth lowered down onto mine, kissing me so slow and so deep I didn't ever want to come up for air.

'You are such a bad influence,' I groaned, his mouth moving to

47

my neck, brushing over it so gently, so lightly, it was crazy!

'You don't know how bad I can be,' he growled, swinging me around so I was backed up against the wall, at his mercy, silently willing him to do all manner of unspeakable things to me, right there and then. I didn't really care. Not anymore.

'I'd quite like you to show me,' I whispered, taking hold of his t-shirt and pulling him against me, smiling as my mouth rested against his. 'Right now.'

6

Kicking my hotel-room door shut behind me, our lips still locked together, I fell back against the wall, my fingers burying themselves in his hair as we kissed. And kissed. And, oh God, we kissed!

'You okay?' he asked, pulling away only slightly, his breathing heavy, his fingers running lightly along the top of my dress.

'I'm fine,' I whispered, aware that my chest was heaving, and whether that was because his fingers were almost skimming the curves of my breasts, or whether it was because I was still out of breath due to our practically running here all the way from the elevator, I didn't know. I just knew that, what was happening here, I was ready for it. I wanted it. I wanted *him* – this tall, dark, dangerous stranger with the beard and the bikes. My Harley Davidson-riding hero. I couldn't stop myself from smiling, and he looked at me, smiling too.

'You sure? Because…'

I shut him up with a kiss, sliding his jacket back off his shoulders, hearing it fall to the floor with a soft thud.

'Well, I think if we're playing fair here, darlin', then you need to lose some clothing too.'

I laughed quietly, my mouth still touching his. 'I'm not wearing a jacket. You were. I'd say we're pretty much even now.'

'Oh, I gotta feisty one here.'

I closed my eyes again as I felt his hand slide up and under my dress, resting on my thighs. I bit down on my lip, our eyes locked together as I silently gave him the permission he was looking for.

'You sure you're okay with this?' His gaze dropped to my still-heaving chest, the fingers of his other hand sliding just underneath the top of my dress, causing me to gasp out loud as they touched my breasts.

All I could do was nod, the need to take this to its somewhat inevitable conclusion achingly painful.

'I'm okay with this,' I whispered, aware that he was tugging at my knickers, and I helped him slowly slide them down until they gathered around my ankles. Kicking them away, I stared into his eyes as I pushed my dress down over my breasts, my hips, letting that drop to the floor too, stepping out of it, leaving me naked, bar those spike-heeled boots. And I felt nothing but a sense of overwhelming freedom. No fear. No nerves. I was naked, in front of this man I'd only just met, and I felt incredible.

'Oh, Jesus, Lana, sweetheart… you truly are beautiful.'

Yeah, and so was he, in that rough, edgy way I was finding so sexy. But, right now, I was done with the talking. It was time for the action we'd probably both been looking for since the second we'd met in the elevator just a few short hours ago.

I backed right up against the wall, raising my arms above my head, closing my eyes as his fingers slid between mine, his mouth gently brushing over my neck with kisses so light I couldn't help but moan out loud.

'Are you sure, Lana?' His fingers tightened around mine, and I had a feeling that, as long as he kept talking to me, his voice could more than likely bring me to orgasm without him even having to touch me. But I wanted to be touched. Oh, God, did I want to be touched! 'Really sure?'

I didn't want to think about it anymore. I didn't want to think about the reality of the situation – that we were, quite obviously, going to have sex and then our lives would go their separate ways. I didn't want to think about that. I just wanted to do this. For me. This man, he wanted me. I wanted him. We both wanted *this*. Even if we *had* only known each other a few hours.

I nodded, and then he was holding me tight, his mouth crashing against mine with a force that literally took my breath away as he lifted me up, my legs wrapping firmly around his hips. I should have been scared. Or at least had the decency to feel just the tiniest hint of nerves – I hadn't had sex in so long, not since I'd left Adam. I hadn't even wanted it. Until now. Until this very second.

Throwing my head back slightly, my eyes closed again as his mouth moved down to my breasts, covering them in the lightest of kisses, his rough beard tickling my skin, and I couldn't help giggling slightly, a giggle that fast turned into a long, low, drawn-out moan as his tongue circled my nipple, causing goose bumps to break out in epic proportions all over my skin.

But then, a wave of ice-cold reality swept over me, hitting me from right out of nowhere, and I unwrapped my legs from around him, pushing him gently away. 'I'm sorry, Eddie, but I... I don't think I can do this,' I whispered, retrieving my dress from the floor, hurriedly pulling it back on.

'It's okay.' He smiled, and I felt that wave of reality start to retreat almost as quickly as it had appeared. 'Really. Believe me, darlin', I'm not just here for the sex.'

Did he mean that? How the hell could I possibly know? When I didn't know *him*. Which was why I really shouldn't have even been *thinking* about having sex with him. But we'd been so close to it just then, and my body had almost let itself go there, because I'd wanted it, I really had. I'd wanted *him*. But was that not just because my head was all over the place, because of my divorce, and the fact that this man wanted me? Wanted *sex* with me?

I closed my eyes for a couple of beats, turning and walking over to the bed. My skin felt warm, those tiny goose bumps that had appeared just seconds earlier still covering it, the tingling between my thighs growing stronger by the second.

'Lana?'

I turned around, my eyes meeting his, and they stayed fixed on him as he walked over to me. I didn't want him to go. I really didn't want him to go. There was still some crazy connection here that went way deeper than a physical need, and I was starting to find it all slightly confusing now. This was so out of my comfort zone.

'I'm… I'm fine,' I stuttered, feeling my heart start to race faster as he stood there in front of me, those dark eyes of his so intense I could feel every defence I was trying to put up weakening, crumbling down around me. There was still a part of me that was struggling for identity… Fuck it! You only live once. And whatever this was, whatever it turned out to be, I was taking it all, and I was going to enjoy it. I deserved *that* much, didn't I?

He smiled a slow smile as I once more slipped out of my dress, kicking it across the room in a manner verging on vicious, almost as if I didn't want to give myself another excuse to grab it again.

Moving closer, he slid a hand around the back of my neck, his fingers winding into my hair as he gently pulled my head back, his mouth lowering down onto mine in another of those incredible kisses. I could lose myself in those kisses. Completely and utterly lose myself. They semed to go on forever, both of us separating only when he pulled back to take off his t-shirt, revealing an array of tattoos that took my breath away. Covering both his arms, his shoulders, chest and back, I'd never seen ink like it. Skulls and knives, fire and flames, vibrant colour and deep, deep black; designs I'd never seen before. I could have spent a good half an hour just checking them out. And maybe I would, later.

I felt my heart start to pound, hammering hard inside of me, the anticipation both terrifying and exciting. I'd never done anything like this before. Ever. I'd only made love to one man my entire life, never really needing to know what another body felt like until I'd pulled my safe and comfortable world down around myself. Then everything had changed!

Once again he lifted me up, my legs briefly wrapping themselves back around him as he lay me down on the bed, my heart still trying its hardest to escape the confines of my chest with a heavy, almost painful, rhythm. I closed my eyes, pulling my legs up slightly, stretching out as I waited for him to undress, trying not to over-think this, because doing that just increased the nerves I was already feeling. Yeah, they'd suddenly hit me, those nerves. And I didn't want to feel nervous. I just wanted to let this happen.

I kept my eyes closed, feeling his hands on my knees gently push my legs further apart, allowing him to lie between, his body warm and hard against mine. A shockwave coursed through me, merging with an excitement I was finding hard to control and I breathed out deeply, desperately trying to push the old Lana further away. She needed to go, and take the past with her. She needed to go, now.

Keeping my arms stretched up above my head, I arched my back as his fingers slowly intertwined with mine, and I clung onto him, my eyes finally opening, meeting his.

'Okay?' he whispered, gripping my fingers tight.

I nodded, letting that tingling between my thighs take over, feeling it spread further up my body, causing the goose bumps to grow and my heart to continue racing at a rate I was finding hard to cope with. It really was quite difficult to breathe now, my throat was so tight.

But then, almost as if he was injecting me with a shot of something calming, I felt him push inside me, so slowly and carefully it caused that breath I'd thought was stuck in my throat to shift, giving way to a low groan I couldn't keep down.

I could feel him, his thrusts slow and gentle, the grip he had on my fingers intensifying as our bodies picked up a steady rhythm, moving together, and I pulled my legs up around him, arching my back again, pushing my hips up against his. I was giving him permission to push harder, go deeper, do whatever it was he needed

53

to do because I was going to take it all. He was setting me free, making me realise what I'd been missing all that time I'd been unhappy and unsure of the life I'd once led. It was like the floodgates were finally opening, and this time I really was emerging as the new me, instead of all those practice sessions I'd been going through these past few months. Could sex with a new man really do that? Could it really make me feel that way?

Throwing my head back I closed my eyes again, moaning quietly as his mouth began covering my neck in the tiniest of kisses, starting at the base of my throat and working upwards, his hips grinding into mine as he continued to thrust in and out of me with that same gentle rhythm. And each time he pushed back inside me I felt a beautiful shot of something – like the sweetest of electric shocks – hit me, causing my body to buck slightly, forcing more low groans out of me. He was making me crazy, and I was loving every wrong, confused second of it.

But then, as his fingers gripped mine so tight it verged on painful, I felt him stop, just for a second, then shudder slightly. And that was when the rush hit me. He was coming fast and hard, and I couldn't help but cry out loud as I felt my own climax start to build, my whole body shaking with the force of an orgasm the like of which I hadn't experienced since – I hadn't experienced. Ever. Every inch of my skin felt like it was on fire, burning up with the heat that seemed to spread through me, diminishing only slightly as both our bodies began to slow down, that rhythm fading, his grip on my fingers loosening.

I kept my eyes closed for a few more seconds, just listening to his breathing, heavy and ragged.

'You okay?' he asked, gently stroking my hair from my eyes, which I slowly opened, my heart still racing as I looked at him.

'Hell, yes!' I smiled, because what had just happened here… how could that *not* make me smile? Even though I wasn't entirely sure *what* I should be feeling now. I'd had sex with this man, just hours after meeting him. What did that make me? Crazy? Cheap?

54

Lucky? All three?

'You felt incredible.' His voice was so low, his mouth almost resting on mine as he spoke. It was the most erotic thing I'd ever experienced, but then, to be fair, anything even verging on erotic wasn't something my I'd experienced all that much of before. Adam just hadn't been the type to go in for all that. He'd been a very practical man, in every sense of the word. Guarded, almost. But I'd loved him. I really had loved him. Once upon a time.

I didn't know what to say now. I wasn't even sure I could speak anymore, my throat had gone all tight again. And my body, Jesus! That was still tingling in a way I hoped would never disappear. I could live with that feeling forever.

I felt him slowly pull out of me, rolling over onto his back. I turned onto my side, propping myself up on one elbow. 'Thank you.'

He did the same, leaning forward to kiss me gently. 'For what?'

'For waking me up.' In more ways than one. But he didn't need to know all the other stuff.

He smiled, reaching out to run his fingers lightly over the curve of my waist. 'Baby, it was a pleasure.' His eyes dipped to my breasts, his hand moving up to touch them, something that brought back that wonderful tingle as his fingers grazed my nipples. 'Has anyone ever told you you've got the most incredible tits?'

'No,' I laughed. 'Actually, they haven't.'

'Well, somebody should have done,' he whispered, his mouth resting against mine as he spoke in that deep, raspy accent of his. 'Because they are fucking amazing.'

I smiled, running my fingers through his even more messed-up hair, letting him pull me closer as he kissed me again, so slowly it drew another tiny moan out of me.

'Stay with me, Lana. Don't go back home. Stay here. In Vegas. With me.'

7

All I could do was stare at him. I certainly couldn't get any words out, not that I'd know what to say anyway. Was he being serious? Or was he just a little bit drunk? Because I was positive *I* must be. None of this was making sense anymore. If it ever *had* made sense. What on earth had I just done? What the hell was he asking me to do?

'Look, darlin', I'm the kind of guy who likes to take a risk, and you look like the kind of girl who feels the same.'

As a woman about to turn forty, I silently thanked him for calling me a girl. But this still wasn't making any sense. 'I don't know what kind of risk you're asking me to take here, Eddie. But I'm not sure I…'

He shut me up with a kiss. A long, deep, sexy-as-hell kiss. And that just pushed me under, killed me dead. I was gone. Finished. Another kiss. Another deadly blow to any common sense I might have still been clinging onto.

'I know you're looking for something, darlin'. And whatever it is, maybe you can find it here.'

'In Vegas?'

'It's as good a place as any.'

'You have no idea what I might be leaving behind back home.'

'I don't believe you're leaving anything important.'

'You don't know me, Eddie.'

'But I want to. I want to know every, single, beautiful inch of you.' His mouth was back on my neck, leaving a trail of tiny, soft kisses along my skin, my entire body shuddering as those kisses travelled lower. 'Spend the day with me tomorrow, Lana. We'll take one of the Harleys, go riding, grab some food at this great little diner I know on the edge of the desert... Let's have some fun, darlin.'

'You make everything sound so easy,' I groaned, unable to stop my body from shuddering again as his fingers gently stroked my hip.

'It *is* easy,' he whispered, his lips gently brushing my shoulder, his beard tickling my skin again. I was beginning to love that feeling. 'I can guarantee, sweetheart, that after you've spent the day with me, you aren't gonna *want* to go home.'

I couldn't help laughing, a small, slightly hysterical, laugh. It was the nerves and the shock and the total confusion this entire surreal scenario was throwing my way.

'You're actually serious?'

'I'm serious.'

I was thrown now. Completely. 'Okay, I... I mean, that's just... I can't even find the words... We only met yesterday.'

His thumb stroked my cheek again, his mouth so close to mine I could feel his breath on my skin. 'And you still don't believe in fate?'

'I told you. I'm cynical. I don't believe in fairytales.'

'Who said anything about fairytales?'

'Why, Eddie? Why do you want me to stay here? A complete stranger you don't know from...' I stopped talking, the sudden realisation that I was about to mention my ex-husband's name hitting me like a smack to the face.

'I've just been inside you, Lana.'

Oh, Jesus, was this really happening?

57

'And I want to go there again, and again.' His mouth was back on my neck, moving slowly upwards, kissing that spot just below my ear, sending a shiver through me I couldn't control.

'I can't just up and leave everything behind, Eddie.' Why not? I'd already done it once and even though that had only involved me moving a few miles down the road, it had also involved breaking up my marriage. But this…this involved a whole new country.

'Don't you want to know what it feels like to take a chance?'

I'd already taken one. Was it not a little too soon to be thinking of taking another?

'It's a crazy idea,' I groaned, arching my back as I felt him start to stroke my thigh, his hand warm and soft against me.

'I like crazy.'

Oh, God, he was inside me again, his fingers pushing their way in, touching me, teasing out of me another long, loud moan. 'This is so unfair.'

'Stay with me, Lana.' He kissed me slowly, and I could feel reality being pushed further and further away with every movement of his lips on mine. 'Stay with me…'

The thick white robe felt soft and comforting against my skin and I folded my arms against myself as I stared out of the window. Outside another Vegas day was dawning, the sky slowly changing colour, the darkness gradually being replaced with swirls of red and orange that cast an almost eerie shadow over a town that never really slept. It was beautiful to watch, my mind completely captivated by something I just didn't get to see back home. Back home there was too much reality. Here I could leave all that behind. And it felt good. I felt free for the first time in so long.

'Come back to bed.'

I closed my eyes as I felt his arms slide around my waist, pulling me against him from behind. 'I couldn't sleep.'

'I'd gathered that much, darlin'. But I didn't say anything about sleeping.'

I smiled, remembering the past few hours with a surprising clarity, given that we'd both drank quite a bit last night. But not enough to dim the memories of sex I never wanted to forget. My whole body felt almost re-energised this morning. In fact, everything about me felt different today.

'Were you serious, Eddie?' I opened my eyes, but continued to stare out of the window, watching as Vegas became bathed in soft, early-morning sunlight. 'About me staying here?'

He kissed my neck, his fingers intertwining with mine as our hands rested on my stomach. 'Baby, I've never been more serious.'

'I just thought, you know, because we'd been drinking...'

He loosened my robe, pulling it open, his hands sliding over my naked skin. 'I'm as sober as the next man now, kid. And I still meant every word I said last night.'

I leant back against him, sighing quietly as his fingers ran over my breasts, not caring that we were in front of the window, not caring about anything except the way he was touching me. His touch was like nothing I'd ever felt before – it was new and different and I was beginning to crave it.

'I meant every word,' he murmured, his fingers running over my hips, down over my bottom. I was lost. In just a few, incredible hours he'd opened up a whole new world for me and it was a world I was becoming more and more reluctant to leave.

I reached back to touch his face, my fingertips grazing his rough skin, burying themselves in his hair as he continued to tease me. I'd never been touched like this before. Ever. And I loved the way it made me feel: alive, beautiful – and sexy. This man made me feel so fucking sexy!

'I know it sounds like some crazy, spur-of-the-moment thing, Lana...' He pulled my robe back off my shoulders, and I let it drop to the floor, gasping softly as he kissed my shoulder, pulling me against him. 'It's what I do now, darlin'. Crazy, spur-of-the-moment things. It's how I live my life.'

What he was doing to me, what he was saying... Just being

here was spinning me out of control yet I knew what was going to happen the second I came to a standstill. I'd already made that decision last night, as we'd had sex over and over again, until our bodies could take no more. I hadn't been able to sleep, so I'd just lain awake, watching him, listening to his breathing, thinking everything over; the craziness of the situation. What I'd be leaving behind. What I might find if I just took a chance – the biggest chance of my life.

'You said something about taking one of your Harleys and going for a ride.' I turned around, the urge to kiss the life out of this man overwhelming. Because I knew how his kisses felt now. I knew what they could do to me. 'So, Eddie Fletcher, we're gonna have sex, then we're gonna go get that bike, and you can start showing me every reason why I should stay here.'

Leaning back against the windowsill, I turned my head to look out of Eddie's living-room window. His house, not all that far from the Vegas Strip, was simple and somewhat sparsely furnished, but it was clean and fairly spacious, with the welcome addition of a little splash-pool out in the back yard, which was more than any house I'd owned had ever had. Not that there was all that much call for splash pools in north-east England.

I'd felt a slight hint of trepidation walking into his home, and I didn't even know why. Maybe there was still a tiny part of me that felt this was all going a bit too fast, which it was, in reality. Yet, the second I'd stepped inside, the nerves and the doubt disappeared, to be replaced by something verging on familiarity. It was strange, but I'd decided to stop questioning everything. To stop over-thinking it all. It wasn't helping, it was just getting in the way.

His home also had a lovely, lived-in feel to it, which seemed to make it all the more welcoming. Probably another reason why I'd felt comfortable the second I'd walked inside. His somewhat bohemian neighbourhood had the most wonderful friendly atmosphere, something I couldn't really explain, but as soon as we'd pulled up outside on the bike there were people shouting hello, conversations striking up before we'd even reached the front door. It seemed like a nice place to hang out. A nice place to live.

'There's a barbecue at Hank's across the road on Wednesday night.'

I turned to see Eddie standing in the doorway. He'd changed his clothes now – the reason why we'd detoured here first before heading out of town. He was still in jeans, of course, but he was managing to pull off a white t-shirt that clung to his toned chest quite magnificently, and it was all I could do not to, audibly, show my appreciation. The addition of a red-and- black bandana tied around his head and a cigarette hanging from the corner of his mouth only seemed to make the biker in him more obvious, and that was an even bigger turn-on in my eyes. I could feel my thighs physically ache for him, despite the fact we'd only had sex less than an hour ago.

'I might not be here on Wednesday,' I said, allowing my mouth to curl up into a slight smile.

'Well…' He walked over to me, stubbing the cigarette out in an ashtray on the windowsill before he slid his arms around my waist, pulling me against him, '… you used the word *might*, so, I'm gonna look at that as a positive sign.'

'Eddie?'

'Hmm?' he murmured, his mouth nuzzling my neck.

'You said you never felt the need to get married. Why was that?'

He pulled back slightly, and the look on his face made me wonder if I'd made a mistake asking him that. Was it really any of my business? But this was a man who'd just asked me to stay here in Las Vegas. To give up my life in England and start a new one, with him. Surely I had a right to at least know *something* about his past?

'There was never anyone special enough, darlin'. Simple as that.' His expression softened, and I breathed a sigh of relief. The last thing I wanted to do was upset him. And anyway, I wasn't exactly being open about *my* past, was I?

'I'm sorry,' I whispered, letting him pull me back into his arms, his forehead resting against mine, my fingers lazily stroking the back of his neck.

'You've got nothing to be sorry for, sweetheart.' His mouth lowered down onto mine, and I allowed his kiss to wash everything else away; all the doubt and the fear and the rationality that *should* be pushing its way to the surface here. It was all being slowly washedaway with every movement of his lips against mine. 'I'm saying this again, Lana, because you need to know I'm serious. Stay with me.'

'Eddie…'

'You think it'll be a mistake?'

I kissed him slowly, my fingers stroking the back of his neck, his hands pushing me harder against him as I continued to live out this fantasy I'd thrown myself head-first into. It also gave me a few more seconds to think. To get my head straight. To make sure I was certain about this. 'I don't know. I have no idea whether this is going to turn out to be the biggest mistake of my life, or the best thing I've ever done. But I'll never find out unless I take that chance.' I smiled, my stomach contracting as he returned that smile. 'And I think I'm… Yeah. What the hell. I'm gonna take it.'

'Okay.' His smile widened, his eyes coming alive right there in front of me, and I couldn't explain the atmosphere that seemed to surround us at that very second. I just knew it felt right. Like pieces of some messed-up jigsaw puzzle were finally coming together. 'So, what do you say then, darlin'? You ready to start the ride of your life?'

As far as I was concerned, it had already begun.

8

I clung onto Eddie's waist, the wind blowing my hair back off my face, the roar of the Harley's engine the only sound I could hear as we sped along the deserted road. On either side of us there was nothing but an expanse of deep, rust-coloured land, the dust and dirt interspersed with patches of green cacti and desert plants. It seemed to go on forever, the colour changing only when it seemed to merge with the pale-blue sky, making it feel as though we were riding on the same stretch of road, over and over. The view didn't seem to change, bar the fleeting glimpse of a bigger cacti patch, or the odd cloud that had dared to show itself in that crystal-clear sky. It felt as though we were the only two people there. Nobody else could touch us, because nobody else existed.That's how it felt.

Leaning forward, I rested my head against his shoulder, closing my eyes for the briefest of seconds, letting the sound of the bike wash over me. I'd ridden pillion on Finn's Ducati a number of times back home, but it had never felt like this. This was something else completely. I felt as though, somewhere between me leaving the tattoo convention yesterday afternoon and meeting Eddie again in the elevator – I felt as though I'd somehow walked into a different world, crossed some kind of parallel timeline into another existence. And I was clinging onto that feeling like my life depended on it.

As Eddie pulled the bike up at the side of the road, I opened my eyes to see a small building a little way off in the distance.

'The diner I was telling you about,' Eddie said, killing the engine, pulling off his helmet and laying it down in front of him as he climbed off the bike.

I pulled off my own helmet, laying it down beside Eddie's, but I stayed where I was for a few more seconds, looking out ahead of me. That building was like an oasis, stuck in the middle of nowhere, even though I knew we were really only a few miles out of Vegas.

'This is so different to everything I've ever been used to,' I whispered, my eyes still fixed straight ahead.

'Different can be good sometimes.'

I turned to look at him, standing there all biker-hot and handsome. What I felt for this man was something I really couldn't explain. I'd known him all of one day – not even that – yet the thought of leaving him behind was the most terrifying feeling. Which was why I'd made the decision to stay here in Vegas. With him. A stupid, crazy decision, but I knew I wasn't going to change my mind now. I was living a fantasy, and I wasn't going to walk away from that; from something not many people ever got the chance to do.

I climbed off the bike, leaning back against it, my eyes locked with Eddie's as he came closer. 'I have no idea how I'm gonna tell my brother I'm not coming home.'

'Well, he's probably gonna try and make you change your mind.' He rested his hand against my cheek, his thumb stroking my skin in slow, gentle movements as his eyes sought to reassure me.

'Probably,' I whispered, my mouth almost touching his now, my lips physically aching to feel his against them. 'But I'm a big girl now, Eddie. I can make my own decisions.'

I felt my whole body relax into him as he finally kissed me, every part of me falling against him, giving into him. He was that dream I'd never even realised I had. That person I'd been looking for, the one who could open up all those locked doors that were still firmly closed inside of me. I believed that. I truly believed that. With every touch of his lips on mine, his fingers on my skin. When he was inside me everything just felt right. How could I walk away from that?

'You haven't really said that much about your life in the UK,' he said quietly, pulling back just a touch, his hand still resting against my cheek.

'You haven't said all that much about yours.' I laid my hand gently over his. 'Have you never felt like going home? Back to Scotland? Don't you miss it?'

He shook his head, his eyes burning into mine with a strange kind of intensity. 'America's my home now. My life's here, in Las Vegas. I don't have any reason to go back to Scotland.'

'There's nobody waiting for you back there? No family?'

He smiled slightly, just a small smile, which I wasn't entirely sure reached his eyes. 'My family aren't all that accepting of my lifestyle. We've never really been that close.'

'And what *is* your lifestyle, exactly?'

His smile grew a little wider, his eyes suddenly lighting up, which only served to make my heart beat that little bit faster. 'I'm a free spirit, Lana. The bike shop, and my stake in the garage my MC owns earns me enough to get by on. I live pretty simply. My home's quite basic, you've seen that… When I'm not working I ride, because when I'm out here, on the open road, it's the only time I think clearly. It really is the best kind of therapy.' His eyes were staring into mine with that strange, yet beautiful, intensity again, something that caused a ripple of excitement to bubble up inside of me. 'I'm an old-school biker, darlin'. I wear my colours with pride and loyalty is everything. But freedom – that's the most important thing in the world for me.'

I couldn't tear my eyes away from his. This tall, handsome man with the tattoos and the beard and a voice so low and sexy – he really was everything I'd ever dreamt of. I just hadn't realised it, until now. And everything he'd just said there, it was everything I'd wanted to hear.

'What about *you*?' he asked, his thumb still stroking my cheek, his hand warm yet rough against my skin. I didn't want him to take it away. I liked it, I liked him touching me.

'What *about* me?' But even after all of that I was still reluctant to open up to him. Maybe because opening up, talking about the past brought it all back to the forefront. And I didn't want to look back. I wanted to move forward.

'Last night, in the elevator – you told me you were divorced.'

I looked down, finally breaking that stare, because looking him in the eye and talking about Adam – that didn't feel right. 'I am. It's just not something I really want to get into.'

'Things didn't work out, huh?'

I raised my gaze, my eyes meeting his again. 'Yeah. Something like that. We were together a long time and... We grew apart, that's all. It happens.'

'Yeah,' he sighed, finally pulling his hand away from my face. 'A lot of shit happens.'

I frowned slightly as I watched his expression change, the look in his eyes something I couldn't read. Sadness? I didn't have time to really let it register as his face broke back into a slow smile. But what he'd said there...

'You still think about him?' Eddie asked, a question that surprised me, because it wasn't something I'd expected him to ask.

'Sometimes.' I was being honest now. Because I did still think about Adam. He'd been a huge part of my life – he'd *been* my life. So of course I still thought about him. 'I was with him for almost twenty years. And you can't just forget all of that as though it never happened.'

'No.' Eddie's expression changed again, the smile once more disappearing from his face, his eyes clouding over. 'No, you can't.' But then, as quickly as if someone had just flicked a switch, the smile was back. The sadness in his eyes gone. 'You said you worked in a tattoo studio…' It was as if he'd sensed a change of subject was needed. He wasn't wrong.

'Yeah. Finn's – my brother's – tattoo studio. One of those major life changes, you know? I used to work in the theatre, now I'm training to become a tattoo artist.'

'You've got some beautiful ink there yourself. Your brother do that?'

I nodded. 'They're all part of the new me.'

'And what about the old one?'

My gaze dropped once more, focusing on my biker boots, the road, anything but him. 'I'm moving on, Eddie.'

I felt him take my hand and I looked up at him, the feeling of his fingers sliding between mine was comforting. 'Hey, I'm all about the here and now, baby. The past, it should stay where it belongs. You let it back in, it's only gonna drag you down, believe me.'

'How can you be so perfect?' I smiled, my fingers lightly touching his slightly open mouth.

He laughed, that low-down dirty laugh that made my thighs ache for him. 'I'm anything but perfect, darlin'.'

I cupped his face in my hands, kissing him slowly, enjoying the taste of him; that taste of beer and cigarettes, his mouth opening as his arms fell loosely around my waist. 'Well, perfect can be boring,' I whispered.

'And boring is one thing I'm not, sweetheart.'

Oh, God, he was making me feel like that infatuated teenager I was trying not to be, but it was hard not to get caught up in the fantasy of this situation. Because the reality was still something I was struggling to get my head around.

'So, you've definitely made your mind up, then?' Eddie asked, letting his hands fall a little lower, his fingers sliding down the back of my jeans. 'About staying here, in Vegas?'

It was still the craziest idea; the kind of thing that didn't happen in real life, not to people like me, anyway. People like me didn't just up and leave everything behind to stay with a person they'd only just met, in a strange country, just because the sex was great. No, the sex was mindblowing! But this was so much more than sex. I knew that. I could feel it.

'Oh, I'm staying, biker boy. So you better get ready for a wild ride of your own.'

'You're joking, right?' Finn folded his arms as he leant back against the wall, watching as I brushed mascara over my lashes. I hadn't expected him to take the news well, and he wasn't. He wasn't really taking it at all.

'Finn, I'm too bloody exhausted to joke about anything.'

'So, let me get this straight. The reason why none of us have seen you since yesterday afternoon is because you've been spending all your time with a Scottish biker called Eddie who owns a motorcycle shop and lives here, in Vegas.'

'That's about the size of it, yes.'

'And tonight, you're going out with him again?'

'You've been listening, then?'

'Yeah, I have, and all of that – *all* of that is fine. It's what I wanted you to do, start having some fun. Have as much of that as you can, kiddo. But… staying here, staying with *him*…? Staying in *America*? What the hell is *that* all about?'

I swung around on my stool. 'I need distance, okay?'

Finn's expression was, of course, confused. I couldn't really expect him to feel any other way. 'What the fuck are you talking about?'

'He's still there, Finn.'

'Who is? Jesus, Lana, you're not making any sense here.'

No. I wasn't. Because all of this had come from nowhere. I hadn't even been aware it was what I'd been feeling until I'd said the words. 'Adam.'

'Adam? Why the hell is Adam on your mind all of a sudden?'

I looked down at my hands, which I'd balled up into fists

without even realising, my nails digging into my palms. So why wasn't I feeling any pain? 'He's not on my mind *"all of a sudden"*, Finn. He's always been there. And what with the divorce and everything…'

Finn came over to me, crouching down in front of me, taking one of my hands and unfurling my fingers. 'Why didn't you talk to me, hmm? I thought you and Adam…'

'We are. We're over. Of course we are. But it doesn't mean I can just push him to the back of my mind and forget about everything, just like that. We were together almost twenty years.'

'But you weren't happy, Lana.'

'I *wasn't* happy, not all the time. But he wasn't a bad person, Finn. He just wasn't the *right* person. For me. And I just wish I'd faced up to that sooner.'

'Okay. But, that's why you left him, isn't it? Because he wasn't the right person for you? You finally found the strength to make that decision, to move on. And that takes guts, kiddo.'

I pulled my hand away from his and turned to look back in the mirror, saying nothing.

Finn sat down on the arm of the couch. 'I'm more confused than ever now. Lana, I… Are you telling me that you're gonna up and leave the new life you've made for yourself back home and… You're actually gonna *stay* with this guy? Just like that? Because you do realise how crazy that sounds, don't you? And you're gonna do that because, what? You think you need distance between you and your ex-husband? The same ex-husband you haven't seen for months? And it doesn't seem to have bothered you being in the same postcode as him since the split. The risk of you running into him, of seeing him, I wasn't aware it was a problem.'

'It isn't.'

'Then all of this is crazy.'

'You're making it *sound* crazy, Finn.'

'No. It *is* crazy, Lana. It's off-the-page crazy. It's ridiculous. You've known this guy for all of a day, had one night out with him, fucked him a few times, and in your eyes that constitutes a good enough reason to ride off into the sunset on some ridiculous notion that you could actually have a life with this man?'

I swung round again, surprised by how calm I actually felt, considering everything Finn was saying made more sense than anything I was doing right now. 'Nobody's talking about making a life with anyone, Finn. This isn't some kind of fairytale happy-ever-after. I'm not *that* naïve?' Or was I?

He just raised an eyebrow, but thankfully kept his mouth shut.

'It's just… This past year, it's been exhausting. And strange. And amazing, and… and I'm still trying to get my head around it all. And you… you are my rock, Finn. I am so glad I found you again, had the chance to get close to you again and you're not just my brother, okay? You're my best friend – you know? The one I will always turn to because you are so important to me now. I love you so much, I really do…'

'And I love you too, beautiful. You walked back into my life as this woman who wanted to change her entire world, and you'd started to do that in a matter of days, Lana. Because you are stronger than you think you are. Than you ever *thought* you were. But this… this is just crazy. And as somebody who loves you, I'm not sure I can stand by and watch you make a mistake like this.'

I shook my head, getting up and walking over to him. 'You can't stop me.'

He stood up, too, his hands in his pockets, his eyes staring deep into mine. 'I can try. Look, I know I pushed you into going out with the guy but, Jesus, Lana, I only meant for a drink. I didn't expect this shit to happen.'

'Neither did I, Finn. But, you know, sometimes things happen for a reason. Sometimes a chance will appear that you never dreamt would or could happen, and you've just got to grab that chance before it disappears forever. Sometimes, you have to rely on fate, whether you believe in it or not.'

He raised that eyebrow again. 'You're believing in fate all of a sudden? You? Miss cynical?'

'I didn't say I believed in it. I'm just taking a risk, okay? Isn't that what you told me I should be doing?'

'I'm absolutely positive I never mentioned running off with a Scottish biker. That wasn't exactly the kind of risk I meant.'

'I know,' I sighed, sitting down on the couch, pushing both hands through my hair. 'I know that isn't what you meant, but... Something happened here, Finn. Something clicked inside of me. Something I can't explain.'

'Are you sure you haven't just been blinded by too much sex? I mean, I know you haven't had any for Christ knows how long...'

I threw him a look as he sat down next to me. 'I don't know, okay? And you're right. This *is* crazy. It's ridiculous, and unreal, and incredibly selfish of me but...' I looked down at my clasped hands. 'Maybe I'm having some kind of middle-age meltdown. But Eddie he's... he's just as crazy as I am, Finn. And maybe crazy is just what I need right now.'

Finn sighed, throwing himself back against the couch cushions. 'Lana, babe, you know nothing about this guy.'

'And he knows nothing about me. But don't you think that's what makes it so much more exciting?'

He just looked at me, but didn't offer up any kind of answer.

'I'm almost forty years old, Finn. And I have spent most of my life in a box I thought I was never going to be able to escape from...'

For the next twenty minutes I found myself pouring my heart out about my marriage break-up. And I had no idea why these floodgates had chosen to open now; why I was suddenly telling Finn all these things I'd kept from him before. I just knew that I needed to get it out. All of it. In order for me to really be able to walk away from the past. Keeping it bottled up inside had only held me back, I knew that now.

'If there's something else out there you want, something that might just make you happy; something you know you can have if you just have the balls to go out there and grab it, then... then

71

nobody should feel guilty about doing that. Nobody. And *you* helped me see that, Finn. You gave me the confidence I needed to go out there and be this person I so badly wanted to be; *needed* to be. The person I should have become a long time ago.'

'So it's my fault you're eloping with Scotty, then?'

'Finn…'

'And what about your apprenticeship at Black Ink?'

'Look, Finn, I'm not saying this is forever, okay? It might not even be something that lasts more than a few weeks but I… It's something I need to do. And I can't really explain it, or give you a reason that would make any kind of sense, I just… I *need* to do this. I kind of want to see where it takes me. And, it'll give me the time I quite obviously need to get my head around those things I'm still finding hard to let go of. You'll still train me, won't you? If I come back home?'

'*If?*'

'Will you?' I fixed him with a look and he sighed.

'You know I will.'

I leant over and kissed his cheek, ruffling his dark hair.

'You're fucking nuts, do you know that? Certifiably crazy.'

I stood up and walked over to the full-length mirror by the bed, cocking my head as I stared at my reflection. 'Yeah. I know I am.' I swung around, smiling as I looked at him. 'Like I said, you made me this way, remember?'

He sighed again as he hauled himself up off the couch. 'I created a frigging monster, that's what I did.' He walked over to me, pulling me into his arms, his expression suddenly turning serious. 'Don't do it, Lana. Please. Think about this, okay? Think about what's happening here. What you're planning to do, it's not the most sensible idea you've ever had.'

'I'm done with sensible, Finn.' I snuggled in against him, holding him tight. 'I've been sensible for almost forty years, and I think that's long enough. Now I want to do crazy and stupid and all those things I never had the chance to do before.'

72

'But this isn't just…' He let go of me, pushing both hands through his hair as he let out another heavy sigh. 'It doesn't matter what I say, does it? You're actually gonna do this.'

'Yeah. I'm gonna do this.'

'Then know that I think it's a bad idea.'

'I need you to be with me on this one, Finn. Please.'

He shook his head, and I felt tears start to prick the backs of my eyes. 'I can't, Lana. I can't support you on this because I think you're making a mistake.'

'Finn, please…'

'Go out with him tonight, and you will be that amazing person I know you are, okay? You do that, you go out there and have some fun, spend the night with him, have as much sex as you want, wear the bastard out for all I care. But in the morning, I want you to tell me you're coming home with the rest of us.'

'I can't promise you that.'

'Think about this, Lana, please. What you talked about just now, everything you said about finding something that makes you happy, about starting a new life, you're doing just fine on that score, kiddo. You really are. You don't need to stay here to prove anything to yourself…'

'That isn't why I'm doing it, Finn. I don't need to prove anything to anyone… Jesus… I just want to… I just want to be with him… There's something about him that makes me feel – I don't know. He makes me feel alive. He makes me feel like somebody I never knew I could be. It's like he's awakened something inside me that's been lying there, dormant, for all those years.'

'Just come home, Lana. Come home and let's get back to normal. Let's carry on doing what we were doing because we were having a blast, kiddo. I thought you liked our life.'

'I *love* our life, I really do, I just… I need that space, that time to really push Adam to the back of my mind…'

'I don't think this is all to do with Adam. Not really.'

I stared at him, right into his eyes. 'I'm staying, Finn.'

He let out another heavy, frustrated sigh. 'I can't believe you're doing this… You know I'm always gonna be there for you, don't you? Always. And when this crazy, stupid, rash act you're about to undertake falls down around you – when it all turns to shit and you realise what a huge mistake it really was, I'll *still* be there, ready to pick up the pieces. I'll still be there. But I can't pretend this is a good idea, Lana. Because I think it's wrong.'

I backed away from him, folding my arms against me again. 'I've told you, I'm not under any illusion this is gonna last forever.'

'That's just as well, then, isn't it?'

'I'm staying, Finn. And there isn't anything anyone can do to stop me.'

9

I stared at the bottle of beer in front of me, my thumb absent-mindedly stroking the label.

'Second thoughts?' Eddie asked, his hand touching mine, pulling me back to the here and now.

'No.' I smiled, watching his thumb as it ran over my knuckles. 'No second thoughts.'

'Lana, darlin', I don't want to…'

I looked up at him, my eyes meeting his. He was still a stranger, this man who'd crash-landed into my life without any warning. This man who'd asked me to stay with him, start a new life – *another* new life – with him, in a strange country. This man who'd made love to me just hours after meeting me and made me feel something I'd never felt before. Even if I wasn't quite sure what that was just yet.

'I only have whatever's in that suitcase back in my hotel room, Eddie. That's all I have to start a whole new life.'

His fingers continued to stroke mine, his eyes almost burning into me, making sure I had no choice but to hold that stare. 'Don't you find that quite liberating? The chance to *really* start again? With nothing of the past to hold you back.'

My smile grew a little wider because he was making this whole crazy idea sound like the biggest adventure. 'Yeah, I do, actually.'

'Do you have dreams, Lana?'

I looked at him, cocking my head slightly. 'We all have dreams, don't we?'

His eyes were still fixed on mine. 'So, tell me yours.'

I looked briefly down at the table before raising my gaze. 'The dreams I have now?'

He just raised his eyebrows, his thumb still running over my knuckles.

'I guess… Well, some of those dreams have already come true. I got the tattoos, showed myself I was capable of changing my life…'

'What would you *really* love to do, darlin'?'

I stared at him, letting those dark, dangerous eyes of his pull me further under, holding me there. 'I want to escape,' I whispered, the words falling free without me even realising.

'From what?'

'Everything.' *Except you*, I wanted to add. *I want to escape from everything, except you.* Because he was the only thing I wanted right now. Him, and the way he made me feel.

'Everything?' He raised another eyebrow, his fingers sliding between mine.

'Just after I left Adam, not long after I'd started my apprenticeship at Black Ink, I remember this group of guys coming into the studio. They were from a local motorcycle club back in Newcastle and they were about to head off on a road trip, riding across France and Spain. It was for charity, but they'd done it a couple of times before, and when they spoke about it, about the freedom it created, just getting on their bikes and riding, for hours… Something hit me, right here, you know?' I tapped my chest, my eyes still staring into Eddie's. 'Because I'd never experienced that kind of freedom before. Never knew what it felt like. Riding pillion on Finn's Ducati through the streets of Newcastle wasn't the same, and I just…' I looked down, watching his thumb as it moved across my skin. 'I know what it feels like now. Being with you… I know what that freedom feels like. And it's something I've dreamt about, ever since hearing those guys talk. The idea of just climbing on a bike and getting away from everything, it always seemed like something people only did in movies. But to be able to leave reality behind, just for a little while…'

His mouth curled up into a smile, something in his eyes making my head spin with a heady excitement. 'Let's do it.'

'Do what?' I frowned.

'Escape. Not right this second, but, in a few days, let's just throw some things into a rucksack, jump on the Harley and ride. Across America. We'll do the west coast, see California, spend our days on the road and our nights fucking until we wear ourselves out. Who's stopping us, baby?'

'I… Are you serious?'

'I think you already know the answer to that one, darlin'.'

I couldn't stop the widest smile from spreading across my face. 'Can we…? We can really *do* that?'

'Like I said, who's stopping us? We're gonna go live those dreams, baby.' He brought my hand up to his lips, kissing it gently, his eyes still on mine as he did so. 'I can see myself in you, Lana. Someone who wants to escape everything that once dragged them down; a free spirit…'

'I'm no free spirit.'

'Well, maybe you should try it sometime. You might get one hell of a kick out of it.'

I laughed, his hand still holding mine as he pulled me down from my stool and into his arms, his eyes once more burning into mine. I felt my heart start to race again – that unexplainable rhythm, that heavy beat I wasn't used to. And before I had time to even take a breath he'd pushed me back against the wall, kissing me, long and slow, the heat of his body as it pressed against me overwhelming. His tongue slid into my mouth as the kiss deepened and I could feel myself responding, almost as though I was being worked by some invisible strings because it really was like I had no control over this.

'Don't ever let go of your dreams,' he whispered, his breath warm against my skin, the musky scent of his cologne heady and strong. 'And don't ever let anyone stand in your way.'

Slipping a hand around the back of his neck, I wound my fingers in his hair, kissing him back just as hard and just as determined, and I was lost, falling deeper and deeper into something I didn't understand. I just knew that he was kissing me like I'd never been kissed before, and all of a sudden I didn't want to be in this crowded bar with its loud music and smell of stale beer. I wanted to be alone with this man.

'You want to escape? Then let me show you *my* kind of escape, Lana. Let me show you my world. Let's make those dreams come true, darlin'.'

My head was spinning, his words dancing around in there like the most beautiful of promises. Except, I had a feeling they were promises he was going to keep. And it was at that second that I knew I was falling into something I didn't want to get out of; sinking deeper and deeper into a life that was sweeping me along at a pace that was breathtaking, but I would run until my lungs hurt to keep up with it all. Eddie Fletcher had changed my world. And there wasn't a thing I would do to change that now.

'We need to get out of here,' he murmured, his mouth still resting against mine.

I nodded, my thumb lightly stroking his neck as he kissed me again. And again. Each kiss dragging me further and further under. 'And I think sooner rather than later, don't you?'

I returned the smile he gave me, reluctantly pulling my fingers out of his hair but keeping my other hand in his, holding it tight as we left the bar, walking out onto the Strip, the bright lights and the noise, and the whole feel of this unreal place reminding me of just where I was – so far away from that life I'd used to live. That person I'd once been. Somewhere, and someone, I didn't

78

ever want to go back to.

With his arm slung across my shoulders, I clung onto his waist as we walked the short journey back to my hotel. As we walked he pointed out places he was going to take me, told me about the things we were going to do; he talked about his shop, his MC, his love of Harleys and why he'd settled so easily in Las Vegas – a place that didn't ask questions. In that short space of time he made me fall in love with the idea of my new, unexpected life a million times over, the excitement inside me building up to breaking point as we finally reached the hotel.

'Days like we had today, baby…' He pulled me into his arms as the elevator doors closed. 'Days where we do nothing but fuck for hours and drink until we can't think straight, they're ours for the taking. Why settle for reality when you can have something so much more exciting?'

'You make it sound like some kind of utopia,' I whispered, running my fingers over his slightly open mouth, my eyes following their every move.

'I can't promise you that, darlin', but I *can* promise you enough great sex to guarantee there'll be days when your legs ache so bad you won't be able to get out of bed, and whisky that'll give you the kind of hangover only a Scotsman can ease.'

I slipped my arms around his neck, pushing myself against him, laughing, a sudden calm taking over as his fingers began stroking the small of my back, up and down, strokes so light he was barely touching me. 'You can promise me that, can you?'

'I can promise you a lot of things…' His mouth rested on mine, and I felt myself breathe in sharply as his fingers slid up under my top, touching my skin. 'You ever fucked on a Harley, darlin'?'

Oh, Jesus, my heart had just skipped a whole bunch of beats there, my stomach dipping so low I literally couldn't catch my breath. These feelings I was experiencing here, they all felt so new and I was having trouble getting my head around them, they were all happening so fast.

'No,' I whispered. 'No. I haven't.'

I closed my eyes as he kissed me again, letting any last lingering doubt that might still be lurking in the recesses of my mixed-up mind evaporate before it had time to show itself. Because it wouldn't be welcome.

'Come on.' He smiled, taking my hand as the elevator doors opened. My heart was beating so fast it hurt as we almost ran along the corridor to my room, so desperate were we to gain some privacy.

The second we were through the door he pushed me back against it, the kiss he gave me hard and rough, a turn-on I hadn't expected. It was almost brutal in its force, and I felt my whole body shiver as his hands pushed up my short leather skirt, his mouth trailing over my neck and collarbone as he yanked down my knickers, giving me no other option but to step out of them. He was taking control and I was happy to submit.

'You're like a fucking drug I can't give up now,' he murmured, my legs wrapping around him as he pushed me back against the door.

I couldn't speak, couldn't get any words out my throat was so tight, my chest so constrained. All I wanted to do was hold onto him and let this happen, whatever it was. Because it was everything I'd been missing in my life – passion, excitement, sex that was raw and animalistic, that both hurt and brought with it a pleasure so intense it was indescribable. And he was giving it to me, right here, and no matter how sordid it all was, or how wrong some people may have found the whole scenario, I didn't care. I only cared that I felt free and alive and about to do something I would never have dreamt I'd ever do. Finn was still right, of course. This *was* crazy. And stupid. And, yeah, probably a little bit selfish, too, but going back home – it wasn't an option. Not anymore.

So what if I was staying here with just a suitcase full of clothes and nothing else to my name? I was giving myself something far more important as far as I was concerned. I was giving myself a chance to do something I'd wanted to do for so long now – I was about to start living.

10

Trailing my fingers in the warm water, I gently kicked my feet underneath the surface of the clean, clear splash-pool out in Eddie's back yard, the sun burning down on the back of my neck. I'd been here all of two days and I was still waiting for the regret to kick in; the realisation that I really had made that huge mistake Finn still assumed I'd made. But nothing was making its presence felt just yet. Maybe it was because, in some weird kind of way, it still felt as though I was only on an extended holiday. All I knew was I hadn't felt like this in a long time. Correction – I hadn't *ever* felt like this. I felt re-born, even if that did sound a little far-fetched.

'Hey.'

I looked up at the sound of that now-familiar voice. Yeah, just four days of knowing him and I could use that word – familiar. It didn't get any easier to understand, I just knew that's how I was feeling. And after years of repressing the way I'd really felt, I wasn't going to let that happen again. I just wasn't. It was all going to come out now. Everything. And I wasn't ever going to care.

'Hey back.' I smiled as he reached down to take my hand, pulling me to my feet. 'You going out now?'

'Aye. I'm gonna head off downtown in a bit. Check out what's going on at the shop.'

I smiled, cupping his cheek in my hand, stroking his skin with my thumb as we kissed. We'd spent a lot of time kissing over the past couple of days, in between me trying to get used to my new surroundings, because Vegas was more than a little different to Newcastle-upon-Tyne. It was warmer, for starters. But Eddie's neighbourhood was also one of the most welcoming places I'd ever encountered. In the short space of time I'd been here I'd already spoken to three of his neighbours, all of them so friendly and willing to do anything they could to help me settle in. It just all added to the rather surreal feeling that still washed over me every now and again. The realisation of what I'd actually done. But waking up next to Eddie, it didn't feel wrong. It still, in some strange way I didn't think I'd ever be able to explain, felt right. As though I'd waited my whole life for this. For him.

'You gonna come with me?'

His voice shook me back to reality and I looked at him, smiling. Yeah, he still made me want to smile. Every single, wonderful, day.

'I'll show you the bikes. We can hang out with some of the guys from the club, maybe go for a ride later on. What do you say? You up for that?'

'You really have to ask?' Riding was something I'd quickly become addicted to. I couldn't get enough of that feeling of freedom, the sound of the Harley's engine, the breeze cooling my skin.

He laughed, a deep, low, throaty laugh that was so unbelievably sexy. 'I haven't even scratched the surface with you, kid. Have I?'

I smiled again, running a hand through his hair, watching as it fell forward over his eyes. That's what I loved about him. Everything was so out of place, nothing was ordered. So unlike everything I'd lived with for so long. 'There's really not that much to know,' I whispered, pulling off my bikini top and tossing it aside. I knew he was never going to turn me down, just as I couldn't say no to him. I couldn't even think of a time when that was going to happen, but I also wasn't naïve enough to think these initial feelings of lust and urgency were going to last forever, so I was enjoying every heart-stopping, breathtaking minute while they were still here. Because I'd almost forgotten how magical they could feel, those early days of just being with someone.

'Well, you see, I think there is,' he murmured, his mouth almost touching mine, his fingers running lightly over my naked breasts. 'Do you ride yourself, Lana?'

'Never had the chance to learn. But it's something I'd love to do.' How I was getting the words out I didn't actually know, because my breath was, quite literally, catching in my throat. It always did when he was this close.

'Maybe I can teach you, huh?' His voice was so quiet now, and way too sexy to even be legal, in my opinion.

'I think you're teaching me enough, Mr Fletcher,' I gasped, throwing my head back as he started to kiss my neck, his fingers slowly untying my bikini bottoms until they fell away from my body, into his hands.

'The lessons are only just beginning, darlin'.'

I shivered inside as his lips rested gently against mine, his body so close now, the inevitable endgame on its way, as had been the norm these past couple of days. We got up, we had sex, sometimes we ate, sometimes we just had sex again. We'd gone out a couple of times, to get some food, to ride; to let him show me around the area. But we'd never stayed out all that long. We'd just gone home again, and had more sex. All night long. I'd only been here two days but it already felt as though I'd been here forever, he was so familiar to me now. I knew every inch of his body, recognised the way he talked, the mood he was in just by looking in his eyes. He didn't ask questions and he didn't judge me. He just wanted to be with me. And I wanted to be with him. Oh, God. Did I want to be with him!

He sat down on the edge of a large wooden sun lounger next to the splash-pool, pulling me down onto his lap, our mouths locked together in a deep, deep kiss, the sun continuing to burn down on my naked body. 'Have we got time for this?' I whispered, reaching down to free him.

'All the time in the fucking world, sweetheart. One of my MC brothers is helping Kyle in the shop, keeping an eye on things for me until I get there. I'm sure he won't mind hanging around for another hour.'

'That's so selfish,' I breathed, lifting my hips up slightly to guide him inside of me.

He laughed quietly, pulling me back down. 'You have no idea how good for me you are, Lana.'

I buried my fingers in his hair, closing my eyes as I moved against him, wanting to feel him, to know this was really happening, because despite everything we'd done, all the time we'd already spent together, sometimes it still felt like one long dream that I was going to wake up from any second now. And I just wasn't ready to let it go. Not yet.

'Jesus, Eddie... You are making me *crazy*!' I groaned, arching my back, pushing myself right down onto him, groaning again as I felt his mouth cover one of my breasts, his tongue working a magic I could barely understand. I only knew it was the most intense feeling; the most incredible sensation. All those years of being with Adam and we'd never made love anywhere other than the bedroom, apart from the one or two times we'd only just made it to the couch. But those times had usually been the rare occasions we'd been fuelled by alcohol, after a friend's wedding or a works' Christmas party. It had never been something we'd made a habit of, spontaneous sex. And I'd just had no idea what I'd been missing. It was like someone had opened the gate to a prison I'd been locked up in for years and now I was finally running free.

'You have no idea how crazy I can make you, darlin'.' He almost growled the words, and I swear to God that's what caused a wave of pleasure so intense to shoot through me I had to bury my face in his hair to stop me from crying out loud. His back yard may have seemed private enough, but I still didn't want to attract any unwanted attention. And as that wave swept rapidly over my entire body, I shook in his arms, feeling the force of his own climax as he came just seconds after me, kissing me this time to soften the sound of our moans. But, oh, God, I had never felt anything like it; an all-consuming, powerful feeling of something I couldn't explain. And I didn't really want to. I quite liked the mystery. It was a pretty big turn-on, if truth be told.

'That was crazy enough,' I breathed, resting my forehead against his as we tried to catch our breath.

I felt his hand slide into the small of my back, his thumb gently stroking it, the sound of his breathing still heavy and uneven. 'You regretting staying yet?' He smiled, and I found myself smiling back, my hands either side of his face as I looked into his eyes. Dark, deep, soulful eyes.

'No. Not yet.' My eyelids flickered shut as he kissed me again, long and slow, and I let myself fall into him; lose myself in a moment I wanted to live over and over again. I still had so much to learn about this man I'd let into my life. This man I'd given my life up for. And I couldn't wait to get started.

The late-afternoon sun bounced off the sparkling chrome and I squinted slightly, wishing I'd put my sunglasses on before coming outside.

The huge, imposing Harley Davidson was one of a handful of bikes on display in the small yard that surrounded Eddie's motorcycle shop. There were many more inside, and I'd spent most of the day checking them all out, listening as Eddie had explained the differences between them. His passion was infectious, and I'd found myself eager to learn as much as I could about this world I was only just beginning to immerse myself in; these machines and the men who rode them. But my heart belonged to the Harleys. There was something about the chrome and the leather, the colours that ranged from my favourite – black – to deep, metallic reds, blues and burnt oranges; from the low-slung Sportsers to the wide-shouldered 1200 Custom cruiser. The whole history of those bikes, it fascinated me. And now that I'd finally had the chance to ride one – albeit pillion on Eddie's Road-King Classic – that had only strengthened my new-found love. And I was in deep now.

'You okay?'

I turned to see Eddie standing behind me. Dressed in battered old jeans, just as battered heavy boots, and a black t-shirt, his hair pushed back off his face, dark glasses covering his eyes – unkempt and untidy... Yeah! So fucking sexy!

'I'm absolutely fine.' I leant back against the bike, placing my hands behind me on the Harley's leather seat, the feel of it soft beneath my fingers.

'I thought we'd head off for that ride now. Maybe stop for something to eat while we're out. And later, if you feel like it, why don't you come with me to the clubhouse?'

I frowned slightly, my fingers refusing to leave the Harley.

'There's a party, over at my MC tonight,' Eddie explained. 'We're welcoming a couple of new members into the club, and it's a bit of a tradition, these welcome parties. But if you think it might...'

I shut him up with a kiss, finally pulling my hand away from the bike to rest it on his hip instead. It had much the same effect as the Harley; making my skin tingle and my stomach flip with a new-found excitement. 'I didn't think you'd want me there just yet, I mean...'

'Why wouldn't I?' he asked, running his thumb lightly over my bottom lip, his eyes following its every move.

I smiled, feeling a slight hint of nerves at the prospect of meeting his MC brothers. I'd heard a lot about motorcycle clubs, never sure how much to believe and how much was just hear-say. Finn and I had friends back home who were members of such clubs, but I'd never set foot inside of one. Never been that close to the reality. Never really asked them what went on within the confines of one. I guess I was about to find out now.

His mouth closed in on mine again. Was there ever going to be a time when we didn't skate close to sex every time we were near each other? 'I want to be with you, darlin'. So much, it's like an ache in my gut that won't go away, this need I have to…' He broke off, kissing me gently, slowly. So slowly it messed with my head, big time. A kiss so hot, so sensual. 'I just want to be with you, Lana.'

No. I still wasn't getting tired of him saying my name. 'I want to be with you, too,' I whispered, staring up at him. Jesus! Did I want to be with him? He had no idea…

He smiled, and I couldn't help smiling back. 'We got that sorted, then.'

I laughed, something he made me do quite often. Real laughs. Laughs that I felt from deep within, because I was genuinely happy in his company.

'I'll be two minutes, okay? Just want to have a quick word with Kyle. Got a couple of guys coming to collect bikes around six, so I just need to bring him up to speed and make sure he's okay to close up for me, then we'll get going.'

I nodded, watching as he walked back inside, that swagger he had still so unbelievably sexy I could have watched him walk all day, as well as listen to him talk. And I was starting to sound like some infatuated teenager again, which I definitely wasn't.

Leaning back against the bike I pulled my phone out of my back pocket, finding Finn's number there at the top of my speed-dial list. It took a few rings before he answered, and when he did he sounded more than a little groggy.

'Jesus, Lana, do you know what fucking time it is?'

I looked at my watch. 'Yeah, it's almost…' I slapped a hand over my mouth, trying not to laugh. 'Oh. Sorry. I forgot about the time difference.'

'Again. You forgot about the time difference *again*.'

'Before you left Vegas you told me you didn't give a shit about the time difference. You said I could call you any time.'

'Yeah, I know, and I'm kind of regretting that now.'

'What time *is* it over there?' I asked, biting down on my lip to stop myself from laughing.

'Almost midnight!'

'Since when did you start having early nights?'

'Yeah. You're hilarious. I take it everything's okay with you and Scotty?'

'Will you stop calling him that?'

'I've called him worse, believe me.'

'Everything's fine.' I ignored his previous comment. I knew Finn still felt I should just get this out of my system and come straight back home, and I wasn't doing anything to stop him. It was easier that way. 'We're just about to head off out on the bike.'

'It's alright for some. The honeymoon period not over yet?'

I smiled, bowing my head, pushing a hand through my hair. 'Thanks, Finn.'

'For what?'

'For not going on at me. For not asking me to come home…'

'Oh, I still think you should come home. Don't for one minute think I'm okay with what you're doing because I'm not, Lana. I still miss you so fucking much, still wish I was walking into Black Ink every day and seeing your face, but right now – right now it just feels like you're on holiday.' He felt that too, then. 'It just feels like I only have to miss you for a couple more weeks and then you'll be back in Newcastle, back where you belong…'

'I'm not coming home, Finn. Not yet, anyway. And I didn't call you to start all this again.'

'I know. I know that. But I can't help the way I feel. I'm worried about you, for Christ's sake. You're over there with a complete stranger…'

'He isn't a stranger, Finn.'

'You don't *know* him, Lana.'

I closed my eyes, breathing in deeply, because I didn't want to argue with him. It was naïve of me to think he'd suddenly just be fine with this, with what I'd done. 'Don't do this, Finn. Please.'

'Lana, listen to me.'

I opened my eyes, exhaling slowly, watching Eddie inside the shop as he leant over the counter, talking to Kyle. 'What?' I wasn't in the mood for this conversation anymore. I just wanted to get on the back of Eddie's bike and get as far away from reality as I could, for as *long* as I could. Yeah. Because I wasn't far enough away from it already.

'There's something you should probably know.'

That got my attention. 'Like what?'

There was a sudden silence on the other end of the phone.

'Finn?'

'Nothing. It doesn't matter.'

'No, come on. You wouldn't have said something like that if it wasn't important. What is it I should know?'

'It's nothing, Lana, really. I just… It's nothing. Just me being stupid.'

'For a change, huh?'

'I'll give you that one, seeing as you're thousands of miles away.'

'Finn, are you…?'

'You just stay safe. Okay? Forget about me.'

'That's not really possible.'

'Yeah, that's what most women say. Once encountered, never forgotten.'

'Not always for the right reasons, huh?'

'I'm banking all these insults up, I hope you realise that. Because when you come back home…' He stopped talking, aware that starting this up again wasn't a good idea. And he'd be right. 'You take care, beautiful. You hear me?'

'I hear you,' I said quietly, my fingers fiddling with the leather bands tied around my wrist. 'I'll call you tomorrow.'

'Time difference, Lana. Remember? Later, sis.'

I slid my phone back into my pocket and folded my arms, looking around me. The sun was still beating down, its intensity almost overwhelming, the sky a colour blue I wasn't sure I'd ever seen back in the UK. All around me was the noise of a busy, vibrant town going about its business, and I felt another jolt of nervous excitement shoot through me. This was where I belonged now – here. With an incredible, heartbreakingly hot biker and the kind of life I hadn't even known could exist. There was no way I was going back home. Ironically, *that* would be the crazy idea now.

I looked over towards the shop as Eddie walked out, all sexy swagger, a smile on his face that promised so much and I was lost again in this world I'd thrown myself into without really thinking about it. Properly. And I still didn't care. I wasn't giving myself time to.

'Hey, gorgeous.' Eddie smiled, taking off his dark glasses and slipping them into the neck of his t-shirt.

'Hey, handsome.' I slipped my arms around his neck, pressing myself against him, and he wasn't resisting, his hands on my hips pulling me closer still.

'About that road trip of ours,' he murmured, his mouth ever-so-lightly brushing the base of my throat. *Jesus*! How could he do this to me? Seconds, that was all it took, to turn me into a weak-kneed mess.

'What about it?' I breathed, my fingers buried in his hair as his mouth moved down to my cleavage, neither of us in the least bit bothered about the fact we were very much on show here.

'I thought we could head off in a couple of weeks.' He raised his head, that sexy-as-hell smirk on his face, his eyes dancing about with an excitement that almost matched mine. 'Let's just do it, Lana. You, me, the Harley, and nothing but the open road.'

It had sounded good when we'd talked about it just a few days ago, and it sounded even better now. 'Who needs anything else, huh?'

'Who needs anything else,' he whispered, his mouth closing in on mine, his kiss once more pulling me further into my very own crazy-stupid love story. And there was nowhere else I wanted to be. Everything was perfect, because I had Eddie. We had the bikes. And that was the only combination I needed. Eddie Fletcher was slowly starting to show me that dreams really could come true. And I wasn't going to let anything ruin that, for either of us. Anything, or anyone…

11

I clung onto Eddie's hand as we walked into the clubhouse, a large, grey-brick building on a private compound owned by Eddie's motorcycle club – a place where he and the other guys in the club held their meetings, hung out, drank, partied; it was their own personal space. Although, anyone was welcome to pop in and hang out with them, so Eddie had told me. It wasn't some kind of secret society.

The sound of heavy rock music and loud chatter filled the air. People were everywhere, both inside and spilling out into the yard, which was lit up by strings of bulbs hanging from any available lamppost, fence or canopy, the flames from a rather primitive-looking barbecue lending a warm-orange glow to the atmosphere outside.

This wasn't my first time in a place frequented by bikers. I'd been to a few bars and clubs back in Newcastle, but I'd never set foot inside a real-life MC clubhouse before. And even though I hadn't been entirely sure what to expect, this one felt like a pretty friendly place. Eddie was right – there wasn't anything dark or sinister about it.

The music was my kind of thing – heavy on guitars and turned up loud enough to make your ears bleed. Everyone was dressed in dark denim and leather, short skirts and skinny jeans, biker cuts, heavy, battered boots and heels so high they looked impossible to walk in. As far as the men were concerned, it was a mass of beards of all descriptions and hair that ranged from crew-cut short to longer than mine, but the women – they were beautiful. I'd never seen so many stunning girls in one room before, and for a second or two I felt slightly inadequate. I was older than most of them and looking around at everyone, I felt it.

'You look incredible, you hear me?' Eddie's mouth was so close to my ear as he murmured those words, his breath warm on my neck, and I shuddered slightly as his hand squeezed my waist. How did he have this knack of almost reading my mind? There was no doubt I'd *felt* incredible when I'd left the house earlier in skin-tight, leather-look jeans, black, spike-heeled ankle boots and a loose-fitting black and dark-grey top that managed to both hug and flatter my curves. Curves I was quite proud of, and Eddie seemed to like them. I'd left my hair loose, my make-up all dark eyes and pale lips and, yeah, I really had felt incredible when I'd climbed onto the back of Eddie's Harley. I'd felt like that biker chick I wanted to be. But was I really just playing at it? I mean, the girls here in front of me, they were true biker babes: all hard beauty and attitude. I was still learning. Although, Finn would probably argue that, as far as the attitude was concerned, I was learning fast.

'Lana, baby, did you hear me?'

I turned to look at him, reaching out to touch his cheek, leaning in for a quick kiss. 'I heard you.'

'There's nothing to be nervous about, okay? They're a great bunch of people here. Whatever you might have heard about biker clubs, whatever you might think goes on, just spend some time here. You'll see we're just a group of guys who love bikes. And beer. And women.' His smile sent a wave of confidence flooding through me. 'You'll be welcome here with open arms, darlin', I promise you.'

'Okay.' I smiled, running my fingers over his beard. 'I believe you. Now, that beer you mentioned? I could really do with one.'

He pulled me against him, kissing me a little bit harder this time, and my body responded in the only way it knew how, moulding itself against his, my arms falling around his neck. 'You got it, gorgeous.'

I watched him walk over to the bar at the far end of the room, absentmindedly biting down on my thumbnail, my eyes never leaving him.

'You known Eddie long?'

I swung around, coming face to face with a very pretty, dark-haired woman, probably a few years younger than me but not by much. I was almost relieved to see someone who was at least in the vicinity of my age range. 'No. Not really. I only met him a few days ago.'

The woman smiled a friendly smile. It seemed to reach her eyes, anyway, which made me feel a bit more relaxed. 'You must be something quite special then, honey, because we ain't seen Eddie with anyone for a long time.'

I didn't really know what to say. All of a sudden I was feeling just a little bit lost.

'I'm Kaley.' The woman smiled again, and I returned it.

'Lana.'

'Well, it's lovely to meet you, Lana. I take it Eddie's getting you a drink?'

I nodded, taking a quick look back over at the bar. Eddie was talking to a tall, well-built, heavily bearded man with shoulder-length, dark-blonde hair covered by a black bandana.

'That's Nate,' Kaley went on. 'The club president.' She led me over to a huge, slightly worn, brown-leather corner couch by the pool table. 'Him and Eddie have been friends for ages, ever since Eddie became a member of this club, and that was about fourteen or fifteen years ago now, I think.' She looked at me as we sat down, curling her legs up underneath her. 'You look a little bewildered, honey. This all a bit strange for you? Only, you *look* as though you belong here.'

That was nice to hear, but I wasn't ready to share my life story with another stranger just yet, not when I hadn't even started sharing it with the man I was sleeping with. 'Things have moved quite fast for me in the past few days, that's all,' I said, leaning forward and clasping my hands between my knees. 'Me and Eddie it's… it's been a bit of a whirlwind, let's put it that way.'

She smiled again. And again a wave of calm washed over me. I was beginning to really like Kaley. Whoever she was, she seemed to be someone else who could make me feel instantly comfortable in this strange environment. 'Eddie's a great guy, Lana. You're very lucky. I know a lot of the women who hang around here would do anything they could to become a part of his life, but he's just never shown any interest in that side of things. He can be a bit of a closed book in that respect, when he wants to be.'

I looked at her, and she laughed, reaching out to touch my arm.

'Oh, honey, I'm not one of those women. I belong to Nate. I'm *his* old lady, which means I'm out of bounds to anyone else, but I'm sure you already know that.'

I knew enough. I knew that when a woman became a biker's 'old lady' – a term that wasn't, in any way, meant as derogatory – it meant commitment. It meant monogamy. It meant nobody else touched her, or even looked at her in that way. I knew enough bikers back home to have picked that much up.

'Yeah. I know that.'

'So, has Eddie asked you to be *his* old lady yet?'

I looked down at my clasped hands, aware that I was wringing them slightly, and I pulled them apart, trying to adopt a more relaxed position. 'I don't think our relationship has quite reached that point,' I replied, kind of wishing Eddie would hurry up with that beer now.

'You look good together. You should know that.' She smiled

again, standing up and leaving me with a wink.

'You've met Kaley, then?' Eddie sat down next to me, handing me a bottle.

'Yeah. She seems nice.'

He took a long drink of beer, looking over at Kaley as she slid her arm around Nate's waist, leaning in to him for a quick kiss. 'She's a good person. She's good for Nate. And he needs someone like her, after everything he's been through.'

I frowned slightly, wondering if it would be too forward of me to ask exactly what it was Nate had been through because, even though I didn't know the guy, I was kind of curious. Everything about this place was making me curious. Especially the way Eddie seemed to have adopted a slightly harder edge to him since we'd walked in here.

He turned to look at me. 'Nate's wife, Deanne, she died a few months back. There was a...' He looked down at his hands for a brief second before meeting my eyes again. 'Sorry, you... you don't need to know all this. It's not important.'

'You want me to be a part of your world, Eddie? Then let me in.'

He looked over at the bar again, his expression changing slightly, a look of something I couldn't really describe clouding his features. It was too soon for me to be pushing my way this far in, quite obviously. But *he'd* brought me here.

'There was a bit of a run-in with another club, an MC operating just outside of Boulder City. Deanne she...' He turned to face me again, his eyes serious, '... she got caught in the middle, trying to stop Nate from...'

I felt my heart start to race because, somehow, I knew what was coming next.

'She was shot. Bled out before anyone could do anything to save her.'

'Oh, my God,' I whispered, my heart now hammering away inside me, my eyes refusing to leave his. 'Oh, Jesus, Eddie...'

He put his beer down, reaching out for my hand, his fingers

96

sliding between mine and I clung onto him. So tight I never wanted to let him go. 'Kaley she… she was there for him, you know? She got him through it, because without her I think he would have crumbled, lost it…' His eyes dipped, focusing on our joined hands. 'Maybe I shouldn't have told you that, but…' He raised his gaze. I'd never shifted mine. 'If this is too much for you, Lana…'

I shook my head, although, what he'd told me was still something I was trying to take in. And all of a sudden his world seemed a million miles away from mine. Even the new one I'd made for myself with Finn. Even that was so far away from this. This was a reality I wasn't sure I could ever have been prepared for.

'There's no need for you to feel scared or in any danger because that kind of thing, that run-in with the other club, that's rare. I can't say things like that never happen, because sometimes… sometimes they do. But what happened with Deanne, that's not the norm, baby. It really isn't.'

I felt my fingers tighten around his as I continued to stare at him. 'Are you…? Do you…? You said you were just a group of guys who love bikes, Eddie.' Christ! How naïve did that make me sound?

'We are, darlin'. That's all we are. Everything else is just shit that happens, but we deal with it.'

'Is that supposed to make me feel better?'

He smiled, his hand cupping my cheek, pulling me forward, his mouth touching mine in the lightest of kisses. And once again it was like he was injecting a dose of something calming into me, a beautiful toxin I needed from him. 'Spend some time here, Lana, and you'll see how safe it really is. Do you think I'd bring you here if I thought you'd be in any danger?'

I kissed him back, running my fingers through his hair, pressing my mouth against his that little bit harder. 'If this is your world, Eddie, then I just want to be a part of it, okay? Look, I started whatever this is – *we* started whatever this is and I'm all for seeing where it takes us.' That didn't mean to say that what I'd just heard hadn't shocked me, because it had. It had shocked me to the core, because it was like something straight off a TV show and being so close to the actual reality was a little unsettling. But I was learning to deal with a lot of things that were out of my comfort zone. This was just something else to add to the list.

He smiled, pulling my legs up and over his, letting one hand run slowly from my ankle to my thigh, his other arm around my waist as he kissed me again. His kisses could calm the strongest of storms going on inside my head. They were capable of blanking out anything I didn't really want to think about; of making crap disappear. I was starting to find out more about Eddie Fletcher's world than I'd bargained for and, yeah, it unnerved me slightly but not enough for me to want to give him up. I was a big girl now. I just had to trust him and make sure there were some things I just didn't share with Finn.

'We don't have to hang around here long,' he whispered, pulling me over so I straddled him, his hands sliding up under my top, the touch of his fingers on my skin causing goose bumps to appear and another of those unfamiliar tiny gasps to escape.

'Eddie, I'm fine with it. Really.'

'I haven't scared you off?' he asked, arching an eyebrow.

I smiled, leaning forward so my mouth rested against his. 'You'll have to try a lot harder than that to scare me off, biker boy.'

He grinned, standing up and lifting me up with him, causing me to let out a little cry of surprise, my legs wrapping around him, my arms clinging onto his neck. 'Come on, gorgeous. We're gonna go grab ourselves a few private minutes, alone.'

'In the bathroom?'

He kicked the door to the rest room open, backing into it. 'You think you've had some great sex so far, darlin'? Just wait 'til you've had sex with Eddie Fletcher in a bathroom stall. This is gonna blow your beautiful mind, kid.'

I gave a surprised shriek, laughing out loud as he backed into one of the stalls, finally putting me down, locking the door behind us. 'You certainly know how to show a girl a good time,' I breathed as he pushed me back against the wall, but my heart was racing again, this time for all the right reasons. Suddenly, everything he'd just told me about Nate and Deanne; all those warning bells I'd tried to silence, they were well and truly shut off now as his mouth closed in on mine.

'You have no idea how good a time I can really show you.' He smiled, his mouth almost touching mine, but then he pulled away slightly. 'Turn around.'

I cocked my head, narrowing my eyes just a little.

'I won't hurt you, Lana. I promise.'

I waited a couple of beats before saying anything, letting the intensity build. 'Unless I want you to,' I whispered, letting a slow smile spread across my face, and he returned it, causing another spark of electricity to fly between us.

'Unless you want me to,' he said quietly, his hand resting lightly against the side of my neck, his thumb stroking it, pressing just that little bit harder. 'Now turn around.'

I did as he said, turning so I faced the wall, closing my eyes as he gently pushed my hair away from my neck, kissing it so lightly I felt the most incredible shiver wash over my entire body. His hands slowly moved down, loosening my jeans, pulling them down around my ankles, along with my underwear, and I couldn't stop the tiniest of moans from escaping as his knee pushed my legs as far apart as they would go. I knew what was coming, and I both craved it and feared it. But I wanted him so much, whichever way it had to come.

His hands covered mine either side of my head, our fingers sliding together, his mouth close to my ear again, whispering into it, words that excited me so much I could literally feel myself becoming wet, and that need for him intensified, an almost unbearable, physical pain taking over as I waited for him to push inside me. And when he did, when I finally felt his body join with mine I didn't care that I couldn't hold down the long, low moan that seemed to come from somewhere deep within me. I only cared about what was happening, right there, between us.

His body slammed against me, each thrust becoming harder and faster, and I pushed back against him, taking him as deep as I could because when he hit that spot… I'd never felt anything like it. Never even known that feeling could exist; that he could touch me so deep inside and make my whole body shudder with something so intense, so incredibly beautiful that I almost cried when I came. With his body right up against mine, our hands joined, his mouth touching the back of my neck – I was in the kind of heaven that even my dreams hadn't let me enter. So what if some people saw this as something sordid and dirty – sex in a bathroom stall wasn't exactly classy. But, Jesus, it was exciting!

I felt my muscles tense as his turn to hit the home run came, clenching tight, causing him to moan so loud it vibrated off the walls around us. And when I finally released my inner hold on him, I clung onto his hands, biting down on my lip as he let it all out, pushing himself up against me, his face buried in my hair as the wave subsided. Until his body finally relaxed. He was done. So was I.

'Jesus Christ, Lana… baby…' He almost growled those words again, something I loved to hear him to do. As if his voice wasn't sexy enough, he could somehow make it even hotter.

He slowly pulled out of me and I reached down, yanking my knickers and jeans back up, turning around to face him, unable to keep the smile off my face. 'Where did you come from, Eddie Fletcher?'

He smiled, too, zipping himself back up, his hand on my hip pulling me against him. 'It's where we're going that matters, darlin'.'

I felt my insides shift on their axis, if that was even possible. In the space of a few days this man had turned my whole world upside down, pushing everything I'd once known further and further away. I was slowly starting to see the kind of future I wanted now. I just didn't know that the past had other ideas…

12

Propping myself up on my elbow, I ran my fingers lightly over the tattoo that covered most of Eddie's back – a huge eagle etched in deep-black ink, dark-red blood dripping from its outstretched wings, its mouth wide open as though some terrifying cry was being forced from it. It was both disturbing and fascinating, but beautifully crafted.

'MC tattoo?' I asked, tracing the outline of one of the eagle's wings, my fingers lingering on the dripping blood.

Eddie looked at me, reaching out to push the covers further down over my hip. 'Aye. It is.'

'Is it true what they say? About these clubs sometimes being like a surrogate family for some people? Is that what it was like for you?'

He moved onto his side, so he was facing me. 'They were there when I needed them, Lana. That's all. And I guess I ended up liking the warped sense of security these places can provide.'

I smiled, moving that little bit closer to him, the heat of his body as it touched mine charging my senses and feeding my habit like a shot of caffeine. '*I* could give you a new tattoo, if you like. I'm not a complete novice anymore.'

In a move so quick I didn't even have time to think about putting up a protest, he'd pushed me onto my back, his hands pinning mine to the pillows either side of my head. 'You may be the most beautiful woman I have ever had in my bed, darlin', but you ain't coming anywhere near me with a needle in your hand.'

I laughed, a low, husky laugh I hadn't even known I was capable of. The things this man could do to me! The way he could make me feel...

'*You* should get more, though.' His eyes scanned my naked body, his grip on my hands showing no signs of loosening. It was a strangely erotic sensation, because that was the only part of him that was touching me – his hands. Yet, it felt as though every inch of my skin was pressing against his. 'Those hips of yours would look fucking incredible with ink snaking around them… all the way up your back. And those tits…'

I closed my eyes, throwing my head back as his knee nudged my legs apart, and I felt him thrust into me almost immediately; hard, rough thrusts that sent my body rocking back into the mattress. I'd never felt so turned-on. It was going to be quick, it was going to be fast, and it was going to make me scream so loud I just hoped the neighbours were already up, but it was every reason why I was here, with this man. He made me want to stay awake all night because sleeping was only wasting time we could be spending together. Doing this. And when sleep did hit, he was even there, in my dreams, letting me know he was still around. Neither of us really knew where this was going. Neither of us was looking for any kind of commitment, and right now it didn't really matter. We had our road trip to look forward to, all that time together with nobody else around to get in the way. Maybe then, after that, we'd know more about a future I didn't really need mapping out. I'd been there and done all that. The not knowing for sure where your life was going to end up, that was so much more exciting.

Letting go of my hands, he pushed my legs as far apart as they could go, and I gripped the pillow tight, crying out in a mixture of pain and pure ecstasy, his body bucking and jerking as he came in a series of short, abrupt waves, each one hitting me with a white-hot heat that seemed to fill every inch of me. Angling my hips just a touch, his fingers once more intertwining with mine, I felt my own climax start its journey and I pushed up against him, letting him rub against me, helping me on to my own, glorious endgame, screaming out his name… 'Eddie!' I was filled with a hope I'd never experienced before; an excitement that scared me because it all seemed too good to be true and I didn't want anything to spoil what we had here. I didn't want anything to get in the way.

'Jesus, Lana…' he breathed, letting his whole body collapse onto mine, his grip on my hands finally loosening. '*Jesus!*'

I breathed out slowly, running my hand over the back of his neck, catching his mouth in a long, deep kiss. 'Is this crazy, Eddie?' I whispered, a brief moment of fear enveloping me.

He rolled over onto his back, gently pulling me on top of him. '*Life's* just one short, crazy, fucking ride, darlin'. And all we can do is roll with it. See where the journey takes us.'

'Have you ever been in love?' I wasn't sure I'd meant to say that out loud, but somehow it had slipped out. And I was kind of intrigued to find out if there was another reason why he'd never married. Had he even had a serious relationship before?

His eyes bored into mine, a momentary glimmer of darkness turning them from brown to almost black, which in turn sent a river of trepidation running through me. 'I'm not sure love exists, Lana.'

That was a strange thing to say. At least, *I* thought it was. 'It does,' I whispered. 'I promise you, it does.'

He gently pushed me off him, climbing out of bed, and I watched as he pulled a packet of cigarettes from his jacket pocket, lighting one up as he stared out of the window.

I got up too, walking over to him, running my hands lightly over his hips, kissing his shoulder. He didn't say anything for a few seconds, just took another long draw on his cigarette, blowing smoke out of the slightly open window.

'We didn't say this was gonna be forever, Eddie,' I said, breaking the brief silence.

He stubbed out his cigarette and turned around, leaning back against the windowsill, pulling me in between his legs. 'Do you know how you make me feel, Lana? Have you any idea how…?' He stopped talking, but his eyes never left mine. 'I'm all about the here and now, remember? Because forever is a long time. But right now, darlin', I just need you here. I *want* you here.'

'Good.' I smiled, cupping his face in my hands, running my thumb over his mouth. 'Because I've got no intention of going anywhere just yet.'

His face broke into a grin, any remnants of the seriousness that had been there seconds earlier now gone. 'I have never wanted to fuck a woman as many times in one night the way I've wanted to fuck you, do you know that?'

I laughed, throwing my head back as his fingers grazed my nipples, his head dropping so his mouth could take over, turning my laugh into a growling moan that rose from the pit of my diaphragm.

Nobody had said this was going to be forever. Forever wasn't even something I believed in anymore. Because I wasn't sure I needed to…

'What's up, Finn? You sound distracted.' I tucked the phone between my shoulder and chin as I spooned coffee into the machine, looking over at Eddie as he came into the kitchen all showered and dressed, his hair pushed back off his face.

'Do I?'

'Yes. You do. You okay?'

Eddie slid an arm around my waist, whispering something in my ear that caused an unexpected groan to escape.

'I'm fine. What's up with *you*?'

'Nothing.' I gave in to Eddie's kiss, holding the phone against my chest for a second to block the mouthpiece. 'Just realised we're out of milk.'

There was a pause on the other end of the line. 'Whatever.'

Eddie mouthed something at me – something that I now knew was going to make me start wishing the rest of the day away just so he could come home and deliver that filthy promise – before leaving me with a wink and a smile, closing the back door behind him.

I leant against the counter, swapping the phone over to my other ear, my voice rising just a touch so I could be heard above the roar of Eddie's bike coming from outside. 'Are you sure you're okay, Finn?'

'Shouldn't I be the one asking *you* that?'

'I'm fine, thanks.'

'Any closer to coming back home?'

I closed my eyes, rubbing the bridge of my nose with my thumb and forefinger. 'Can we please just have one conversation where you don't nag me?

'Who's nagging? I'm asking. There's a difference.'

'Really?'

'It's been a fortnight now, Lana. Isn't the novelty wearing off yet?'

'No.'

There was another slight pause, and I opened my eyes, looking out of the window, into the back yard, for no reason other than I needed something to focus on.

'What time is it over there?' Finn asked.

I frowned. 'Early afternoon. Why? I thought we were over the whole time difference thing?'

'I just wondered. What you been up to today?'

'You're genuinely interested?'

'I miss you, Lana. Okay? Like you wouldn't believe. Hearing what you've been up to is the only way I can feel close to the sister who deserted me for some ex-pat Scot with a Harley.'

'Two.'

'What?'

'Eddie's got *two* Harleys.'

'Yeah. Of course he has. Is he treating you alright?'

'Finn, he's treating me fine. Better than fine. And I don't *need* looking after.'

'So, you're familiar with your new surroundings now, are you? You know Vegas like the back of your hand after just two weeks?'

'I'm gonna hang up in a minute.'

'What you been doing today?'

'Nice diversion. I've been with Eddie.'

'Do you ever leave his side?'

'I really am gonna hang up now.'

'I'm sorry, alright?'

'Are you, though?'

I heard him sigh down the line and I closed my eyes again. 'Yeah. I am. I'm sorry. Really. Lana, look I… I love you. Okay?'

'Okay… Finn?'

'Yeah.'

'I feel like I'm losing you again. And I hate that. I don't *want* to lose you, but I feel like…'

'You're not losing me, Lana. I promise you. I'm just… I'm just worried about you, that's all.'

I waited a couple of beats before speaking again. 'There's nothing to be worried about. I promise.'

'I still can't believe what you're doing. That you stayed over there with a complete stranger. Do you know how hard that still is for me to get my head around? And having to explain it to everybody… They all miss you, Lana. Everyone. They miss you. You had a great life here, and I don't understand… Don't you miss it?'

'Of course I miss it. I miss *you*, like crazy, I really do. But being here… It's so hard to explain, Finn, it just feels as though… as though I have to *be* here. For some reason.'

'You're talking crap again.'

'Okay. I'm going now. Say hi to the guys for me.'

I ended the call and threw my phone down onto the counter, pushing both hands through my hair, throwing my head back and sighing loudly. Why did everything feel like such a battle now? But fighting to try and make Finn understand why I'd done this, it was bound to be hard, when I still didn't really understand it myself.

I let out another frustrated sigh as my phone started ringing. I picked it up and answered it without even checking to see who it was, something I never usually did. But I just assumed it was Finn again. 'Yeah?'

'Lana, sweetheart? It's me.'

I felt my heart almost leap into my throat as I heard his voice, my head spinning so fast I had to grip the counter behind me to steady myself. 'Adam?'

'How are you, darling?'

The way he called me 'darling' was so different to the way Eddie said it. So, so different. I hadn't spoken to Adam in months. Hadn't heard his voice in so long, and I was struggling to get my head around the fact I was hearing it now.

'Lana? Are you still there?'

It was as if a part of me thought I was dreaming this conversation, and I actually held the phone away from my ear for a second or two, bringing it back to see if it really was him on the other end of the line.

'I... Yeah, I'm still here. But... why are you calling me, Adam? I thought the divorce... I thought we were done.'

'Lana, I... I need to talk to you.'

'Why?' I whispered. 'What's left to talk about?'

'Darling, please...'

'Why are you calling, Adam?' But then the penny slowly started to drop, and I threw back my head, sighing quietly. All of a sudden the reason for Finn's distracted tone became clear. And that thing he'd thought I should know... 'Has Finn said something?' An obviously rhetorical question.

'He's worried about you.'

'He had no right… He had *no* right to say anything, especially not to you. It's got nothing to *do* with you…'

'He didn't say anything because he knew how you'd react.'

'And he'd be fucking right! *Jesus!*' I was so angry I couldn't even get the words out. And confused. Both emotions I didn't want to feel.

'*I'm* worried about you, Lana.'

'I'm fine, Adam.' My voice was quieter now. Calmer. But this was a conversation I didn't want to continue. 'So, whatever Finn's asked you to do, don't waste your time.' I hung up before he could say anything else. I couldn't believe Finn had gone behind my back – it stung. Because if there'd been one person in this entire world I'd thought I could trust now, it was Finn. And what he'd just done… He must really be desperate to make me see what he considered to be sense if he was turning to a man he'd never really got on with for help.

I looked at my phone, wondering whether I was just a bit too angry right now to call my brother. He was more than likely expecting to hear from me at some point soon, because he quite obviously knew Adam would ring me. But I wasn't sure that spilling forth a tirade of abuse at him was the best idea, not just yet. Even though it was exactly what I wanted to do. But the sensible side of me was telling me that waiting was the best way to handle this, even though some people seemed unable to believe that I actually *had* a sensible side. I was beginning to doubt it myself.

I put the phone down, then picked it straight back up again, wondering whether to call Eddie this time. But what good would *that* do? He was on his way to the club for a meeting, and I wasn't sure he needed to be bothered with this. Adam would get the message, eventually. Because I wasn't planning on indulging him or anything Finn had asked him to do. Our marriage was over. He had no say in my life anymore, no right to tell me how to live it. He'd never had the right to do that, but I'd allowed him to. For too many years I'd let too many people tell me how to live my life, but I'd broken that habit now. And I wasn't going back to it.

I opened the nearest drawer and flung my phone into it, slamming it shut before walking over to the fridge, taking out a bottle of vodka and pouring myself a shot, downing it in one before pouring another. But I just looked at that one, remembering the kind of headache I got when I downed vodka shots too quickly.

Putting the glass down on the counter top I walked back over to the drawer, wrenching it open to retrieve my phone. But I must have thrown it so far back in there, I couldn't see it. Sliding my hand inside I rummaged around, reaching right to the back of the drawer, but instead of finding my phone my fingers touched something cold and hard, something unfamiliar; something that made my skin turn clammy, my stomach turning as I pulled it out, because I'd known what it was the second I'd touched it. A gun. As it sat there in the palm of my hand, all I could do was stare at it, not quite sure what to do next. It was like someone had pressed the pause button. Everything around me stood still, even my eyes couldn't seem to move, their gaze never leaving the black metal object that was balancing precariously in my shaking hand. But then my fingers began to curl around it, slowly, almost as though someone else was making me do it, because holding this, even looking at it, was the last thing I wanted to do. So why was I running my thumb over it? Why was I letting myself do that?

And then, as if someone had flicked another switch, as though they were writing a scene from a book and had suddenly changed their minds, erased that paragraph, and re-written it all, I threw the gun back into the drawer, retrieved my now-visible phone and slammed the drawer shut so hard it made the whole cupboard shake.

Picking up the glass of vodka I'd discarded just minutes ago, I downed that second shot in one mouthful, keeping my eyes closed as the clear liquid burned my throat, a feeling I welcomed. I needed it. And it wasn't as though I was naïve enough to think guns didn't exist in some households in this country. It was just that, I'd never seen a real one before. Never been that close or held one in my hand. Never realised how heavy something like that could be; how cold and terrifying it had felt in my hand. It had shaken me slightly, that was all and because of that, along with the phone call from Adam, two shots of vodka weren't feeling like anything near enough now.

I reached for the bottle again but stopped myself. Getting drunk fast was never a good idea. I'd tried that a lot in the early days following my split from Adam, and Finn had had to cope with the aftermath on more than one occasion. I didn't really want to put Eddie through all that. But I couldn't help thinking about what he'd told me at the clubhouse a couple of weeks ago, about Deanne getting shot, and the run-in with a rival MC. And then I quickly shook those thoughts out of my mind. Now wasn't the time for my overactive imagination to start working overtime.

The doorbell ringing brought me back to a now-confusing reality, and it was because of that that I blindly headed out into the hall, swinging the door open without even thinking about asking who it was first.

'Did you honestly think I was just going to let you hang up on me like that and not pursue this?'

13

I couldn't say anything. I was too busy staring at him. Too busy trying to get my head around the fact my ex-husband was here, in Las Vegas. And to make matters more confusing, if that was even possible, the man standing there in front of me, that wasn't the man I'd walked out on almost a year ago. At least, he didn't *look* like the man I'd walked out on. The man standing there in front of me, his voice was still the same, he was still tall and handsome, and his dark hair was still short, but instead of it being perfect with not a strand out of place it was messed-up and ever-so-slightly ruffled, his usually clean-shaven face now sporting a neat, slightly greying beard. And, for some reason, all of that seemed to make his ice-blue eyes stand out even more – seemed to render me unable to break the stare. Because I couldn't believe what – who – I was looking at. I was struggling to believe it really was Adam. That he was here. Invading a world I didn't want him anywhere near.

'I… hang on…' I took a deep breath, quickly composing myself. There was no denying this had thrown me, but I had to get a grip on the situation, and soon. 'What are you doing here?'

'I needed to see you, Lana.'

'No, Adam, please… No.' I was shaking my head, so vigorously, as though hoping that, if I shook it hard enough, he'd go away. That *this* would go away.

'Lana, sweetheart…'

'Did Finn ask you to come over here?'

'No, darling, he didn't. He asked me to speak to you, to try and talk some…' He stopped dead, bowing his head, aware that what he'd been about to say probably wasn't something I wanted to hear.

'He wanted you to try and talk some sense into me. Right? Because I'm largely ignoring him, is that it?'

He raised his gaze, his eyes meeting mine. And I still couldn't believe he was there. Couldn't believe this was happening. 'I knew you wouldn't listen to anything anyone had to say over the phone…'

'So, you thought, what? You'd come all the way over here, make me listen to whatever it is you and Finn want me to hear, and then bring me home, is that it?'

'Yes. If you want to put it that bluntly.'

Now I was just stunned. Surely this – *this* – had to be a dream. It had to be. Otherwise, what the hell else was it? The grown-ups banding together to bring the errant child back into line?

'I don't believe this is happening…' I trailed off, leaning back against the doorpost, pushing a hand through my hair as I quickly tried to get my head into some kind of order. This *was* happening. And I was going to have to deal with it, whether I liked it or not. 'I'm assuming Finn gave you this address,' I sighed, my voice little more than a whisper. And I couldn't look at him now, couldn't face him anymore. I didn't want to. He wasn't welcome here. I didn't need this. Everything had been good, so good. Me and Eddie – things were so bloody good! And I really didn't need this.

'Yes. He did.'

I took another deep breath, exhaling slowly as the situation began to finally sink in.

'Come home, Lana. Whatever this is, this… this mid-life crisis you appear to be having…'

It was like we'd come full circle, back to the day I'd walked out on him. He was still saying the same old things, accusing me of the same old stuff. I started to shut the door on him but he put his foot out to stop me, and this time I allowed my eyes to meet his again, staring straight at him. 'Don't do this, Adam.'

'We need to talk.'

'You see, you keep saying that, but I don't think we do. Whatever's going on in my life now, it's got nothing to do with you.'

'So, I'm just supposed to stop caring, am I? I *never* stopped caring, Lana. Never. If I didn't care about you, do you think I'd have come all this way?'

'I didn't ask you to come to Vegas, Adam. That was *your* decision.'

'I know,' he sighed, pushing a hand through his hair. 'Look… You do know you're acting like some adolescent trying to prove a point.'

'I'm not having this conversation.'

He moved his foot away from the door, sticking his hands in his pockets, looking briefly down at the ground before his eyes met mine again. 'Just listen to what I have to say, Lana. That's all I ask. Just humour me. Please.'

'Eddie'll be home soon. Now's not really the time.'

I didn't miss the way he flinched slightly when I mentioned Eddie's name.

'Then meet me, tomorrow. We can have some lunch, just talk things through. I'm staying at Caesar'sPalace. I assume you know where that is?'

I nodded, folding my arms tighter against myself, my fingers digging into my upper arms. 'I'm just not sure there's any point, Adam.'

'Please, Lana. Just hear me out, okay?'

I looked at him again, this man I'd spent almost twenty years of my life with. Twenty years I'd thrown away, just like that, and all of a sudden a completely unexpected rush of guilt swept over

113

me, so strong it almost knocked me off my feet. Mixed with the confusion Adam's arrival and finding Eddie's gun – I assumed it was Eddie's gun – had thrown up, it might have only been early afternoon, but all I wanted to do now was sleep and hope that when I woke up I'd realise this had all been nothing but an elaborate dream.

'Please, Lana.'

I breathed out, looking down at the floor because looking at him was just way too surreal for me right now. 'Okay,' I said quietly, raising my gaze to meet his.

He smiled, and all that did was make me feel sad. Sad for what we'd once had. For everything I'd wanted our life to be. For all those years I'd just thrown away because, seeing him standing there, it hurt. Like someone was slowly nipping at my heart, picking away at it bit by bit. This man had once been my world, and now…

'I really need you to go, Adam.'

He reached out, gently touching my cheek with the palm of his hand and for the briefest of seconds I allowed fleeting memories of me and him to flood my mind, before pushing them back where they belonged.

'When did you get so beautiful?' he whispered, cocking his head slightly as his eyes locked with mine.

'Please, Adam. I can't do this right now.'

'Is he treating you well?'

'Adam…'

He smiled – a small smile – before pulling his hand away and stepping back. 'Tomorrow. I'll meet you in the foyer of the hotel, around one o'clock?'

I nodded, watching as he backed away down the path before turning around and walking to his hire car. And all of a sudden the old Lana was racing back to invade my head with everything I'd tried to forget, everything I'd tried to push aside. She was edging her way in, making an unwelcome return, and the only person I wanted right now was Eddie. At that very second I needed him like

I'd never needed him before. My world had, once more, shifted on its axis and that, more than anything, was what scared me.

14

'Hey, what's happened, darlin'?'

I looked up as Eddie walked into the living room, swinging my legs down from where they'd been tucked up underneath me, the bottle of vodka now half empty on the table in front of me.

'Nothing's happened,' I sighed, pulling my legs back up, crossing them underneath me this time.

'You sure?' Eddie frowned, sitting down beside me.

'Everything go alright at the meeting?'

'Fine. You gonna talk to me?'

I looked down at my fingers, watching as they picked at the frayed knee of my jeans. 'Adam's here.'

He said nothing for a second or two and the silence was almost deafening. 'Here in Vegas?'

I nodded.

'Have you seen him?'

I nodded again, mainly because I had no idea what to say. My head was all over the place, and I still hadn't called Finn. So part of me couldn't help wondering if it would have been better to have got that conversation out of the way, to have vented some of the anger and confusion I was currently feeling before Eddie had got home. The last thing I wanted to appear in front of this man I still barely knew was weak.

'What does he want?' Eddie went on.

I raised my head, my eyes meeting his. 'He wants to talk. I'm meeting him tomorrow.'

'Lana…'

'He just wants to talk, Eddie.'

'He's come all the way from England to talk? He could've done that over the phone.'

'I know.'

'When you left him, Lana…'

'We'd just grown apart. I already told you that.' My voice was quiet as I realised that was about all I'd told Eddie about my split from Adam. He had no real idea what had brought it about, or how I'd really felt when I'd walked out on twenty years of my life. I hadn't thought it mattered. Until now. 'There was no fighting, no bad feeling, nothing like that. We'd just grown apart.' I looked down at my hands again, my fingers still pulling at a stray thread in the torn knee of my jeans. 'I found a gun, Eddie. In the kitchen drawer.' I wasn't even sure I'd meant to say that out loud, or maybe I had. Maybe I'd seen it as the perfect diversion from a conversation I really didn't want to have.

I heard him sigh, looking back at him as he pushed a hand through his unkempt hair, his expression almost stoic. 'I meant to put that away.'

'Is it legal?' I asked, waiting until his eyes met mine, holding his gaze.

'Aye. It's legal. And no, it isn't loaded.'

Whether it had been loaded or not hadn't even crossed my mind, and that caused a small wave of nausea to rise. I really shouldn't have touched that thing.

'Look, Lana, sweetheart, things are bound to be different…'

'I know that. I'm not stupid, Eddie. It was just a shock, that's all. Guns aren't something I'm overly familiar with in my world.'

That deafening silence fell between us again, but still my expression didn't waver. Our eyes were still locked together and all I could feel was my heart beating so hard inside me it almost felt out of control.

'Do you *want* to talk to him?' Eddie asked, his voice tinged with a slight hint of irritation.

'I have to,' I whispered.

'Do you? I thought that part of your life was over. I thought you were moving on.'

'I am. I'm trying to, but... I've got to do this, Eddie.' I just wished I knew why.

He reached out, touching my face, his thumb stroking my cheek, his mouth moving closer to mine and I closed my eyes, falling against him as he kissed me slowly.

'Things are changing for me, too, Lana. You, being here, it's changing everything I've ever known.' I rested my hand lightly over his, our eyes once more locking together. 'For most of my life I've been alone, because that's the way it's...' He broke off, looking down, his fingers clinging onto mine. 'It's the way I wanted it. I've never needed anyone else, never *wanted* anyone else.' He looked back up at me. 'There were always enough women out there willing to accept that all I wanted was sex and a quick goodbye. But you...'

I shook my head, resting my forehead against his. 'Adam being here, it changes nothing between us, do you hear? I'm not going back to him, and I'm not leaving here. Whether you want me or not, I'm going nowhere. This past year, I really thought I'd started to make progress, you know? I thought I was finally starting to get everything into some kind of order; that I knew what I was doing, where I was going, who I actually was. But there are still so many things I need to work out. I'm finally that person I really want to be, or I'm getting there, anyway. And being here, with you, this was the adventure I needed, Eddie. I needed *you*. You've made me feel... For the first time in my life I actually feel like *me*. It's taken me a long time to find that person and I'm not going to let Adam turning up ruin that; ruin *us*.'

He kissed me again, and again I fell back against him, letting that kiss take over, pushing aside any thoughts of Adam and the confusion his arrival had kicked up. A confusion I hoped was only momentary.

'Come on, gorgeous.' He stood up, taking my hand and pulling me to my feet. 'We're going for a ride you ain't ever gonna forget.'

I rested my chin on Eddie's shoulder, my arms wrapped tight around his waist. All I could see was desert either side of us, the quiet, almost traffic-free road stretching out in front of us, as far as the eye could see. The sun was about to set, the only noise the sound of the bike – it was perfect. I'd become so used to these rides in the short time I'd been here. I craved them now. They were my drug of choice– holding onto my biker boy, the two of us alone, with just the Harley and the open road for company. I was in a bubble I didn't want to escape from now. Everything I didn't want to think about was gone, pushed away for the time being. I wanted to bottle this experience and keep it forever, so I would always remember, at this very second in time, how free and alive I felt. How nothing could touch me, nobody could get to me. I was who I wanted to be, doing what I wanted to do, with the person I wanted to be with. Right at this very second in time, my life was perfect.

Burying my face in his shoulder, I briefly closed my eyes, breathing in the smell of leather and engine oil, my fingers gripping him tighter as he pulled the bike into a lay-by, the tyres screeching, kicking up dust as he spun it around, putting a foot down on the ground to finally bring it to a stop.

I let go of him, pulling off my helmet and shaking out my hair.

'Good?' He turned his head slightly, smiling at me.

'Yeah.' I smiled back, the feeling of exhilaration still lingering. I wasn't sure anything could surpass it. 'Good.'

He climbed off the bike, laying his helmet down on the ground.

I made to get off too, but he put a hand on my shoulder, pushing me forward slightly, straddling the bike again, but behind me this time. 'I asked you if you'd ever fucked on a Harley, remember?' His mouth was so low, and so close to my ear I felt my stomach almost hit the ground, and I took a deep breath, exhaling slowly as his hand slid around to rest on my stomach.

'I remember,' I breathed.

'And you haven't, right?'

'Right,' I whispered, leaning back against him, his lips now travelling along my neck, his breath warm on my skin.

'So, maybe it's time to change that, huh?'

His voice was deep and gruff; so sexy I felt the ache between my thighs intensify within seconds.

'You gonna be my bad, beautiful biker girl?' he growled, and I couldn't stop a groan from escaping. Right now, I was going to be anything he wanted me to be. I had no intention of putting up any kind of fight.

I kept my eyes closed as he continued to kiss my neck, his fingers pulling at my jacket, yanking it off and tossing it aside. I did the same with my t-shirt, and it wasn't particularly warm out there in the desert, with the rapidly darkening sky, but my body was burning up so fast he was the only heat I needed.

'Swing your legs out to the side, baby.' In an action that shouldn't have been, but actually was, incredibly erotic, he helped me wriggle out of my jeans, pulling off my underwear, leaving me completely naked. And I didn't care. This was freedom personified. Whoever I'd become now, whoever this person was who seemed hell bent on taking me places I hadn't even allowed my dreams to go, I liked her. I liked her a lot. 'Now put the boots back on,' he murmured. 'And get back on this bike. Keep your back to me, darlin'.'

Slipping my knee-high biker boots back on I once more strad-dled the leather seat, leaning forward, my fingers gripping the handlebars as he held onto my hips. I'd never felt so sexy, so wanted; never felt more like acting the low-down dirty bitch for a man who could, quite honestly, turn me on just by opening his mouth.

Pulling me back, just slightly, I closed my eyes as I felt him slowly push into me, his groans merging with mine, the denim of his jeans rough against my skin, but that was good, that was *so* good! I was naked, on a Harley, in the middle of the Nevada desert, with one hell of a hot biker fucking me from behind. And the angle of my body the bike's seat had caused me to adopt – *Oh, Jesus!* The pleasure was indescribable! Everything that was happening, everything I was feeling, it was worth every single sacrifice I'd made to be here, with this man. It was worth it all, to feel what I was feeling right now.

Arching my back, pushing myself harder against him, I cried out loud, almost screaming his name, the sensations I was experiencing so intense I couldn't hold them in, and why even try? We were alone. And even if we weren't, I didn't care. The whole world could watch him fucking me and I wouldn't mind. In fact, the thought of that just turned me on even more.

I gripped the handlebars tighter, arching my back deeper, his fingers digging into me as he thrust in and out, my body slamming back against his, the cool breeze on my skin heightening everything, every nerve ending standing to attention. And when he came, his almost animalistic cries filled the air, echoing around the silence that surrounded us, his body stiffening slightly, his hands still holding tightly onto my hips. It was just seconds before I felt myself start that climb, thanks to him and the friction of the leather seat against me; felt it building up, washing over me, causing me to cry out twice as loud as him. Because I could. Because I wanted to. Because he was making me feel like the most incredible woman in the world.

I kept my eyes closed as he pulled me up, and I leant back against him, listening to his breathing, letting what we'd just done sink in. 'Bad enough for you?' I gasped, reaching up to bury my fingers in his hair.

He laughed, low and deep, and I felt the tiniest of shudders hit me, his hands covering my breasts, his mouth kissing my shoulder. 'Bad enough for *me*, darlin'.'

It was dark now, the only illumination available coming from the beam of the Harley's lights, and I was amazed at how calm I felt, out there in the middle of nowhere with a man who was, in reality, still a stranger to me. Yet I'd never felt closer to him than I did right now.

Winding my fingers in his hair, my eyes still closed, I groaned quietly as his hands moved down, running over the curve of my waist, my hips, lightly stroking my thighs, moving inwards. I arched my back again as his fingers found home, touching me gently, easing out of me tiny gasps that seemed to get just a touch louder as his fingers probed deeper. And when he finally slid them inside me, those tiny gasps all seemed to roll into one, long, drawn-out moan, my head thrown right back against his shoulder, his mouth finding mine in the most erotic of kisses. I opened my legs wider, giving him permission to push deeper, not that he needed permission to do anything. Right now, he could do what the hell he liked to me and I'd take it, all of it, whatever it was. Because this – this was my fantasy, a once make-believe world I was finally living. And I needed it. Craved it. Wanted it. I wanted Eddie Fletcher. Oh, God, did I want him!

'Tell me if I'm hurting you,' he whispered, his fingers keeping up a steady rhythm as they continued to push as deep as they could possibly go.

'You're not hurting me,' I breathed, willing him to keep going, to push as hard as he wanted because I could take it. I wanted to feel it, to feel *him*, and know that I was really living this.

'My beautiful bad girl,' he growled, and I was sure he was doing that deliberately now, because the shiver it sent coursing through my body seemed to accelerate another impending climax brought on by his finger-fucking and the way his mouth seemed to travel over my skin without touching it, yet I could feel it. Right there. Almost burning me. 'Jesus, Lana, baby…' he groaned as my muscles gripped his fingers, holding him there, until the white-hot wave of pins and needles he'd caused had washed right over me, my body shuddering in his arms, my legs instinctively opening as wide as they could go, my cries loud and long as he held me. And when it was over, when the wave had subsided and he'd pulled free of me, I felt as though I'd just been through the most incredible out-of-body experience, because it still took some getting used to, the fact I was here, in Las Vegas, with this man I was fast becoming addicted to. He was my sordid drug, my bad-boy biker. And he was making me love my life like I'd never loved it before. 'You should never have to put clothes on that killer body,' he murmured, and I stretched out, my fingers still buried in his hair, a long, satisfied groan escaping my slightly parted lips. Nobody had ever described my body as "killer" before. And I liked it. No, I loved it; loved the way he made me feel.

'Yeah, well, as much as I'm quite liking being naked, with your hands all over me, I think it's probably illegal to ride like this.'

He laughed that low, downright filthy laugh again, and once more my body reacted by shivering slightly, those post-sex tingles still very much evident as his hands ran lightly up over my thighs and hips. 'I needed this, Lana. What we've just done. I needed this.'

I turned my head just a touch, our mouths meeting, the kiss slow and deep. 'Yeah. So did I, baby.'

'I told you I'd give you the ride of your life.'

It was my turn to laugh, feeling my stomach turn somersaults as his hand rested on it. 'As long as this isn't the only ride I get, biker boy.'

'Believe me, darlin', this is just the first of many.'

And all I could do was close my eyes, lose myself in another deep, soulful kiss, and hope with every beat of my heart that he meant that.

15

Walking into the foyer, I stood completely still, staring out ahead of me at the huge expanse of space that seemed to stretch out for miles. The hotel I'd stayed in just a couple of weeks ago had been breathtaking enough, its foyer also bigger than the length of my entire street back in Newcastle, but this one – this was something else. From its ornate ceiling with the brightly coloured glass centrepiece that you couldn't take your eyes off, to the sheer number of people that were making their way across the marble floor, veering off in various directions, off to do whatever their own Vegas adventure entailed. And I knew better than anyone that this town could certainly throw up a few surprises.

Doing a quick spin around on the heels of my faithful biker boots, I started walking towards reception. He was already there, my eyes falling on him immediately. He was leaning back against the desk, his hands in his pockets, his head down. Dressed in dark jeans and a pale-blue shirt, the sleeves rolled up over his forearms, I noticed he still hadn't shaved, and his hair was still slightly ruffled. In fact, the only familiar thing about him was the smell of his cologne, which hit me the second I drew closer to him.

'Adam?'

He looked up, smiling slightly as I approached. 'You look… you look, different.'

I wasn't sure whether he meant that as a compliment or not, but in my skin-tight black jeans, biker boots, and a t-shirt that clung to me, showing off both my curves and my tattoos, my long, blonde, black-tipped hair loose around my shoulders, I certainly wasn't the woman he'd once been married to. The one who, yes, might have dressed in jeans and boots and had more than a slight aversion to dresses and skirts, but I'd never pushed it as far as I was pushing it now.

'I'm sorry, I meant… I mean, you *do* look different to the last time I saw you, back in England, and I know I saw you yesterday, but, I didn't really look at you properly, take in what…' He looked down, running a hand along the back of his neck before his eyes once more met mine. He almost sounded a touch intimidated, which was strange. For a man like Adam. I'd never known him be intimidated by anything. 'You look beautiful, Lana.'

Okay. He *had* meant it as a compliment. I just didn't know whether to believe him or not. The Adam I used to know would've hated all this shit. But this wasn't the Adam I used to know. This was a completely different man. Well, he *looked* different, anyway. I just had no idea why. Maybe he'd found someone else. I wouldn't blame him if he had. Someone who could love him the way I'd once loved him. Someone who wouldn't stop trying. Someone who wouldn't give up. Because he deserved someone so much better than me.

'Even with these?' I questioned, holding out my arms, his gaze dropping as he scanned the tattoos that covered them.

'Even with those,' he whispered.

Our eyes locked for a few, brief seconds, and it felt strange, looking at him like this. I was still having trouble believing he was actually here. And after last night, out in the desert with Eddie; everything we'd done, the way he'd made me feel, being here now, with Adam, it was more confusing than I wanted it to be.

'You wanted to talk,' I said, trying to sound casual. But it was actually quite hard to sound relaxed when I wasn't feeling it. As I stood there, looking at him, it felt like I was looking at a stranger. And that wasn't right. That wasn't how it should be.

'Come on. We'll go outside, by the pool. Well, one of the pools. You wouldn't believe how many this place has…'

I watched as he bowed his head again, his hands back in his pockets.

'Adam, I…'

He raised his gaze. 'I'm sorry, Lana.'

I frowned.

'For everything that happened. For the person I couldn't be…'

'Adam, please… Don't.'

'Because it makes the guilt creep back in?'

My frown deepened, and I took a couple of steps back, shaking my head. 'I'm not doing this…' I turned to walk away. Because I really *didn't* want to do this.

'No, Lana, hang on!'

I slowly turned back around, staring straight at him.

'I didn't mean it like that, I… This is just hard, you know? Confusing. Because I… I still love you, Lana.'

I shook my head again, more vigorously this time, but for some reason I was rooted to the spot now. I couldn't seem to move. 'No, Adam…'

He held out his hand, but I kept mine in my pockets. All those years of never holding hands, and he wanted to do it now?

'Adam, I can't.' My voice was barely a whisper. I couldn't make it go any louder. And the expression on his face almost broke my heart, a wave of confusion, so strong it almost knocked me sideways, washing over me. I took a deep breath, trying desperately to pull forward images of last night, of Eddie and the Harley and sex so incredible my body still wasn't letting me forget it, even now. I could still feel the tingling in my legs. The mere thought of it brought my skin out in goose bumps.

'We're divorced, Lana. That doesn't mean we can't touch each other anymore.'

I hesitated for a second, before I reached out and took his hand, feeling his fingers curl around mine, a feeling so unfamiliar. And how the hell had we let it get to that?

He smiled, but I just couldn't return it, not yet. The confusion was still too strong. 'Let's go.'

'Adam, I…'

'I just want to talk. Okay? I just want to talk.'

'You shouldn't have come here,' I said, my voice still unable to rise above that whisper. 'Finn shouldn't have called you.'

'I'm glad he did.'

His eyes locked with mine, and I felt almost resigned. But there was also this wave of anger simmering up inside me that I couldn't push aside. I wasn't a wayward teenager who'd run away to try and prove some kind of point. Yet that's how I felt both Finn and Adam were treating me.

'You shouldn't have come here,' I repeated.

His eyes wouldn't leave mine, and as much as I wanted to look away it felt as though something was keeping my head fixed in place. I couldn't seem to move it anywhere.

'Maybe we should go somewhere a little quieter?'

I frowned. Again. I was doing a lot of that lately, frowning. 'No. Adam, this really isn't fair.'

'You want to talk about fair?' His expression had darkened slightly and I finally found the strength to pull my hand away from his, shoving it back in my pocket. 'What isn't fair, Lana, is what happened to *us*.'

'There is no *us*, not anymore.'

'And don't you find that sad?'

I looked at him again but I couldn't say anything; couldn't find any words that felt right. Why was he doing this now?

'Twenty years, Lana, and we just stopped trying. That's something I regret with every beat of my heart.'

I shook my head, taking another couple of steps back. 'Why now, Adam? Why…? Look, I… I really can't do this…'

'So run away. Again. Go on, run away, and hope all of this will just disappear, but what you're doing…'

I moved closer to him. 'Not here, Adam. Don't do this here.'

He stared deep into my eyes, almost daring me to turn away, but I couldn't. I just couldn't. 'Room 3126. It's up to you, Lana.'

I watched him walk away towards the elevator, my heart beating so fast I had to lean back against the wall to catch my breath. What was going on here? What was I doing?

I almost ran outside, reaching for my phone to call Finn, closing my eyes for a second or two as I waited for him to answer.

'Jesus, Lana… You really have to…'

'I don't give a fuck about the time difference, okay?'

'Shit. He's there, then?'

'I thought it best to wait a few hours, you know? See if I'd calm down a bit more but, well, that's just not happening, so… Why, Finn? Why did you do that?'

'Because I love you, Lana. And I don't think you're acting the grown-up right now.'

'So, what? You just thought you'd take control of my life, is that it? Call the ex-husband, tell him I'd gone off the rails, needed pulling back into line.'

'It wasn't like that…'

'What *was* it like, then? Do you want to explain why you felt the need to contact Adam, after everything I told you? I mean, why not go a step further and get our parents out here too?'

'Lana, listen to me…'

'No. You had no right, Finn. No right at all.'

'I care about you. *That's* why I did it. And Adam he… he's not as bad as I thought he was. Not really. He still cares about you, Lana.'

'I don't believe this…' I threw my head back, feeling more confused than I'd felt in a long time. It was almost as if every step forward I'd taken over this past year was slowly being erased, flinging me right back to square one, whether I liked it or not.

'You're over there, in a strange country, with a strange man, somebody you only met a few weeks ago, and you can't see how odd that is? How weird it sounds?'

'Jesus…'

'Adam just wants to talk to you, Lana.'

'No. Adam has just told me he still loves me. Adam is piling guilt on me, telling me I haven't been fair. Adam wants to change my mind, turn me back into that woman I used to be and I'm not going there, Finn. So, no, Adam doesn't *just* want to talk.'

'Would it be such a bad thing? To listen to what he has to say? Maybe he's changed…'

I hung up. I wasn't even in the mood for a fight anymore. All of this was messing with my head and for a brief second I wondered why I hadn't just done what my mother had always wanted – stayed in a steady job, married to Adam, had those grandkids she'd always nagged me about. If I'd chosen that life this confusion I was feeling right now wouldn't even be a problem. None of this would be happening, and everybody would be happy. Everybody except me. But, hey, at least my life would be a whole lot easier. Settled. Ordinary. Normal.

Sliding my phone back into my jeans pocket I stared out ahead of me, taking a few seconds to just gather my thoughts, try and work out what to do next because I didn't know now. I really didn't know. It was almost as if a lightning bolt of reality had been fired straight at me, and I couldn't ignore the damage it had caused.

16

Sitting on the wall outside Eddie's MC clubhouse, my legs tucked up underneath me, an almost-full bottle of beer hanging from my fingers as I stared straight ahead at nothing in particular, I willed my mind to go blank. Adam turning up had really shaken me, and I didn't know why, why his presence was getting to me so much, but today I just wanted to forget all about it, if that was possible. He quite obviously wasn't going to go away, but I wasn't in the mood to deal with him right now. I still had to get my head around the fact he was here at all before I could even begin to think about anything else.

Looking down at the bottle in my hand I sighed quietly. It was only eleven in the morning and I was already turning to alcohol. Were things really that bad?

'Want some company?'

I looked up, smiling at Kaley as she leant back against the wall beside me.

'You look miles away,' she went on, taking the bottle from me and helping herself to a mouthful before handing it back to me.

'I'm fine.'

She shrugged. 'You don't have to tell me anything, honey. I

ain't gonna pry.'

I stared back out ahead of me, watching Eddie as he talked to Nate over in the garage adjacent to the clubhouse. He'd brought a couple of Harleys over to the club compound because, as well as selling bikes he also fixed and customised them. But with no on-site garage over at the bike shop he brought everything here, to the garage at the compound, for any repair work or customisation to be carried out. I'd felt like coming with him today. It was a change of scenery. A different place for me to sit and think. About shit I didn't really want to think about, but I didn't have all that much choice now.

'It's nothing,' I said, finally taking a sip of the beer, even though I didn't really want it. 'Just a few things going on I need to sort out.'

'Anything to do with Eddie?' She looked at me. 'Oh, crap, and there's me saying I wasn't gonna pry.'

I threw her another smile. 'It's okay. And, no, it's nothing to do with Eddie. Not really.'

She raised an eyebrow. 'Not really?'

I took another sip of beer, wanting this conversation to end now. I didn't need to confide in anyone about what was going on. I'd handle it myself. Eventually. 'It's complicated.'

'Well, there's an explanation that's used all the time when someone's talking about something they really don't want to share.'

'Kaley, I'm sorry, it's just…'

'It's alright, honey. I'm only messing. You really don't have to tell me anything. I just hate to see people looking down, is all.'

'I'm fine, I am, it's just… It's taking a bit of time to get used to things; a new life, a new country…'

'Missing home, huh?'

I looked down at my left hand, my third finger having now lost that indentation my wedding ring had left there for a good few months after I'd finally taken it off. And, strangely enough, it was the first time I'd actually acknowledged that.

'No. I'm not missing home.'

'Okay. Listen. I know just what you need.'

I looked up again, frowning slightly.

'We're gonna have a girls' day out.'

That was the last thing I needed. Or wanted. Coffee mornings, shopping expeditions, gossip sessions; all things I'd never really gone in for. Which was why I'd always chosen to work, predominantly, with men. I just seemed to get on better with groups of them than I did with women. Big groups of women intimidated me, because I just didn't feel like I had anything in common with them.

'Biker style,' Kaley winked, and I laughed, relief washing over me as she took my hand, pulling me up from the wall. 'And whatever's on your mind, honey, I guarantee this'll make you forget all about it. For a little while, anyway.'

We headed across the compound towards Nate and Eddie, both of them turning to look at us as we approached, their conversation suddenly stopping dead, which I thought a bit odd, but I shrugged it off. They obviously didn't want us to overhear anything, and whatever they were talking about, it was none of my business anyway.

I let go of Kaley as she walked over to Nate, watching as he took a set of keys from a hook on the wall and handed them to her.

'You heading out somewhere?' Eddie asked, wiping his hands on a cloth he'd pulled out the pocket of his jeans.

I nodded, folding my arms. He reached out and unfolded them, pulling me loosely against him.

'What's all this, huh? This arm-folding shit, this looking all preoccupied? This isn't the fun-loving, ass-kicking Lana I know. And you've been like this for days now. Ever since your ex rocked into town.'

'It's got nothing to do with Adam.' I couldn't believe I'd actually said that out loud. Because it had *everything* to do with Adam. How could it not?

'Forgive me if I don't believe that.' He kissed me gently, and like they always managed to do, his kisses injected a shot of calm straight into me; a brief wave of serenity flooding my body. 'If he's making you this unhappy, darlin', then make him leave.'

'How can I do that, Eddie? I can't *make* him do anything.'

'Do you *want* him to leave?'

'Yes.' I'd said that without missing a beat, because I meant it. I wanted him to leave. I wanted him to go, and stop invading a world he wasn't welcome in.

'Lana, listen, I just… I know that me and you… what we've got here… I know it's confusing. But this is me, darlin'. This is how I live – no ties, no commitments, and I just… I guess what I'm trying to say is… If you need to see him, to see Adam… If you need to…' He pushed a hand through his hair, looking away for a second before his eyes met mine again. 'Whatever you need to do…'

What exactly was he saying here? It was like he'd, all of a sudden, just thrown another layer of crap and confusion onto an already-growing pile.

'What's your point, Eddie?' I pulled away, narrowing my eyes as I looked at him.

'You know the score, Lana. No commitment, we said. No ties. Neither of us wanted that.'

'Yeah, I know the score, and I *still* know it. I understand the way this is all working, I get it. Okay? And I'm still not entirely sure what it is you're trying to say, but, if I'm sending out messages you're not happy with then you're reading them wrong.'

'Lana…baby, come on… What the hell's going on here, darlin'?'

'You tell me, Eddie. Because I don't have a fucking clue.' I looked over at Kaley. 'We ready to go?'

'We sure are, honey.'

I turned to look at Eddie again, his expression as confused as I felt. This whole surreal conversation was just one more thing that had succeeded in throwing me. I wasn't sure where it had come from. I just felt like I needed some time out now – an escape from the man I wanted to escape *with*. How ironic was that?

I started to walk away, but Eddie stopped me in my tracks, his hand on my arm making me turn back around to face him, the kiss he gave me almost verging on violent, yet, at the same time it had a calming effect that was instant.

'I need you in my life, darlin',' he murmured, his mouth resting against mine as he spoke, and I felt my knees almost give way beneath me as his hand fanned out in the small of my back. 'And whatever I said just there, however it came out… There are reasons why I…' He bowed his head, his thumb lightly stroking my cheek and I frowned, waiting for him to finish that sentence. 'Just know that I need you, Lana. We're good together, baby. We are so good together.'

Resting my hand against his cheek, I stared into his eyes. Sometimes he seemed so far away from that man I'd met in a Vegas hotel just a few weeks ago – was that because he was finally starting to feel real? Was the fantasy now fading and the reality beginning to show itself? I kissed him back, but I said nothing in reply. I just pulled away from him and headed over to Kaley.

I didn't understand anything that had just happened there. Maybe we both needed a little bit of time away from each other. Just a little bit of time. Because, right now, it felt as though that feeling of freedom I'd started to experience was beginning to slowly disintegrate, and a wall of doubt and confusion was quickly taking its place. And if I didn't knock it down as soon as possible, it had a real chance of surrounding me completely.

'Three, two, one!' Kaley shouted as we both downed the shots in one mouthful, slamming our glasses back down on the table. 'And I'm gonna have to wave the white flag now, honey, because I'm in charge of that bike out there. But that don't have to stop you. I'm guessing you could kinda do with the release.'

I leant forward, clasping my hands together between my knees as I looked out around me, taking in the dimly lit bar we'd ended up in with the loud music and the eclectic crowd. It was only three in the afternoon yet the place was filled to the rafters, everybody partying like it was Saturday night. But I had to remember I was in Vegas. A place so far away from my other world. The real world?

'Thanks for this, Kaley. I really needed a bit of time out and this has helped like you wouldn't believe.'

'Yeah, well, a few vodka shots and a little bit of help from our friend Jack Daniels never hurts, does it? I could tell you needed to get away for a while, even if you won't tell me why. And, like I said before, you don't have to tell me anything, and I ain't gonna pry, but, you and Eddie, back there at the compound… Is everything okay between you guys?'

'It's complicated.'

'Eddie's probably the least complicated person I know, Lana.'

'The *situation* is complicated.' I looked down, once more focusing on my naked left hand. Why was I doing that now? When I'd never done it before. Not in all the time Adam and I had been apart. I lifted my head, my eyes meeting Kaley's. 'Has he… has Eddie ever been involved with anyone? Seriously, I mean. Only…'

'He doesn't talk about his relationships much – at all, if I'm being honest. So I really don't know. I have no clue what his life was like back home in the UK, because he doesn't talk about *that* much, either. All I know is, in all the years I've known him, he ain't ever had anyone living with him. And he's never brought anyone to the clubhouse before. So I know that you – you're different.'

I looked down again. The alcohol may have blurred the edges slightly, but some things were still way too clear.

'He's a dreamer, Lana, and sometimes he feels as though he doesn't always fit in with the way the rest of us live because Eddie he… he's old school, you know? And he *can* be a bit of a loner. But at the same time he needs to know he has something to fall back on. People he can turn to. Because I'm not sure he wants to be alone *all* of the time, and that's where the club comes in. He doesn't hang around the place as much as some of the other guys do. Some of them practically live there. But Eddie… he prefers his own space more than anyone I know. He has his own way of doing things. He's different. And I guess it's just taking a bit of time for you to get your head around that, huh?'

I shrugged, reaching for the bottle and pouring myself another vodka shot, knocking it back in one. 'There's something I need to do.' I looked at Kaley. 'Can you take me back to the Strip?' I wasn't even sure why I'd asked that. The words had almost fallen out of my mouth without me realising.

'Sure I can, sweetheart. Come on. Let's go.'

As we headed back to the main drag, I clung onto Kaley as she handled the bike as well as any man, picking up speed when necessary, taking corners in a way that was both exhilarating and nerve-jangling. She was one real-life, kick-ass biker chick, and I was beginning to really like her. *Really* like her. If she could inject just a little bit of her 'take no shit' attitude into me I was sure I'd be able to handle Adam and Eddie and everything else I had to deal with a whole lot easier than I had done so far. Because I was beginning to realise that, maybe, I wasn't quite as 'kick-ass' as I'd thought I was. I still had a way to go on that score.

Pulling up outside the hotel Kaley brought the bike to a halt. 'You gonna be okay?' she asked as I climbed off.

'Yeah. I'm gonna be fine.'

She threw me a small smile. 'Okay, darlin'.' She started the bike back up. 'You need anything, you know where I am, you hear me?' she shouted, raising her voice above the roar of the engine.

'Thanks, Kaley.'

'Don't mention it, honey. I'll see you later. You take care now.'

I watched her speed off, back out on to the Strip, taking a second to wonder if I was doing the right thing here. But I obviously wasn't going to settle until I got this out of my system. Until I found out what he really wanted. Because he wasn't going to go away until I did.

Reaching into my pocket I pulled out my phone and without hesitation punched in his number. He answered almost immediately.

'Lana?'

'You're right, Adam. We do need to talk.'

17

Stepping into the elevator I closed my eyes, leaning back against the grab rail, breathing in deeply, quietly. My head was spinning slightly, the alcohol finally beginning to take hold now, but I knew I couldn't – *wouldn't* – have done this sober, whatever *this* turned out to be. Because right now I wasn't altogether sure. I was kind of playing it by ear.

As I walked along the corridor, checking the room numbers as I went, a tiny part of me wondered if this was such a good idea. Should I not just turn around and head back to the bike shop? Back to Eddie? Back to what I really wanted? Because I'd been happy – happy with the uncertainty and the freedom and the utterly mind-blowing sex. I'd been happy with everything just the way it was. Until Adam had turned up. So I needed him to go, to leave me alone to get on with the new life I'd been building for myself. A life without him in it.

Finally finding Adam's room I hesitated for just a second before I knocked on the door; the tiniest of raps. It was almost as if a part of me deliberately didn't want him to hear, then I could pretend he wasn't in there, turn around and leave this alone. But I could hear him coming towards the door, and now my feet felt as though they were glued to the spot, so I couldn't really go anywhere, even if I'd wanted to.

I took a step back as the door opened, and there he stood, all tanned and bearded and different. And that's what was confusing me. This wasn't the Adam I'd been married to. This was someone else completely.

He said nothing, just stood aside to let me through, closing the door behind us. I walked inside, taking in the oversized room with the enormous bed and the dark walls and the stunning views of Vegas that greeted me from the huge picture window.

'I'm glad you came.'

'You didn't leave me much choice, really.' I turned to face him. 'Did you?' Had he always been that handsome? Had his eyes always been that blue? Why couldn't I remember that? Had we really lost sight of each other *that* much? 'I mean, you obviously aren't going to go anywhere until you've said whatever it is you want to say to me, so, come on. Whatever you've come all this way to say, just say it.'

'What I *want* to say to you and the reason I came here are two completely different things. Now.'

I frowned. I didn't have a clue what he meant by that.

'I came here to tell you that I think... What you're doing is a mistake, and I still think that. I still think it's a crazy, stupid thing you've done. But the second I saw you, after all these months... I still love you, Lana. I *still* love you.'

I shook my head, my eyes refusing to leave his. This wasn't what I'd wanted. This wasn't supposed to be happening. 'Adam, please. Don't. I only came here this afternoon because I... I want you to understand that I need you to leave.'

'And I want *you* to understand that I'm not going anywhere. Not now. A couple of days ago, maybe, I could have been persuaded to leave you alone, to let you get on with whatever the hell this is you're doing, with a stranger. A stranger, Lana.'

'He isn't...'

'He is. Grow up, sweetheart, and realise that's *exactly* what he is.'

My eyes still wouldn't leave his, and my feet wouldn't move either, so all I could do as he came closer was watch and feel my heart pick up a steady rhythm that was continuing to confuse the hell out of me.

'Twenty years, Lana. We shared twenty years of our lives. And you can just push that aside, can you? Just like that?'

'No,' I whispered, shaking my head again, wishing he'd stop this. I needed him to stop this. 'Adam, please…'

He was right there in front of me now, so close I could smell that familiar cologne, something that sent more memories rushing forward to flood my brain. 'Do I look different, Lana?'

I breathed in deep as he slid a hand around the back of my neck, gently stroking it with his thumb.

'Because *you* look different. So different to the girl I was married to.'

'Adam…'

'And I like that. I like that we're different now. We're not the same people we were a year ago. We're not the same people…' He trailed off, his mouth moving closer to mine and I closed my eyes, waiting for the inevitable, until a wave of reality washed over me, suddenly sobering me up. Something inside me snapped and I pushed him away, stepping back from him. He held up his hands in surrender, bowing his head for a couple of beats before looking back up at me. 'I'm sorry.'

'I don't want you to be sorry, Adam. I just want you to go home.'

He shook his head, his hands in his pockets as he continued to stare at me. 'All those tattoos, the hair; the way you look now, Lana… Yes, a while back I would have hated it all. I can't deny that. But the more I look at you…'

I felt another rush of blood to the head and whereas a second ago I'd felt almost sober, now it was as though the alcohol I'd been drinking all afternoon was having a staggered, almost delayed, reaction, hitting me in waves every now and again.

I moved closer to him, reaching out to run my fingers over his rough chin. He was right. We weren't the same people anymore. And all of a sudden I found that incredibly exciting. Something was happening I couldn't control, and it was probably the alcohol's fault, and I may well regret every second of it in a few hour's time, but what the hell? That had been my mantra for the past year. Why change things now? 'The tattoos turn you on, huh?'

He grabbed my wrist, his eyes boring deep into mine, but he said nothing.

I laughed quietly, not caring that his grip was hurting me. 'We play hard now, do we?' He'd never really met the new Lana. He didn't know her, didn't know what she was capable of. He didn't know the things she'd learned in such a short space of time. But if he wanted to find out…

'Do they turn you on, Adam?' I whispered, watching as his eyes scanned my right arm, taking in the shapes, patterns and the rich, vivid colours that covered my skin. 'Do they turn you on? Make you think you're dealing with a bad, bad girl?'

'Jesus, Lana…'

Oh, this was good. I was having fun now. If this was the way he wanted to play this, I was quite willing to take charge, and teach my once straight-laced ex-husband things he probably never even knew existed. He might even like what I was about to show him. Maybe. It was worth a try. I was here now. And I was curious. I wanted to push him, see how far he was willing to go. I wanted to show him who I was now. And if he still loved me after that…

'You ever fucked a bad girl, Mr Saunders?'

He groaned as I slid a hand down over his neck, sliding it inside his shirt, touching his chest. He felt harder than I remembered, more toned. He'd quite obviously been hitting the gym more frequently than usual. Turning himself into that different man he claimed he'd become?

'Do you *want* to fuck a bad girl?'

He grabbed my waist, pulling me against him with so much

force it knocked the breath right out of me, and I had to hold onto him to steady myself. But it had also knocked some sense into me, too. Brought the reality of this situation rushing forward like a tidal wave. I must have drank way more than I'd thought I had this afternoon because my head really wasn't straight at all. I was all over the place here.

'Adam, I'm sorry, this isn't fair on you…' I disentangled myself from his arms, stepping back, but his grip on my wrist was firm. He wasn't letting me go anywhere.

'No, Lana. Baby, I need this.'

He'd never called me 'baby' before. Never used that kind of language. And all that did was confuse me more. I didn't know who he was. And I didn't know who *I* should be when I was around him.

'I need *you*.'

'You don't know me anymore, Adam.'

'I do. Lana, I do. And, right now, I want you more than I can even begin to describe.'

He wanted sex, that's what he meant. Because I'd pushed him to that point; it was my fault. And even though I hated myself for it, it was what *I* wanted, too. God help me.

I felt my heart start to pick up that rhythm again; that fast, painful rhythm. And I found myself thinking about Eddie, remembering our confusing, almost surreal, conversation earlier today before Kaley had taken me away from it all for an afternoon of drinking and dancing and talking to strangers who, for a short while, had made me forget all of this; everything I'd done. The mistakes I'd made.

I searched his face for something, anything that could tell me he was being honest here. Because I didn't know what to do anymore. A part of me wanted to close my eyes and let a man I'd known half my life take me again, draw me back into his world, back into his bed. But another part of me wanted to walk right out of here and go back to that new world I'd thought I was settling into. That ridiculous, crazy, stupid world. Eddie and me, we were planning our trip. Preparing to take to the road, just me, him and his Harley. I didn't need *this*.

'I want to fuck a bad girl, Lana.'

Hearing him talk like that, his voice low and deep, it sent a shiver so sharp, so red-hot running through me I couldn't stop my body from shuddering as his lips touched my neck, his hand sliding down onto my hip.

'I want to fuck a bad girl.'

I pulled away, just a touch, shaking my head, a slight smile on my face as my fingers ran lightly over his unfamiliar beard. 'No. You want the bad girl to fuck *you*. I promise, it'll feel so much better.'

He groaned again, probably because I'd pulled right away from him now, slipping my t-shirt off over head, my eyes locked with his. He wanted to see how much I'd changed since I'd walked out of his life? He was going to see it all.

'Oh, Jesus, Lana...' His groans grew louder, his eyes dipping as I unclasped my bra, tossing it aside, continuing the slow strip in front of him, letting it turn *me* on as much as him. We were going there now, heading in one direction only. Any doubts I had about this situation would have to be pushed aside because it was way too late to turn back. Way too late.

He walked over to me, lifting me up and sitting me down on the dressing table, helping me slip off my jeans, sliding my knickers down so slowly, his eyes burning into mine. I was verging on desperate for him now, the ache inside me growing by the second. Or was I just desperate for sex? Desperate for some kind of release?

'Why did I let you go?' he whispered, stepping between my legs, his thumbs flicking over my nipples, drawing loud gasps from me as my head fell back, my legs wrapping around him. 'Why didn't I fight harder to make you stay?' I could feel his hard-on through the denim of his jeans, feel it pushing against me, and I wanted it inside me. I wanted *him* inside me. But I'd told him a bad girl was going to fuck *him*, and right now *he* was taking the lead. And that had to stop. So, despite a need to just unzip him, grab him, and put him where I needed him to be, I drew back a leg and kicked him away, which must have hurt because I was still wearing spike-heeled boots.

'We're doing this *my* way, remember?' I slid down from the dressing table, running both hands through my hair before shaking it out. 'You wanted to play dirty…'

'Jesus Christ… I was *married* to you?'

I smiled as I watched him throw off his clothes with an almost indecent haste, trying not to show my obvious appreciation at the body that was being revealed in front of me. He really had been looking after himself since we'd split up. He was more toned, harder; he truly was a different man. And I wanted to see if he *felt* different, if he fucked different. Until Eddie had walked into my life, Adam had been the only man I'd ever slept with. And I was more than ready to see if the familiarity was still there, or if something inside both of us had changed everything.

I walked over to him, slowly, making sure his eyes took in every movement of my hips, the slightly exaggerated swagger I was putting on, before I reached out to touch his chest again, fanning my fingers out, letting my hand slide down until it was wrapped around his rock-hard dick. 'You ready for this, Mr Saunders?' I breathed, squeezing him tight, the sound of his moans as he threw back his head causing my knees to almost give way. He was ready. And I was more than ready for *him*. For this. Whatever it was. 'Lie down,' I whispered, pulling my hand away from him and giving in to the urge to touch myself. Just briefly, but enough for him to see it. For his expression to let me know he wanted to see more.

He did as he was told, lying down on the bed and I straddled him, kneeling up, sliding my hand back between my legs, watching him as he watched me continue to touch myself. I was deliber-ately playing with him now, something I'd never done before. Sex between us had always been pretty straightforward; good, but never all that exciting. And maybe that was why, in the end, it hadn't even interested me anymore. But now – now I wanted to play with him. Physically and metaphorically speaking. This handsome man with the piercing blue eyes and a body so hot I couldn't quite get my head around the fact he'd once been my husband.

Pulling my hand away – even though I could have quite easily brought myself to the most incredible of orgasms within seconds – I ran my fingers up and over my thighs, my hips, touching my breasts, stretching out as another shiver shot through me.

I felt him reach out to touch my thigh, but I pushed his hand away, shaking my head as I looked at him. 'My rules, Adam.'

'Lana, come on,' he groaned. 'This isn't fair.'

I leant over, arching my back, letting my breasts lightly brush over his chest, my fingers intertwining with his. 'It'll be worth the wait. I promise.'

With Eddie, he always took the dominant role where sex was concerned. In the short time we'd been together that was the way it had always been. And, okay, sex with Adam had never been like sex with Eddie but, thinking back, I'd always allowed *him* to take the lead, too, to instigate everything; to control it. Now *I* wanted to take some of that control back. To make my own rules and play them hard. And I liked it. I could get used to it. Control suited me. I'd probably never be able to dominate Eddie, and I wasn't sure I wanted to, but Adam was different.

I inched up slightly, lowering myself down onto his stomach, letting the wetness between my legs touch his skin. And that action had the required result, eliciting another long, deep groan from him, his fingers tightening around mine as I rubbed against him and I leant over again, licking that space just below his ear, arching my back down so my breasts once more pressed lightly against his chest.

'Lana… Jesus, I'm going to explode here… I'm begging you, sweetheart, if I don't… Jesus *Christ!*'

'Don't be such a baby.' I let go of his hands, slowly trailing my fingers across his chest, down over his stomach, moving myself back a touch, finally taking him in my hand again. 'We're almost there.' I kept my eyes on his, holding his gaze as I raised my hips slightly, pausing for just a second before I lowered myself down onto him.

It was like coming home, to a newer, slightly upgraded, home that could give you so much more than the old one ever could, and I closed my eyes, leaning back to take him deeper; to feel him there inside of me. My husband – my *ex*-husband. A man I'd walked away from because I'd thought this was over. Finished. Done. And yet now, somewhere in the back of my mind, I knew it was so far from over. He'd seen to that by coming here. And I didn't know whether I still hated him for doing it, or whether I was glad that he had. My emotions were all over the place.

Leaning forward, his eyes once more meeting mine, I pushed down harder onto him, forcing him to go deeper. Did he feel as confused as I did right now? Or was everything I was feeling just down to the alcohol I'd consumed today? Should this even be happening at all?

I felt one of his hands in the small of my back, the other one cupping my breast, and when his mouth finally touched mine I knew I wanted to kiss the fucking life out of this man until my lips hurt and neither of us could take any more. *Shit! What the hell was going on here?* We'd not been divorced five minutes and yet, *this* was happening. But as I felt that rush of white-hot pain start to build, creeping up my legs until it hit me right where it mattered, I couldn't think about that. Couldn't think of anything except what he was doing to me – what I was doing to him. The way he was making me feel. The familiarity of his body in mine as he came fast and hard.

'Lana, Lana, Lana…' he murmured, his face buried in my hair as our bodies stayed locked together, taking in every last second of what had just happened. 'What are we doing?'

I slowly pulled myself up, climbing off him straightaway, walking over to where I'd thrown my clothes down on the floor.

Prolonging this wasn't a good idea. I needed to get away, needed to think.

'Lana?' He got out of bed, coming over to me, pulling me into his arms, and for a few seconds I felt like I'd been transported back to a time when his arms had been my place of safety. Somewhere I'd never wanted to leave. Until I'd realised I'd begun to rely on him just a little too much; that depending on him wasn't a good enough reason to stay together when everything else just wasn't working. And I didn't need to depend on him anymore, did I?

'I should go.'

'I don't want you to go. Lana, we can do this, me and you. We can make this work again. Start over...'

I shook my head, pulling away from him, reaching down to retrieve my clothes, hurriedly pulling them back on. 'It shouldn't have happened, Adam, I'm sorry. It wasn't fair...' This hadn't been the plan. This had been so far from the plan. I was only supposed to have let him talk, listen to what he had to say, then tell him to leave. I wasn't supposed to have done *this*. Was I really that weak?

'You walking out on me again isn't fair, Lana.'

'I didn't walk out on you, Adam. Our marriage was over. There was nothing there, nothing to...'

'Didn't you feel it? Just now? Didn't you *feel* that?'

'It was sex, Adam. That's all it was.'

'That wasn't just sex. There was a connection. I felt it, and I think you did, too. Something is still there, Lana. It's still there.'

I looked at him, knowing that what we'd just done here, this had only made everything worse. 'Don't, Adam.' I pulled on my t-shirt, raking my hands through my hair. It was time to go. Time to get out of there.

I started making my way to the door, but he grabbed my wrist as I walked past him, swinging me around to face him. 'I mean it, Lana. What happened there, all that has done is reinforce everything I already knew – I still love you. I'm still *in* love with you. Can your biker boyfriend say the same, huh? Does *he* love you

147

like I do? Does he love you at all?'

'Don't, Adam, please…'

'Do *you* love *him*?'

I stared at him, feeling his fingers tighten around my wrist. 'I'm not here to find love.'

'Then why *are* you here? I mean, I thought you'd found your new life back in Newcastle? Finn, the tattoo studio, all your new friends… Is that not enough for you anymore?'

'Where is this going, Adam?'

'Whatever you want me to be, Lana, I will be it. You want a new man? Then you got him.'

'It isn't that simple… Jesus!'

'I love you.'

'And you saying that constantly really isn't helping.'

'I'm trying, darling…'

I shook my head, his grip on my wrist loosening slightly. 'This isn't you,' I whispered, pulling back from him. 'All of this… It isn't you.'

'I don't want to *be* me anymore, Lana. You walked away from *me.*'

'Adam, please…'

He pulled me back into his arms, his mouth closing in on mine in a kiss so deep and gentle I had no choice but to accept it, to kiss him back just as deeply, just as gently.

'Come back, Lana,' he whispered. 'Please. Come home.'

I rested my forehead against his, stroking the back of his neck with my fingertips. 'I have to go, Adam.' Yeah. I had to go. Before I did something I really would regret. Something I regretted even more than what I'd already done.

I pulled away from him and headed towards the door.

'Lana…'

The sound of his voice made me turn back around, my eyes locking with his.

'I'm serious, sweetheart. I'm not going home. I'm not going anywhere. I'm not leaving Vegas unless you're leaving with me.'

18

I loved hanging out at the bike shop. Eddie was teaching me more and more every day, building my understanding, making my love for those two-wheeled machines grow. We rode almost daily, whenever we could, and those were the times I looked forward to more than anything, especially the early-morning rides when we'd get up just before dawn and head out onto the open road as the sun began to rise. Out there, surrounded by an expanse of nothing but desert, the sound of Eddie's Harley the only thing piercing the silence, the rising sun turning the sky a sea of reds and oranges and colours so beautiful I truly felt, sometimes, like I was in a kind of temporary heaven.

We'd stop for breakfast in a small diner off the beaten track, make love outside and not care if we were caught, then we'd ride back to Vegas and open up the shop, knowing we'd already had the best day. That's what Eddie Fletcher did for me. He took me away from the crap and confusion and made me feel alive. No ties. No commitment. No shit to deal with. We'd got that sorted now. We knew where we stood.

But there were also times when the reality of what was really happening kicked in. When I realised pushing Adam and the fact he was still in Vegas to the back of my mind wasn't going to work long-term. I still had to face up to what was going on. Choosing the usual head-in-the-sand option wasn't something I could keep up forever, although for the past couple of days that was the option I'd taken – avoiding Adam since that afternoon at the hotel, because I wanted to be with Eddie and the escape he could provide. Adam had tried calling me, of course he had. But I was ignoring him, even though I knew I couldn't do that for much longer. I just wanted a bit more time to think things through, that was all.

Should I have told Eddie that I'd slept with Adam? That was something else that kept going round and round in my head. The guilt I felt at what had happened was a regular visitor. It tore me apart, what I'd done to Eddie. I'd been weak and stupid and the last thing I'd ever wanted to do was hurt him. So there wasn't a day went by when I didn't regret what had happened with Adam; when I didn't regret being so weak. So selfish. I'd taken what I'd thought I wanted at the time, without even considering the consequences. But every time I came close to saying anything, to telling Eddie the truth, he'd kiss me, or tell me something that made me laugh, and the moment was gone. The decision to just forget it had happened winning over. I knew it was wrong, but I was terrified of losing what I had with Eddie. Terrified of losing this new life I was building, even though I had no idea where it was heading.

I looked up as I heard someone come into the shop, a slow smile spreading across my face as Eddie and that still unbelievably sexy swagger of his headed towards me.

'Hey, big guy.' I slid an arm around his waist, kissing him quickly and he grabbed me, pulling me in for a deeper, longer kiss.

'Hey, darlin'.' He pulled back slightly, his fingers running lightly over my cheek, his eyes staring into mine with an expression I just couldn't read. 'Everything okay here?'

'Everything's fine,' I replied, walking back behind the counter.

His mood seemed a little strange. For the past few days I'd had a feeling he was slightly distracted, by what I had no idea, but it seemed to be more evident every time he headed out to, or came back from, the club. Every time he saw Nate.

'What's happening here, Lana?'

I felt something inside me shift. I'd thought everything was okay between us. Despite the fact he'd seemed distracted at times, I hadn't thought it was anything to do with me. But now I wondered if I'd been slightly naïve in thinking that. The past few days had almost felt like normal, though. Before Adam had turned up. Before I'd let *myself* become distracted. 'There's nothing wrong, Eddie.' I slowly looked up, my eyes meeting his. And he held my gaze, his stare carrying a hint of coldness that hadn't been there a few seconds ago.

'I didn't ask if anything was wrong. I asked what was happening.'

I could feel the guilt rushing forward again, spreading through me like wildfire, bringing with it the fear that one stupid mistake could have messed up everything I was starting to love.

'You slept with him.' It wasn't a question. Somehow he knew.

I felt like I'd just been floored by a punch so hard to the stomach I couldn't breathe for a second or two. And I couldn't face him, I couldn't. I needed a minute to get my head straight, to work out how to handle this. So I walked through to the room at the back of the shop, but he followed me, of course he did. What else had I expected him to do?

'Did you sleep with him, Lana?' Eddie kicked the door shut behind him, his voice tight.

'I… Jesus!'

He bowed his head, raking both hands backwards and forwards through his hair in an almost manic fashion. 'Kaley told me she dropped you off outside a hotel on the Strip, a few days ago. And it doesn't take a genius to work out that the only reason you'd be there, at a hotel on the Strip, would be to see him. I don't mind that. I don't. I said if you needed to see him…'

151

'Eddie…'

He looked up, right at me, his eyes dark and dangerous, a nervous shiver trickling down my spine. 'Did you fuck him, Lana?'

I took a deep breath, backing up against the wall, determined to keep calm as he moved closer. 'It was a mistake,' I whispered, breathing out slowly, his hand resting gently against the side of my neck.

'Aye, darlin'. It was.'

His thumb stroked the base of my throat, his eyes searching my face for – what? Checking to see if the guilt was obvious?

'Did I push you, Lana? To do that? To fuck him?'

I frowned, aware of how close he was now, his mouth almost touching mine as he spoke. 'I don't… don't understand…'

'That morning, at the compound, the conversation we had. I told you, to do whatever you needed to do… Did I push you towards him?'

I shook my head, my breathing becoming lower, shallower, the heat of his body almost unbearably hot as he closed in on me. 'No, Eddie… I'd been drinking, I was confused, I just wanted to hear what he had to say…'

'And you had to sleep with him to do that, huh?'

'I'm sorry… Baby, I am so sorry.'

I closed my eyes as his mouth bore down on mine, the kiss surprisingly soft, given his manner and how tense the atmosphere was. 'What we have, darlin', I don't know what the hell it is, I really don't. And I thought I'd be able to handle this, I thought I could…' He looked down, his hand still resting against my neck.

'Eddie?'

He slowly raised his head, his hand pressing a little harder now, his eyes still dark, still dangerous. But I wasn't scared. I didn't feel threatened in any way. In fact, what I was really feeling was a flicker of excitement; a twisted kind of turn-on.

'I need you, Lana,' he murmured. 'Jesus, baby, I fucking need you. Right now.'

I didn't feel like I was entirely there. It was almost as if I was watching from the sidelines, witnessing how warped and fucked-up this relationship really was because, until now, until this very moment, I hadn't realised that's exactly what it was. But I needed him, too. I needed him.

He moved his hand from my neck, winding his fingers into my hair, pulling my head back slightly as his other hand slid up and under my dress, yanking down my knickers with such force I was sure I heard them tear, but all that did was draw the longest moan out of me. He was taking me in a way that was rough, verging on brutal, but at the same time so hot I could feel how wet I was. How wet he'd made me.

As his mouth crashed down onto mine he pushed inside me, a beautiful pain shooting through me, causing me to groan loudly against him. And we laughed, both of us, we laughed as we kissed, as he fucked me, my legs wrapped tight around him. It was the craziest, most unreal moment. And I didn't understand it, didn't even try to. I just let it happen. Let his body invade mine, because I liked it. He was pushing Adam away, and that's what I needed – to push Adam away.

'Jesus *Christ!*' Eddie shouted as he came so fast, so quickly, he almost lost his balance. '*Jesus!*'

I held onto him, my eyes closed, my face buried in his hair as I tried to catch my breath. Now we were done, had it changed anything? Made the situation any clearer? What had happened here, there was a reason for that. A reason why the sex had been hard and the words confusing.

'It's over, Lana.' His voice was quiet as he gently put me down, his eyes almost burning into mine as my messed-up head tried to process what he'd just said. 'Us. It's over, darlin'. We're done.'

19

Kaley passed me the joint and I took a short drag. I didn't really want to because I wasn't used to it, and I didn't particularly *want* to get used to it. But, right now, as I lay back on the couch in Eddie's front room, listening to Pink Floyd and Joe Bonamassa, drinking beer with some of the guys from the club, I needed the release it was giving me.

'Eddie tells me your ex is in town,' Kaley said, taking the joint from me.

'Eddie had no right to tell anyone anything.'

She looked at me. 'Touchy subject, huh?'

I didn't reply.

'So, what's he like – your ex?'

'Nothing like Eddie,' I replied, sitting up and picking up my beer, taking a long swig. The alcohol, combined with everything else I'd been drinking and smoking over the course of the night, was beginning to make me feel more relaxed than I actually was, but that was okay. It was good. It was necessary.

'I'm gonna go find Eddie,' I sighed, knocking back another mouthful of beer as I stood up.

'Lana, I'm sorry.'

I sighed, turning back around. 'It's not you, Kaley, okay? Things are just... Well, you know how things are between me and Eddie right now and... I need to talk to him.' I headed out into the hallway, checking my watch as I walked, although I had no idea why. It wasn't like I was going anywhere.

'I wasn't sure if you'd still be here.'

My head shot up at the sound of his voice, and I felt my heart almost physically break as I looked at him. He'd told me it was over, but it was like I was in some kind of denial. I was still in the process of moving out of his place, of finding somewhere to stay, and being here, being around him, it was sad and hard for me to take in. Because it was only when I'd heard him say the words – that it was over – that I realised how much I really wanted him. Needed him. Distancing myself from him, it wasn't something I was in a hurry to do, which was why I was spending my time in the company of Kaley and alcohol and cigarettes I shouldn't be smoking – anything to help me try and understand what was going on. Or forget it all. Neither was happening. 'Do you want me to go?'

He stood there, all dark and dangerously handsome in that sexy, almost dirty way, a cigarette hanging from the corner of his mouth, a bottle of Jack Daniels in his hand. And I just found that unbelievably hot. So hot I temporarily forgot we weren't together anymore.

He bowed his head, taking a draw on his cigarette before he looked back up at me. 'No. I don't want you to go.'

I moved a little closer, taking the Jack Daniels from him and helping myself to a mouthful.

'Come here,' he murmured.

And I should have said no; shook my head and just walked away. He'd ended it, he didn't want me anymore, so why put myself through more pain by sinking deeper into this increasingly surreal situation? But I was weak. So bloody weak.

Stepping into his arms, I let him fold them around me, nestling myself against his hard body, the smell of cigarette smoke and beer something I now found strangely sexy. On him. He tilted up my chin so I looked right at him, his mouth brushing gently over mine, the confusion so painful; so real. What were we doing?

'I never meant to hurt you, Eddie,' I whispered, snuggling into him as he leant back against the wall. 'And I'm so sorry I did that. I'm so sorry.'

'I can't do it, Lana. Not anymore.'

His hand ran lightly up and down my spine as he held me, and I just wanted to close my eyes and stay there, in his arms. I wanted to wind the clock back and erase everything I'd done to cause this. 'I don't want to go.'

'I know, baby.' He tilted my chin up again, kissing me slowly, another shot of calm rushing through me, albeit for a very brief second. 'I know. But I…' He threw his head back, letting out a loud, almost tortured, sigh. 'Lana, darlin', this is so hard for me to…' He took my hand, leading me over to the stairs and we sat down, his hand still holding mine, but his head was down, his hair falling over his eyes and I felt an overwhelming urge to lean forward and push it back, tuck it behind his ears, just like I'd used to do.

'What's going on, Eddie?'

'Do you love him, Lana?' He finally raised his head, and there was a sadness in his eyes that I'd never seen there before. An almost heartbreaking sadness. 'Adam. Do you still love him?'

I'd really wanted to say no, without missing a beat, so sure was I that any feelings I might still have for Adam were gone. But more beats than I cared to count had already passed, and I hadn't given any kind of response.

Eddie's head went down again, and he let go of my hand, an action that filled me with a sudden, painful emptiness. 'I was in love, once. A long time ago.' His eyes dropped to the floor, his hands clasped tightly together. 'Back in Glasgow. We'd met when we were just teenagers, hanging out with the local bikers at a fair that had rolled into town for the summer. Best summer of my life, that was.' He seemed to drift off some place else for a few seconds and I let him go there. I sensed it was a place he needed to re-visit, even if it was only for the shortest time. 'She was beautiful, Lana. Really beautiful. All long auburn hair and a smile that could floor any man. She had an attitude from hell, of course, but that's what I loved about her. She took no crap from anyone. Knew how to stand up for herself.' He raised his eyes to the ceiling, closing them briefly before he once more dropped his gaze, staring back down at the floor. 'We were together a long time, almost thirteen years, and I… I loved her, so fucking much. She was everything I'd ever wanted. She was… she was everything…' He lifted his head slightly, and I watched as his expression changed, a fresh wave of sadness engulfing him. And I felt my heart break, felt it shatter into pieces for this man I hadn't ever really understood. But now I wished I'd tried harder. I wished I'd tried. 'When I woke up that morning, and she wasn't there, I knew something was wrong. Something wasn't right, it hadn't felt right for a while, but I'd just ignored it.' He gave a short, cynical laugh, dropping his head again. 'She'd been having an affair. With my brother. It had only just started, that was their defence. It had only just started… Aye… It was all in the note, all the details, all the necessary crap needed to break my fucking heart…' He pushed a hand through his hair, a heavy, pain-laden sigh escaping him. 'They were gone. The two of them. Left, just like that. They didn't even say where they were going, just upped and ran off, leaving only that fucking note.'

'Oh, Jesus, Eddie… I had no idea…'

He looked at me, his expression a little harder now. 'Why would you? I've never told anyone this. Never shared this with any other person. But that's why – that's the reason I left Scotland. I needed to get away, from everything that reminded me of that life I'd wanted. The life I'd almost had; the woman I'd wanted to spend it with. I just walked away from everything, left it all behind – my job, my family, everything. I wanted to forget it all, pretend none of it had existed, that's how much it had affected me. And coming here, it worked, you know? I started again, built a new life for myself, and I love that life. So fucking much. I love the bike shop, love Vegas; love the fact Nate and the guys gave me a new kind of family. One I could rely on. One that wouldn't cheat or lie or take away everything I'd ever loved. It's just that… after what's happened…' He dropped his gaze, and I felt my heart shatter all over again, crumbling into dust inside of me. 'I said I didn't want commitment, but that was a lie. I fucking lied, Lana. Because I knew I was falling in love with you, and that scared the fucking crap out of me.'

I took a deep breath, desperately trying to keep tears that had started welling up behind my eyes at bay. I didn't want to cry. I didn't deserve to cry.

'Oh Jesus, Eddie…'

'I can't do it, Lana. I thought I could. I thought putting up those barriers and pretending I didn't care; I thought doing all of that would stop this from happening. I thought you'd be nothing more than a beautiful escape…' He pushed a hand through his hair, but it just fell straight back down over his eyes because his head was still bowed. 'But knowing you slept with him… I can't do it, darlin'.' He looked up, his eyes staring deep into mine. 'I can't let myself go there again. I thought I could, thought I could deal with all this shit now but… I can't.'

I shook my head, reaching for his hand, and he let me take it. Let me wrap my fingers around his. 'I'm so sorry, Eddie.'

His smile was weak, and it didn't reach his eyes, but as he touched my cheek, his thumb gently stroking my skin, I felt a pain I hadn't known could even exist cut right across my chest. 'It's a mess, baby. It was a mess from the start. Because I don't think either of us were ready for this.'

I closed my eyes, feeling tears start to slowly slide down my face as I rested my forehead against his.

'If you think there's even the slightest chance you might still love him, Lana…' Eddie whispered, his thumb still stroking my cheek, brushing away the tears that were still falling. 'Just the slightest chance…'

'I want *you*.' I wanted the warped and twisted love I had with Eddie, not the conventional kind I'd once had with Adam. That kind had only dragged me down, made me hate the person it had turned me into.

'Any chance, Lana. *Any* chance. Don't let him go until you know for sure, darlin'.'

'No,' I whispered, shaking my head. 'No.'

'There's so much for me to get my head around right now, baby. And I can't… I just… I can't…' And then we were kissing; his mouth moving against mine in the most beautiful way. I don't know how it had happened, whether it was just the emotional situation, or the fact neither of us really wanted to let this go, I didn't know. I just knew that we were kissing, that he'd pulled me onto his lap, that my skirt was pushed up over my hips and we were making love, right there, on the stairs. He was inside me, and I never wanted him to leave. It was fucked-up sex, for a fucked-up situation. 'I'm sorry.' His mouth rested against mine as he spoke, so quietly the words were barely audible. 'I'm so sorry, darlin'…' And when he came, I cried. Slow, silent tears, the worst kind of self-pity taking over as I held onto him, moving with him, taking everything he was giving me because this could be the last time I was ever this close to him. So when the tears finally stopped I still clung onto him, closing my eyes, trying to keep the world shut out for as long as I could because all I wanted to do was live these final few minutes with him. These final, few, beautiful minutes.

'I'll tell him to go,' I murmured, running my fingers through his hair, aware that he'd done what he needed to do now. He was finished. And with that realisation came the crushing reality of what was going to happen next. 'We can work this out, Eddie.' I pulled back slightly, so I could look at him. 'We can take that road trip, baby. Just you and me. We can talk this through…'

He took my hands, moving them away from his face before

lifting me up and off him. 'It's over, Lana.'

I stood up, following him as he took the stairs two at a time. 'You really want me to go? Huh? Can you look me in the eye, Eddie, and tell me you really want me to go?'

He swung around, the sadness that had taken over his eyes just seconds earlier having been replaced by an almost cold steeliness as he stared at me. 'Of course I don't want you to go, Lana.'

'Then tell me to stay. And I'll make Adam go.'

He shook his head slowly, his eyes still fixed on mine. 'It's too close to home, darlin'. What you did, it's too close to home. It's brought back too many memories, memories I was done with, and you brought them back.'

'Then you have to tell me you want me to go, Eddie. You have to tell me, and you have to make me believe you really mean it.'

In a movement so sudden I couldn't have seen it coming, he'd grabbed my wrist, pushing me back against the wall, his mouth once more crashing down onto mine, sucking the breath out of me. 'Every fibre of my being is screaming out for you to stay, darlin'. Because I don't want you to go. I want *this* – the messed-up sex and the days spent planning our escape, just like we'd talked about. I want that so much it hurts like fucking hell. But knowing what you did, knowing that you might still love him, knowing that he touched you… That hurts so much more. Loving you and losing you, baby, that's something that could rip me in two and I can't go there. Not again. I can't take that risk.'

Lifting up my leg I kicked him away, running my fingers through my hair and shaking it out. 'Then I'm wasting my time here.'

Our eyes locked together, the stare long and hard and achingly brutal. He wanted me, I needed him. And neither of us was going to win this one.

'You're really that weak, Eddie?'

'Because I don't trust you? Because that's what it comes down to, Lana. Trust. Loyalty is everything – remember?' He dropped his gaze, running a hand over the back of his neck. 'I know this…' He

160

looked back up at me. 'This thing we had, I know it was compli-cated. It was confusing. And we both tried so hard to believe that we didn't need – didn't *want* commitment, but…'

'Don't you even want to *try* and work things out? We could be so good together, Eddie, you said that yourself. When I'm with you I feel like I can take on the world…'

'You don't need me to be able to do that, darlin.'

I felt fresh tears start to well up behind my eyes and I blinked a few times to stop them from falling. 'You have no idea how *much* I need you, Eddie.'

Once more a deep, painful silence fell between us, our eyes still locked. 'If you love him, Lana, in any way – if you love him, you need to make sure you don't lose him.'

'I don't love him, Eddie.'

'I don't believe you.'

'I slept with him. That doesn't mean I'm still in love with him.'

'You'll regret it, baby. One day. Maybe not now, maybe not even in a few years, but one day you'll regret it, regret not taking this chance to find out just what you really need…'

I walked over to him, running my fingers down over his cheek, resting my mouth against his, kissing him so slowly, every move-ment of my lips on his tearing another piece of me away. 'You said we shouldn't let the past drag us down, Eddie.'

'But he's not really your past, Lana. Is he?'

'Eddie…'

'If you'd really wanted to let go of the past,' Eddie whispered, his eyes staring deep into mine, '… then why keep his name?' He gently took hold of my wrist, stepping back from me, his eyes never leaving mine. 'Come get your things tomorrow.'

I watched him disappear into the bedroom – *our* bedroom – before a wave of something I could only describe as anger took over, and I followed him, slamming the door shut behind me. 'You want to walk away from this, Eddie, you do that, okay? You throw it away before we've even had a chance to see where it could go…'

'No, darlin', *you* already did that.'

His eyes were blazing, but I was sick of all this shit now. I was fighting for what I wanted here. I was going to fight until every last breath had been wrung out of me.

'Why, Eddie? Hmm? Why did I decide that fucking my ex-husband would be a good idea? Because *we* messed-up. You're spinning me all this crap about stepping back from commitment when that's exactly what you're looking for, you've just said so yourself. But do you know what the ironic thing is here? I'm not. I'm really not. Or I wasn't, anyway. I walked into this relationship not wanting to be tied down, I just wanted some fun, and I got that. In fucking spades. You were so good for me, Eddie. So good. And I don't know when all that started going wrong, I don't know when the early-morning bike rides and sex by the side of the road stopped being what we *both* wanted...'

'There's something going down at the club,' he sighed, leaning back against the wall, pushing a hand through his hair.

I looked at him, frowning slightly. 'Like what?'

'You don't need to know.'

'Don't I?'

He fixed me with a look that almost froze my blood. 'You don't need to know, Lana. That way you don't become involved in shit you need to steer well clear of.'

My frown deepened. 'You in some kind of danger?'

'I got distracted, that's all.' He sighed again, his head turned away from me, his eyes fixed on nothing in particular. It was like he was just staring into dead space. 'I got distracted, took my eye off the ball.' He turned to face me, sliding a cigarette between his teeth and lighting up, taking a long, deep drag on it, blowing smoke upwards. 'I let go of *us*, Lana.'

'Jesus, Eddie...'

He took another drag on his cigarette, looking down as he flicked ash onto the dark wooden floor. 'I need to move on.'

'Without me?'

He raised his gaze, his eyes showing just a touch of that sadness they'd expressed earlier. 'Loyalty is everything to me, Lana. Loyalty is everything. Without that, darlin', we are done.'

20

I almost ran along the corridor, my heart beating out of my chest, my head spinning, but I knew what I was doing. Knew he was to blame for all of this. I'd played my part, I'd let weakness take over, but he should never have come here. He should never have reopened a past that was finished with. It should never have been brought into the present.

Hammering hard on his door, it took just seconds for him to answer. I hadn't even considered the fact he might not be in there. I just assumed he would be.

'What the hell…?' His eyes widened in surprise as he saw me.

I was slightly out of breath, but that anger was still there, kicking its way to the surface with every second that passed.

I pushed past him, slamming the door shut behind me. 'Go home, Adam.'

He stood completely still, a small laugh escaping as he folded his arms, a slightly amused expression on his face. 'I'm sorry?'

'Go home. This is crazy. You, being here, it's crazy. And it's messing everything up.'

He continued to stare at me, which only served to make the anger inside me grow, masking the pain I'd felt at walking away from Eddie. Because I hadn't wanted to do that, hadn't wanted to leave, but I'd had no choice. And I needed someone to blame, someone to focus that anger on because I'd already beaten myself up so many times I wasn't sure I could take any more.

'I told you I wasn't leaving here unless you were leaving with me, Lana. And that still stands.'

'I don't love you, Adam.'

'Don't you?'

'Go home.'

'Would a drink help?'

'Everything we did that afternoon; sleeping together. It was a mistake.'

'If I thought you really meant that I'd probably pack my case and book my flight right away. But I think you know as well as I do that…'

I'd slapped him before I'd even realised my hand had been raised, my palm connecting with his face in an action that, for a split second, shocked me. I'd never done anything like that before, never felt the need, never felt this level of anger. And why? In reality it wasn't even him I was angry with. It was me. He hadn't forced me to sleep with him, I'd made that decision all by myself. Me. My fault. It was my fault I'd lost Eddie – my fault I'd hurt him. My fault I'd lost that life I'd been loving.

Adam grabbed my wrist before I had a chance to go there again, and that second's worth of respite that had appeared suddenly vanished, to be replaced by another wave of confused anger.

'Is this really what you've turned into, Lana,' he hissed, still holding onto my wrist, his eyes burning into mine. 'Is the denial that much of a killer, huh?'

I wrenched my arm free, backing away from him. 'You really want me, Adam? Do you? You *really* want me? Even after this? After I come in here shouting crap and hitting you? You still want me?'

He turned his head away from me, his hands in his pockets, his eyes closing for the briefest of seconds, as though he was quickly trying to take in the whole situation. 'I want my Lana back,' he said quietly, slowly turning his head to face me again. 'I want *my* Lana.'

I shook my head, my eyes fixed on his. 'She's gone.'

'No, she hasn't.'

He moved closer, and I could feel my heart beating faster now. 'She's still there, somewhere. Underneath all of this, she's still in there.'

I backed away from him, not wanting him to come any nearer. 'She's gone, Adam. That woman you used to love, she's gone. And when you said you still loved me, you couldn't mean that, because you don't know me anymore. You don't know the person I became. So you can't love me.'

'I can learn,' he whispered, placing his hand on my cheek, but I pushed him away. Eddie's touch was still too fresh in my mind, the memory of his body inside mine still too raw.

'Please, Adam, just go home. Leave me alone to live my life…'

'I'm not leaving Vegas without you, Lana. And *you* more than anyone should know that when I say something, I mean it.'

He looked so deep into my eyes, I felt as though he was reaching right into my very soul, stepping all over those shards of my shattered heart, making his mark, whether it was welcome or not.

'You *really* want me?' I repeated.

'Any which way you come, Lana, I want you.'

I laughed, a mild hysteria taking over from the anger and the pain. But I couldn't forget how my world had changed once more in a matter of hours. Because of this man. Because I'd been too weak to resist him.

I felt his fingers slide between mine, the feel of his skin against me warm and soft.

'Any which way you come,' he whispered, his mouth touching mine. 'Forget him, Lana. Get him out of your system and forget him. He's gone.'

'Fuck you!' I spat, trying to push him away, but he was stronger than me – or was it just that I didn't really want to resist?

166

He smiled, and that just made the anger return ten-fold, which gave me the strength I needed to push him away, kicking him back with the full force of my boot. But nothing seemed to deter him, and confusion started to erase the anger. This wasn't the man I remembered – that safe, conventional man who wanted sex at weekends and considered spontaneity to be something that only got in the way of a well-ordered world. That man would have backed away from this, not welcomed it. That man would have rather walked away than deal with confrontation from me. But now he seemed to be almost encouraging it.

'Does this get you excited, Lana?'

'Well, it certainly seems to be doing it for you,' I drawled, reaching down to touch his obvious hard-on, slowly pulling his belt away from his jeans, my head spinning with something I didn't even want to get into. It was too tiring to even think about it. This past couple of days had been exhausting, and I just wanted a release now. An outlet to enable me to rid myself of whatever this was. And if Eddie didn't want me, this man did.

'You can hate me, Lana,' Adam whispered, sliding my skirt down over my thighs, 'All you like, you can hate me. Tell me to go. Scream at me, blame me, tell me it's all my fault but I'm not leaving this place unless you're leaving with me.'

I closed my eyes, letting his mouth cover my shoulder in the softest of kisses, moaning quietly until his lips on mine stifled the noise, a kiss so deep and beautiful rising from out of nowhere. When the hell had he learned to kiss like that?

I could feel the heat burning up from inside, and I knew I was crossing lines again, making the same mistake I'd made just two days ago, but I needed this. I wasn't sure how much I really needed Adam, but I needed this. Sex. Hot, angry, confused sex.

We almost ripped each others' clothes off, tearing at material like it was nothing but rags, my skin burning up, despite the goose bumps. I needed to see how this was going to play out now. That line – I was well and truly over it.

167

Throwing my arms up above my head I cried out as he slammed me back against the wall, his fingers tightening their grip on me, his mouth crashing against mine. My skin felt like it was on fire, every nerve ending on red alert, every tingle shooting through me intensifying by the second, causing long, drawn-out moans to spill out of me.

I had no idea what was happening here; no idea *how* it had happened, apart from the fact I'd barged into his room angry and upset because me and Eddie were over. And that had somehow led to this. To sex. The one thing that shouldn't be happening. But it *was* happening. *Oh, God, it was happening!*

And I didn't really know who this man was, the man who was touching me in ways he'd never touched me before. But I craved it, whatever it was. I ached for it.

Letting go of my hands he let his own fall, travelling down my body until they were stroking the curve of my waist, my hips, moving around until they cupped my bottom, lifting me up, my legs instinctively wrapping themselves around him. And I cried out again as he thrust into me almost immediately, once more slamming me back against the wall, but all it did was turn me on more, make me scream louder, grip tighter, my fingernails digging into his shoulders as I buried my face in his hair. It was going to be quick, I could feel it. His movements were speeding up, becoming harder, rougher; he was pushing so far into me I felt him hit his limit. He could go no further. And then he was coming so fast I felt his grip on me become almost painful, his own cries merging with mine, filling the room, loud yet low as all the tension flooded out of him. Out of me. Until the silence took over. All I could hear now was our breathing and the vague sound of Vegas getting on with things outside.

He lowered me down and I looked at him, running my fingers through his hair as I watched him struggle to catch his breath, the exertion almost too much for him; as I waited for the regret to kick in. The realisation that I'd made the same mistake twice.

And then he laughed, and it was infectious, the mood lightening instantly. That regret didn't seem to be coming, and that confused me slightly. But the intensity returned within seconds, his eyes staring deep into mine and I felt my whole body shiver; a deep, sexy shiver that hit right at the very core of me.

'We're not done yet,' he whispered, parting my lips with his thumb before trailing it down over my neck, along my collarbone. 'We are so far from done.'

Oh, he was right there. Despite everything else that was going on, all both of us wanted now was this – hot, dirty, different sex. Sex like we'd never had before. All those years we'd been together and we'd never, ever had sex like this. Ever. Was this all we'd really needed? Hard, hot sex? I knew *I'd* certainly needed it.

Gently pushing him away I backed over to the bed, our eyes locked together as he came closer, reaching out for me. And just the touch of his fingers on my skin made my breath catch, the excitement rising all over again.

'When did we lose this?' he whispered, pushing the hair back off my shoulder, leaning in to kiss it so lightly his lips barely touched me.

'It was never ours to lose, Adam.'

He looked at me, right at me, and I felt the deepest, wildest shiver wrack my body, the heat between us almost unbearable as we fell onto the bed, the kisses rough, the confusion mounting, the need for each other taking over everything that threatened to get in its way.

'It's ours now,' he said quietly, sliding a hand between my legs, his eyes burning into mine as his fingers pushed inside me. 'And I'm not letting it go.'

I held his stare, his eyes mesmerising, so intense I could barely take it. It was almost as if I was seeing him for the very first time, feeling him for the very first time and that, in itself, was painfully exciting, his fingers thrusting in and out of me only adding to it all. And when he pulled out without bringing me to that climax my body ached for, I couldn't stop a long, frustrated groan from escaping, only for it be replaced with one of pure pleasure as he moved down, lowering his head, his hands pushing my thighs wider apart as his tongue set to work. I gripped the pillows behind me, my hips bucking as he moved in harder and I closed my eyes, not caring that my moans were growing louder. He was making me crazy, something he'd never done before, not in the latter years of our marriage, anyway. But now – now he was killing it, killing *me*, just by being here. By doing this. By walking back into my life and, in the space of a few minutes, making me rethink everything. *Everything*.

I could feel that delicious tingle start to make its presence felt, feel it working its way up my body, and as he pulled away from me the cry of sheer frustration I let out was almost primal. I hadn't even realised it was me making that sound until I heard it, felt it from deep within – where I needed him to be.

'I want to know every part of you, Lana,' he whispered, his mouth close to my ear, and I gasped quietly as I felt him push into me. He *knew* every part of me – the old me. The new me was still a mystery to him. I wasn't even sure she was my *own* best friend just yet. But I was more than willing to introduce this man to her now, let him get to know her better. Let him invade her, use her; make him understand why she'd had to appear. Maybe that was something we *both* needed to understand.

I opened my eyes as his fingers intertwined with mine up beside my head, an almost electric stare causing sharp flickers of white-hot pain to shoot through me. A beautiful, exciting pain, a constant pain that stood its ground as he pushed my hands back into the pillows, his thrusts growing harder and more frequent and I drew my legs up, pulling them back, forcing him to go deeper, the sound of his groans making me wetter, so wet I had to grip him tight to keep him inside me.

I could taste myself on his lips, which caused another groan to escape, my fingers tightening around his. I didn't want this to end, didn't want him to stop doing what he was doing, because when he did, once this was over, that reality I was so scared of now was going to throw itself upon us in such an unwelcome way it would taint everything. And I wasn't sure I was ready for that. Not yet. So I kept my eyes closed, held onto him as tightly as I could and gave in to the moment, letting him flood my body with everything he had and I took it because this man was twenty years of my life and I really had been naïve to think I could just walk away from that the way I had done. Naïve to think I could just forget about it, forget about *him*. And yet, for almost a year, I'd done exactly that. Until now.

'I love you, Lana.' His voice was so low I could barely hear it, his mouth touching mine as he spoke.

I let go of his hand, reaching up to touch his face. I needed to feel that he was real because the sex wasn't enough, although my body would beg to differ. It was over, but he was still inside me, and I loved that he was. That he wasn't going anywhere yet. But then I allowed Eddie to enter my head. His dark, rough good looks invading my thoughts, hitting me with a guilt I didn't need right now. He didn't want me anymore. I'd walked away from him and he hadn't tried to make me stay. So the guilt was unnecessary, or at least that's how I tried to convince myself, and not too successfully at that.

'Adam… I can't…'

'Come home, darling. Please.'

I felt tears start to trickle down my face, and I really hadn't wanted that to happen. Crying was something Lana Saunders had done enough of in her thirty-nine years on this earth. And I was almost positive she'd vowed never to let that happen again. Had I really got a handle on this new me? Or was I still just playing at it?

'I'm falling in love with the tattoos and the black-tipped hair,' he whispered, his mouth on my neck, leaving a trail of tiny kisses in its wake as he moved lower, '… with the killer body and the attitude, and the fact you can open those incredible legs of yours wider than you ever could when we were together.'

I couldn't help laughing now, burying my fingers in his hair as he kissed my breasts, the short, sharp touches of his lips on my skin sending a million shots of something beautiful coursing right through me, his own laugh lightening the mood again.

'I'm serious, Lana. When I say I'm not leaving Vegas without you, I really do mean that. I want you to come home. I want you to come back to *me*.'

I drew my legs up around him as I felt him withdraw, but I still wanted to keep him close. I didn't know what to say. I'd come here with one plan in mind, and now everything had changed.

'Let's make tomorrow day zero, Lana. A new beginning. A whole new start.'

He seemed to have jumped a few paragraphs all of a sudden, taking us off the same page, if we'd ever been on it. But I was too tired to get into that right now. I just wanted to sleep. To hold him. To feel him holding me. Tonight I was going to lie in the arms of this man and tomorrow – tomorrow I had to make a decision. Once and for all.

21

I turned over onto my side, watching him as he slept, those piercing blue eyes of his closed to the world. I wanted to reach out and touch him so badly, but I also didn't want to wake him just yet. I hadn't slept much at all. I'd lain awake for most of the night, unable to grab even a few minutes' worth of sleep as I'd tried to come to some sort of decision, something that made any kind of sense. But there was really only one thing I could do now, and that was go home. Back to England. I couldn't stay in Vegas indefinitely, and if Eddie and I really were over, then there didn't seem much point in me being here. It was a place that carried too many memories now – insanely happy ones, and ones that were heartbreaking.

Sliding carefully out of bed, trying not to disturb Adam, I quickly pulled on my clothes and went into the bathroom, looking in the mirror above the double marble basins. Rough didn't even begin to describe how I looked, and not in a good way. Eddie looked rough in a good way. I just looked like someone who hadn't slept all night. Just thinking about Eddie again caused my chest to tighten, my heart literally aching for him and what we could have had, my eyes closing as if trying to push him out of my mind.

Quickly composing myself, I took a long, deep breath, splashing my face with cold water and running my fingers through my hair as I looked in the mirror again. Better. Slightly.

'Going somewhere?'

I spun around to see him standing there, leaning against the doorpost, dressed only in jeans that hung loosely on his hips, his arms folded against his toned chest. And how come *he* looked sexy-as-hell, all ruffled and just woken up? Jesus! Men got away with so much more than women did.

'I need to go collect the rest of my things, from Eddie's.'

He walked over to me, pushing me back against the basins, taking me by surprise with a kiss so soft I could've curled up in his arms and not moved all day. And as much as that sounded like a pretty nice idea, there were things I had to do. Things I had to sort out.

'It's really over, then?' he whispered, pushing my messed-up hair away from my eyes, his hand resting against my cheek, his thumb stroking my skin. 'Between you two?'

I nodded, once more feeling that pull on my heart that was so hard to take. So hard to get used to. 'I threw it away, Adam. By sleeping with you.'

'You don't belong here, Lana. You don't belong with him.'

'I belong with you, is that what you're trying to say?'

His hand was warm against my skin, and I had no desire to push him away or make him go, but I had to forget what had happened last night. Last night had been crazy and mixed up and incredible. But what he was doing here – he was making me believe that this was what I could have if I came back to him, and I wasn't sure that was going to be the case because, right now, we were still inhabiting fantasy land. None of this was real. It was fucked-up, all over the place, and I had to see beyond what *this* was to know what the reality could be.

'I'm coming home, Adam. I don't have a lot of choice, and I can't stay here, but… I'm not coming back to *you*. That would be a mistake. And I don't want either of us to get hurt. Again. You don't deserve that.'

'Why not let *me* decide what I deserve, Lana.'

'I just need to get my life back on track and I think, maybe, that's what you need, too. Things happened here that changed me. They made me... made me realise I need to think about things a lot harder before I act. Because that was something neither of us did last night.'

'You regret it?'

'I didn't say that.'

He leant back against the wall, his hands in his pockets. It was all I could do not to keep staring at him. He really was the most incredible-looking man and I'd just forgotten that, lost sight of it. When? Why? When had it all started to go wrong? Had we met too young? Married too soon? Taken each other for granted too early?

'I'll meet you downstairs in a couple of hours. Alright? We can go somewhere, because I think we really need to talk. Just talk.'

'Okay. We'll talk.'

I turned to leave.

'Lana?'

I spun back around, my eyes once more meeting his.

'I love you. Remember that.'

'I thought you weren't going to be here,' I said, continuing to throw the rest of my things into the suitcase, looking up as Eddie walked into the room.

'I'm meeting Nate.'

'Something to do with what you were talking about last night?'

He didn't reply to that.

'Eddie?'

'Jesus, Lana, darlin', what are you doing to me?' he sighed, sliding a hand around the back of my neck, his fingers winding in my hair, his body pressing up against me, all hot and hard. 'I really wanted the thought of you fucking another man to be some

175

kind of twisted turn-on, you know?'

'Don't, Eddie.' I stepped back, putting distance between us, even though the only place I wanted to be was close to him. 'I just came to get my things. I didn't think you were gonna be here.'

He leant back against the wall, sighing again, a little heavier this time. 'I'm sorry, Lana. For asking you to stay here, asking you to move in with me when… when I was obviously in no state to handle any of it. To handle the things you were making me feel.'

'It's done now, Eddie. I don't want to stand here raking over everything again. It won't change anything. We're moving on now.'

'Aye,' he sighed, bowing his head. 'Aye, we are.'

'Eddie!' Nate's voice shouted up from downstairs, breaking the brief silence that had ensued.

Eddie went straight over to the door, leaning out into the hallway. 'Be there in a minute, Nate!'

'Come on, brother! Time's not on our side with this one, I need you now!'

I frowned as Eddie turned back to face me. 'What's going on?' I asked, a sudden wave of uneasiness sweeping over me. I just had no idea why.

'Nothing,' Eddie replied. But his body language told me otherwise. 'Just a favour we promised to do for someone. Look, Lana, I'm… *Jesus!*' He walked back over to me, his hand once more sliding around the back of my neck, his mouth lowering down onto mine in a kiss so hard and so deep; so beautiful it tore me apart. Because it was a final kiss. A goodbye kiss. 'You take care of yourself, darlin'.'

I watched him go, my fingers lightly touching my mouth, the feel of his kiss still tingling on my lips.

'You and our sexy Scot definitely over, then?' Kaley asked, walking into the room, her eyes going straight to my case.

'Yeah. Yeah, I guess we are.' Saying it out loud made it seem final, somehow, and another wave of sadness washed over me, engulfing me, but I shook it off. I'd killed our relationship before it had even started, so self-pity wasn't something I was about to indulge in.

Kaley looked at the case again, then back at me. 'So, where are you staying? Because, if you need a place to crash…'

'No, thanks. I've booked into a hotel for a couple of nights, then it's back home. Back to the UK. Listen, Kaley, is… is everything alright? I mean, Eddie and Nate…?'

'It's just something they need to sort out. Something that should have been sorted a long time ago.' Kayley leant back against the doorpost, folding her arms.

'Like what?'

She lit up a cigarette, her eyes fixed on me as she took a long drag. 'Word of advice, honey – don't ask too many questions. Okay?'

My frown deepened, that uneasy feeling washing over me again. 'I'd better go.'

Kaley took another drag on her cigarette, watching me as I hauled the case off the bed. 'You were good for him, Lana.' She stubbed the cigarette out on the doorpost and walked over to the window, throwing the butt outside. 'I think Eddie needs someone like you in his life.'

There was a part of me that wished she hadn't said that. And I wasn't entirely sure Eddie Fletcher needed anyone, anyway. Not now. Not anymore.

'I really should go now,' I said, pulling the handle up on my case and wheeling it to the door.

'You stay in touch, you hear?' Kaley smiled, a genuinely warm smile, and I couldn't help but return it.

'Yeah. I will.'

'And I meant what I said, Lana.'

I looked at her, narrowing my eyes slightly.

'Eddie needs someone like you.'

22

'I didn't think places like this existed in Las Vegas,' Adam said as we walked through Sunset Park, the sun beating down on us, the low hum of chatter and children playing filling the air. Just a short distance from the Strip, the huge and sprawling park was like an oasis away from all the glitz and bravado of Vegas, an almost never-ending expanse of grass and trees and a lake so big I couldn't see where it ended. It was a place that seemed to usher in a feeling of calm that didn't always exist back in the heart of this town.

'Well, neither did I, to be honest.' I sighed, shielding my eyes from the bright sunshine. 'But I guess we all have our own, rather fixed views of Vegas. We assume it's just what we see on TV or in holiday brochures – all the brashness and glitz. But I've realised there's a lot more to it than that.' I looked out ahead of me as we walked, slipping my sunglasses down over my eyes. 'It's a nice escape, away from the noise and the lights and the masses of people out there on the Strip.'

A comfortable silence fell between us as we continued to walk, but then I noticed Adam's head drop, his expression changing. 'Did you love him, Lana?'

I breathed in deep, turning my head away from him, even

though the dark glasses were hiding my eyes. 'A few weeks isn't enough time to know if you love someone.'

He stopped walking, turning to face me. 'It was enough time for me to know I loved *you*.'

Pushing my sunglasses up onto my head I looked right into his eyes. 'Things are different here, Adam.'

He sighed quietly, raking a hand through his hair. 'This is crazy. All of this, it shouldn't be happening. We should never have let it get this far, Lana.'

'But we did. And there were reasons why it happened. We can't just go back to how it was, Adam. That can never happen now, and I think you know that.'

He leant back against a tree, his hands in his pockets, his head turned away from me slightly. I sat down on the wall opposite, looking down at my clasped hands.

'How's David?' I'd never got on all that well with Adam's older brother. He'd never really thought I was good enough for Adam, always thought his younger sibling could have done better than me. And he'd never been subtle in letting me know his true feelings. Once upon a time it had bothered me. I couldn't have cared less what he thought now.

Adam hung his head, scuffing the heel of his boot against the tree. 'David's fine. He's doing a good job of looking after the business while I'm over here.'

'I'm surprised he isn't begging you to come home. You know – quit while you're ahead.'

His eyes met mine, holding my gaze. 'You know, when Finn came to see me, to tell me what you'd done... I'd accepted the fact you weren't coming back. I'd started to move on, got used to you not being around, but, when he turned up... It brought it all home, Lana – how stupid we'd been, how we'd let so many things get in the way; how we'd ignored *us*. *That's* why I came here. To Vegas. All of a sudden nothing made any sense – you walking out, me just letting you go without putting up any kind of fight...'

'We didn't talk, Adam. We never talked. And we should have done.'

His eyes were still locked with mine, and I felt a sensation deep in the pit of my stomach, a feeling I'd thought was long gone as far as this man was concerned, but it was there now, it was back, twice as strong and taking me completely by surprise.

'Would that have made a difference? If we'd talked?'

I waited a couple of beats before replying, letting those ice-blue eyes of his penetrate deep into mine. 'It might have done.'

'I didn't know you were so unhappy, Lana. I had no idea.'

'Like I said, Adam, we didn't talk. So how *could* you have known?'

'The last thing I ever wanted was for you to be unhappy. I just thought…' He pushed a hand through his hair again, breaking the stare. 'I thought everything was okay. I thought we were good, that we were just getting on with our life. I thought we were settled, thought we…' He broke off, still staring out into the distance. 'What did we do, Lana?'

'We let go. We just let go.' I stood up, sliding a hand around the back of his neck, pulling him down so our mouths lightly touched, barely kissing him. All of a sudden I just needed to feel him close. In the space of a few, short minutes memories had returned, and feelings I'd thought were gone forever had been reignited. But it still didn't change the situation. It didn't suddenly make me want to jump straight back into his arms and sail off into the sunset towards some kind of happy-ever-after I wasn't sure existed anymore. 'We let go, baby,' I whispered, moulding my body against his as his arm fell around my waist, pressing me against him.

'Maybe if… if we'd found the time to have kids, be a proper family…'

I shook my head, running my fingers over his beard, letting myself continue to grow used to the fact that he had one. And how different it made him look. 'Who's to say that wouldn't have made things worse?'

'But I know…' His eyes hit me with a look that almost broke

my heart, a faint pain crossing my tight chest as yet more memories of our confused past flooded my brain. 'I know it was what you wanted, Lana. A family. And I didn't even consider that at the time. How much it meant to you. I was selfish, thinking only of the business, of how I could build the company up... I was too busy to put *us* first...'

'Adam, don't. Please.'

'We can fix what's broken, darling. Start putting things right. And we aren't too old to start that family...'

'Things have changed.' I looked down, realising my fingers were still stroking the back of his neck and I pulled them away, stepping back from him. 'What I wanted then and what I want now – it's all changed. And... and what it feels like here, in Vegas, how *we* feel here, everything that's happened... and what it's going to be like if we... They're different things, Adam.' My eyes met his again. 'If we got back together, how could we be sure we wouldn't just slip back into those old ways, make those same mistakes? How could we be sure we wouldn't lose each other all over again? You really want to put yourself – put *us* – through all of that? Because *I* don't. I don't want to hurt you. I don't want to do that.'

'You wouldn't hurt me, Lana.'

'I've already done it once. You're saying you could really trust me not to do it again?' I felt my stomach dip. Just talking about trust made me think of Eddie, and the way I'd hurt him. The way I'd thrown everything I'd ever dreamed of away just because I'd needed some kind of stress-release fuck. How old was I? Too old for some kind of teenage rebellion. But that's how I'd acted. And now I had to live with the consequences.

'Lana?'

I looked up, momentarily losing my train of thought. What had I been talking about? Oh, yeah. Trust. 'I made a huge decision when I walked out on us, Adam, and even though I spent months afterwards wondering if I'd done the right thing, I know now that I did. If I'd stayed... if we'd carried on the way we had been doing, it would have destroyed us. Both of us.'

'And you think I'm feeling good about everything *now*?'

'Nobody said it was going to be easy.'

'I love you, Lana. I love you so much.'

I moved closer, laying my hand against his rough cheek, such a different feeling to the usually smooth, clean-shaven look he'd always sported before. 'All of this…' I ran my fingers lightly over his beard again. 'This isn't you. You hate all of this; you hate tattoos, hate bikers and rock music and everything *I* love, Adam. I know now that for most of my life I wanted to be somebody else, a different person to the one I became, but for most of my life I was weak and scared; too scared to do what *I* felt was right so I bowed to the pressure to conform, to stay in that comfortable, safe life we'd built…'

'Is that how you thought of me? Safe?'

I closed my eyes, resting my forehead against his. 'No, Adam. Baby, I loved you, I really did love you. I loved you *so* much, and for those first few years we were amazing together. For those first few years you were all I wanted, everything I needed, but… It was a mess, in reality. When we look back at what happened to our marriage, at the way we ended up living our lives, almost separately, like strangers, it was a mess. And *we* couldn't see that because, on the outside, everything seemed fine. Everyone was happy, or that's the way it looked, anyway. That was the image we portrayed – the happy, successful couple. But it was a mess. And we just didn't realise that until it was too late.'

He sighed, a little heavier this time, throwing his head back, his arm still loose around my waist. 'I had no idea, Lana. I just couldn't see it. What the hell was going on all that time? What stopped us from seeing what was happening?'

'Life,' I whispered. 'I guess we just let it pass us by because, on the surface, everything seemed okay. *We* seemed okay. But we weren't. We weren't okay.'

'Why didn't you talk to me?' he asked, an almost desperate tone to his voice now. 'When you started to feel like this. Why didn't you talk to me?'

'Because you were so busy. Because you were working away so much, you were hardly home. Because I didn't want to bother you with something I saw only as *my* problem… Because I didn't think you cared.'

'Jesus…'

'Everything I wanted, Adam… everything I wanted to do, everything I wanted to *be*, it was so far away from the things *you* wanted and I…'

'I only wanted *you*, Lana. That was all I ever wanted.'

'You didn't know that at the time.'

'I just thought… I thought you were going through some sort of mid-life crisis. I thought you just needed to get whatever it was out of your system and then when you asked for a divorce I just… I didn't even fight it. I didn't… Why didn't we fight it?'

I closed my eyes again, my thumb stroking his cheek, his arm pulling me just that little bit closer. 'Maybe this was always meant to happen,' I whispered.

'When you left me, were you happy?'

I nodded, breathing in deeply as he took my hand, clutching it tightly. 'Eventually. I felt free, Adam. For the first time in so long. And I know you never meant to make me feel trapped or anything like that, but I did. Do you understand? I just didn't like who I'd become. I knew that person wasn't me, it wasn't who I was supposed to be, who I *wanted* to be. That's why getting the tattoos, dyeing my hair, changing the kind of clothes I wore… I needed that to happen. I needed a complete change. Because, doing all of that, that's when I slowly started to become *me*. When I started to become someone I actually liked. Our marriage hadn't been a bad one, it had never, ever been that. We'd just let it die, Adam. We hadn't looked after it. We'd let it suck the life out of us. I lost who I was, lost all the confidence I'd had when we first met and I just needed to get that back. And Finn, he was great. Getting close to my brother again, that helped me so much, you have no idea. He brought me out of that shell I'd been hiding under for too long; he taught me how to live again. He didn't ask questions and he didn't judge me. So, yes, I was happy. But I was also sad that it had taken the breakdown of our marriage to make that happen.'

He gave another sigh, his fingers gripping mine even tighter. 'We got it so wrong, Lana.'

'I know.'

Those blue eyes of his bored deep into mine, sending the tiniest shot of electricity surging through me. 'But we can put it right. Can't we?'

I broke the stare, looking down at our joined hands, watching as his thumb stroked my knuckles. I wasn't really ready for this conversation. The pain of losing Eddie was still too raw. Too confusing. 'I don't know.' My eyes locked with his again, a million questions flying around inside my head. Questions I really couldn't answer.

'And what about Eddie? How do you feel about him, Lana? How do you *really* feel?'

Just hearing Adam say Eddie's name caused tears to well at the backs of my eyes and I had to turn away from him for a second or two.

'Lana? Are you okay?'

I nodded, sitting back down on the wall, my head still turned away from him. 'I… I guess he epitomised everything I'd wanted out of life, but never thought I could have. He's a free spirit, a dreamer. He doesn't care what people think, he just gets on with his life the way *he* wants to live it. And that was all I ever really wanted to do.'

'So, you loved the *idea* of him?'

'I needed him.' I still did. 'I needed that experience being with him gave me. I needed to know that passion, that excitement; that raw, aggressive lust for everything that he just seemed to have.' I finally turned to face Adam again. 'It was the best adventure, being with Eddie. We'd ride any time we could, out into the desert, just us, the bike and nothing else for miles. We'd…' I stopped talking, looking back down.

'I know you slept with him, Lana. I'm not naïve enough to think you and him didn't have some kind of physical relationship. Come on, baby, we're not together, you weren't doing anything wrong.'

'Sleeping with *you* was wrong.' My voice was little more than a whisper. 'Because I was with Eddie.'

I felt Adam sit down beside me, but I still couldn't look at him. 'It was a different life out here, huh?'

I nodded, my fingers fiddling with the leather bracelets on my wrist. 'We'd ride out into the desert, make love on his bike, not caring if we were caught because it just felt so…' I slowly looked up, turning my head to face Adam, his eyes boring into mine. 'It felt incredible. To not be tied down, not have to dance to anyone else's tune and I know that makes me sound like some adolescent who doesn't want to do anything they're told, but that's not how it was. I'd just spent so long being someone I didn't always want to be, that once this new me finally had the courage to show herself to the world, I wanted to do it all, Adam. Have sex outside, ride a Harley, dress in leather and drink whisky and beer with a man who didn't give a fuck what the world thought. You *cared* what the world thought; the people around us, our friends, they all cared what the world thought. But I didn't want to. Because it doesn't matter. What the world thinks… it doesn't matter.'

He reached out to touch my face, cupping my cheek as his eyes continued to stare into mine. 'We didn't really know each other at all, did we?'

I shook my head. 'And that makes me so sad, Adam.'

'I love you, Lana…'

'You love the old me. You don't really know the new one.'

'But I want to.' He smiled, just a small smile, but it made me smile too, and I closed my eyes as he leant in to kiss me. A soft and gentle kiss that sent a beautiful, unexpected shiver coursing right through me, the roughness of his beard against my skin an unfamiliar feeling, but I liked it. 'Let's go back to the hotel.'

'No, Adam…'

He kissed me again, a little harder this time, a little longer, his hand sliding up under my t-shirt, his fingers stroking my skin. 'We can do this, Lana. You and me. We can do this. And we can make it work this time.'

'We're allowing the sex to cloud everything, Adam.'

'I need you, Lana.'

'It's getting in the way.'

'We need to find each other again…'

I stood up, backing away from him. 'I'm coming home, Adam, you know I am. I've told you I'm coming home. But I'm not coming back to you. I've told you that, too. And you need to start remembering that. Start getting used to it. I'm coming home, but not to you.'

'Lana…'

'I don't know how I feel. Do you understand that? I don't know how I feel about anything. I wanted to be with Eddie so badly and now it's over. So I think going home is the best thing for me to do. But going back to you, that would be a mistake. For both of us. Because I don't think *you* know what you want either, Adam. Not really. What's happening here, I don't… I don't know what it is or what we're supposed to do, I just know that the sex is clouding everything. It makes me want you, for a few wonderful minutes, and then it just confuses me. We can't build a relationship on that. It isn't fair on anyone.'

He stood up too, coming closer, his hand resting lightly on my arm, but I pulled back again. 'If you want me, Lana, even if it's just for the briefest amount of time…'

'When we get back home could you *really* live with the woman I am now? Could you cope with Finn, our friends, their lifestyles; the bikes, the body art and the places we hang out? Could you cope with your partner working in a tattoo studio, cope with her ink-covered skin and the clothes she wears; the music she likes to listen to? Would you really want to take me to those business dinners with my tattoos on show or would you make me cover them up because you don't want people to know they're there? Even if *I* want to show the world. Could you cope with all of that, Adam? Really?'

He leant back against the tree, raking both hands through his hair as he looked down at the ground. 'I don't know.'

'And that's not good enough.'

He raised his head, his eyes meeting mine, his expression so sad it really did break my heart – if it was possible to physically feel it break, that's what I was feeling right now. 'Lana, baby, please…'

I shook my head, standing my ground, knowing I was right. Sleeping with him was confusing everything. Masking the reality.

'I'm going back to the hotel and I'm going to start making plans to fly home. Maybe that's what you should do, too, Adam.'

23

I leant against the reception desk, checking my watch to see what time it was. After speaking to Adam I hadn't really been in the mood to come back to the hotel straightaway, so I'd spent the rest of the day checking out some of the other hotels, looking in the shops, losing myself in this crazy town and feeling sad that I was leaving it. I didn't really want to go but I had to move on now. Had to leave all this behind and what it could have been to find the future I needed.

I'd eaten dinner in the Harley Davidson café out on the Strip, got chatting to a few people, joined some of them for a drink in a nearby bar, and somehow or other the time had just flown by. It was late now. Almost half past two in the morning, and the day had finally started to catch up with me, a wave of tiredness suddenly washing over me.

Looking up, I focused on the still ridiculously busy foyer of this huge, impressive hotel and I couldn't help but be in awe of somewhere that was so full of people at this hour of the morning. The whole place felt alive, pumped up; the atmosphere electric. A reminder of why I'd grown to love Vegas. It had been good for me. A necessary adventure. But it really was time for that adventure to end now. It was time for me to go back to Newcastle; back to reality.

I continued my scan of the foyer, letting my eyes roam slowly around the vast space in front of me. I'd never been a huge people-watcher, but this was the perfect place to indulge in that pastime as all walks of life went about their own personal Vegas adventure, each one different to the next. And I couldn't help wondering what people's reasons for coming here were – were they all just here for a vacation? To throw themselves into that stereotypical Vegas experience? Or were there a number of them out there just like me? Using it as a place to escape to.

Scanning the foyer one last time I squinted slightly as I tried to focus on a familiar-looking figure standing by the entrance. Was that…? Yeah. It was him. But he wasn't alone. It looked like *he* hadn't wanted to come straight back to the hotel either. I kept my eyes on him, watching as he continued his conversation with a tall, slender, dark-haired woman, a little older than him, I guessed, but she was stunning. All tousled curls and red lips, and I felt something I could only describe as a surprising, and unexpected, stab of jealousy cut across my chest as he leant in to kiss her quickly on the cheek. I watched as they hugged before she turned and left the hotel, him waiting until she was gone before he started making his way across the foyer to the elevator. I still couldn't break the stare, so it was no surprise that he eventually turned his head, his eyes locking with mine. It was almost as if I'd, subconsciously, kept that steady stare in the hope that he'd see me. Notice me. I didn't know. I didn't know all that much right now, except that it really was time for this extended holiday to end. Normality needed to be resumed.

He started to make his way over to me, looking casual and relaxed in dark-blue jeans and a light-blue shirt, the sleeves rolled up to the elbows, his short dark hair still not-so-perfect, that beard he now sported still making him look twice as handsome; those ice-blue eyes of his intense as he held my gaze.

'Night out go okay?' I asked, trying to sound not-that-bothered, when I was actually more bothered than I wanted to be.

He slid his hands into his pockets, smiling slightly as he stopped just a few centimetres in front of me. 'It wasn't a night out, Lana.'

'It's none of my business…'

'She's the CEO of an LA-based company I've been talking to while I've been over here. I thought that if I was going to be staying in Vegas for a while, I might as well make myself useful. It was a business dinner, that's all.'

'At half past two in the morning?'

He shrugged. 'This is Vegas, baby.'

I couldn't help smiling back now. Yeah. This was Vegas. And I was fast beginning to realise that it had a time zone all of its own.

'I'm telling the truth, Lana.'

'Like I said, Adam, it's none of my business.'

'But I want it to be.'

That stare of his seemed to grow more intense, and neither of us appeared to be in any hurry to look away.

'Come upstairs, Lana. Let's quit all this crap, all this dancing around the subject, and just…'

'No, Adam.'

'You and Eddie are over, right?'

I narrowed my eyes as I looked at him. 'You know we are.'

'Then what's stopping *us* from trying again? Baby, come on. Remember what it felt like when we made love.'

I breathed in deep as his eyes held mine. 'It was sex, Adam. And, yes, it was great. The best. But you can't build a relationship on sex alone.'

'We can try,' he said, the corners of his mouth twitching up into a smile that I couldn't help but return. 'Look, Lana, I get it, okay? I get it now. You're scared…'

'Who said I was scared?'

'You're scared of trying again. Of giving us another go…'

'I never said I was scared, Adam. I just don't want to go jumping straight into something I'm not sure of. The situation's complicated.

And when did *you* get so loose in your way of thinking? What happened to the man who liked everything planned out and ordered?'

'He disappeared not long after you walked out.'

I looked at him, cocking my head slightly. 'You booked your flight home?'

'Have *you*?'

I smiled again, sticking my hands in my pockets as I leant back against the reception desk. 'Not got round to it yet.'

'Then we'll do it together. Tomorrow.'

I raised an eyebrow. 'Will we?'

'We're both going home. Back to the same place, whether we're "together" or not. So it makes sense to book the same flight, don't you think?' He reached out to gently touch my cheek, his thumb stroking my skin, his breath warm on my face as he took a step closer to me. 'Just come upstairs, Lana. I get that a second go at a relationship isn't on the cards just yet, but that doesn't mean to say we can't still have some fun, hmm? You up for some fun?'

What was I supposed to do? He had me cornered here. And, yes, I was up for some fun. There was just a part of me that still wished I was having fun with Eddie. But I really had to start forgetting him now. It was over. My beautiful escape, my biker boy – he was gone. And I had to get used to that.

I laid my hand over Adam's, closing my eyes as he kissed me slowly, our fingers sliding together. 'This means nothing, Adam. Okay? It means nothing. It's sex. That's all it is. It's sex.'

He smiled, taking my hand and squeezing it gently. 'Just sex. I promise. Come on. Let's get out of here.'

Sitting on the bed, watching Adam pour two large shots of whisky, I knew I probably wouldn't even touch mine. I'd had enough for one night. And anyway, breakfast was only a couple of hours away. Dawn was almost here. So why wasn't I tired anymore? I'd been up half the night. And for a brief moment downstairs I'd felt exhaustion engulf me. Yet now I was wide awake.

'Here,' Adam said, handing me a drink, which I immediately placed on the bedside table. 'You okay?' He raised an eyebrow, taking a sip of whisky.

'I'm fine.'

He bowed his head, staring down into his glass. 'I'm glad you're coming home, Lana.' He looked up, his eyes meeting mine. 'I wish you were coming home to *me*...'

'Adam...'

He sat down on the bed, and I felt my heart start to beat that little bit harder, that tiny bit faster. 'I'm never going to stop hoping that you *will* come back to me. One day.'

'You will. You'll stop. Eventually.'

'Then you really don't know me very well, Lana.'

I closed my eyes, breathing in deeply as he brushed my hair back off my shoulder, leaning in to kiss me so lightly our mouths almost didn't touch. Why had it never felt like this before? When had we just stopped trying? And as he pushed me back onto the bed I put up no resistance. What was the point in pretending I didn't want this to happen? He'd worn me down, made his presence felt too much for me to keep on ignoring the way I felt about him. Had Eddie really been nothing more than a distraction? Because it was starting to feel that way, and I hated that. Hated that that's what was happening, because Eddie had meant so much more to me than a distraction. I just hadn't realised that – until it was far too late. I seemed to be realising everything far too late. If these confusing feelings I had for Adam were there and I was accepting them, acknowledging them, then why wasn't I willing to give us another chance?

Our eyes locked together as he slowly pulled off my t-shirt, unhooking my bra, leaning over to brush my breasts with his mouth and I arched my back, sighing quietly, my fingers gripping the sheet beneath me. Did I still love him? Was I still *in* love with my ex-husband? Or was I just overcome with the fantasy being here, in Vegas, was creating? A place where we could be two completely different people – not the people we'd been when we'd been together. But were those the people we were in danger of reverting back to once we were home? Was that what was stopping me from taking another chance with a man I still felt something for? That fear? Maybe. Or maybe it was just because Eddie was still there.

'I'll never stop hoping, Lana,' Adam whispered, loosening my jeans, pulling them off before sliding his hands back up my legs, my skin breaking out in a million goose bumps as he hooked his fingers into the sides of my knickers. 'I'll never, ever stop doing that.' I lifted my hips up slightly, arching my back even more as he slid my knickers down, leaving me naked and desperate for him again. He hadn't really left me much choice, and I was fine with that. Fine with this. I was happy to run with it. I needed the distraction, even if sex only confused things.

He was in no rush, though. He was taking his time, letting his fingers explore, his kisses driving me crazy until I could barely take any more. I was one step away from crying out in frustration, my body aching for him with a pain so real it physically hurt.

So when he finally pushed inside me I felt a relief so huge sweep over me I couldn't stop the long, deep moan from escaping as I stretched out underneath him, his hands slipping into mine. And I clung onto him, enjoying the slow, steady rhythm our bodies had fallen into, moving together like we'd never been apart. Like this was the way it had always been, and maybe it had, I couldn't remember. I just knew that, somewhere along the line, we'd forgotten how to love each other. And now we were slowly beginning to remember. Did I really want to let go of that? Did I want to let go of *him*, for what? Some fantasy I'd thought I'd wanted?

I could feel his breath on my neck, his fingers gripping mine tighter as he pushed that little bit deeper and I drew my legs up, groaning quietly as I felt him respond. Hips crashed against hips,

193

mouths touching, bodies burning up as it all started to come together. His breathing speeded up, became more ragged, more uneven as he pushed harder, and I answered back, bucking up against him. And when that climax hit it took over both of us, almost simultaneously; a feeling so intense I couldn't help but cry out loud, my fingers crushing his as I clung onto him. He was coming so quickly, I'd never felt anything like it before, not even with Eddie, and it was both beautiful and painful and I didn't want it to end. I didn't. I hadn't felt this way, with this man, *about* this man, for so long. Too long. And the fact I wasn't sure I could walk away from him now terrified me more than I thought possible. One minute I was telling him I was coming home, but not back to him, and the next he was making love to me and the only thing I could think about was waking up beside him, every day. Of loving him this way for the rest of our lives. So what I did next, the next move I made – it was something I had to think really hard about, and I wasn't sure I was brave enough or strong enough to make the decision that needed to be made. All of this, it was pushing the new me a little further away, allowing the old Lana to make a reappearance – something I really didn't want to happen. And that's what was making me think twice. My heart was breaking for this man now, but my head was telling me he might not be good for me. Not anymore. The reality of what we could become again – I just couldn't face going back there. I couldn't. And all of this, this sudden rush of feelings, they could all be because I wasn't yet over Eddie – hadn't yet worked out what he and I had lost. The need to forget him could be causing everything I was feeling for Adam so I couldn't know what was real and what wasn't. And that was dangerous.

'Jesus, Lana, that was incredible,' Adam breathed, still holding onto me, his body still inside mine. 'Fucking incredible.'

I let go of his hand, stroking his face with my fingertips, my eyes meeting his as he continued to try and catch his breath. 'Maybe it's the tattoos and the hair and the fact you're making love with a whole new woman, huh?' Because he had to accept that I was a new woman, and he had to accept *her*, fully. No compromise.

He smiled, just a small smile, but it was there. 'Maybe.'

And then that conversation we'd had in Sunset Park came flooding back, hitting me completely out of the blue because, for a short time there, I'd forgotten all about it. Forgotten his reaction when I'd asked him if he really could cope with the changes in me, the new friends I'd made, the new job I was training for; the body art I refused to cover up. In fact, I was planning more. And, somehow, remembering all of that broke the mood.

I closed my eyes as I felt him pull out of me, rolling over onto his back. Sitting up, I drew my knees to my chest, waiting a few beats before I got out of bed and started gathering my clothes together.

'Lana?' He propped himself up on his elbows, his expression slightly confused.

'I should go.'

'No, hang on…' He jumped out of bed, quickly pulling on his jeans. 'Wait, come on…'

'It won't work, Adam.'

'What won't?'

'This. Us. In the bedroom, yeah, it's great. It's better than it ever was when we were together. I feel like… like we're re-discovering each other all over again and that feels so good. *You* feel so good. It's exciting, but… but this isn't reality. All the incredible sex in the world isn't gonna take away the fact that we can't build any kind of life together if you can't get your head around who I am now. Because I'm not the woman you used to know. I'm not the woman you used to be married to. And I never will be. I'm not going back there, Adam.'

He frowned, moving a few steps closer to me and I backed up against the wall, dropping my t-shirt. 'Is this because of what happened in the park?'

'You know it is.'

'You took me by surprise, that's all. And, okay, at the time, maybe, I didn't really know how to respond but… I've had time to think now, Lana. Time to get my head around the way you are now…'

'The way I *am*?'

'The tattoos, the hair, the people you hang out with, the job you do… I just needed some time to get used to it all, do you understand? You've changed a hell of a lot – a *hell* of a lot. You're almost a completely different woman, and that's not an easy thing to get my head around.'

I said nothing for a beat or two, just stared deep into his eyes, not really sure what I was looking for. Honesty, maybe? Hope that he wasn't just telling me this because he thought it was what I wanted to hear?

'It can't happen just like that, Adam. It can't, it won't, it… If *I'm* still trying to get used to the person I am now, then how the hell can *you* even *pretend* to know who I really am?'

'Lana, baby, if we love each other…' He stopped talking, suddenly aware that I'd never actually told him I still loved him. Even though I probably did, I was almost sure of that now. But whether I was *in* love with him was still something I *couldn't* be sure of. There was so much more to all of this than I was willing to think about right now. 'We can work anything out, sweetheart, I know we can.'

'I don't know, Adam…' My phone ringing interrupted us, and I crouched down to retrieve it from my jeans pocket, answering it immediately. 'Kaley? Is that you?'

'I need you to come to the clubhouse, Lana. Can you come to the clubhouse? Please? It's Eddie…'

24

'Eddie?' All of a sudden my blood ran cold, a wave of fear sweeping over me.

'He's asking for you.'

'What's happened?' I was trying to keep my voice steady, trying to stay calm because, until I knew what was going on...

'It didn't go to plan,' Kaley said, her own voice as steady as mine – almost. But she couldn't hide the faint trace of an underlying panic hidden within hers. 'We were all here, at the compound, thinking it had... thinking it had gone okay, that it was all sorted, but... I told him they shouldn't have done it. It was a crazy idea, I told them... They just turned up, Lana... So many of them... Laid into Eddie and Nate like they were nothing but punchbags...'

'What... what are you talking about, Kaley? I don't...'

'Eddie needs to get to a hospital, he's... he's hurt... He wants to see you first. Before we take him... Are you coming? Can you get here?'

'Yeah. Yeah, I'm on my way. I'll be there as soon as I can.' I looked down at my phone as I hung up, trying to take in what I'd just heard, because none of it really made any sense. I just knew I needed to get to Eddie.

'Lana?'

Adam's voice made me look up sharply. 'I… I need to be somewhere.' I pushed past him, hurriedly pulling my clothes back on as I tried to keep the panic at bay. I didn't even know if I had anything to panic *about*, but the tone of Kaley's voice had sent an unwelcome shiver up my spine.

'Need to be where? Lana, look at me. Look at me… Lana!'

I stopped what I was doing and stared at him. 'I've got to go.'

'Where?' His voice was slightly agitated now, but all I could think about was Eddie. And then that uneasy feeling I'd experienced yesterday, at Eddie's, it came flooding back. I'd sensed something was up. I'd felt it. And it looked like I'd been right to feel that way.

'Eddie needs me.'

'Lana, will you just stand still for a second. *Lana*!' He grabbed my wrist, swinging me around to face him. 'I'm coming with you.'

'No…'

'I'm coming with you.' He quickly pulled on his shirt, running his fingers through his hair.

'Adam, I don't need…'

'I don't *care* what you *need*, Lana. I'm coming with you.' The touch of his hand on my cheek sent a wave of calm flooding through me, allowing the panic to subside for a few, brief seconds. 'I'm coming with you.'

'What the hell *is* this place?' Adam asked, following me into the clubhouse. I didn't answer. I just wanted to get to Eddie. But it was hard to ignore the broken furniture lying around, the shattered glass all over the floor, the smell of spilt alcohol and the faint trace of something I couldn't quite place, but it smelt like smoke, like a fire had just been put out, hanging heavily in the air. Something had gone on in here that caused that uneasy feeling I still had to multiply ten-fold, and a part of me wanted to turn around and leave, to get out of there, because this wasn't my world. But Eddie – I needed to see Eddie.

'Kaley…' I almost ran to her when I caught sight of her leaning against the bar, and when she turned to face me I could clearly see the panic etched on her face, something which made my stomach sink, that wave of fear washing over me yet again. 'Where is he?'

She looked at me, then at Adam. 'Who's he?'

'My ex-husband. He drove me here… Where's Eddie?'

'Is he…?' She was still looking at Adam.

'It's okay, Kaley.' I turned to face Adam, taking his hand. 'Wait for me outside. I won't be long. Stay in the car, please, Adam.'

'Lana, I'm really not comfortable…'

'She'll be fine,' Kaley said, and I looked at her, still holding onto Adam's hand.

'Will she?' Adam's eyes were narrow and serious, his expression stern; his tone of voice less than convinced.

'She'll be fine,' Kaley repeated, holding Adam's gaze for a few seconds longer before turning her attention to me. 'Eddie's through here.'

I looked at Adam again, squeezing his hand. 'I won't be long, I promise. Okay?'

He threw back his head, letting out a deep sigh. 'Jesus Christ, Lana…'

I let go of him, not wanting to listen to any more. I just wanted to see Eddie.

I followed Kaley into a dimly lit room behind the bar – a room I'd never been in before, despite my numerous visits to the clubhouse. It was dominated by a huge, darkwood table which was surrounded by chairs of differing styles, and it had a strange, almost oppressive, feel to it, but it wasn't something I dwelled too much on as my eyes followed Kaley's gaze. Eddie was sitting up on a battered old couch at the back of the room, flanked by a few of the guys from the club. Nate was sitting next to him. On first sight the club's president looked untouched, but a closer look revealed Nate's badly bruised arms, cuts and slashes decorating his heavily tattooed skin. But Eddie – it was his face and chest that seemed to have taken the brunt. His shirt had been removed, and I could clearly see the bloodied cuts, the bruises beginning to form; the swelling that was just starting to set in. One of his eyes was practically closed, unable to open due to the damage that had been inflicted on it by – by who? Did I really want to know? Because this part of Eddie's life really was a world I was unfamiliar with. It was almost unreal, except, I was standing here, right in the middle of it, which made it very real.

'What happened?' I asked, barely able to raise my voice above a whisper.

'You don't need to know the details, Lana,' Eddie said, looking up at me.

'Don't I?'

Kaley leant back against the wall, lighting up a cigarette. 'No. You don't.'

I threw her a look, but she just shook her head, blowing smoke up into the air.

'Sit down, darlin', please,' Eddie continued. 'Please, Lana.'

I sat down beside him, taking his hand, feeling him wince and I loosened my grip on it, looking down to see his bruised knuckles, his slashed skin. 'Why ask me to come here if you aren't gonna tell me anything,' I said quietly, gently running my thumb over the back of his hand. He was cold, his skin clammy.

'I needed to see you because… because things between us… They didn't work out the way I wanted them to, Lana. And that's *my* fault, and I'm sorry…'

'I thought we'd been over this, baby,' I whispered, my fingers absentmindedly stroking his hair, almost forgetting we weren't together anymore.

'The way we said goodbye… It wasn't enough, Lana. It wasn't enough.'

I shook my head, looking back down at his hand in mine. I wanted him to stop talking, to not say any more. It was too hard. Too painful. 'You need to get to a hospital,' I said, letting go of

200

his hand, reaching out to gently touch his face. 'And I need to go.'

'Lana…' He grabbed my hand again as I tried to stand up, pulling me back down. 'It was stupid retaliation…'

'Eddie…' Nate interrupted, but Eddie ignored his warning tone.

'Retaliation for what they did… For what happened to Deanne. They needed to know… They needed to know we hadn't forgotten.'

I looked briefly over at Nate, who had his head in his hands now.

'Maybe we didn't try hard enough, you know? Maybe we went in too soft, didn't get the message across in quite the way we wanted to but… We aren't like them. We aren't outlaws here. We're just trying to get on with our lives. But what happened to Deanne, what Nate needed to do to… We needed to finish that chapter.'

'I should have let her memory rest,' Nate said quietly, pushing both hands back through his dark-blonde hair. 'But ever since that day… I just couldn't get it out of my head, what they did. How she got caught up in the middle of it all; how *I* let that happen. I didn't protect her… I couldn't… That's what made me want to change this club, change the way we did things, because all that crap, the fighting and the stupid, senseless wars… And yet, I let myself carry out a revenge that…' He sighed heavily as he stood up, and I watched as Kaley went over to him, taking him in her arms and holding him as he cried. This big, strong, tough man was broken, and I wondered if this was the first time he'd let that happen. If this was the first time he'd really let himself grieve for his wife. Properly grieve for her, instead of letting the anger take over.

'It's gonna be okay, brother,' Eddie said, looking up at Nate. 'It's gonna be okay.'

Nate reached out to Eddie, placing a hand on his shoulder and squeezing it gently. 'I owe you, Eddie. I owe you so much.'

Eddie shook his head, smiling as best he could at his friend before he looked back at me. 'It looks worse than it really is,' he said, trying to smile again, and I returned it, reaching out to very gently touch his battered and bruised face.

'You need to get checked out. I'll call you later – make sure everything's alright.'

He took hold of my hand, bringing it to his lips and kissing it lightly. 'Lana...'

'Don't do this, Eddie. Please.'

'Do what?'

'I'm going home. Back to Newcastle.'

'When?'

'Soon.'

He bowed his head, his thumb stroking my knuckles. 'Lana, I...' He took a long, deep breath before he looked back up at me. 'I think we're unfinished business, darlin'.'

25

'What the fuck are you involved in?' Adam threw the car keys down onto the sideboard, pushing a hand through his hair as he paced the floor. 'Because that – *that* back there... Jesus Christ! That is messed-up, it's wrong.'

I leant back against the wall, looking out of the window, watching as a new day broke over Las Vegas, this city that, apparently, never slept. A place full of dreams and magic; the perfect escape, or so I'd thought.

'Lana?'

I looked up, Adam's expression a mask of anger and confusion and a million feelings I couldn't read, and I didn't blame him. What we'd just seen, that was so far from the world either of us knew. 'I found a gun,' I said quietly. 'In Eddie's house. The day you arrived in Vegas... I found it, in the kitchen drawer...'

Adam leant back against the wall beside me, pushing a hand through his hair again, sighing heavily. 'What the hell are you doing, Lana? This man, he's dangerous...'

I shook my head, refusing to believe what Adam was saying. Was that naïve of me? Maybe. But I still refused to believe Eddie was a violent man. 'People have guns in this country, Adam. For all sorts of reasons.'

He looked at me, moving so he stood right in front of me, one hand pressed against the wall beside my head as he leant in towards me. 'Are you going to stand there and tell me you weren't scared?'

I looked into his eyes, desperately trying to get my head together, but the fear and the confusion and the tiredness that was starting to flood my body was fast taking over. All I wanted to do now was sleep. 'A lot of things scare me, Adam.' What I still felt for *him* scared me. More than anything now.

He cupped my cheek with his hand, resting his forehead against mine. 'You're still coming home.' It wasn't a question.

'I'm still coming home,' I whispered. That decision had been made. I wasn't going to change my mind.

Adam smiled, breathing a sigh of relief that came from so deep within him I almost felt it myself. 'Come back to *me*, Lana. Please. Let's leave all this shit behind and start again, just you and me.'

I shook my head, not ready for this conversation, not now. I just needed to sleep. Then I needed to see Eddie. 'Can we talk about this later, Adam? Please?'

He tilted up my chin, making me look at him, those eyes of his drawing me in, pulling me down; making me want him, when I really didn't know if that was something I *should* be feeling.

'You don't belong amongst all that crap, Lana. That isn't you.'

'You don't know what *me* is anymore, Adam.'

'It isn't *that*, I know it isn't, and so do you. Baby, please, listen to me… listen to me, okay? I love you, and you can tell me to shut up, make me stop saying it, but I will never stop feeling that way about you. You are my life, Lana, do you understand? The only woman I have *ever* loved, and somehow… somehow I let go of that, I took you for granted, but I promise you, sweetheart, that will never happen again. Whatever you want me to do, whoever you need me to be…'

I shook my head again, gently pushing him away. 'I need to get some sleep. I can't do this now.' I started walking towards the door.

'Sleep here. Please. Lana, I... I don't want to let you go, not after...'

I turned back around. 'After, what? After tonight?'

'Yes, after tonight. That was some serious crap your biker boyfriend's mixed up in, and you think I'm happy that he's putting you in danger?'

'Jesus, Adam, he's not my boyfriend.' Not anymore. 'And he isn't putting me in danger...'

'For Christ's sake, Lana, will you grow up? Open your fucking eyes and look at what's happened. You were involved with a man to whom guns and knives are a part of his everyday existence...'

'That isn't true. You're wrong, Adam. Eddie isn't like that.'

'You know that for sure, do you? You found a gun in his fucking kitchen, Lana. And the next thing you know he's carrying out some mindless revenge at the request of a man who claims to be his friend, an act which resulted in him being beaten half to death! Does me spelling it out for you make it any easier to understand?'

'I'm not doing this now,' I said, opening the door, but he ran over to me, grabbing my wrist to stop me from leaving.

'Does it make it easier, Lana?'

I stared at him. This man I'd spent half my life with. This man who'd come here and made me rethink everything. He'd turned the world I'd thought I'd finally settled into on its head, made me take steps backwards, and I wasn't comfortable with that. Or maybe I really did just need to sleep.

'Stay here, Lana. Please. Stay with me.'

I let go of the handle, leaning back against the door and closing my eyes, a feeling of defeat washing over me. I was too exhausted to fight him anymore. Too exhausted to do anything except curl up and sleep. It was a new day, but I still had to say goodbye to the old one.

Raising my hand I tapped lightly on Eddie's front door, bowing my head as I waited for him to answer. Adam hadn't wanted me to do this, but Adam didn't make my decisions for me. I couldn't just walk away from here not knowing how Eddie was. And, yes, maybe I *did* just want to see him, one last time. But that was my choice. My decision – my mistake – to make.

I looked up as Eddie finally answered the door, and I couldn't hold in the gasp of shock that escaped when I saw him. His face wasn't as swollen as I'd expected it to be, that seemed to have settled slightly, but more bruises had flared up now, the cuts still raw and angry. He looked a mess.

'Jesus, Eddie,' I whispered, unable to take my eyes off him.

'I'm fine,' he said, standing aside to let me in, closing the door behind us.

'They give you painkillers?'

'Aye. Lots of them.'

I followed him into the living room, sitting down on the couch, looking up as he sat down beside me. 'I'm going home, Eddie.'

He sighed, leaning forward, his head dropping, his hands clasped between his open knees. 'Lana, darlin', I am so sorry.'

'For what?'

He looked up, and I tried to hold in another gasp because his eyes were so red and tired, they looked sore, one still barely open, looking only slightly better than it had done the other night. 'For all of this. For not saying no to Nate when I knew... I knew we should have just left it alone. But...' He let out another heavy sigh, '... you have to go with your president's decision. You have to...' He pushed a hand through his hair, turning away for a second or two. 'What we did, it didn't change anything. It hasn't made Nate feel any better, not really. All it's achieved is more crap, more tension. All we've done is re-open old wounds. And the way I've been behaving, some of the things I said... I put *us* in jeopardy, Lana. Because I couldn't think of anything else except getting this shit over with. It took over. And I let it affect everything.'

'Eddie, we both made mistakes.' That was the painful reality of it all because I still felt something for this man, I really did.

But then Adam had arrived. And turned everything on its head.

He looked down again. 'You and Adam...'

'There *is* no me and Adam.' Wasn't there? 'I just think – I need to go home, Eddie. Being with you, staying here, it was something I needed to do. Something I had to experience. But we always knew it was never gonna be forever.'

'And if I'd been able to... to commit...' He looked straight at me. 'If I'd let myself fall in love again?'

I frowned as I studied his broken face. Even though his eyes were red and tired, I could still see a sadness there behind them that I'd never seen in him before. And it hit me hard, seeing him like that – vulnerable, almost. I took his hand, gently running my fingers over his bruised knuckles, wishing I could get the words out, tell him something, anything, but I didn't know what to say. And my silence caused him to turn his head away from me, his hand still in mine.

'After everything that's happened... I want out, Lana. It's time for another new start.' He looked down, closing his eyes for the briefest of seconds. 'I'm moving to LA. I've been putting feelers out about premises for a new shop, and I've got a few contacts over there who are willing to help get me up and running as soon as possible. I've even got a place to stay in Culver City.' He looked at me again, his expression a touch softer now. 'I didn't treat you the way I should have done, darlin'. I let the past get in the way, and I allowed the present to distract me. For so long I've shut my feelings down, closed myself off to any emotion that could hurt me again but... I was wrong. I was stupid. Because you... you walked into my life, and I should have told you how I really felt instead of backing away from it all.'

'Eddie...'

'Come with me, Lana. To LA. I'm not that person you saw the other night, baby. I'm really not. And I don't ever want to be. But that club – what Nate has done... It probably won't ever be free of that crap now. And, yeah, it might look as though I'm running

207

away, but I can't stay here. Not now. Too much has happened. I need to get away. I think we both do. But you don't have to go back home, Lana. You don't. Come with me, let me show you the kind of man I can really be. A man who wants to fall in love again. A man who wants to change his life. Just like you changed yours.'

Listening to him talk, hearing him say the words I'd wanted him to say ever since I'd walked away from him, it was just making everything here harder to deal with now.

'Just me, you and the bikes, Lana. That's all we need.'

I stood up, walking over to the window. 'I'm going home, Eddie.' I folded my arms across my chest, still staring outside.

'You don't *have* to, darlin'.'

I slowly turned back around. 'I know. But I *want* to.'

He let out a quiet, almost defeated, sigh, digging his hands into his pockets, his head down.

'I never meant to hurt you, Eddie. That was never my intention, and I am so, so sorry for what I did to you…'

He looked at me, shaking his head. 'You didn't hurt me. Everything that's happened here… I was weak, too weak to listen to my own feelings. Too weak to face up to things. You came into my life for a reason, Lana, and I just ignored it, me, the one who kept banging on about fate, so… so everything that happened…'

I walked over to him, reaching out to gently touch his bruised face. 'Adam turning up didn't help. And if we're talking about being weak, I think I've been more than guilty of that myself. If anyone killed this for us, Eddie, it was me.'

He took my hand, his fingers curling tight around mine. 'Do you love him, Lana?'

I looked at him for a few, long seconds before I said anything. And the words that came out surprised even me. 'I don't know if I ever really stopped loving him.'

'Then don't lose him, darlin'.'

'Eddie, I…' Before I could do anything he was kissing me, holding me tight and kissing me, a reminder of those wonderful,

208

almost magical, kisses we'd shared over the past few weeks. A reminder of a time I would never regret, because being here, being with him, it had focused my mind more than I'd realised. I knew what I had to do now. But still nothing was guaranteed. There was a lot of fighting to be done yet. Happy-ever-after was a long way off.

'I want you to stay with me, Lana. And I know I said… I know trust is…' He threw his head back, sighing quietly, but it was a sigh that seemed to wrack his whole body. 'When I told you I needed you, that was no lie. And I still need you now, despite everything I've said, but… If you love him…' He dropped his gaze, letting go of me, and I felt as though a distance was slowly growing between us now. A gap that had been getting wider without either of us realising, whilst the one between me and Adam had been closing.

'I'm sorry, Eddie.'

He looked back up, his hand resting against my cheek, his thumb stroking my skin. 'You have nothing to be sorry for, darlin'.'

'You were good for me, baby, you were so good for me.'

He laughed quietly, a sound I hadn't heard from him in a while. 'Was I?'

I smiled, placing my hand over his, needing to touch him, for just a little while longer. 'Yeah. You were. And I'm always gonna to think of you as my beautiful escape. You gave me the chance to live a little bit of a life I hadn't even known existed until I met you. I had sex on a Harley, I mean, come on!'

He laughed again, and my fingers curled around his, holding tightly onto his hand as he kissed me one more time. One *last* time.

'I had sex on a Harley,' I whispered, tucking his hair behind his ear, lightly running my fingertips over the deep cut on his face. 'And I will never forget that, Eddie. I'll never forget *you*.'

'You could live more of that life, Lana. You've only scratched the surface, darlin', you… you could live so much more…'

I shook my head, and it was sad, because he was right. I could have that incredible, wild life he'd started to show me. I could have that. All I had to do was reach out and take it. But it would be a life without Adam. And that was the kicker. I didn't want a life without Adam. Not anymore. And as much as that realisation shocked the hell out of me, it was the truth. It was how I felt. I didn't want a life without Adam.

He squeezed my hand, a small smile still on his battered but oh-so-handsome face. And another wave of sadness washed over me. 'You've got my number, okay? And you keep hold of that, you hear me? You keep hold of it. And if you ever need me…'

I let go of him as I began to slowly back away. 'You take care, Eddie. Please.'

He stuck his hands back in his pockets, his head down. 'Aye. You too, sweetheart. You too.'

And without looking back, I walked out into the hall, and out of Eddie Fletcher's life…

26

Closing my eyes, I felt him pull me back against him, his mouth warm on my skin as he covered my shoulder in tiny, soft kisses, his hand moving around so it laid on my stomach. I reached behind me, burying my fingers in his hair, his beard rough against the back of my neck, a sensation that made my whole body tingle.

I sighed quietly as his hand moved down, sliding up under my nightdress to rest on my hip. 'Adam…' I groaned, pushing back against him as he slipped his hand between my legs, touching me gently, whispering things in my ear I hadn't even realised he'd been capable of thinking. But I guess I'd been teaching him good, taking him to a whole other level as far as sex was concerned – turning him into a bad boy in the bedroom, while letting him stay that sexy businessman in the boardroom. It was a turn-on we made use of quite regularly now. A game we played a lot. And he, in turn, loved the idea of the suit-wearing CEO and the tattooed biker chick. It worked for us in ways neither of us could ever have imagined.

'Just lie back and let it happen,' he whispered, his other hand taking mine, keeping hold of it as he manoeuvred himself inside me, squeezing my fingers tight as he pushed deeper.

'Your early-morning alarm call's here, Mr Saunders,' I murmured lazily, biting down on my lip as his thrusts built up a slow and steady rhythm.

He laughed quietly, a deep, sexy laugh that made my stomach cartwheel so many times I almost couldn't breathe. This man had been mine for so long, yet it only felt as if I was beginning to know him now. And for all I'd fought this; fought us getting back together, it had been pointless. Him turning up in Vegas had changed everything. I'd finally had to face up to that. And now we were back home, I kind of wanted to see where this second chance was taking us. Because nothing was set in stone yet. We were still getting to know each other all over again, and so far that had been fun. So much fun!

'I love you, Lana,' he murmured into my shoulder, his body so much a part of me now it was like we were locked together. And it made me feel safe. I liked how it felt – how *he* felt, after so many years of not feeling him at all. Of not feeling anything except sad, that our marriage was failing. That we were losing each other. But finding each other again... oh, that was the best part, something that was almost worth all the pain and heartache we'd gone through.

I gripped his hand tighter, drawing my legs up, his body moulding against mine as I moved position. 'I love you, too,' I breathed, and I meant it. Oh, God, I meant it. With every beat of my racing heart.

'We *could* just stay in bed all day,' he said quietly, his hand on my hip again, keeping me pushed back against him. 'Stay here, fucking, until we can't take any more.'

I moaned long and low, laughing quietly. 'You know I like to look at you when you talk dirty, Mr Saunders. Because you never *used* to talk dirty. Words like that never once left that super-sexy mouth of yours.'

'Yes, well, my mouth has been on a bit of a learning curve lately, and it's having one hell of good time in the process.'

I laughed again, a low-down, dirty laugh, arching my back and pushing my bottom into him as his lips trailed over my neck and shoulders, a never-ending surge of tiny electric shocks piercing my skin. It was the most beautiful sex; a slow, lazy way of making love, just perfect for this time of the day.

'You ready?' he asked, his mouth close to my ear, which sent another shiver scurrying up my spine.

'Not yet,' I whispered.

He slid his hand back between my legs, his fingers instantly finding that place they needed to be, bringing me to the edge within seconds. 'You ready now?'

'Jesus, yes!' I gasped, my hand gripping his so tight I almost cut off his blood supply. '*Yes!*' I bit down on my lip, my breath coming out in short, sharp gasps as it all came to a slow and beautiful end, his body pressed so close against mine it truly did feel as though we were one. He was a part of me. He'd always been a part of me. He always would be.

'I've got to go in a little while,' he said quietly, his lips gently brushing over my shoulder as he pulled out of me.

I turned around so I was facing him, kissing his slightly open mouth. 'So, we never really *were* gonna stay here all day, fucking until we couldn't take any more.'

He smiled, and I felt my insides react, leaping about like an over-excited jack-in-the-box. 'No, but, I'm a huge fan of the idea.'

'Yeah,' I whispered, resting my mouth against his. 'Me too.'

I closed my eyes as he kissed me, the most incredible, slow, drawn-out kiss that I didn't want to end. We'd never used to kiss all that often once married life had kicked in. In the beginning, yeah, I realised that we had. In fact, I was starting to remember a lot of stuff I'd obviously just chosen to forget. In the beginning we'd been all over each other like a rash, at times, with friends having to pull us apart just so we could come up for air. How on earth had I let myself forget all that? Forget the way I'd once felt about him; lose those memories like they'd never happened. We'd just pushed it all to one side while real life had taken over, and in the end the need to remember it had waned. Dissipated. But we were changing all of that, finding that time we hadn't bothered to find before, making sure those simple things we'd once taken for granted – or forgotten altogether – weren't pushed aside again. I wasn't into repeating mistakes, not anymore. So we kissed a lot now. Oh, God, did we kiss a lot!

'I don't want to go into work today,' I groaned, falling onto my back and stretching out. My whole body felt like it had just undergone the most intensive workout. Sex with my hot and handsome ex; the best kind of exercise.

'I thought you loved going into work these days,' Adam said, his fingers running lightly over my stomach, pushing my nightdress up and I helped him pull it off, throwing it down on the floor beside the bed.

'I do.' I turned my head to look at him, a slow smile spreading across my face. 'I'd just rather be here. With you. Naked. Having lots of dirty sex.'

'You are such a bad influence,' he whispered as he leant over me, his mouth covering one of my breasts and I buried my fingers in his hair, arching my back, pushing myself up against him, moaning quietly as his beard once more tickled my skin. 'But…' He raised his head, kissing me quickly. 'I really have to go. I've got a meeting in an hour and I need to get to the office to prepare.'

'Spoilsport.'

He grinned, climbing over me, kissing me once more before he got up and headed into the bathroom.

I sat up, pushing both hands through my hair and shaking it out before I reluctantly forced myself out of bed. Walking over to the mirror I looked at my reflection. Sometimes it was still a shock to see the woman I'd become, because she was so different to the woman I'd once been. But I liked the new me, ink and all.

'You look beautiful.'

I swung around, smiling at Adam as he stood there, all just-out-of-the-shower sexy, wearing nothing but his own smile and

214

a towel tied low around his hips. 'Yeah. Of course I do. The just-got-out-of-bed look was always a favourite of mine.'

He came over to me, tucking my hair back behind my ear, leaning in to kiss me gently. I was beginning to wish he'd stop that now. It was only making me less keen to leave this room. Right now I wanted to act like a rebellious teenager, call Finn, tell him I was sick and stay in bed all day. My ex-husband still had a lot of things to learn about the new me. We were nowhere near done with those lessons yet.

'You look beautiful,' he repeated, pulling my naked body against his almost-naked one.

'Okay.' I slid my arms loosely around his neck, trying hard not to let the touch of his fingers stroking the small of my back turn me on too much. But it was already too late. 'I believe you.'

He looked down, his eyes scanning every inch of me, and that did nothing but send the most delicious shiver running right through me, up and down my spine so many times I thought it would never stop. 'I really do have to go, darling.'

I reluctantly let go of him, leaning back against the sideboard, watching as he began to get dressed.

'There's a fundraising dinner tonight,' he said, as he pulled on a clean white shirt, slowly transforming himself from hot bedroom bad boy to sexy businessman. I just wanted to keep him all ruffled and untidy – and naked. Oh, God, I wanted to keep him naked. And maybe I really did need to get to work, focus my mind on something other than sex. But that's what you got when you'd spent almost the entire weekend in bed with a man as beautiful as Adam. How many years had I wasted not realising just how beautiful he really was? 'Lana, sweetheart? Did you hear what I said?'

'Hmm? Oh, sorry, I'd drifted off there for a second.' To a lovely place I fully intended to go back to, very soon. But maybe not when I had a tattoo gun in my hand. That wouldn't be good for business. 'What did you say?'

'There's a fundraising dinner tonight, at Calbrook Hall.'

'Calbrook Hall?' I frowned. 'Isn't that the country-house hotel up in Northumberland? The one that's just had a massive refurbishment?'

'Yes. That's the one. A lot of local businesses are lending their support, and it should be a good night, so, I was just wondering if you... if you wanted to come with me.'

I looked at him with a slightly wary expression. 'Why wouldn't I?'

He looked down for a second or two, his hands in his pockets. 'Well, I know how you feel about these kind of events now, Lana. I know you didn't always feel comfortable and... and I don't want to force you into doing anything you don't feel comfortable doing, I just...' He raised his gaze, his eyes locking with mine. 'If you don't want to go, that's fine. I'll understand.'

'Do you *want* me to come with you?' I asked, my tone probably more defensive than I'd intended. I was letting paranoia take over, and I instantly regretted it.

'I wouldn't have mentioned it otherwise, Lana. I just didn't know if it was too soon, that's all.'

'Too soon for what? For you to be taking me out in public? For your high-powered business colleagues to see how much I've changed? To see what I've done to myself?' I walked away from him, into the ensuite, grabbing a robe from the door and wrapping it around myself.

'Jesus, Lana, come on.' He followed me into the bathroom. 'I don't care about any of that, okay? But maybe *you* do, huh? Maybe it's *your* problem, not mine. Maybe you're the one that isn't ready to show the real you, because me – I don't care, sweetheart.'

I stared at him, right into those beautiful blue eyes. But I couldn't quite read him. There was something there that unsettled me. The fact he'd hit a nerve? No. He was wrong. He was so wrong. 'You really don't care?'

'No, darling. I don't. I really don't care what anyone else thinks, okay? Have you got that yet? You're not the only one who's changed, Lana.'

'It's just difficult for me to believe, Adam, that's all. Hard for me to believe that you can change your opinion on so many things in such a short space of time.'

'I lost you, Lana. And when Finn told me you'd found someone else… When I saw you there, in Vegas, I hadn't actually prepared myself for just how much that was going to hurt. I hadn't realised how much I missed you until that very moment. And I certainly hadn't realised how much the idea of another man touching you…' He sighed quietly, pushing a hand through his hair. 'That tore me apart. That really hurt, more than I ever thought it could. And forgive me for bringing up an age-old cliché but, it's true – you really don't know what you've got until it's gone.' He bowed his head, leaning back against the wall. 'I love you, Lana.' He raised his gaze, his eyes meeting mine. 'And, okay, I'll admit, there are a few things that are taking a bit more getting used to than others. Everything's different, *you're* different and… and it's just something I need to get my head around. But I will. I promise you, I will. Because I am not prepared to let you go again.'

I folded my arms, my expression softening. Maybe I *had* over-reacted slightly. Maybe the paranoia was uncalled for. 'Nobody said it was gonna be easy, Adam. And I don't expect you to be on board with everything that's happened in my life just like that.It would be selfish of me to expect that. But you need to know that the woman you married, she's gone. And she really isn't coming back. If you want the perfect corporate wife, then you're gonna have to look elsewhere, because I'm not it. I never will be. The tattoos, the hair, the new job, they're all staying. This is who I am now. This is who I want to be. But I also want to be with *you*.'

'I don't want the perfect corporate wife.'

'You used to.'

'I used to want a lot of things.'

It was my turn to drop my gaze, looking down at the cream marble floor of Adam's pristine bathroom. The house we'd lived in together for so many years had been sold now, the money split between us. He'd bought this place, a large four-bedroom detached on the outskirts of Newcastle city centre, and I'd moved in with Finn until I could find a place of my own. But this house – it still screamed the old Adam, that neat, tidy, almost-perfect man who loathed anything out of place; a man who liked order and routine. And that was something I fought against now, because it was something I'd once felt trapped by. I preferred the idea of spontaneity, a little bit of chaos, and, all of a sudden thoughts, of Eddie filled my head. The way he'd lived his life, that was how I'd wanted to live mine – free from the shackles of everyone else's opinions.

'Maybe it's best you go alone tonight,' I said, a feeling bordering on defeat washing over me. 'I'm not sure I'm ready for all that just yet.' Our perfect weekend was over now. The bubble had been burst, and he'd just brought the reality of our still-fragile situation crashing back to face us head-on – the one thing I'd feared from the second we'd decided to give our realtionship another go. But I should have known it would happen, sooner or later. It was naïve of me to think it would never be an issue.

'Lana…'

'You're right. I'm not ready for all of that just yet.'

I heard him give a frustrated sigh before he turned and left, grabbing his suit jacket on the way out. I closed my eyes as the door shut behind him. *Was* I letting paranoia get in the way of things? I mean, in reality, if I really did feel comfortable in my new, inked skin why should it bother me what anyone else thought? Because I cared about Adam, that's why. And I still wasn't completely convinced that he was ready to show me off in all my tattooed glory just yet. He might be getting some kind of kick out of it all in the bedroom, but was he really ready for the reality? Was *I*?

I gripped the edge of the sink tightly, my fingers clinging on until my knuckles started to turn white. I'd told Adam it wasn't going to be easy. But I hadn't realised just how hard this battle could turn out to be.

'I reckon one would look good on my other shoulder. What do you think?' I asked Finn as I watched him tidy up after a busy morning of consultations and one highly intricate design he'd etched onto the skin of a young man who was turning out to be a regular customer at the studio. Finn had already done a few tattoos on the guy's arms and back over the past year, and he was slowly building up a rather impressive collection of ink.

'I think we're talking tattoos so you can avoid talking about what's really on your mind.' He leant against the workbench at the back of the room, folding his arms. 'What?' He raised an eyebrow and I couldn't help smiling.

'You. You look like you're about to give me a lecture.'

'Something up with you and Adam?'

'No. Why would it be?'

'You are such a bad liar, do you know that?'

I picked up a book of designs, absentmindedly flicking through it. 'I don't know, Finn. I mean, we woke up this morning and everything's good, you know?'

'So, what happened between getting up and now?'

'Adam's got this fundraising dinner thing tonight,' I went on, still flicking through the design book.

'And?'

I put the book down and looked at my brother.

'And what?' he asked, widening his eyes.

I pushed a hand through my hair, throwing my head back. 'This is exactly what I was afraid of.'

'Are you gonna start making sense any time soon? Because I've got someone coming in at three who wants a sleeve tattoo starting and I'd like some lunch before I begin that job.'

'What if he's embarrassed by me, Finn?'

'For Christ's sake… The man came all the way to Vegas to show you how much he still loves you. What more do you want him to do?'

'No, he came to Vegas because *you* asked him to.'

'Do you know how annoying you are sometimes?'

'It's a talent.'

He took me by the hand, leading me over to the mirror by the door. 'Look at that person there. Not the handsome one at the back, although I think we both know how insanely attractive he is…' I nudged him gently in the ribs. 'That woman there in front of you. The beautiful one with the blue-grey eyes and the heart-shaped face and that incredibly stunning sleeve tattoo on her arm… Who did that, by the way? Because whoever he is, he must be ridiculously talented.'

'I'm getting bored now, Finn.'

Our eyes met in the reflection, and I felt his hand squeeze mine tight. 'Remember who she is, Lana. Remember why she's here.'

'I don't think I could take losing him,' I said quietly, my fingers curling around Finn's. 'Not now I've found him again. Now that we've found each other… But if he can't… If everyone else is…'

Finn turned me around, holding me by the shoulders as he looked straight at me. 'You don't give a shit what people think, beautiful. You don't care. And that's because it doesn't matter. It really doesn't. So stop moving backwards, sort yourself out, and when you go out with Adam tonight – because you *are* going to go with him tonight, do you hear me? – you hold your head up, look amazing, and know that every bloke in that room will be as jealous as hell of your man. Okay, one or two might throw a disapproving look your way, or stare at those unbelievable tattoos of yours, which, I have to say, really are a work of art…'

'Finn!' I laughed. I couldn't help it. He was so good at doing this – helping me get my head around crap I thought was a problem, when it really, really wasn't.

'They might stare, kiddo. But, believe me, inside they'll all be wondering how Adam managed to snare someone as beautiful and different as you.'

'I love you so much sometimes, do you know that?'

He dropped a quick kiss on my forehead before walking out

into the main reception area. 'Just call me the best brother in the world, kiddo.'

I followed him out, pulling myself up onto the front counter, watching him as he laid out the design book I'd been looking through with a couple of others on a large coffee table in front of two huge black-leather couches. 'Well, I'm not sure I can go *that* far.'

He looked at me, smiling slightly. 'Just be yourself, Lana. That's all you need to do. And remember, nobody else matters except Adam, and you. Whatever anyone else thinks…' He shrugged. 'Just let it go, sis.'

'Yeah. Maybe you really aren't that bad a brother after all.'

'And don't you forget it, missy.'

Both our heads turned as we heard someone come into the studio, and I couldn't stop the smile from spreading across my face as I saw who it was because, despite the fact things had been a bit fractious between us earlier, just seeing him there, all handsome in his suit and tie, I was close to forgiving him anything. Almost. And I still thanked God every day that he'd grown used to the beard, because I found it unbelievably sexy on him. And I kept telling him that, in the hope he wouldn't make a quick return to his clean-shaven days.

'Hey. What are *you* doing here?'

He looked at me, a serious expression on his face, one that almost wiped the smile from mine, and I felt my stomach dip in a not-all-that-pleasant way.

'Just shut up and listen to me, Lana. Okay?'

I stared at him, blinking a few times in surprise. He'd come over all dominant, which was rather nice, not to mention unexpected. Especially at ten to one in the afternoon. 'Yeah. Okay.'

His eyes bored into mine and he left a couple of what seemed like extrememly long beats before he spoke again. 'Marry me.'

27

I was, to say the least, a bit gobsmacked, and Finn couldn't hold back his surprised expression either. I was just glad everyone else was out at lunch.

'Have you been drinking?' I asked, because I couldn't actually think of anything else to say.

'No, I haven't been drinking.' Adam walked over to me, stepping between my legs and I wrapped them around him, accepting his kiss. Even if I still didn't know what the hell was going on.

'Oh, Jesus, I'm out of here,' Finn groaned, grabbing his jacket. 'I'll be back in half an hour, okay?' He winked at me. 'Don't do anything I wouldn't. But just in case you do, don't forget to disinfect the work surfaces afterwards, alright?'

'Fuck off!' I laughed, waiting until he'd turned the closed sign around on the door and locked it behind him before I looked back at Adam. He had an eyebrow raised, his mouth curled up into a slight smile. 'What?'

'That mouth of yours,' he sighed, lifting me down from the counter.

'What about it?'

He smiled, sliding his hands up and under my t-shirt and I

flinched slightly as his cold fingers touched my warm skin. It was a pretty nice shiver, though. 'Every time you talk like that, I just want to…' He broke off, leaning in to kiss my neck, sending more shivers to join the party. 'Are we going to get married again, Lana?'

I looked at him. 'Oh, Christ, you were serious about that?'

He ran his hand lightly up my back, his fingers sliding gently up and down my spine. 'We should never have got divorced.'

'Maybe not,' I whispered, my mouth almost touching his now.

'So let's put that right.'

'You're not just doing this because of what happened this morning, are you?'

'I'm trying to prove something to you, yes. I'm trying to make you believe that I really do love every beautiful, tattooed inch of you. I love the way you look, Lana, the way you move because you hold yourself differently now. Your head is up, the confidence you never seemed to show before is so prominent and I find that such a bloody turn-on. You're stronger, more determined, and I'm sorry for being the kind of person who made you hold back from all of that for so long but… I love you, baby. I love *you*. I loved the old you, and I love this new version. Jesus, Lana, you're making me crazy here, making me face up to feelings I never knew existed, and I love that you challenge me.'

I kissed him slowly, letting my lips linger on his for as long as possible, wanting to taste him, to feel him. 'Well, fighting *can* be really, really sexy sometimes.'

He laughed quietly, resting his forehead against mine, his hand fanning out in the small of my back, pushing me against him. 'I don't want to lose this, Lana. I don't want to lose *you*. You're back in my life and you've changed me, changed the way I think about things, the way I *feel*… I love you. It's as simple as that. I love you.'

'I love you, too,' I whispered, stroking the back of his neck. Because I did. I loved him. And I wanted this to work, I really did. I just wasn't sure that getting married again, right now, was such a great idea. We were only at the beginning of a very long journey as far as I was concerned. We both still had a lot to get used to. A lot of things to work through.

'I can't stay long,' he said, his fingers still stroking my back. 'I've got a meeting in Durham at half past one. But you – you make me want to forget all about meetings and conference calls and contracts. You make me want to cancel everything and spend the afternoon with you, doing whatever the hell we like.'

'That'll be lots of dirty sex, then' I murmured, running my fingers through his short, dark hair, deliberately messing it up.

'Yes… probably.'

He pushed me back against the counter, his hand sliding down onto my hip, his mouth touching mine and I literally melted inside. It was like the first time all over again, that wonderful moment all those years ago when we'd shared our first kiss. I remembered it so vividly now, after years of it being nothing but a hazy memory. It was playing out inside my head like a movie clip, so clear and so real. I remembered it like it was yesterday. Because everything I'd felt back then, all those feelings that first kiss had kicked off, they were happening again, happening here as he kissed me.

'I really have to go,' he whispered, running his thumb lightly over my lower lip before kissing me again, his body pressed so hard against mine I didn't know if he'd ever be able to pull away. I didn't want him to, I knew that much. 'Think about it, Lana. Please. I'll see you later, okay?'

I reluctantly let go of him, watching as he left the studio, wondering if he really had turned into the man I wanted to spend the rest of my life with. Because, if he had, then he was leaving me with very little choice here…

28

Adam took my hand as I stepped out of the taxi, his fingers sliding between mine, and I held on tight, not ready to let go of him in a hurry.

I watched him out the corner of my eye as we started walking towards the hotel entrance, the bright lights and loud chatter of the guests already inside filtering out through the huge, open doors of the beautiful, upmarket country house that was hosting this fundraising dinner. It wasn't somewhere I would usually frequent now. Me and these kind of places, we just didn't fit anymore. If we'd ever fitted at all.

'Would you rather I'd covered up?' I asked, a question I'd been thinking, but hadn't really meant to say out loud.

Adam stopped walking, turning to face me. 'Lana, come on. No.' He rested a hand against my cheek, kissing me quickly. 'You look amazing.'

I *felt* amazing. In a black, figure-hugging, knee-length strapless sheath dress and high-heeled black ankle boots, my hair loose and curled around my shoulders, I felt a million dollars. But every tattoo I had was on show, which meant I was going to stand so far out from that crowd of other women here tonight – the beautiful wives and girlfriends of Adam's colleagues, friends and business associates. With their perfectly styled hair, expensive dresses and manicured nails, I was nothing like them, and I never would be. I'd tried to fit in before, tried to be the woman Adam had wanted me to be, but I'd never felt comfortable in these situations. Never liked coming to these kinds of dinners and the various other functions we'd had to attend because of Adam's status as one of the region's leading businessmen. I'd failed as the corporate wife on every level, and even though he'd told me that wasn't what he wanted from me, I was still unsure he really meant it. He couldn't change who he was any more than I could change who I was now.

'I know I look amazing,' I deadpanned, and he smiled, laughing quietly. 'I think I look as hot as hell, but what are *they* all gonna think, Adam? That lot in there, all your colleagues with their perfectly groomed partners. I'm walking into the cast of *The Housewives of Hexham* here and I'm still not sure you're ready for how they're all gonna look at me.'

'Their reactions might surprise you, Lana.'

I raised an eyebrow. 'Listen, handsome, they weren't all that over-welcoming when I was the old Lana, and now I'm covered in ink with a new-found love of skin-tight clothes and a mouth that can sometimes be a bit too loose, you think they're gonna be any more welcoming?'

He was still smiling. 'Who cares?'

It was my turn to laugh. 'Am I hearing right? Did Adam Saunders just utter those words? Again?'

'Adam Saunders has a red-hot new wife, and right now *that's* all he cares about.'

'I haven't accepted your proposal yet, mister. Although, I agree with the red-hot bit.'

He gave my waist a small squeeze. 'Seriously, though, Lana. Have you thought about it? Getting married again?'

'I've thought about it, yeah.'

'And?'

'One step at a time, baby, okay? I think we need to take things slowly.'

'Do we?'

'Yes, we do. Come on. Let's get this over with.'

He took my hand again, and I shook my hair out, remembering Finn's words – *head up, look amazing, and be yourself*. I could do that.

'You okay?' Adam asked as we walked up the steps, the music and the chatter growing louder now.

'I'm just fine,' I replied, because I was. Adam loved me. He'd told me he was willing to accept me as I was now, and I had to believe he meant that. The successful businessman and the biker babe – just thinking about that sent a little tingle rushing through me and all of a sudden I just wanted to pull him into the nearest bathroom and show him how much of a bad girl I could be. But, maybe not right now. I had to cut him a bit of slack here. These people were his peers. *I* might not have to see them on any kind of regular basis, but Adam had to do business with them. So I'd try and behave.

Walking into the main hall confirmed at least one of my fears, though – most of the women in there had, quite obviously, spent a good part of the day being groomed to within an inch of their lives. Perfect hair and stunning dresses were everywhere, designer handbags hanging from their flawless, spray-tanned arms. So it was no surprise that heads turned when we made our entrance. And not all for the right reasons. I could see the expressions on their faces, see them whispering, trying not to stare. The men were less obvious. Oh, I could feel their eyes on me, there was no doubt Finn was right on that score. But at least some of them had the decency to talk to us, rather than *about* us.

For me, though, it was all having the opposite effect to how I'd thought it was going to make me feel. Because, looking around at those women who didn't seem to want to come near me, it just brought back memories of how much I'd hated this before.

But that was because I'd been pretending – to be something and someone I wasn't. They weren't bad people, these women. They just weren't the kind of people I wanted in my world. I'd never be like them. I didn't want to be. I'd tried, and it had only made me miserable. But now – now I was here with the man I loved, as the woman I wanted to be. And if they didn't like it, that was *their* problem. I just wished I'd been able to pull up on a motorbike. I should have got Finn to drop me off, or better still, Bobby and all his biker friends. How much would I have enjoyed *that* entrance? Just the thought of it made me smile.

'Everything alright?' Adam asked, giving my waist another quick squeeze.

I looked at him, leaning in to kiss him, long and deep and not giving a fuck who was watching. I didn't care where we were. I was Lana Saunders, and it was about time people got used to me, tattoos and all.

'Lana…' He pulled away slightly and I narrowed my eyes as I looked at him.

'Something wrong?'

'No… Look, don't get all defensive, it's just… There's a time and a place, darling. Okay?'

I touched his cheek, running my fingers down over his beard. 'Yeah, you're right. I'm sorry.'

He took my hand, squeezing it tight, his expression changing to apologetic, with just a hint of panic in his eyes. Almost as if he knew he'd said something wrong. Something that hadn't quite come out the way he'd meant it to. 'It's not that I don't… because I do, but… When you do this, Lana, it messes with my head, do you understand? The way you look, the way you act now, it's one hell of a turn-on, but somewhere like this – I can't handle that. I can't do it.'

Eddie would be able to handle it. Eddie would have dragged me, not all that discreetly either, off to a quiet place and taken me hard and fast just to release all those pent-up feelings. Oh,

228

God, why did I keep thinking about Eddie? The memories were obviously still too fresh, still alive inside my head. But I didn't love Eddie. He wasn't a part of my life anymore and I had to get used to that. I had to start forgetting him and move on. That's why I'd come back here, wasn't it? Back to the UK? To move on. Because, when you scratched below the surface and started looking at the reality, Eddie's life hadn't been one I was sure I could have lived for long. Or was that just me letting a small part of the old, over-cautious Lana slip through?

'Come here,' Adam said, his voice jolting me back to the here and now as he took my hand and pulled me to one side. 'Listen to me, baby, okay?'

I leant back against the wall, my fingers still curled around his, our eyes locked together, those memories of Eddie still lingering, refusing to go just yet. 'What?'

'Don't look at me like that, Lana. I'm trying here, darling, I really am.'

'Is this how it's gonna be from now on, Adam? Both of us constantly on our guard, both of us trying, twenty-four hours a day? Do you know how exhausting that's gonna be?'

'Do you want to stop? End it? Give up, all over again? We've been here five minutes, Lana, and just because…'

I threw him a look and he stopped, bowing his head briefly, breaking the stare. 'I want this to work, Adam. I do. I really do. But I guess I'm only just beginning to realise how much give and take it's actually gonna involve. From both of us. Over in Vegas I didn't have to…' It was my turn to stop talking, his eyes once more meeting mine.

'Didn't have to what, Lana?'

'I didn't have to worry about anything. About *anyone*. But I'm back home now. And it's time to stop being so selfish. I guess we're *both* gonna have to do some compromising, huh?'

He reached out to gently touch my cheek, cocking his head slightly as he looked at me. 'Did he feel different?'

I frowned, placing my hand over his, rubbing it gently. 'I'm not getting into this, Adam. Eddie's gone. It's all about you and me now.'

'Did he feel different, Lana?'

I shook my head, squeezing his hand. 'No, Adam. I'm not doing this.'

'Is he the one who taught you all those things you're teaching *me*? Did he get to experience them first, get to feel you touch him in that way? Did he break those inhibitions down...?'

'Adam, no. No!'

His mouth lowered down onto mine, kissing me gently, his arm pulling me to him and I just fell against him, aware of the low hum of chatter coming from the main part of the room, of the fact we weren't completely alone. But I wished we were. I wished we didn't have to do this, be around these people and these places because I just didn't feel at ease here. I still couldn't completely be me, because being me was what was making Adam uncomfortable. Whatever he was telling me, I could see by his body language, the look in his eyes. I could feel how tense he really was.

'I need a drink,' I said, pulling away from him.

He looked at me, and I threw my head back, sighing quietly.

'Don't worry, Adam. I won't be knocking back beer straight from the bottle.'

'Lana...'

'Leave it.' I held out my hand, and he hesitated for a couple of beats, gauging my mood. So I smiled, lightening the atmosphere, letting him know I was running with this. I was going to try and get through this night as best I could. 'Come on. We're here now, so we might as well enjoy ourselves.'

He took my hand, pulling me back against him. 'Lana, darling, you have to believe me when... I'm still learning, sweetheart. I'm still getting to know you, because there are times when it feels like I'm with a completely different woman to the one I used to know, and that's exciting, it really is, but, sometimes... sometimes it scares me, too.'

230

I gently stroked his cheek, kissing him quickly. 'I know, baby. I know.'

'And I'm sorry if tonight…'

'I'm still learning, too, Adam.'

He returned my smile, and I let the fluttering in my stomach remind me why I'd come back to this man. 'Let's go get that drink.'

'Okay.'

'Listen, Lana… when we get home…'

I leant in against him, my mouth resting on his as I spoke. 'That bad girl inside me is gonna be so frustrated by that time that she is almost definitely gonna want to come out and play. And she's probably gonna want to play pretty hard, I'm guessing.'

He groaned quietly, his hand slipping down into the small of my back. 'You are killing me.'

'Come on, Mister CEO. Time to get your business face on and mingle. That'll take your mind off anywhere else it might be tempted to wander off to.'

'You think?'

I winked at him, squeezing his hand but saying nothing. He was on a promise. And that was the only thing that was going to get *both* of us through a very long evening.

'Lana Saunders?'

I turned around to see a tall, slim woman standing beside me. Dressed in a salmon-pink cocktail dress that screamed expensive elegance, her honey-blonde hair knotted into a perfect chignon, her make-up subtle and understated, I desperately tried to place her, because she obviously knew *me*. I just didn't have a clue who she was, but then I never had paid much attention to any of Adam's colleagues' partners.

'Emma Grayson.' She smiled, quite obviously realising my memory needed jogging. 'I'm married to Oliver, Adam's accountant.'

Yeah. I still wasn't all that much the wiser, but I vaguely remembered talking to Oliver Grayson at a Christmas party a few years ago. Not sure I'd ever had a conversation with his wife, though.

'Are you and Adam...? Oh, I'm sorry. Forgive me for being so upfront, and please, tell me to mind my own business but, I thought you and Adam had separated? Oliver told me your divorce hasn't long been finalised.'

'A few weeks ago, yes.'

'So, you're back...? Look, this really is none of my business...'

'No, it's alright.' Our separation had been common knowledge, so it stood to reason that me suddenly appearing back in Adam's life just over a year later was bound to raise questions from people in his work and social circle. Especially *this* version of me. Nice, safe Lana had gone, to be replaced by this blonde-and-black-haired woman with the figure-hugging clothes and inked arms. 'We're back together.'

Emma gave me an almost relieved smile. 'I thought as much. Oliver said Adam had tried dating a few times since you separated, but nothing ever came of it. Although, I do seem to remember him having a brief relationship with a lovely girl from Hexham – her father runs an agricultural machinery business near Wooler. The family are very prominent on the Northumberland social scene...' She stopped talking when she noticed the look on my face. 'Anyway, I... I see you've been...' I toyed with the idea of letting her squirm for a few seconds longer, because it was quite obvious she was trying to find a way to address the fact that I'd changed somewhat since the last time she'd seen me. But I decided to play fair instead and put her out of her misery.

'I've changed careers,' I said, deliberately running my hand up over my tattooed arm. 'I've left the theatre now, and I'm training to be a tattoo artist.'

I quite enjoyed watching her expression change. It wasn't shock, exactly, more something akin to confusion, as though that kind of career was almost unheard of to her. 'Oh, I... And... what does Adam think of your... of your career change?'

'It's got nothing to do with Adam.' Her eyes widened even

more, as if I'd just uttered the most shocking words possible. But I was standing my ground on this one. She might do everything that was required of her in her role as the perfect wife in order to make sure the lifestyle she was accustomed to stayed permanent, but that wasn't me anymore. In hindsight, it never really had been. I didn't care about the lifestyle. I only cared about being happy.

'I, erm... They're... they're very... distinctive.' Her gaze dropped to my arm and I watched as she slowly scanned it all the way from shoulder to wrist.

'*I* like them.' My eyes met hers and I held her stare. 'And they're growing on Adam.'

That one got her. But I didn't really want to make her feel uncomfortable. That wasn't fair and I was trying to be good tonight, for Adam's sake. So I softened my expression and threw her a warm smile instead, which seemed to relax her slightly. But I imagined she was probably sorry she'd come over now.

'Adam said you'd been in the States for a few weeks. Las Vegas, wasn't it?'

I nodded, taking a sip from the glass of ice-cold champagne I'd acquired from one of the many waiters and waitresses hovering around the place. I was craving a beer, though. Or a whisky. Straight up, no ice. Just how Eddie liked his scotch. 'A bit of an extended holiday,' I replied. I wasn't getting into this one. She'd had enough information out of me. There was nothing else she needed to know. Besides, I'd just seen David, Adam's older brother, start making his way over to me, and that was a meeting I was looking forward to. I hadn't seen him in over a year. He wasn't exactly a member of my fan club after everything that had happened, and I'd never really been a member of his.

'Anyway, it was lovely to see you again,' Emma said, leaving me with a smile as David approached. 'I really hope it works out for you and Adam this time, Lana.'

'Thank you.' I returned her smile before I turned my attention to David. 'Not sharing her enthusiasm on that one, I take it?' I looked straight at him. If I'd thought Adam was straight-laced, his older brother had taken it to a whole other level. But with David a lot of it was front, because he wasn't half as savvy as Adam and deep down he knew that. But he loved his brother, I'd give him that much.

'Vegas didn't work out, then?' David's expression was stoic, but the sarcastic undertone in his voice didn't escape me.

'No. All the twenty-four-hour sex and debauchery had started to play havoc with my sleep patterns.'

He narrowed his eyes as he looked at me. 'You hurt him.'

'I never meant to. But I'm sorry it happened. I'm sorry for everything that happened.'

'It might have been kinder to say no to him this time, Lana. To let him move on, get on with his life. He'd started seeing other people...'

'Yes, I heard.'

He narrowed his eyes even more. 'And you were seeing some biker, I gather.'

He'd almost spat out the word *biker*, and I couldn't help but let out a low laugh. 'Yeah. I guess I finally found my level, huh, Dave?' He hated being called that, which was why I did it.

'Look, Lana,' he sighed, pushing a hand through his greying hair. He wasn't anywhere near as handsome as Adam was. In fact, to look at the two of them together it was hard to believe they were brothers. Maybe that was because of the six-year age gap, I didn't know. I just knew that whereas Adam was a truly beautiful man, inside and out, David had a much harder face, more worn, and not in that sexy, lived-in kind of way that Eddie had. 'It's not that I don't...' He couldn't keep his eyes off me, and he wasn't even hiding the fact he was staring. 'I'm just worried about Adam. If this doesn't work out...'

'I know I was never the kind of girl you thought Adam should be with,' I interrupted, placing my empty glass down on the table behind me. 'Even before all the ink appeared you never thought

I was good enough for him. I get that. I do. But maybe it's time to stop fighting it now, David, don't you think? Adam's a big boy and he's quite capable of making his own decisions.'

'Do you honestly believe it'll be any better second time around?' David asked, moving that little bit closer to me. 'If it couldn't work when you… when you were normal…'

I raised an eyebrow at that one, but kept my mouth shut.

'… how can you possibly expect it to work when you're on some ridiculous quest to become a… a tattoo artist, of all things, covering yourself in…'

I held up a hand. I'd had enough. 'I'd stop now if I were you, before you become really offensive.'

'It's how I feel, Lana. I mean, look at you. And you expect Adam to bring you to these events and feel comfortable about that? Do you honestly think people are going to find it easy to accept that *you're* his partner?'

'I said, stop,' I hissed. 'Try getting your head out of your arse and quit with the generalisations, okay? Me and your brother, we messed up first time around. Somewhere along the line we forgot how much we love each other, how much we need each other, and me walking out on our marriage, I think it probably saved us, David. It brought him back to me, brought us back together, as changed people. Because we needed to change. Staying as we were – it was destroying us. And I love him, you know? I love him so much. I never *stopped* loving him. But I wasn't happy being that person I was before. I was miserable, and because of that I let go of everything I felt for your brother. But now… now we're trying to find a way to make it work, and it's not easy. Tonight has shown me just how bloody difficult it's going to be, and people like you… You're not helping. But I *want* me and Adam to work this time. So you and everybody else in this room, all those who are judging me on the way I look, you can think what you like because now… now I don't care. What *you* think doesn't matter. What Adam thinks does. He is the only one around here who gets to decide whether I should be in his life or not. Not you, not anybody else. So back off.'

He gave a small laugh, briefly glancing down at his perfectly polished shoes. 'And if you start being bad for business?' I didn't even flinch at that remark. 'What do you think he'll do then, Lana?'

'Back off, David.' I'd kept my voice steady and calm, because that's how I felt. David and I had clashed on many an occasion, for a number of reasons, but this – he'd brought this down to a purely personal level now. He was crossing lines he had no right to be anywhere near. 'Let your brother get on with his life the way *he* wants to live it, not the way you think he *should* be living it because, believe me, both Adam and I know how that feels and we know how much it can push people away.' I held his gaze for a few seconds more, making sure he got the message, before I headed off to find Adam. He was out in the foyer talking to a man I vaguely recognised from a few of the dinner parties we'd been to over the years; just the thought of dinner parties sent a cold shiver creeping up my spine. Was I going to have to go *there* again, too? I watched as Adam and the man shook hands and said their goodbyes, waiting until Adam was alone before I went over to him. I wasn't really in the mood for any more introductions. I was a bit tired of the same old conversation now.

Adam looked up as I approached, a warm smile spreading across his handsome face, and that made *me* smile, too. I couldn't help it. He had that effect on me sometimes. Most of the time. All of the time, tonight.

'Everything okay?' he asked, sliding an arm around my waist.

'A girl from Hexham, huh? Daddy own a country retreat and appear in *Horse & Hound* a lot?'

He threw back his head, sighing quietly. 'Did David tell you that?'

'No. David's been offensive on a whole other level. It was Oliver's wife – Emma, I think she said her name was. She told me you'd been out a few times since our separation. She seemed to like Ms Socialite a lot, though.'

236

'It wasn't like that, Lana.'

I raised an eyebrow. 'Oh, really? I mean, she would have been so much more suited to all of this, wouldn't she? What with all those hunt balls and dinners she must attend. And coming from money…'

'Lana…'

I put my fingers to his lips, shutting him up. 'And you'd rather be with *me*? A woman who loves motorbikes, rock music, inked skin… beards…' I removed my fingers from his mouth, moving my own closer to his as I spoke, '… and sex that is all kinds of wrong.'

He groaned quietly, a sound that, because his mouth was resting on mine, almost seeped into me. It made my whole body shudder with the low reverberation it caused.

'She would have suited you so much better, don't you think? She would have known how to conduct herself at these things; how to behave.'

'I didn't want her, Lana.'

'I know, baby. I know you didn't.'

'What's David been saying?'

'I don't want to talk about David. I want to go home and I want you to fuck me until it hurts. That's the only thing I want right now because being here, I'm bored now, Adam.'

He took my hand, taking me completely by surprise as he pulled me outside, pushing me back against the wall and kissing me so hard I almost couldn't breathe. But, oh, it felt good. *He* felt good. His kiss was slowly beginning to push tonight and everything I'd hated about it to the back of my mind. His kiss was reminding me, all over again, why I was back here. With him.

'Come on.' I smiled, dragging him around the side of the hotel. It was quieter there. Darker. There was less chance of us being seen.

'Lana, I… We can't…'

'Can't, what?' I asked, taking his hand and sliding it up and under my dress. 'You brought me out here, handsome. You took the lead.'

'Jesus!' he groaned. 'Have you been wearing no underwear all night?'

'Look at the dress, Adam. It wasn't designed to have underwear worn with it.'

'You are one *bad* girl,' he whispered.

'I know,' I murmured, kissing him slowly, and just the way his lips moved against mine was enough to make me forget everything else going on around us. I'd already emerged from *my* shell, now I was slowly bringing Adam out of his. And I was enjoying every single second of watching that happen.

He pushed my dress further over my hips, lifting me up and holding me tight as I wrapped my legs around him. I was ready to feel him become a part of me again, because it was the only time I didn't think about everything too much, dwell too deeply on the things that weren't working; the long road we still had ahead of us. I didn't think about any of that when he was making love to me.

I buried my face in his hair as he pushed into me, rocking my body back against the cold brick with every beautiful, harsh thrust. This was a new Adam here. A man who was willing to give me what I wanted, step out of his comfort zone and try new things. And I loved him for that. Loved that he was still here, after I'd pushed him so far away.

'Lana, baby, I'm sorry it's so quick...'

'Sshh, it's okay' I held onto him as I felt him come, my legs tightening around him to keep him steady. 'It's okay, it's all good.'

I didn't care that it was over in the blink of an eye. I really didn't. I'd just wanted to feel him inside me, to know that he still wanted me, that's all I'd needed after the night I'd had. But why had I felt so insecure? Why was I letting other people's opinions get to me? None of that mattered. *They* didn't matter. They didn't.

He put me back down, still holding onto me. His hair was all ruffled, his suit jacket a little creased, and I couldn't help but think how sexy it made him look. How much it made me want this man – a man who still wanted *me*, after everything I'd done.

A good, kind, caring man, who I'd almost pushed away forever.

'The answer's yes, by the way,' I whispered, the words falling out of my mouth before I'd had a chance to realise I was saying them. 'Let's get married. Again.'

29

'You're looking pretty miserable for a woman who's just got engaged. To her ex-husband.' Finn threw me a smirk as I leant back against his bike, drinking beer from the bottle.

I looked at him. 'I'm not miserable.'

'Really?' He raised an eyebrow. 'How'd it go the other night, then? Seeing as you didn't seem to want to talk much about it before.'

I shrugged. 'Okay. I suppose. People stared, they asked questions… David stuck the boot in and voiced his disapproval that I'm back in Adam's life. Nothing I didn't expect.'

'No ring?'

I looked down at my still-naked left hand. 'I don't want one.'

'You don't want a ring?'

'That's not why I got engaged, Finn. I did that because… because I just want to be with Adam.'

'I'd believe you if you could sound just a little bit more convincing.'

I turned to face him, giving him my biggest smile. 'I'm happy, alright? But I'd be even happier if I had another beer.' I gave him a gentle push. 'Bar's over there.'

We were at a biker's festival on the outskirts of County Durham. It was a blisteringly hot August afternoon, the music was loud and heavy, the people friendly, the drink flowing, and I was having a blast, despite what Finn thought. Adam wasn't with us, of course. This wasn't his kind of place, and I couldn't expect it to ever *become* his kind of place, so he was at home, working. Well, I say home. *His* home. It certainly wasn't mine. I was still reluctant to move in with him, even though I was spending most of my time at his place. There was just something stopping me from making that move permanent.

'Why is that?' I directed that question at a surprised Finn as he returned with more beer.

'Why's what?'

'Why am I stalling about moving in with Adam?'

Finn shrugged. 'How should *I* know? Because you hate the idea of not living with *me* anymore?'

I looked at him, smiling slightly. 'Yeah. That'll be it.'

'Listen, Lana, can I ask you something?'

I took a sip of beer. 'Fire away.'

'Are you sure you want to get married again? Are you sure you want to marry *Adam* again?'

I took another sip of beer, staring out ahead of me, at the crowds of people milling around the site, all of them the kind of people I felt comfortable around. Unlike the people I'd been surrounded by at the fundraising dinner. These people here, they didn't judge, they accepted. Some of the people Adam mixed with, they judged. They only saw the tattoos, heard the strong Newcastle accent. They judged. But I needed to get past that. It just wasn't turning out to be as easy as I'd thought it would be. 'I'm sure.'

'So, Mr Perfect's managed to snare you a second time, huh?' Finn smirked.

I couldn't help smiling. 'He's a long way off perfect, okay? We both are.'

'Christ, don't start with the self-fucking-pity again, sis. It's an

241

ugly trait and one you never used to have. Adam quite obviously still loves you like crazy, although God knows why. I'm not entirely sure the poor guy knows what he's letting himself in for this time around. Maybe I should have a word with him…'

I slid an arm around Finn's waist, smiling as I hugged him tight. 'How do you always know what to say?'

'Because I'm a fucking genius, that's why.'

'Whatever. But you *can* talk a lot of sense sometimes. Even if you do look a little weird.'

'Yeah. I could go off you, beautiful. So, if you want that new tattoo doing any time soon, I'd start being nice to your brother if I were you.' He winked as he let go of me. 'Back in a minute. I'm off to check out the portaloos.'

'Too much information,' I laughed, as he backed away from me, still grinning, before he turned around, digging his hands in his pockets as he walked.

I leant back against the bike, taking another sip of beer before throwing my head back and closing my eyes, letting the hot afternoon sun hit my face, the music filling my head.

'Looking good there, darlin'.'

I almost froze at the sound of that voice. That still-too-familiar voice. A voice I hadn't been sure I'd ever hear again.

Slowly opening my eyes, I looked at him, standing right there in front of me, large as life and twice as hot. His hair was still that messed-up mid-length with the ability to fall over his eyes unless he slicked it back; his beard was still goatee style, those dark eyes of his still as deep as I remembered. He was wearing battered dark-grey jeans and his old faithful biker boots, a white t-shirt clinging to his strong, toned torso. Eddie Fletcher. Back in the UK. But, why?

'Good to see you, Lana.'

Jesus! The way he said my name, it still had the ability to floor me. 'I… What are you doing here? I mean, I thought you… I thought you were moving to Los Angeles?'

242

'I am. I have. Got a new shop in downtown LA, just like I wanted, an apartment in Culver City, and things are good. Everything's working out, but… My mum, she passed away a couple of weeks ago and despite everything that's happened with my family, I had to come home – I *wanted* to come home. I wanted to lay her to rest and make my peace.'

'Oh, Eddie. I'm so sorry.'

He shook his head, dropping his gaze. 'It's okay, darlin'. It was expected. She hadn't been well for a long time, so…' As he looked back up at me I couldn't help but see a touch of sadness in his eyes, a vulnerability he didn't show all that often, but it was there. 'It wasn't such a huge shock.' He threw back his head, shaking it slightly, almost as if he was trying to rid himself of any remaining negative feelings that were still lingering somewhere inside of him. 'Anyway… I came home, I did what I had to do. What I *needed* to do…' His eyes met mine again, and I could do nothing but stare at him. Because I still couldn't quite believe he was there. 'I'm not flying back out to LA for a few days, so when I heard about this biker get-together going on this weekend I called a couple of mates I know in the area, told them I was stopping by. This seemed like a great excuse to spend a bit of time hanging out with them, do some catching-up. One of them's pretty friendly with a guy you know, apparently. Bobby Gardener?'

I continued to stare at him, not really knowing what to say. 'Yeah. Yeah, Bobby's a good friend. He's one of the tattoo artists at Black Ink.'

'Well, he said you guys might be coming here this weekend so I… I kind of hoped he was right. And fate seems to have worked in my favour. Again.'

I briefly looked away, running my hand along the back of my neck.

'Still having that love-hate relationship with fate, huh?'

I faced him again, smiling slightly. 'You could say that, yeah.'

He stuck his hands in his pockets as he leant back against the bike beside me. 'So, you and the ex-husband…'

'Not so ex anymore,' I interrupted, looking down at my boots. Eddie stayed silent.

'We're getting remarried,' I continued, finding it hard to meet his eyes now I'd told him that.

'Really?'

But I finally managed it. Finally I looked straight at him. 'Really.'

'Things are working out, then?'

I looked away again. Why? Why had I done that? That made it look like I wasn't sure, and I *was* sure. I was absolutely sure that remarrying Adam was what I wanted.

'Lana?'

'Yeah. Things are working out.'

It was his turn to look away, his arms folded across his chest as he stared down at the ground. 'Then I'm happy for you, sweetheart.' His eyes once more met mine. 'I really am. I'm happy that you've finally found what you were looking for.'

'How's Nate? And Kaley?' I asked, desperate to change the subject now.

'They're doing just great. Getting married themselves in a couple of months, in Vegas. Got a baby on the way, too.'

'Oh, that's fantastic news!' I gasped, and I genuinely meant it. Maybe that's what Nate had needed, to focus his attention on something that mattered, something that would help him forget the past.

'Well, I hope so, darlin'. Because the trouble Nate kicked up when we…' He trailed off, looking back down at the ground. 'Retribution isn't always the best idea. And none of what we did helped, at all. The trouble hasn't exactly gone away, but…' He sighed, pushing a hand back through his hair and I watched as it did its usual trick of falling straight back over his eyes. 'I don't think anyone's in any danger anymore, let's put it that way.'

'Glad to be out of it?' I asked, willing him to look at me. I needed him to look at me for some reason.

He finally raised his gaze, his deep, dark eyes meeting mine. 'I needed it, you know? That new start, and... Aye. Things are much more laid back in LA.' He left a couple of beats before he spoke again. 'I think you'd really like it out there, Lana.'

And the moment was gone, just like that. I had to push it away. I had to.

'Finn's bike, is it?' He'd obviously sensed we'd needed another change of subject. And he wasn't wrong.

'Yeah. This is Finn's bike.'

Eddie ran his fingers along the black and red paintwork of Finn's beloved Ducati. 'Never been much into racing bikes myself,' Eddie went on, turning around to get a proper look at the bike. 'But this one's pretty impressive.' He turned back to face me. 'You gonna be here for the whole weekend?'

I nodded. 'We've all got tents over on the site. God help us. You?'

'Aye, I'm experiencing the whole camping thing too. Not spent the night in a tent for a while, though, I have to admit.'

'No. It's not my favourite sleeping place either. I'd much rather be at home, in my own bed...' I stopped talking, my eyes down on the ground.

'Are you happy, Lana?'

I couldn't look at him. In fact, part of me was becoming a little irritated now, that he'd turned up here, out of the blue, just when things were starting to settle down between me and Adam. It was almost like the whole situation in Vegas had been reversed, and I didn't need this. I didn't need – I didn't *want* the memories to return. That would hurt just a little too much. 'I love him,' I said quietly.

'That isn't what I asked, darlin'.'

'It's the answer you're getting.' I slowly raised my head to look at him, my eyes meeting his, holding the stare. He was the first to break it, looking down again, his arms folded back across his chest. 'Why did you come here, Eddie?'

He raised his gaze, his folded arms feeling almost like a defence mechanism now. 'When I said I'd done everything I needed to do, that wasn't entirely true. There's still something I need to finish. Still something that has to be done and I need to do that before I even think about getting on that plane back to LA. You and me, Lana – I need to see if there's still something there.'

30

'Oh Jesus…' I pushed a hand through my hair, sinking to the ground, pulling my knees to my chest.

He sat down beside me, mirroring my stance. 'Unlike you, sweetheart, I still believe fate plays a big part in our lives, and now I'm back in the UK, I couldn't leave here without trying to find you. Without talking to you. Without trying one more time to make sure you're doing what you really want to do with your life.'

'I'm fine, Eddie. Everything is fine.'

'Fine is such a beige word, Lana. It doesn't scream that you're happy, that life is exciting…'

I looked at him. 'Life can't always *be* one long round of excitement, Eddie. Sometimes reality gets in the way.'

He stared at me. Right at me. And for a few seconds he said nothing, just fixed me with a look that made my stomach sink in a way I couldn't explain. 'Who's talking now, darlin'? Because that sure as hell sounds like the old Lana to me.'

I turned away, staring out at the crowds of people, feeling the sunshine burning down on my bare shoulders.

'You *know* life can be exciting, Lana. You know that. You've *lived* it.'

'For a few weeks. But it was never gonna be forever. That kind of life *can't* be forever.'

'Can't it?'

I looked at him again. I didn't know what to say now. This was making my head spin in a way I didn't welcome.

'Let's go for a ride,' he said, those dark eyes of his boring into mine. 'I've got a mate's Harley I'm using for the weekend. We can get out of here for an hour or two. Give me a chance to remind you how exciting life *can* be.'

'Eddie, I… I don't know…'

He pulled himself to his feet, pushing a hand through his hair. 'It's up to you, Lana.'

I stood up too, looking around to see if I could find Finn. 'I need to… I need to think, Eddie. I don't… I don't know…'

'I'll be over there, for the next ten minutes or so. You want to come with me, you know what to do. And if you don't… well, you take care of yourself, kid, you hear?'

I watched him walk away, blinking a few times to make sure it really was him. That that had really happened. Because a huge part of me wished it hadn't.

'Was that…?'

I turned to see Finn back beside me. 'Yeah. That's him.'

'What the hell's *he* doing over here? I thought he was in LA now?'

'He is. He's over for a funeral. He's going back to the States in a couple of days.'

Finn frowned. 'So, this is all pure coincidence, is it?'

I slowly shook my head. 'No. Not really. One of his friends knows Bobby, and he told him we'd be here this weekend, so, Eddie he… he came here to find me.'

Finn let out a low whistle. 'He's persistent, I'll give him that much.'

'Don't make light of this, Finn. Please.'

'I'm not, believe me.' He eyes scanned my face for some sort of reaction. 'So, how do you feel about seeing him again?'

'I'd rather he hadn't turned up.'

'You tell him that?'

'I tried to.'

'*Tried* to?'

'He wants me to go for a ride with him. Now. Just for an hour or so.'

'You're not going, are you?'

I didn't reply immediately, and that, in itself, scared me. 'No. I'm not going.'

'Tell you what,' Finn said. 'Hang on a sec... Bobby! Here, mate, take this will you?' He handed his beer over to Bobby before picking up his helmet, handing another one to me. '*We*'ll go for a ride. Okay? You want your head clearing, let *me* clear it for you. How does that sound?'

I smiled, taking the helmet from him and eyeing his bike. 'Well, it's no Harley, but...'

'Just climb on, will you? And don't start getting all picky over your bikes because you want to ride a Harley around this neck of the woods, and you're riding pillion with Bobby. You got that?'

I was still smiling as I straddled his Ducati. 'No, you're alright. I'll make do with this.'

'You're such a biker bitch sometimes,' Finn sighed, winking at me before he slammed his visor shut and climbed on in front of me. 'Hold on tight, beautiful. We're outta here.'

'Do you really have to stay the night there, Lana?'

I leant back against the wall and closed my eyes as the last of the evening sun got ready to set on a festival site that was already enjoying a night of music and partying, biker style, which was exactly what I needed; to lose myself in something other than reality. 'It's one weekend, Adam.'

'Until the next one.'

'For Christ's sake...' I sighed, opening my eyes and looking around me. This was where I wanted to be right now. Here, in this place, with Finn and Bobby and all our friends, listening to loud, thumping rock music and drinking beer and whisky until the sun came back up. 'Don't make me…' I stopped, aware that I was actually thinking out loud now. What I'd been going to say, it wasn't really meant to be said.

'Don't make you what, Lana?'

'You knew the score, Adam. When we got back together, you knew how it was gonna be.'

'And we also talked compromise, Lana. Remember?'

I wasn't in the mood for this. 'You want me to come home, is that it?'

'No,' he sighed. 'No, that's not what I want. Well, yes, I'd love you to come home, I miss you…'

'One night, Adam.'

'You're there with all those other men, Lana.'

'And all those other men have partners, women who are my friends, Adam. All of them. It isn't just me and a huge group of guys… Jesus…'

'I'm finding this hard to deal with, okay? It isn't my world, I'm not used to any of it. I don't know how it's supposed to work.'

'I know, and I'm sorry, baby.' It was my turn to let out a huge and heavy sigh. I couldn't help it. This conversation was draining me. I understood exactly where he was coming from, and I knew that what I was doing.Of course it was hard for him to get his head around. But I wasn't giving this up. Not for him. Not for anyone. I loved him, no doubt about that. I loved him so much. But I loved my life, too – the bits I shared with him, and the bits I didn't. 'I love you, Adam. You do know that, don't you?'

'Yes. I know that. And I love you, too. I just miss you, that's all. I miss sleeping next to you. I miss that incredible body of yours lying next to mine, even if it *is* only for one night. I've spent long enough without you. I was just getting used to you being around again.'

I couldn't help smiling now. 'Yeah. I miss you too, handsome.'

'Lana, we… we *are* going to be okay, aren't we?'

I paused for a couple of beats before I replied. Why had I done that? I hadn't really meant to. Maybe it was just the fact that my usually confident ex-husband had suddenly sounded just a touch needy there. And I wasn't used to that. 'Yeah. Yeah, we're gonna be better than okay, baby. You just keep on looking for wedding destinations, alright? Far away from here, remember? I want it to be just the two of us this time around. I'll see you tomorrow.'

I hung up and slid the phone into my pocket, wandering back over to everyone.

'You hungry?' Finn asked. 'Bobby and Phil are heading over to the burger van if you fancy one.'

I shook my head, sitting down next to him.

'Everything okay?'

'Yeah, everything's fine,' I sighed, pushing a hand through my hair. 'Adam's just… I don't know. There are hints of things happening that I stupidly thought *wouldn't* happen… Forget it. I'm not making any sense. Maybe I *should* eat something. It might kick-start my brain into thinking straight.'

Finn smiled, giving my hand a quick squeeze before yelling over at Bobby to get two more burgers. Then he turned his attention back to me. 'He's still not happy about you being here, huh?'

I shrugged, letting go of Finn's hand to fiddle with the leather bands on my wrist. 'I don't know *how* he feels, really. I mean… Am I being selfish here, Finn? Expecting him to just accept the way I am now? For him to just slot in between everything else I want to do? Because that isn't how I meant it to be. I want him in my life, I really do, it's just that…' I looked back down at those bands on my wrist. 'It's just that, I can't let go of all *this*, either. Because this is where I'm happy.'

'You don't look very happy right now, kiddo.'

I looked at him. He shrugged.

'Just an observation, sis.'

I picked up his beer and took a long swig. 'I'm happy. Really.'

'Okay,' Finn sighed, taking back his beer. 'Whatever you say.'

'Anyway, forget all that. What about you?'

'What *about* me?'

'I thought you were setting up a date with Kelly, from Mikey's Bar?'

'I am. But that's not until next Wednesday, and you're extremely good at changing the subject, do you know that?'

'Just another talent of mine.' I smiled, freeing him of his beer again, taking another sip. But as I settled down next to my brother for some food and time with friends I'd grown to adore over the past year, the relaxing, stress-free night I'd planned to have suddenly came crashing down around me. Because he was still here. I could see him, leaning against the bar, drinking beer and laughing at something the guy beside him was saying. Eddie Fletcher just wasn't going to go away. Should I be reading something into that? Or should I just be passing it off as nothing more than an uneasy coincidence?

I felt Finn's hand on my shoulder, and I closed my eyes as he gently rubbed it. 'Just tell him, Lana. Tell him nothing's going to happen.'

'He's only having a drink, Finn.'

'Tell him, Lana. Say the words out loud, and believe them. Mean them.' He looked right into my eyes, taking my hand again and squeezing it tightly. 'Do you understand what I'm saying? If you don't believe them, if you don't mean them…'

'I understand.' I smiled, leaning over to kiss him quickly, taking one more swig of beer. 'I won't be long.'

'And get yourself one of these while you're over there, alright?' He returned my smile as he retrieved what was left of his beer. 'Stop you from thieving mine.'

I threw him another smile before I turned around and walked slowly over to Eddie, my hands in my pockets, my head down slightly as I got ready to face him again. I knew what I had to do, what my heart was telling me to do; what I *needed* to do. But until those words actually came out of my mouth I had no idea whether I was going to believe them or not; whether I was going to mean them. And that kind of scared me.

'Hey,' I said, keeping my hands in my pockets, looking up as I approached him.

'Hey.' He smiled that wonderful smile I'd loved so much back in Vegas. 'Just a second, darlin'.' He said something to the man he was talking to, waiting until he was gone before he turned back to me. 'So, you didn't feel much like riding this afternoon.' It was more of a statement than a question.

'Finn and me, we went out for a couple of hours.'

'You blew me off for your brother and a Ducati, huh? What happened to my Harley-loving biker babe?'

I smiled, leaning back against the bar. 'She fancied something harder and faster.'

He raised an eyebrow. 'Did she get what she was looking for?'

I looked away, shifting my gaze to the dusty ground beneath us, the day's sun having almost scorched it bone dry. 'Look, Eddie…' I let my eyes meet his again, and the undeniable attraction I didn't want to acknowledge – it was still there. He was still everything I'd ever dreamed of, all rough and hot and living his life the way I'd wanted to live mine. Until Adam had turned up. 'I know that it might look like I'm going back on some of those things I claimed I wanted but… Adam … I can't let him go. I know that sounds weak, and I hate feeling the way I do, but I just can't. I can't let him go.'

'And what about letting go of your dreams, Lana? What about all those things we talked about? What about that road trip we were gonna take? All the plans we had?'

'They're still in here,' I said quietly, gently tapping the side of my forehead. 'They'll never go away.'

'But is anything ever gonna come of them, darlin'? This man of yours, you love him, right?'

I nodded, my eyes refusing to leave his. Even though looking away might have made things easier.

253

'And, does *he* love *you* enough to let you live out your dreams?'

'I'm already living them, Eddie.'

'Some of them, Lana. You're living some of them. Ones you'd already started living before he came back into your life. I'm talking about the dreams you're still reaching for. The dreams you've yet to fulfil. Does he love you enough to allow you to chase those, even if they don't fit with his?'

I finally broke the stare, looking back down at the ground. 'I love him. And loving someone, being with someone, it means you just might have to compromise in order to make it work.'

'Really?'

I looked back at him, but I didn't know what to say. The words had suddenly got stuck in my throat.

'What if the person you loved – what if they *shared* your dreams, Lana? There wouldn't have to *be* any compromise then, would there, darlin'.'

I looked up at the darkening sky, closing my eyes for just the briefest of seconds. 'I love him, Eddie.'

'And you're willing to give up everything for him, are you? You shouldn't let anyone stand in the way of your dreams, Lana, I told you that, remember? Don't let anyone do that.'

'I love him,' I repeated. And I really just wanted him to stop talking now. I didn't want to hear any more. Because he was hitting a nerve? Making me think about things I didn't want to think about?

Eddie's eyes bored deep into mine, holding my gaze, daring me to look away this time. 'Then I really do hope he loves you back, enough to let you live that life you want to live, Lana. Because you only get one of those, remember.' And then he just turned and walked away, leaving me slightly confused and frustrated, because I hadn't even said what I needed to say – that nothing was going to happen; that he and I, we really were done. Or maybe I *had* said that. Just not in the way I'd intended. But that didn't seem to matter. That whole conversation felt unfinished to me.

'Everything okay?' Finn asked, joining me at the bar.

'I don't know,' I replied, my eyes still following Eddie as he pushed through the crowd. 'No. I've got to finish this…' I started to follow Eddie's rapidly retreating figure.

'Lana…?'

'I won't be long!' I shouted back at Finn, not knowing *how* long I was going to be, in reality. I didn't even know what I was going to do once I caught up with Eddie. I just knew that this felt unfinished. Loose ends were still hanging there, and even though a part of me was angry at him for coming back here and re-opening this whole scenario, another part of me – that cynical part that still held fate very much at arm's length – that part of me wouldn't lie down and forget. So I had to finish this. Whatever it was.

'Eddie!'

He stopped, waiting a few seconds before he turned to face me, standing completely still until I was right there in front of him. Before I could even take another breath he'd pulled me against him, his mouth bearing down on mine in a kiss so hard and so deep I wasn't sure that breath would ever come. My arms fell around him as though they were being worked by someone else completely, my body pressing against his, his hand in the small of my back keeping me there. It was a kiss that seemed to go on forever, bringing with it memories that were playing out like a movie reel inside my head – the memories we'd created together; those early-morning rides, having sex on his Harley as the sun came up, eating breakfast in the roadside diner and knowing we still had the best day ahead of us.

Pulling away only to turn me around, he pushed me back against the wall, and I kept my eyes closed as his mouth moved down to my neck, lightly brushing over the base of my throat, his hands sliding up and under my t-shirt, the feel of his fingers on my skin making me flinch slightly. But that was also an action that jolted me back to reality and I took hold of his hands, pulling them away from my waist. 'No, Eddie.'

'There are no compromises, Lana, if someone you love shares your dreams.'

I shook my head, a feeling of sadness washing over me so suddenly it almost took my breath away. 'Life isn't that perfect.'

He raised an eyebrow, leaning in to kiss me more gently this time. A kiss that broke my heart, for reasons I couldn't really work out. I just felt a pain cut across my chest that was all-too real. 'Maybe I'm not as strong as I thought I was,' I whispered, letting go of him and walking away.

'Maybe you just won't *let* yourself be that strong.'

I turned back around. 'I don't *want* to need him, Eddie.'

'You don't need anyone, Lana. You know that.'

I smiled a small smile, not really knowing what had happened here. I just knew that those loose ends, they felt a little more secure now, if not yet completely tied. 'Maybe not,' I whispered.

He walked over to me, gently tilting my chin up and kissing me so lightly it drew the tiniest gasp out of me. Yeah. He still had the ability to make me gasp. 'You look after yourself, darlin', you hear me?'

I smiled again, reaching up to stroke his cheek, running my thumb over his rough skin. 'Yeah. You too, Eddie Fletcher.'

Letting go of him, I walked away without looking back, because I knew looking back was dangerous. I'd done what I'd needed to do. I'd made the right decision.

31

Lying on the couch in Adam's front room, I turned over onto my stomach, picking up another of the many brochures I'd surrounded myself with, all of them showcasing far-flung places that looked like paradise with their white beaches and swaying palms and wedding packages the price of which were making my eyes water. But none of it was doing it for me.

'I'm just not the flowing-white-dress-and-flowers-in-the-hair kind of girl,' I moaned to Finn, the phone tucked between my chin and shoulder as I continued to flick through the pages.

'Blackpool in a tracksuit more your thing, is it?'

'Fuck off!'

'Well,' he laughed. 'What kind of wedding *do* you want?'

'The complete opposite to the one I had last time.'

'That's incredibly selfish of you, sis. The last time you married Adam there was a free bar and a party that went on until four the next morning. You telling me we're not gonna get that this time around?'

'No. You're not. I want it to be just me and Adam this time.'

'Boring!'

'Shut up!' I laughed, glad I'd called him now. I didn't even know why I was stressing over wedding arrangements anyway. We hadn't even begun to discuss dates or honeymoons or anything like that. 'Anyway, I'm going now.'

'Really? And I was just beginning to enjoy this conversation.'

'Yeah. You're hilarious. I need to get ready. This engagement party's starting in a couple of hours and I haven't even thought about what I'm wearing.'

'It's only a house party, Lana.'

'Yeah, but, it's not gonna be like one of *your* house parties, you do know that, don't you? There are gonna be people here who… Best behaviour, Finn. Okay?'

'Scout's honour.'

'Like *you* were ever in the scouts.'

'Listen, Lana, I'm being serious now. You do *want* to get married, don't you?'

'Oh, not this again… Of course I want to get married.'

'To Adam?'

'Are you being funny?'

'No. I'm asking a serious question. It's just that, after what happened with Eddie the other weekend, at the festival… I just want to make sure you're doing the right thing, that's all.'

'I am. I know I am. I love Adam. I love him, Finn, and I'm not willing to let him go a second time.'

I felt a hand on my hip, a body move close to mine, his mouth almost touching my ear as he spoke, sending a huge shiver tearing up my spine. 'I'm glad to hear that.'

I bit down on my lip, closing my eyes as Adam's hand moved lower, sliding down my shorts. 'Gotta go, Finn.'

'Mister CEO home after a hard day's work, huh? On a Saturday, too. He must be keen.'

'Yeah. See you later. And bring beer.' I threw the phone down, keeping my eyes closed as Adam kissed the back of my neck, his fingers stroking my skin, the smell of his cologne overwhelming. 'You still wearing your suit?' I murmured into the cushion.

'I've just this second walked through the door, so, yes. Why?'

I turned over and looked up at him, all tall and handsome with his short, dark hair, those ice-blue eyes and a beard I was continually begging him to keep. In fact, I was thinking of making it a kind of pre-requisite to our engagement – shave it off and the wedding was a no-go. I was that serious about it staying.

He stood there, a slight smile on his face, his hands in the pockets of his navy suit pants. He'd loosened his tie slightly, his shirt now open-necked, his jacket still on, and I couldn't remember ever seeing him look so sexy. Why had I never seen that whole businessman thing as a turn-on before? Because I'd been too busy trying to be the perfect wife, that was why, when I should have been focusing my attention elsewhere, instead of trying to become something I could never be.

'Don't take it off.' I returned his smile, wriggling out of my shorts. 'Well, you can take the jacket off. But leave the rest on.'

He shrugged off his jacket, throwing it over the back of a chair, leaning over to help me out of the rest of my clothes. 'I want *you* naked,' he whispered, rolling up his shirtsleeves and spreading my legs. 'Actually, I'd like you permanently naked.'

'You'd like your own personal plaything, you mean.' I stretched out, locking my fingers above my head as he lay between my legs.

'Have you got a problem with that, Ms Saunders?'

Jesus! When had *he* learnt to talk like that? He'd almost growled those words, all deep and sexy and, for Christ's sake, he'd just made me wet within seconds. 'No problem at all, *Mister* Saunders. After all, you're the boss.'

I got such a kick out of this role-paying shit; couldn't believe we'd wasted all those years not even realising the fun we could have had. Still, we were making up for that now.

I closed my eyes as he bent his head, his hands on my breasts, his thumbs flicking over my nipples.

'I've been dreaming about this all afternoon,' he moaned, lowering his head, his mouth touching my stomach, kissing it ever so lightly, making it contract in the most beautiful way. 'All fucking afternoon.'

His language was almost turning me on as much as his actions, because hearing him use those kind of words, well, he didn't do it all that often. Not in this context, anyway, and I was kind of hoping it was going to become a habit. I'd turn this man into something darker and dirtier if it killed me. He was already getting there.

'I can't believe I'm actually saying this…' I groaned, arching my back as his hands gripped my hips, his mouth moving lower still. 'But, do we have time for sex? The party's starting in a couple of hours…'

The touch of his tongue between my legs shut me up instantly. We'd make time. Besides, he was down there now and if there was one thing I knew about Adam, once he'd started something, he didn't stop until he was finished. So I just left that question unanswered, lay back, and let his mouth bring me to the kind of climax that rocked my body in the calmest of ways. It was so gentle, so peaceful, almost, I didn't want it to stop. Didn't want to leave the place it took me to.

'I love you, Lana,' he whispered, moving back up, the feel of his clothed body against my naked one a whole new turn-on. 'I love you so much.'

I looked up at him, pulling him nearer to me by his tie, wiping his mouth with my thumb, smiling slightly. 'Yeah. I kind of love you back, handsome.'

He laughed quietly, reaching down to unzip himself. 'I just need you to know that I love you and I'm really trying to get my head around all these changes and… You're this whole new woman to me Lana and it's still quite strange but… Jesus…' He bowed his head, watching as he pushed inside me before his eyes locked back onto mine. 'I'm as confused as hell, but I can't…'

I put a hand on his cheek, stroking his rough face, keeping my gaze fixed on him. 'Can't what, baby?'

'It feels new, Lana. And when something is this new it scares me, and right now I am so scared.'

I kissed him, wrapping my legs around him, pulling him deeper into me, wanting him to feel safe and know that this was scaring me, too. All of it. It was scaring me, too. 'We've got to learn to shut out the rest of the world and concentrate on *us*, Adam. Because that's where we went wrong last time. We have to try and focus on what makes *us* happy.'

'But some of those things don't fit, Lana. What makes *you* happy doesn't always make *me* happy, and I don't know…'

I shook my head, stopping him from talking any more. 'I don't want us to live in each others' pockets, Adam. We can *be* a couple, we can have a great life without having to do *everything* together. I know that now, and I think it'll be much better, for both of us, if we aren't glued to one another.'

'I worry about you,' he whispered. 'Out there, riding pillion with Finn, I mean. What if he has an accident, and you're on the bike with him? What if…?'

I shut him up with a kiss, pulling my legs tighter around him, drawing them up slightly, forcing him even deeper. 'Can we not do this while you're fucking me?'

'Lana, please, do you have to call it…'

'You're fucking me, Adam. I don't always want us to *make love*, okay? Sometimes I just want us to fuck… Oh, there you go.' I arched my back as I felt him stop for just a second, before he came so fast it surprised even him. 'You love it when I talk dirty, don't you? Really?'

He couldn't help laughing, looking down at his hands still holding onto my hips as his movements started to slow down. 'Was this always you?' His eyes slowly moved back up, once more locking with mine. 'Was this person always inside you, waiting to be set free?'

I reached out to touch his face again, running my fingers over his beard. 'For a long time, yes, I think she was probably in there.'

'If she'd shown herself sooner…?'

'She's out now and all I want is for her to never feel the need to hide away again. Do you understand, Adam? If you want me, you have to take who *she* is, too. Because she isn't going away.'

He looked down again as he pulled out of me, zipping himself back up before he climbed off me.

'We should be getting ready,' I said, sitting up, pushing both hands through my hair. 'People will be arriving soon.'

'Come here,' he whispered, holding out his hand and pulling me up into his arms. 'You are making me step so far out of my comfort zone, do you know that? Who you are now, what you do; how you talk. It's all so different and…'

I looked at him, trying to read his expression, see something in his eyes that I could understand because all I was getting were words. And they didn't always match what was really going on inside someone's head. 'If you can't handle this, Adam. If you really can't…'

'No.' He shook his head, his arm tightening around my waist. 'No, I… Jesus, I came all the way to Vegas because I knew I needed you back in my life, I just… It's intense, Lana. More intense than I thought it was going to be.'

I narrowed my eyes as I continued to stare at him. 'David been in the office today, huh?'

'Listen, baby…' He tucked a strand of hair behind my ear, kissing me gently, his hand resting lightly against my cheek. 'I'm sorry, okay? For bringing this up tonight, for…'

'Don't,' I whispered, pressing myself against him, stroking the back of his neck with my fingertips, my mouth almost resting against his now. 'We have to shut them out, Adam. Remember? We have to shut them all out because, if we don't, we're in trouble.'

'I can't lose you again, Lana. I *won't* lose you again.'

'Then ignore David. Ignore all his shit and concentrate on what's important, which, right now, is you and me sharing a shower. And believe me, once I start showing you just how useful shower gel can really be, you aren't gonna care what your narrow-minded brother thinks. Anyway, he's probably just jealous. Maybe, deep down, he wants to find out for himself what it's like to fuck a woman with tattoos and a love of hot, dirty sex.'

'Jesus, Lana...' Adam laughed, letting his hands wander over my naked breasts, his eyes following their every move. 'You really don't know when to stop, do you?'

I shook my head, smiling as his eyes once more met mine. 'I promise, I'll be on my best behaviour tonight, though.' I ran my thumb lightly over his mouth. 'Around everyone else, anyway.'

He smiled back, his hands falling onto my bottom, pushing me harder against him. 'You are going to kill me.'

I kissed him slowly, feeling his hard-on make a fast return. 'Let's get upstairs, handsome. We haven't got much playtime left and I haven't finished with you yet.'

'Your favourite brother-in-law's here, I see,' Finn said as we hung out in the conservatory, drinking beer and people-watching.

I looked over at David standing by the fireplace in a pale-grey shirt and tailored charcoal pants. 'Still looks like he's got something permanently shoved up his arse,' I sniffed. 'And his wife doesn't look any more relaxed.'

'Still a big fan, then?' Finn smirked.

'Don't even go there. You really don't want to get me started.'

Finn looked back over at David, and the glamorous Tamsin, his undeniably beautiful but, in my opinion anyway, completely unapproachable, wife. She could, actually, be rather lovely when she wanted to be, and we'd had one or two fairly pleasant days out together in the past, surprisingly. But I'd always felt that she allowed David's opinions of me to cloud her own, which meant I'd kept her very much at arm's length, whenever possible. She intimidated me way too much, or she'd used to. But something told me I wasn't going to let that be the case anymore.

'They really don't look alike, do they? Him and Adam,' Finn continued.

'No. They don't.'

'The lovely Tamsin's still looking hot, though, in that kind of stuck-up way… Man, that is such a fucking turn-on...'

I rolled my eyes, shaking my head. 'You're not still fantasising about her, are you?'

'Always fancied a bit of upmarket posh myself.' Finn grinned, throwing me a wink. 'And you don't get much posher than Tamsin Saunders. Her father still owns that stud farm, doesn't he?'

I just gave him a withering look. 'She'd eat you for breakfast, baby brother.'

'Yeah,' he sighed, taking a swig of beer. 'I know.'

I threw him another look, which he returned.

'Anyway, where's Christian Grey?'

'Will you fuck off?'

'No. You need me tonight, and don't deny it.'

I nudged up against him, quickly kissing his cheek. 'Yeah, you're right, I do. Without you here I'd be drowning in Adam's friends and colleagues. Can't believe Bobby and the guys have that biker's rally in Morpeth this weekend. This would've been so much more fun with everyone here. I'd have paid money to see David's face when that lot turned up.'

'Adam's friends can't *all* be that bad, surely.'

'No,' I sighed, taking another drink of beer. 'They're not. Some of them are really lovely. Mainly the ones I've known since me and Adam first got together. It's just me being paranoid. Ignore me. I haven't had enough to drink yet.'

'So, where is he, then? The gorgeous Adam.'

'Pack it in, Finn.'

'No. I'm enjoying myself. Every time I say his name you go all "girlie", and that is so entertaining for me, you have no idea.'

'I hate you.'

'Yeah. Sure you do. Oh, hang on, here he is.'

I followed Finn's gaze, my eyes immediately falling on Adam. He looked heartbreakingly handsome in dark jeans and a navy-blue shirt, displaying his own brand of casual-relaxed with the sleeves rolled up to the elbows, his hair just a touch messed-up. And that was only because I'd ran my fingers through it not ten minutes earlier when he'd pushed me back against the kitchen wall and grabbed a quick kiss on his way to fetch more wine from the fridge. I bit down on my lip and Finn looked at me.

'You see? You're doing it again.'

'I am not!'

'You are.' He waved his empty beer bottle in my face. 'Re-fill?'

'In the kitchen. You know where they are.'

'You're not the best hostess in the world, are you?'

I threw him a sarcastic smile. 'Those days are well and truly behind me.'

I watched him head off into the kitchen, pulling myself up onto the sideboard behind me, taking a long swig of my own beer.

'Are you doing this on purpose?'

I looked up to see David standing in front of me, but I wasn't about to let him get to me. Not tonight. Not ever. Those days were well and truly behind me, too. 'Sorry. Am I not allowed to drink now?'

'You know what I mean.'

'I don't, actually… Oh, you mean the bottle, is that it? A lady should always be drinking from a glass, right? Am I not displaying the proper manners here?'

'This is supposed to be a celebration, Lana. What's wrong with champagne?'

I kept my eyes fixed on him as I drained my beer. 'Nothing. I'm just not all that keen on the stuff, to be honest. Well, not unless your brother's pouring it over my naked tits and licking it off while he fucks me – hard.'

'Jesus Christ.' David turned away for a second, pushing a hand through his hair before he turned back to face me. 'You've proved your point, Lana, alright?'

'I don't *have* a point, David.'

265

He moved a step closer, but I still wasn't about to let him intimidate me. He was welcome to try, though. I was more than ready for him. 'Why, Lana? Why do this to yourself? You're a beautiful woman, but this – whatever it is you think you've become… I never thought you were right for Adam, but at least before… At least you did what was expected of you…'

'I'm *sorry*?' I laughed, unable to believe I was hearing this. Although none of it really surprised me, I'd always known the way David felt about me. I'd just never heard him say it out loud or in such in a candid way. Back then it would have bothered me. Now, I didn't give a crap.

'Do you really think people are going to be accepting of you walking back into Adam's life…?'

'*He* walked back into *mine*, actually. Get your facts right. Dave.'

'I'm ashamed to say he's acting like any man faced with a woman like you…'

'A woman like me. Do you want to expand on that?'

'You look cheap, Lana.'

'If I were you, I'd be extremely careful right now, David.'

'He's blinded by…'

'Sex?'

He laughed quietly, his stare as determined as mine. 'Whatever you're doing to him, he'll get over it. Eventually. He'll get tired of the attitude and the language and this ridiculous obsession you've acquired that involves branding your skin with that vile ink. He'll get tired of it all. Eventually. He isn't that shallow, Lana. He'll see sense. He'll see that you aren't right for him. You never were. You're even less so now. He needs someone who can accompany a man of his standing to functions and dinners, a woman who holds herself with dignity; someone on the same level as him. Someone who doesn't put him on edge, in fear of what they might say or do. He needs…'

'He needs *you* to keep out of shit that doesn't concern you,' I hissed, leaning forward only slightly. 'And I have no idea where you get off thinking you can say any of this to me because you are so out of line here, it's ridiculous. Now, I really don't care what you or anyone else thinks of me; I've already told you, David, nobody else's opinion matters anymore. So…' I shrugged, '… say what you like, because to me it's nothing but white noise. You're just wasting your breath.'

He continued to stare at me, but I was holding my ground here. Even if, for just a fleeting second, I wished I was somewhere else. Some place where I didn't have to deal with all this crap.

'You really are an incredibly beautiful woman, Lana. I can't deny that. And, you know, if you'd come back into Adam's life the same woman you had been before, maybe things could have worked out. It's just a pity you've seen fit to ruin yourself in the way that you have.'

'Everything okay here?' Adam asked, walking into the conservatory, looking from David to me.

'Everything's fine,' I replied. 'David was just congratulating us, weren't you?' I held his stare for a few more seconds before turning to face Adam. 'Where've you been? I've had to amuse myself annoying Finn.'

Adam walked over to me, kissing me quickly. 'I had to take a phone call.'

'Work-related?' David asked.

Adam looked at him. 'Graham Kenwood. He just wanted to make sure the meeting was still on for Monday afternoon.'

'Do you want me to take charge of that one? Only, I know you're pretty busy with Hendersons, and sorting all that paperwork out for the LA contract…'

'We'll both take care of the Kenwood meeting, David, and can we talk about this on Monday, hmm? Tonight is supposed to be a party.'

'If business needs to be handled at awkward times…'

'Monday, David. Go get a drink and loosen up, will you? Go on.'

I couldn't help smiling at that. Yeah. I was teaching him good.

'Has he been bothering you?' Adam asked, once David had finally left us alone.

'No. He's fine,' I sighed, pulling him between my legs and kissing him slowly, enjoying a few brief minutes to ourselves.

'You sure? Only, I know you two never really got on and...'

I shut him up with another kiss, running my hands up and down his forearms. 'You gonna keep going on about your brother?'

'If this is what I get every time I mention him then, yes, probably.' He grinned, and I smiled back, hooking my legs around his hips as he lowered his mouth back down onto mine. 'But, as much as I would love to do nothing but stay right here, between your incredibly beautiful legs, we really should be more sociable. This *is* supposed to be our party, after all.'

'Yeah. You're right.' I played with the collar of his shirt, keeping my legs wrapped around him for just a few more seconds. 'And anyway, these legs are quite happy to take a rain check.' I kissed him quickly. 'They'll open up again later. When we're alone.' Another kiss. 'Naked.' And another. 'In bed. With nothing to do but make love until the sun comes up.'

'Now *that* sounds like a plan.' He smiled, sliding a hand into his pocket and pulling something out. 'Give me your left hand, come on.'

'Adam! We said no rings. Anyway, I've already got one.'

'From eighteen years ago, Lana. You're not wearing a second-hand ring, okay?'

'It's not second-hand. It's *my* bloody ring.'

'Shut up and hold out your hand.'

'So romantic,' I sighed, grudgingly doing as I was told.

'I didn't think hearts and flowers were quite your thing.'

I looked at him, the smile he gave me making my heart shudder. 'When did I ever say that?'

He just raised an eyebrow as he slid the ring onto my third finger. I looked down, my smile growing a little wider as I stared at it. To say it was different to the first engagement ring he'd given me was an understatement. That one had been simple and under-stated, but you couldn't really call this one understated. This one was almost the complete opposite of that first ring. This one was uniquely beautiful, and I fell in love with it immediately. And that was coming from a woman who didn't do expensive jewellery. I did leather bands and cuff watches, but this ring – a square, black diamond set in black gold – it was so me I couldn't have chosen better myself. I hated to use the word perfect, because nothing was ever that, but this ring, it sailed pretty close.

'It's a cushion-cut black diamond,' Adam explained, his hand still holding mine. 'And I thought the black gold was more your thing, too. Did I do okay?'

I looked up, loving him for doing this, but hating him because he was making me cry, for such a girlie reason. 'I love you so much, Adam Saunders.'

'You like it?'

I nodded, quickly wiping my eyes with the back of my hand. 'Yeah. I like it and I'm gonna show you just how much I like it later.' I kissed him again, sliding a hand around the back of his neck as our mouths moved together, his body close to mine. Exactly where I wanted it to be.

'We'd better go join the party.'

I rested my forehead against his, running my thumb lightly over his mouth. 'I'll be out in a bit. Go on. I won't be long.'

He gave me one last kiss before he headed out of the conservatory to rejoin the party. I crossed my legs up underneath me, cocking my head slightly as I stared back down at my ring.

'Whoa!' Finn whistled, leaning over to get a closer look.

'Isn't it amazing?' I looked at him, scrunching up my nose. 'I went all "girlie" again, didn't I?'

'He's changing you, sis,' Finn mock-sighed, shaking his head and leaning back against the sideboard, nudging me gently. 'Seems like he's got you sussed, though. That really is one hell of a ring. Must've cost him a small fortune.'

'Yeah,' I whispered, looking back down at my hand. 'I suppose it must've done.'

'Oh, Jesus, *now* what's wrong?'

I looked at him. 'Nothing. It's just… David's being an arsehole, and I've stupidly let him get to me, even though I'd promised myself I wasn't going to let that happen.'

'Being an arsehole in what way?' Finn asked, handing me a fresh bottle of beer.

'Telling me I'm not right for Adam, voicing his dislike about the way I look…'

'And that matters, does it?'

'No, but…'

Finn just raised an eyebrow. 'He's always been an arsehole, Lana. I knew that from the second I met him.'

I couldn't help smiling. 'Yeah. He's always been a big fan of yours, too.'

Finn shrugged. 'Well, there you go, then. His opinion means fuck all. Forget it.'

I looked back down at the ring. 'It just…it feels as though me and Adam have such a battle ahead of us, Finn. On so many levels. I hate doing all that corporate shit, I hate it with a passion but, if I'm gonna be his wife again, then surely I just have to suck that up and support him. But does that mean I have to change who I am when we're out together? Am I gonna have to cover up and dye my hair and act like the perfect partner? Because that's not what I'm signing up for here.'

'And I'm sure Adam knows that.'

'I know there are gonna have to be *some* compromises. I mean, I'm not *that* selfish to think everything has to be done *my* way, but…'

'You said yourself it wasn't gonna be easy, kiddo.'

'Yeah, I knew it wasn't gonna be easy. But there are times when I can't help thinking we might be hoping for the impossible.'

He pulled himself up onto the sideboard beside me, taking

my hand and squeezing it gently. 'What really happened with you and Eddie at the festival? I mean, you said you just talked, but...'

I looked at Finn. 'I didn't sleep with him, if that's what you're getting at.'

'Is that what I asked?'

'It's what you meant. Seriously, was I away long enough for that to have happened?'

'Did you want to?'

I looked straight at my brother. Right into his eyes, not missing a beat before I answered. 'Yeah. I did. I wanted to sleep with him.' And that was the truth. I had. For a brief second or two.

'Jesus, Lana...'

'But that was just because, him turning up like that, out of the blue, I was hit with this wall of memories and I...' I looked back down at the ring Adam had just given me. 'I knew it would have been wrong to go there. But he... he said a lot of things that... Look, I dunno. They just hit a bit close to home, that's all.'

Finn threw me a slightly confused look. 'You having second thoughts here, kiddo?'

I shook my head, running my thumb lightly over the black diamond nestled nicely on my finger. 'I'm just letting David get to me more than I should. But, you know, maybe he's got a point.'

'And what point would that be, exactly?' Finn frowned.

'I fell for Adam so hard in the beginning. *So* hard. And because I would have done anything for him back then, I allowed myself to change everything I was, everything I wanted to be to fit in with *his* world – to make *mine* easier. And isn't that what *he's* doing now, Finn? Changing everything he is to fit in with *my* world?'

'Would that be such a bad thing?'

'It didn't work out so well for *me*, did it? In the long run it only made me unhappy. What if all we're gonna achieve is the same outcome here? I mean, I know we seem happy enough now, and for the first half of our marriage I *was* happy. I...'

'Lana...'

'I'm not having second thoughts, Finn.'

'I think you are.'

I looked down, letting go of his hand and clasping mine together. 'I love Adam. I never *stopped* loving him, not really, and I will fight as hard as I can to make it work this time around, I really will, but I don't want him to end up unhappy. I don't want *him* to end up feeling what *I* felt in the end or we're gonna lose it all over again.'

Finn gave my hand another squeeze and I leant in towards him, resting my head on his shoulder. 'When did your life become so complicated, beautiful?'

'When I let it,' I sighed, sliding down from the sideboard, my eyes going straight to Adam, who was over the other side of the living room, chatting to a pretty, dark-haired woman. She seemed to be hanging on his every word, looking right into his eyes, an interested smile on her face. With her beautifully styled shoulder-length hair, smart trouser suit and expensive-looking jewellery she was everything I'd tried to be for him, but had never quite managed to pull off, even after almost twenty years of trying.

'Lana?'

Finn's voice brought me back to reality and I turned to face him, frowning slightly as he slowly shook his head. 'Don't, okay? Don't go there. Don't start moving backwards, kiddo, don't do that. You've come such a long way since I rescued you from oblivion…'

'Shut up!' I laughed, loving him for pulling me back from a mood I didn't want to sink into.

'You see?' He smiled, taking my hand and squeezing it again. 'I told you you needed me here tonight.'

I moved in for a hug, snuggling in against him. I really hadn't realised just how much I'd missed my brother, until I'd found him again.

'Are you *sure* you're doing the right thing, Lana?'

I pulled back slightly, frowning as I looked up at him.

'I mean, I know I practically pushed you into going back to Adam, but that was only because I was worried about you out there, in Vegas, with Eddie, this guy you barely knew. I just wanted you to come back home and I thought Adam might be able to talk you round better than *I* could. And now, after seeing you guys together, I just want you to be sure. I want you to be really sure. Because marriage – even to a guy you've been married to before – it's a huge decision. And you, more than anyone, are putting a lot on the line here. You're putting who you *are* now on the line.'

I ran my hands up and down his arms, lowering my gaze as his words sunk in. 'I know.'

'I want you to be happy, sis.'

I looked back up at him, smiling slightly. 'Yeah. I know you do.'

'Does Adam make you happy? *Really* happy?'

'I love him, Finn.'

'That's not what I asked, Lana.'

It was the same question Eddie had asked me a couple of weekends ago and the answer I'd just given Finn was the same answer I'd given *him*. Was there a reason for that?

'I'm gonna go see him,' I said, kissing Finn quickly, then heading back out into the living room before he could throw any more curve balls at me. This was my engagement party. It was time to find my fiancé and start celebrating properly. But he seemed to have disappeared from the living room, so I tried the kitchen. There was no sign of him there, either. But as I walked past the slightly open utility-room door, I heard their voices – David and Adam's. They were speaking in low tones, so it was hard to make out what they were talking about, and even though I wasn't one to eavesdrop, the one thing I *could* make out was my name. That caused me to stop in my tracks. Leaning back against the wall, as close to the door as I could get without being seen, I was grateful the kitchen was all but empty. I hoped it stayed that way. I wanted to know what Adam and his brother were talking about now I'd heard my name being mentioned. But they were keeping their voices quiet and I had to concentrate really hard to hear anything they were saying.

'Are you sure, Adam?' David's voice was clearer, which told me he was standing closest to the door. 'Really sure. Because some would say you'd had a lucky escape.'

'Jesus, David, come on. Cut her some slack, will you? She was my wife...'

'And she walked out on you. Remember? Almost twenty years together and she walked out on you to become some freak who hangs out with bikers and tattooists and all manner of people you really can't afford to be seen mixing with. Have you any idea how bad it would be for business if our clients thought those were the kind of people you associated with?'

'Do *you* have any idea how narrow-minded you sound right now?'

'It's the truth, Adam. And deep down you know it. Why you couldn't have made it work with Caroline...'

'I didn't want to *be* with Caroline, David.'

'Caroline was perfect for you. Elegant, classy, polite; from a good, well-respected family. She knew how to handle herself in the social circles we mix in...'

'Did you hear what I said? I didn't want to *be* with her. She was a perfectly lovely woman, but we just didn't click.'

'You could've made it work.'

'Have you always been this bigoted? Or have I just chosen to ignore it all these years?'

'Lana's image, Adam – it doesn't "fit" with the company. It doesn't fit with who *you* are.'

'Doesn't...? What the hell are you talking about?'

'Image is everything in business.'

'Is it?'

'Oh, come on... Do you want to lose everything? Are you willing to put it all on the line just because you're infatuated with your ex-wife's need to turn herself into some kind of...'

'Leave it, David. I'm warning you...'

'Think about it, Adam, for Christ's sake. Can you really see her, with all those vile tattoos, and that hair and the language she uses, the way she carries herself now, she looks...'

'Hot.'

I almost laughed out loud at Adam's quick-fire response to that.

'Jesus, Adam...' David sighed. 'She looks cheap. But then, she hardly comes from good stock, does she? Look at that brother of hers...'

'I'm not going to tell you again, David. You don't talk about her in that way, do you hear me?'

'You've built that business up... *We've* built that business up...'

'This isn't *about* you, David.'

'I'm only saying these things because I care about you, Adam. I think she's wrong for you. The way she is now, she's wrong for you. Can you not *see* that?'

'Look...'

I closed my eyes as Adam's voice rose slightly, my heart hammering hard as I continued to listen in to this quite obviously private conversation. But it involved me, so I figured I had every right.

'... maybe this is just something she needs to get out of her system, okay?'

My eyes sprung open at that remark, my heart beating even faster now.

'Maybe she just needs a bit of time to live out these – I don't know – these fantasies. Maybe this is nothing more than her version of a mid-life crisis, but she's back with me and now we're together again, things will probably change, David. They'll change.'

'Do you think so?'

'She's an intelligent woman. She knows what she should be doing. She knows right from wrong.'

I couldn't quite believe I was hearing those words come out of Adam's mouth. It was like a black mist had descended over me and I really had to try hard to stop myself from crashing their conversation and smacking the pair of them. Because now – *now*

275

the truth was coming out. The game was changing again and I was close, I was so close to letting them know I was there and I'd heard it all. But I stayed where I was. I needed to hear where this was going. I needed to hear exactly what else my fiancé had to say now he'd seemingly opened the floodgates.

'The tattoos can be covered up, David. They can be hidden. Her attitude can be changed, all of that can be changed. She loves me, and she knows I need her to do certain things if this is going to work a second time…'

I couldn't listen to any more. I felt sick now. And sad. I didn't even feel confused because I knew exactly what I had to do. The decision had been that instant. That definite. But that feeling of being kicked hard in the stomach; that feeling of having almost every breath knocked out of me was overwhelming.

Walking slowly and quietly out of the kitchen, away from the party, I didn't stop until I was upstairs, in our bedroom. Well, Adam's bedroom, because it wasn't mine. I still didn't live with Adam on a permanent basis, even though I'd left a few clothes here now, a few items of my own I'd brought over from Finn's. Tonight had just proved how lucky I'd been not to let go of an independence I'd slowly gotten used to over the past year.

With my heart still hammering a hard, painful rhythm I sat down on the edge of the bed, taking a brief second to think about what had just happened; to let the consequences of what I'd heard sink in. But nothing had changed. I still knew that what I was about to do, it was the right decision. It was the only decision.

I didn't belong here.

It was time to start packing.

32

Dragging the suitcase down from the top of the wardrobe, I threw it onto the bed, standing back as it hit the mattress with a resounding thud. For a couple of seconds I just looked at it as if, all of a sudden, I'd temporarily forgotten just what the hell it was I was doing. Was that deliberate? Was that actually my own subconscious giving me a little bit more time to think about everything? To make sure this really was the right thing to do?

Leaning back against the wall I closed my eyes, breathing in deeply. My heart was still beating fast, pounding away inside my chest as I tried to shut out the noise drifting up from the party going on downstairs; a party I should be getting back to. But I couldn't. Not now.

"... *this is just something she needs to get out of her system...*"

His words were playing over and over in my head like some never-ending record I couldn't switch off.

"*She loves me, and she knows I need her to do certain things if this is going to work a second time...*"

Yeah. I loved him. But did I love him enough? Enough to strip myself of everything I'd fought so hard to become?

I slowly opened my eyes, taking another deep breath, my gaze falling back on the empty suitcase.

'Lana?'

I swung around so quickly I almost lost my balance, my breath catching in my throat as I saw him standing there.

'What's going on?'

'I'm leaving, Adam.' I'd thought my resolve would weaken the second I saw him but I was obviously stronger than I thought I was. 'And this time, I'm not coming back.'

My voice was surprisingly calm because, in reality, what was there to be angry about? Had I actually expected this to work? All we'd really done was have lots of great sex, and made a mountain of promises that had been nothing but empty words, because we could never be together. Not really. Not with all the crap that still surrounded us. Too much was getting in the way, and I just didn't have the energy for the kind of fight this could turn out to be. Not when I couldn't see anyone winning. That gap that had widened between us over the years, it hadn't really started to close. If anything, it was probably wider than it ever had been.

'Leaving?' He pushed a hand through his hair, a confused look on his face. 'I don't... Lana, baby, I don't understand.'

I stared at him. I was ready for this. 'Tattoos *can* be covered up, Adam. But, the thing is, I'm not ashamed of them.'

'Oh, Jesus...' he sighed, turning away from me for a second. 'Lana, sweetheart...' He turned back around, his eyes meeting mine and I was determined to hold his stare. Because I meant this.

'It won't work, Adam.'

'No, listen, Lana, all of that...'

'Is how you really feel.'

He shook his head, his eyes never leaving mine as he moved a little closer. 'It's just... You know this is hard for me, darling...'

'It isn't hard for you, Adam. It's impossible.' I walked over to him, reaching out to run my fingers lightly over his beard, his ice-blue eyes still holding my gaze. 'All of this, it really isn't you, is it?'

'I'm trying,' he whispered, laying his hand gently over mine. 'I really am trying. Because I love you, Lana. I love you so much.'

I rested my forehead against his, closing my eyes for the briefest of seconds because I needed to stay in control here. I needed to stay focused. 'I know, baby. I know you do, and I know how hard you've tried...' I wasn't going to cry. I was *not* going to cry, even though I could feel my whole world crumbling down around me. And it was worse this time around. So much worse than before because this time I was aware of what was happening, of what I was losing. When I'd walked out the last time I hadn't realised what I was leaving behind. I hadn't realised how much I still loved this man. And I knew he was trying, I knew he was. He was trying so hard to accept me for who I was now, the woman I wanted – needed to be. And that acceptance had to work both ways, I knew that too. I couldn't expect him to do all the compromising. But it was the thought of what *I* might have to compromise that scared me, and after hearing Adam talking to David, I just wasn't sure compromising was even on the cards anymore. I wasn't sure either of us could do what we needed to do. I wasn't even sure we wanted to and if that was the case, what chance did we really have? 'I need to know, Adam. I really need to know... What you said to David, just now...' I looked up into his eyes, because I didn't just need to hear his response, I needed to feel it, too. 'Deep down inside, do you wish I wasn't like this? Deep down inside is it really the old Lana you want back?'

His fingers tightened around mine, and even though he said nothing, the look in his eyes shattered my heart. The pause said it all.

'Then I can't stay here.' I pulled my hand away, stepping back from him, but even though the physical bond had been broken, I knew I'd left a piece of myself with him. Maybe it was a piece of me that needed to be left behind. Maybe I was better off leaving it there, cutting it loose, forgetting about it. Because, maybe, it was a piece of me that was dragging me backwards.

'Lana... please...'

I kept my back to him, shaking my head. 'We can stand here and talk until there are no more words left to say, Adam. But this – it's never gonna work.'

'How can you say that?' His voice carried an almost desperate tone to it and I had to stop myself from turning back around to face him. If I wanted to be the Lana I *needed* to be, then I needed to walk away from this.

Slowly slipping the beautiful black diamond ring he'd given me not half an hour ago off my finger, I placed it down on the bedside table. The second I did that I felt a new strength take hold, sweeping over me with an intensity that almost winded me. 'It's time for us to both get on with our lives now, Adam, because I think we've been stalling for far too long.'

'You're throwing twenty years of our lives away, Lana.'

I was strong enough to face him now. To finish this and move on. 'And most of those twenty years were a lie.'

'No,' he whispered, shaking his head, his eyes locking with mine. 'That's not true. We were in love, Lana. For a long time. I'm still in love with you now, I…'

'It won't work.'

'We need to keep trying.'

'I'm done, Adam. I am done here.'

'You're giving up on us? Jesus… You're not even going to *fight* for this? We need to fight, Lana. We didn't do that before, we didn't fight, and it killed us. It killed us, baby.'

'I can't be what you need me to be, don't you understand?' I was trying to keep my voice calm and quiet, but it was hard. So hard. Because, inside, I was crumbling.

'We can work something out, sweetheart, please…'

It was my turn to shake my head, reaching out to touch his face one more time and the urge to kiss him took my breath away. It was a feeling so strong and all-consuming I had to summon up every ounce of strength inside of me to resist. If I kissed him I'd change my mind, I knew that. If I kissed him it would change everything, and I couldn't afford for that to happen. I'd seen the truth and it wasn't what either of us needed.

'I have to go, Adam.'

He tried to pull me to him, but I was too quick, moving away before he had a chance to get his arm around me. 'Lana, darling, I can't… I need you. Just as you are. I want *you*.'

'No,' I whispered. 'No, Adam. You want the crazy sex and the bad girl in bed, because you like that now. That side of things, you're okay with. But outside – out there, in the real world, you want the woman I just can't be anymore and I'm not willing to split myself in two for you – to be your bad-girl fantasy in the bedroom and the perfect wife the rest of the time. I just want to be me. *All* of the time. And you can't handle that; I saw it in your eyes.' He was the quicker one this time, gently grabbing my wrist as I reached for the suitcase. 'Don't do this, Lana. Please. We can talk about it… I just don't want you to go. I can't let you go.'

I laid a hand on his cheek, lightly stroking his skin, that overwhelming, heartbreaking need to kiss him still burning away inside me. 'I'm sorry, baby. I'm so, so sorry it's come to this because I still love you, so much…'

'Then why are you going?'

'You know why, Adam. You *know* why.'

'Jesus…' he whispered, throwing his head back, his hand once more lying over mine, holding it tight. 'I thought we could do this. I really thought we could do this.'

I took a deep breath, exhaling slowly, pulling that strength I needed to the forefront before I let go of his hand, stepping back for the last time. 'Look after yourself, Adam. Okay?'

'Lana…'

I looked at him, knowing that his face would be etched in my mind forever now. Those ice-blue eyes of his, so sad and tired, would always be with me. The man I loved. The man I could never have. Unless I was willing to lose *me*.

'I love you, sweetheart. Don't ever forget that. I love you.'

281

I managed a small smile, dragging the case off the bed. 'You're better off without me, Adam.'

And I was better off without him. I was. I had to be.

33

Wrapping the fluffy white robe around myself I walked over to the window. From my hotel room at The Bellagio I could see Las Vegas stretching out before me, and if I looked down I had a near-perfect view of the fountain show below. I'd watched about half a dozen of those shows last night, just after I'd arrived here. Back to a place I saw as my escape. I'd found them almost therapeutic, the jets of water rushing up towards the Vegas skyline in rhythm to the music, washing away everything I didn't want to think about. But it was pointless trying to pretend I was over him. I wasn't. I just had to deal with the fact that he couldn't be in my life. Not if this was the life I wanted.

I continued to stare out of the window, hugging the robe tighter around me. Across the road I could see the Paris Hotel, with its model of the Eiffel Tower out front flanked by the Aladdin Resort and Casino on one side and Bally's on the other. While out in the distance I could just make out the mountains that always reminded you that this was a town in the middle of the desert. I think that was what I loved about it the most. Not just the feel of the place, but the fact it was, to all intents and purposes, out in the middle of nowhere. And that's exactly where I wanted to be right now.

In the middle of nowhere. Just for a little while. Until I finally decided what was happening in my ridiculously mixed-up life.

The sound of my phone ringing made me jump slightly, and I swung around, walking slowly over to the bedside table, looking down at the caller ID. Adam had tried to get in touch countless times over the past few weeks, but I just wasn't ready to speak to him yet. I wanted to get used to the idea that he really was out of my life this time before I tried to prove to myself I was over him. But it wasn't him calling. It was Finn, and I smiled as I sat down on the bed to answer the call.

'Hey.'

'Hey back, beautiful. You get there okay?'

'Yeah. No problem. Finn, look, I'm sorry for messing you around…'

'Shut it, Saunders. No apologising, alright? You haven't messed me, or anyone else, around. You take as much time as you need, and we'll just pick up where we left off as soon as you're back home. Okay? Your tattoo gun ain't going nowhere, baby.'

'I love you, Finn.'

'Yeah. Right back at ya, sis. Anyway, how you feeling? You alright out there on your own?'

'I'm fine. It's actually quite nice, you know? To really have some time to myself. I think it's what I need – to get away from everything, just for a few days.'

'Well, you know where I am if you need me. You call me any time, you hear? And forget about the time difference. I don't care if it's stupid-o'clock. If you need me, you call me. You got that?'

I couldn't help smiling, absentmindedly fiddling with the hem of my robe. 'Yeah. I got it.'

'What you gonna do today, then?'

'Thought I might just have a wander around, check out some of the hotels I didn't get to see last time I was here. Maybe spend the afternoon by the pool.'

'It's alright for some,' he sniffed, but I knew he was just messing.

A part of me couldn't help but wish he was with me, though. I missed him and I did need him, probably now more than ever. But I really had to learn to stop leaning on him quite so much, because I knew that's exactly what I'd been doing this past year. Over these past few weeks, it was Finn I'd run to when I'd walked out on Adam a second time. It was him who'd sat with me, night after night, while I'd cried and drank myself into oblivion in the hope it would make me feel better. It hadn't, which meant he'd had to deal with the hangovers, too. It was Finn who'd encouraged me to take a bit of time out, to get my head together. Finn who'd encouraged me to think really hard about what it was I wanted. What I needed. And I loved him so much for all of that. For going through all this crap with me, again.

'I'm hard work, aren't I?' I sighed, closing my eyes for a second or two. It was a rhetorical question, of course. I was *bloody* hard work, I already knew that.

'You're a full-time job, beautiful. But, do you know what? My life was kind of dull before you crash-landed back into it. I'd be bored if you weren't around, and I mean that, kiddo.'

Now I *really* wished he was here. 'I love you loads, Finn Black.'

'Love you back, sis. You take care, you hear? And remember, any time.'

'I know. I'll speak to you soon.'

'Hang on…Listen, Lana…'

'Yeah?'

He paused for a couple of beats, and I frowned as I waited for him to say something. 'Just… stay safe. Okay?'

My frown deepened. Was that really what he'd meant to say? 'Finn? Is everything alright over there?'

'Everything's fine,' he sighed, but I still wasn't convinced. I wasn't going to push it, though. If he really wanted to say something, he'd say it, eventually. 'You go have a good day. Call me later.'

I hung up, staring down at my phone for a few seconds before I finally pulled myself together, standing up and walking into the bathroom. It was time to get ready to face my first full day in Las Vegas. Alone. Just the way I wanted it? No. But it was the way I needed it to be.

The Strip was as busy as ever, teeming with tourists all wandering around in the sunshine, many of them clutching drinks to help with the heat as they took in the sights, merging with the many people milling about advertising the various club nights and shows that were going on in town. The atmosphere was heady and vibrant, and just being out there was good for my soul. It was making me feel like I really could do this. I could finally make that move forward, without Adam. I was here, after all, wasn't I? In Las Vegas, alone, something I would never have dreamt of doing even just a few months ago. I didn't think I had it in me, but it was slowly becoming obvious that I could do anything, if I really wanted to.

Heading out towards the MGM Grand, just a short walk along the Strip from my hotel, I arrived at The Harley Davidson Café, a place I'd visited on more than a few occasions during my recent trip to Vegas. I'd been here with both Eddie and Finn. But not with Adam. I hadn't thought it was his kind of place, but I loved it. The vibe was cool, the food was great and the people were friendly. So I had no qualms about sitting in there on my own with a burger and a beer and all the time in the world to think.

I found a table at the side of the café, gave my order, had a short chat with a couple of staff members who recognised me from my last visit, then sat back and waited for my food and drink to arrive. It was actually nice being on my own, having time to finally think about things properly without someone else being there to, whether they meant to or not, cloud my judgement. I felt free again. My head was slowly beginning to clear and that was exactly what I needed to happen. It was exactly why I'd come back here.

Smiling to myself I looked up, taking in the huge motorcycles suspended from the ceiling, the giant American flag hanging on the wall and the many TV screens dotted around the place. The whole café was buzzing and even though it was a pretty big place, it felt relaxed. That easy-going atmosphere was something I loved. It calmed me, almost instantly. I actually felt at home here, amongst the bikers and the tourists. I was going to be a regular over the next few days, that was a given.

I flicked through a magazine I'd bought at the mini-mart next door as I ate my lunch, enjoying the solitude. I was alone in a crowd but that suited me just fine right now. My world was slowly starting to make sense again and maybe it was strange to some people, that I'd had to come all this way in order for that to happen, but something had pulled me back here. Something had made me come back to Vegas and I hadn't ignored it. I'd acted on it and now I was here, it felt like the right thing to have done. Distance and space was everything.

Pushing my plate away I leant over to slip the magazine into my bag, feeling wonderfully refreshed and ready for an afternoon lying by the pool, listening to some music and chilling out. There was no harm in topping up the tan while I had the chance.

'Anyone sitting here?'

My head shot up as I heard his voice, my heart almost stopping in my chest as I saw him standing there. Because he wasn't someone I'd expected to see. Not here. Not now.

'I… No.' It was all I could get out. No other words were forthcoming.

Eddie pulled out the chair and sat down opposite me, leaning forward and clasping his hands together on the table in front of him.

'What are you doing here, Lana?'

Oh, God, the way he said my name – was that ever going to stop making my stomach flip over like that? 'I could ask you the same question. I thought you were in Los Angeles now.'

'I'm in Vegas for Nate and Kaley's wedding. They got hitched last night, in one of those little white wedding chapels they have here in town. Didn't want a big fuss, just a few club members – and me.'

'Things okay with you guys?'

Eddie smiled a small smile, his eyes dipping for just a second before he looked back up at me. 'Aye. Nate's a good friend, and we kind of need each other, you know, whether I'm a part of the club or not. And anyway, I still hold a stake in the garage the MC owns. We were never gonna lose touch. It's just – it's nice to not have it all on my doorstep anymore. I'm an old-school biker, remember? I like the freedom being out there on my own can give me. I never was one for worrying about anyone else. Takes enough energy to look after myself most days.'

I couldn't help smiling too. Company was the last thing I'd wanted; the last thing I'd needed. But seeing Eddie again… I just had to make sure he didn't kick up any unwanted confusion. I was done with all that now. I was trying to move on, from everything.

'How did you know I was in Vegas?' I asked, my eyes fixed on his. He looked the same as I remembered, but then, it hadn't been all that long ago since I'd last seen him. 'I mean, surely you bumping into me like this, it can't just be coincidence. That would be too weird.'

'A friend of mine saw you come in here. He didn't know I was in town when he dropped me the text, of course, but seeing as I was… I hadn't intended to travel back to LA until tomorrow anyway, so, I thought I'd come see how you are.'

'I'm fine.'

'Adam with you?'

It was my turn to look down, my eyes going straight to my left hand, and that third finger that had worn the beautiful black diamond engagement ring Adam had given me just a few short weeks ago for all of a few minutes. Yeah. That memory still had the ability to make my heart ache. Just a tiny stab of pain, but I could still feel it. That was all I was letting through, though. Just that one, tiny stab. 'It didn't work out,' I said, determined to keep my voice steady.

Eddie raised an eyebrow, but he said nothing. Even though I

could see he wanted to ask why.

'You were right. In a way,' I continued, deciding to answer his silent question. Even though I didn't really think he needed to know any of this.

'I was?'

'It was never gonna work. Me and Adam. We're too different. I mean, he tried, and maybe *I* could've tried harder but...' I shrugged, not really wanting to get into this now. It was almost undoing everything I'd managed to achieve since arriving here. 'I've changed too much,' I said, my eyes back on Eddie's. 'And I don't think it's fair of me to ask Adam to change, too. Not if he doesn't want to.'

'And he *doesn't* want to? Even if it means losing you?'

'I don't think he has it in him to change, Eddie, so, no. I don't think it *is* what he wants. And if he can't feel that, if he really *doesn't* want to change, then... then I can't make him. It isn't fair.'

He held my gaze for a few, long seconds, and I didn't waver once. 'You still love him though, huh?'

'I came here to sort my head out, Eddie, and this isn't helping.'

'I know what would.'

'Come on, then. Surprise me.'

'No surprise, darlin'. Just climb on the back of my Harley and I'll take you some place I can guarantee will clear that pretty head of yours of any crap you want rid of. You won't get it any clearer any place else.'

I sighed, probably a touch heavier than I'd meant it to come out. But I wasn't sure I needed this. I'd been getting used to the time on my own. Things were starting to fall into place, but now *he* was here...

'What do you say, Lana? You up for a ride? For old time's sake?'

I could quite easily say no, get up, and leave him to it, head back to the hotel for that afternoon by the pool I'd originally had planned. But the idea of being back out there, riding his Harley, out on the open road, it was a draw too strong to ignore. More fool me...

34

We'd done this ride before, the thirteen-mile loop around Red Rock Canyon, but it never failed to hit me, the undeniably striking views that surrounded us as Eddie rode his black-and-silver Harley along the quiet roads. It was breathtaking, the colours that seemed to sink into the desert cliffs – the reds and the oranges merging with the creams and browns of the dusty interior they sat in. It was like being in a different world all of a sudden. Nothing like the bright lights and brashness of the Vegas Strip. It was stunning. It had been one of my favourite rides from the second Eddie had brought me here and somehow, it felt like I needed to be back. There was something almost spiritual about this place, a pull coming from so deep within it shook me slightly.

Eddie swung the bike around, killing the engine, the tyres kicking up dust as it came to a halt. Pulling off his helmet he turned his head to look at me. 'You okay?'

I pulled off my own helmet, shaking out my hair. 'Yeah. I'm fine.'

He climbed off the bike, laying his helmet down on the seat, shoving his hands in his pockets as he leant back. 'You still no closer to making friends with fate?'

I swung my leg over so I was sitting sideways on the seat, my hands clasped between my knees. 'I think you already know the answer to that one.'

He stared out ahead of him, and I did the same, taking in the tranquil surroundings, the red-tinged cliffs in the distance, the cobalt-blue sky that was spotted with just a smattering of tiny clouds; the masses of cacti and desert plants that spread out before us in the clay-coloured, dusty-dry ground. The only noise I could hear was the sound of the desert.

'So, you don't think you came back here for a reason?' He was still staring straight out ahead of him and I turned my head to look at him, unable to take my eyes off him. I didn't want to.

'I told you why I'm back here.'

His eyes met mine. 'And you think that's the only reason you're here?'

'Yes, I do. Eddie, I really don't want to go down that route, okay? You may think it's some kind of weird coincidence that both you and I happen to be back in Vegas at exactly the same time but, that's all it is – a coincidence. And I'm not about to start reading anything more into that.'

He shrugged, turning right around to face me. 'Well, whatever it was that brought us back here, maybe we shouldn't completely disregard what it might be trying to tell us.'

'And what *is* it trying to tell us, exactly?'

He said nothing for a few seconds, just let his eyes bore deeper into mine. 'That you and me – maybe we're unfinished business. Because I still think we are.'

I climbed off the bike, shaking my head as I walked away, grabbing just a few feet of space between us, but enough to make me feel slightly less claustrophobic. 'Don't, Eddie. Please.'

I kept my eyes on him as he walked over to me, tilting my chin up with his thumb and forefinger, making me look right at him. 'You have *your* opinions, Lana...'

He was saying my name again. He was saying my name...

'... and I have mine.'

291

'I've just walked out on my husband, for a second time.'

'Ex-husband. He's your ex-husband, remember?'

Yeah. I remembered. 'Don't, Eddie. Don't.'

'That life we talked about, Lana, we could still have it. You'd love it out in LA, and I truly believe that's where you should be...'

'With you?'

His eyes were still burning into mine. 'With me.'

I stared back at him, some invisible force rendering me unable to look away, no matter how much I wanted to. 'I didn't come here for this, Eddie.'

'Which is why you really should try and believe in fate a bit more. You didn't come here for this, but it found you anyway. Doesn't that tell you something?'

I pushed his hand away and walked back over to the bike. I didn't need this. But it was my own fault. I shouldn't have come. So much for not going backwards.

'I should be getting back to the hotel,' I said, without a great deal of conviction, running my fingers lightly over the Harley's leather seat, looking down at the black and chrome machine that had brought us here. So powerful. So beautiful.

'Why? You got somewhere you need to be?'

I looked at him standing there, all biker-hot and strikingly sexy with that messed-up hair and those dark, almost dangerous, eyes. 'Yeah. Away from here. Away from you. When I said I didn't need this, Eddie, I meant it.'

He walked over to me, not stopping until he was right there in front of me, so close I could feel the heat of his body. 'You sure about that?'

I stared up at him, laughing quietly. 'I've made my mind up, Eddie, and I can't...' It was all I could get out before his mouth was on mine, kissing me in that wonderfully deep and dirty way he'd always used to kiss me. And, despite myself, I gave in, for a few, weak seconds. I gave in to his touch, to the feel of his body against mine, and those few, weak seconds grew into longer, weaker minutes because now he was kissing me, now he was this close to me again, every memory of every time we'd had hot, heavy sex came flooding back, swamping me, engulfing me in a blanket of emotions I was quite willing to push aside and ignore, just so I could feel him fuck me one more time.

'Remember the sun beating down on your naked skin,' he murmured, his mouth resting gently against the side of my neck. 'Remember the breeze cooling you down because, baby, we were so hot together.'

'You pushed me away,' I breathed, shrugging off my jacket, hearing it fall to the ground with a light thud.

'I wasn't in a good place, Lana.' He cupped my cheek in the palm of his hand, his eyes burning into mine. 'I hadn't dealt with my demons. I'd let them take over, allowed them to guide me, make me think I didn't need everything I really wanted…'

I took his hand, slowly shaking my head. 'This isn't fair on you, Eddie. Because I'm the one not in a good place now. And if we… if we do this… it isn't fair on you.'

His mouth lowered down onto mine again, and I just melted in his arms, until I forced myself to push those memories aside, to step away from him.

'Take me back to the hotel, Eddie. Please.'

He held my gaze for a few more beats, and the intensity in his eyes was so strong I felt a red-hot shiver physically shake my body.

'No,' he whispered, shaking his head. 'No, Lana. I'm not gonna do that.'

His fingers caressed my neck– so lightly he was barely touching me – tilting my head to one side as his mouth touched my skin, sucking the fight out of me, destroying any last remnants of strength I might have had left.

'We're gonna do this, darlin'.'

Yeah. We were. And I was going to love every single, wrong second of it. But how *could* it be wrong? I wasn't with Adam anymore. I wasn't with anyone. So this wasn't wrong. It was just something I wanted to do. With a man I hadn't really managed to push to the back of my mind just yet

He loosened my jeans, sliding his hands down over my hips, my thighs, pushing them down, and I wasn't fighting it now. I was running with it.

'Sit down,' he whispered, and I did as I was told, sitting down on the bike, leaning back slightly as he pulled off my jeans, reaching back up to remove my knickers, and I closed my eyes, my fingers gripping the leather seat. I felt almost detached from the situation, as though I was letting it happen, allowing him to do this, but I wasn't totally involved.

'Once more on a Harley, darlin'. That's all this biker needs.'

I opened my eyes as he pulled me up, into his arms, his mouth crashing back onto mine with a force verging on violent, yet beautiful in its harshness. Raising my arms up above my head he freed me of my t-shirt, the touch of his hands on my naked breasts drawing a long, deep moan from me. I ached for this man now, for *sex* with this man. I wanted him in the worst way, and I just didn't care.

He straddled the bike, pulling me down opposite him, our eyes locked together, and the anticipation I felt was like nothing I'd experienced before. It was almost painful, and I welcomed it. Craved it. Needed it.

Pushing my thighs apart he freed himself, pulling me onto him, pushing into me before I had a chance to set the breath caught in my throat free and I threw my head back, crying out as loud as I could, all the pent-up frustration rushing forward, escaping in the most beautiful of ways. I wrapped my legs around him, his hands on my hips keeping me steady as his thrusts speeded up, the force of them building steadily, growing stronger, until his cries merged with mine. He was flooding into me, I could feel him, filling me up with every fantasy he'd created inside my head, and I clung onto him, closing my eyes, letting those last few seconds of peace and calm wash over me.

'Lie back,' he whispered, gently lowering me down. 'And keep those beautiful legs wide open, darlin'.'

The fantasy was still ongoing, and I was fine with that. I wasn't sure I was ready to let go of it just yet and as I felt his mouth touch me, his tongue pushing me towards an all-consuming second climax, I let go of everything except this moment. I even let myself, for one brief second, wonder if fate really had played a part in what was happening here. But then I felt his mouth trail lightly up my stomach, his fingers taking the place of his tongue as they pushed inside me and I groaned quietly, opening my legs as wide as I could as he touched me so deep inside. So deep...

Arching my back, I felt him give one last push, his breath warm on my skin as he literally pulled that climax out of me, my body shuddering with the force of it all, the most incredible feeling. I was aware of my cries filling the silence around us, of me calling out his name, of his mouth back on mine, kissing me back to reality as those final few tingles eased their way over my skin. I wasn't sure I wanted to leave here now. Wasn't sure I was up for going back to that reality.

'You still haven't found what you're looking for, have you, Lana?' he whispered, pulling me up, his hands still holding onto my hips.

I didn't answer him. Because he was probably right.

'Do you even *know* what you're looking for?'

It was like a switch had been flicked, and all of a sudden I wished I hadn't come here. Wished I'd been strong enough to say no to him. Wished I'd been strong enough to handle a whole lot of other things way better than I had done. 'I know exactly what I'm looking for,' I said quietly, my eyes once more meeting his. 'I'm just not sure I can have it.'

'Then look for something you *can* have.'

'It's not that easy,' I whispered, holding his gaze, feeling a million different emotions all clashing together inside of me that were painful and hard, but also exciting and confusing.

He took my hand, his thumb gently stroking my knuckles

and I looked down, watching its every move, its slow, rhythmic motion creating an almost calming effect. 'My life's still changing, too, Lana.'

I continued to stare down at his hand in mine, not really knowing what to say. It was like my brain had just stopped working.

'I know I go on about freedom and not wanting to have anyone else to think about but…'

'Eddie, please. Don't do this.' I didn't want him to spoil what had just happened here by talking too much. By making both of us face up to things neither of us were ready to face.

'Together we could take on the world, baby.'

I shook my head, because even though I'd just had sex with this crazy, wonderful man, I still couldn't get past Adam. I couldn't get past the man I really wanted, the man I loved; the man I couldn't have because I was unwilling to be that woman he needed. So, in reality, how much did I really love him? If I couldn't do that, couldn't make that sacrifice to be with the man I wanted, how much did I really love him?

'If you need to forget, then going back home isn't gonna help, darlin'. It isn't. It's gonna make things worse, deepen that pain. You need to harden your heart, Lana. Believe me, it helps.'

Maybe he was right. Going back home wasn't going to help me forget. But neither was staying here. Nothing was going to make me forget. I just needed to learn how to live with it. 'You once asked me if I was going to run away from everything that needed dealing with.' I raised my gaze, my eyes locking with his. 'If I go with you to LA, I'd be running away from something I really need to deal with. Once and for all.'

'Let me help you, Lana.'

'Are you listening to what I'm saying, Eddie? I think I've probably spent most of my life running away from, and refusing to deal with, things that have either scared me, or things I just wasn't strong enough to face up to. And I can't do that anymore. Taking the easy route isn't an option now. I got a lot of things wrong, I messed up, I hurt people – it's time to start changing all of that. Yes, I want to live my life the way *I* want to live it, but…'

'Forget that. Forget all of it. Stop letting it get in the way, stop putting it first, stop letting it drag you down, Lana, come on. You want to live your life the way *you* want to live it? Then just start doing it, darlin'. Just start living.'

My eyes met his again, and I felt the strongest jolt of something shoot right through me. I didn't know what it was, I couldn't explain the feeling in a way anyone would understand, I just knew it had happened. And as his hand rested against my cheek, his touch warm and comforting, his words dancing around inside my head, I closed my eyes and let him kiss me. I let him kiss me until the sky grew dark and nothing else in the world mattered anymore. I let him kiss me…

35

'Shouldn't you be getting back to LA?' I asked, leaning against the wall and folding my arms, but I was finding it hard to keep the smile off my face. 'I mean, you were supposed to leave two days ago, but you're still hanging around here.'

'I'm a man on a mission, darlin'.' He moved closer, his hand resting lightly on my hip, his mouth almost touching mine.

'And what mission would that be, huh?'

He laughed quietly, tucking a strand of hair behind my ear. 'I think you know what I'm talking about, Lana.'

I knew exactly what he was talking about. I was just trying to sidestep the subject. We'd spent the past two days together; the past two nights. We'd gone out on the Harley during the day, spent the evenings in biker bars and clubs both on and off the Strip, and he'd stayed with me, in my room, here at the hotel. We'd slept together in the literal sense of the word – there'd been no more sex. Despite my body aching for him, but I knew it wasn't really *him* I ached for. I'd ached for the sex, because what Eddie could give me, it was a release, an escape; an opportunity for me to be able to push everything aside and forget. So I didn't have to deal with what I was really feeling. But I couldn't do that forever. So this – what was happening here, it wasn't fair on Eddie. Which was why I was calling time on it now. I had to. I needed to start putting the pieces of my life back together and try and find a fit that worked.

'Eddie, I...'

His mouth gently touched mine, pulling me under for a kiss that needed to be the last. It was too much now. Things had gone far enough.

'Kissing you is, you know, something I never tire of doing, but...' His dark eyes looked right into mine. 'Baby, I need to...'

I shook my head, running my fingers lightly over his beard. 'No, Eddie. This stops now. It stops, now.'

'Lana,' he groaned, leaning back against the wall, his hands shoved deep in his pockets. 'Come on, darlin'. What more do I have to do here?'

You have to be Adam, I thought. And then silently cursed myself for even thinking that. If I was going to compare every man to my ex-husband I was never going to be able to move on. 'You don't have to do anything,' I replied, stepping back from him and pulling my hair into a ponytail. 'I just think it's time we stopped confusing things now. We've blurred too many lines, Eddie, and it really isn't fair on you. On either of us.'

He raised an eyebrow, walking over to me, sliding an arm around my waist, pulling me back against him. And I didn't stop him, even though I should have done. I was supposed to be walking away from this. 'Have I helped, Lana?'

'Helped?' I asked, playing with the collar of his leather jacket.

'Get your head straight.'

I wasn't sure if that would ever happen now. And then I silently cursed myself again for throwing more negativity in the way, creating obstacles where there didn't need to be any. Obstacles only I could remove. If I wanted to. I just wasn't sure I was ready to shift them yet. Having them there, letting those memories remain, it was like a comfort blanket I couldn't throw away. 'Yeah. Yeah, I think you have, actually.' As I said the words, I finally started to believe them. This man had given me so much, and I hadn't even realised *how* much, until now. He'd shown me a world I never would have thought I could inhabit. He'd given me confidence and a sense of adventure I hadn't thought it was possible for someone like me to have. He'd shown me the kind of woman I could be; the kind of woman I *wanted* to be. He'd taught me that all I needed to do was reach out and take the things I wanted because I could do anything. I could do *anything*.

'But you're still not coming with me to LA.' It wasn't a question. Because he already knew the answer.

I shook my head, my fingers still holding onto his jacket collar. 'I can't, Eddie. I just can't.'

'You can, darlin'. You just have to take that leap of faith.'

'You're making things sound easy again.'

'The only reason everything feels so hard, Lana, is because you're making it that way.'

'Newcastle is my home, Eddie, and I guess I'm just not ready to leave it.'

He looked at me, his thumb lightly stroking my cheek, those dark eyes of his staring deep into mine. 'You're not ready to leave *him*.'

'That isn't what I said.' But it was what I'd meant, and that in itself was screaming so many things at me the noise inside my head was almost deafening. 'I have a life back home.' I pulled his hand away from my cheek and stepped back from him. 'There's Finn, and Black Ink and I love it there, Eddie. I'm learning a new skill that I'm actually bloody good at. I have friends I adore, so, I don't need to stay here to forget the past. I just need to throw myself into that life I want to start living. Because the past year has really been nothing more than a practice session.'

'And what about me? Don't you need me?'

I reached out to touch his face, running my fingertips over his cheek. I needed him more than he would ever know. Just not in a way that was good for either of us. 'You're a part of my life I can't get rid of now.'

He smiled, and I felt my stomach dip – a reminder of everything I'd once felt for him. Still felt. 'It's called fate, darlin'.'

I threw my head back and sighed, laughing quietly as I pulled away from him. 'Whatever. I just know I like having you around.'

'But not enough for me to be around permanently, huh?'

I looked at him, remembering the day I'd met this man, the way he'd made me feel, the fun we'd had; the promises he'd made me that I had no doubt he could deliver. And all I had to do was, as he'd already said, take that leap of faith. It wouldn't even be a leap into a world I was unfamiliar with – I already knew how Eddie worked, what made him tick. I knew how he liked to live his life, because it was how I wanted to live mine. So why couldn't I just let myself see what would happen if we tried living that life together? What did I have to lose? 'There's so much going on in my head right now, Eddie and this is something I didn't expect. I didn't expect *you* to be here and it's thrown me slightly.'

'These past few days, Lana. They've been a reminder of how good we are together. We fit each other, darlin', we just feel right.'

These past few days *had* been good, I couldn't deny that. Spending every day together, hanging out in Vegas, riding his Harley, talking about everything from bikes to the state of the world, and how we could change ours. It had been almost perfect. At times I'd forgotten I was here to get my head straight, because at times it didn't feel as though there was even a problem. I had Eddie and he was proving to be a beautiful source of solace – the kind of escapism I'd needed. But he wanted to move things forward and I just couldn't do that.

'I can't tell you what you want to hear, Eddie.'

'I don't want promises, Lana. I don't believe in forever.'

But *I* was starting to. I wanted a forever and I was beginning to believe I was the only person capable of making it happen.

I didn't say anything as I walked over to the window, looking out over another bright and sunny Las Vegas day. I felt him come up behind me, felt his fingers gently brush my hair back off my neck before his mouth lightly kissed it, and that still sent shivers coursing up and down my spine. The touch of him still made my skin break out in goose bumps and my heart race that little bit faster. But I didn't love him. I couldn't love him. Because of those obstacles I was so unwilling to remove, I just couldn't go there. So all of this, it really wasn't fair on him.

'I'll call you later,' he whispered, his breath warm on my neck, his hand giving my waist a gentle squeeze before he let me go.

I couldn't turn around. I didn't want to. So I waited until I heard the door close behind him before I moved away from the window, suddenly at a loss as to what to do next. My head had started to spin and I had to sit down on the edge of the bed before my knees gave way. Staring down, I watched as my fingers ran all the way from my wrist to my shoulder, trailing lightly over the bright colours and shading of the sleeve tattoo that stretched all the way up my arm; every single one of those images was a symbol of the new life I'd so desperately craved, and yet now they felt like nothing more than a painful reminder of everything I couldn't have.

Pulling off my top and wriggling out of my jeans I stripped naked and went into the bathroom, staring at my reflection in the mirror. There was no denying the change in me over the past year. I seemed younger, almost. My body was certainly different, more toned and lithe, but the curves were still very much there, the tattoos that now adorned it perfect decoration, adding colour and spectacle to something I'd once thought of as ordinary and dull. That's how I'd used to think of myself in the end, once the sparkle and light had gone out of my and Adam's marriage and things had settled into that routine and rut that had kick-started this whole journey. I'd thought of myself as ordinary and dull. Yet now, as I looked at this completely different person to the one I'd once been, it was like I was looking at someone on a TV screen.

Like that person in front of me was a character, nothing to do with me. I was still that same ordinary, dull person looking in on the woman I really wanted to be, but had lost the strength to become. I'd lost Adam in the beginning because I'd been too weak to fight and I'd lost him a second time because I'd fought too hard. So hard I'd ruined any chance I ever had of being in his life again. That's what hurt the most. My only regret: I couldn't have it all.

I switched on the shower. Hoping to wash away all the negativity? It was worth a try. Give me time to think about everything Eddie had said? It wouldn't hurt, and I was glad, in a way, that Finn wasn't here now because this was something I needed to work out on my own – take a leap of faith and go with Eddie to LA, try and start that completely new life I'd tried to start once before, or go back home to Newcastle and try to get on with a life I loved there. Without Eddie. Without Adam. Those were the choices I had.

Quickly drying myself, I slipped on a robe and pulled my hair out of its ponytail, tipping my head upside down and running my hands through it, shaking it out before flipping my head back. I felt better after that. It was probably all psychological, of course, but what did that matter? I felt better.

Wandering back out into the bedroom I flicked on the TV, leaving it on a channel showing a familiar sitcom while I sat at the dressing table and applied a little mascara, a touch of pink blusher, some pale lip gloss. It was all I needed to complete my short but therapeutic make-over, and I smiled as I stared at my reflection now. Yeah. I could do this. Eddie was right in one respect – I had to let go of everything that was dragging me down, otherwise I was never going to be able to move forward. And I wanted to move forward because, even though I'd thought I had, I really hadn't moved very far at all. I'd turned forty now. It was time to stop playing at life and start living it.

A knock at the door startled me slightly because I'd been so deep in thought and for a second or two I just sat there, not

303

moving. I didn't want any intrusion right now. I was beginning to like my own company. For the first time in days I was actually able to think straight

But then I heard him. Heard his voice. And suddenly everything changed…

36

My world once more shifted on its already unstable axis and I closed my eyes, hoping it had all been a dream because I really, really didn't need this – the pain it could cause. What I needed was for him to go away. I wasn't sure I could bear the torment of raking over a situation neither of us could change, no matter how much we wanted to. That was cruel and I didn't think I could take it. I couldn't.

'Lana? Are you in there?'

I squeezed my eyes tight shut again, hoping that would send him away, make him disappear. But that was wishful thinking and this was a situation I had to face, whether I wanted to or not. *No more running away, Lana, remember?*

Getting up, I made my way slowly to the door, preparing myself for the flood of feelings I knew I was going to experience as soon as I opened it. They didn't hold back, washing over me like the strongest of waves, hitting me like the hardest of punches, taking my breath away the second his ice-blue eyes met mine.

I was gone. It was like the rest of the world had just evaporated around us as he kicked the door shut behind him, pushing me back against the wall without either of us saying a word, his hands already pulling the robe away from my body and I let it fall. The only thing I wanted to feel against my skin now was him. It was crazy; like some weird, erotic dream straight from my subconscious, because what was happening here, it was everything I'd imagined and wanted and hoped for with this man since the second I'd left him behind, but I'd never once thought it would happen. It had all taken place within my perfect, imaginary world and now, all of a sudden, it was playing out for real.

Every pent-up emotion, every held-back feeling was tearing out of me in a rush so strong it was frightening, because all of this was only a prelude to more pain and heartache when it was over. But I needed him so much. I wanted him so badly. So I didn't care about the pain and the hurt that would follow. I pushed it aside, wrapped my legs tight around him and let him take me hard, his body invading mine with a beautiful force that shook me to the very core. I felt his presence in every nerve ending, every fibre of my being was affected and I craved every thrust, every crash of his hips against mine. And when he came he let forth a cry so brutal I felt my entire body shake with the weight of frustration spilling out of him but, oh, that feeling of knowing he was inside me. Knowing he was there, and he was real, I could feel he was real.

I buried my face in his hair, my fingers gripping the material of his shirt as everything started to slow down and that blanket of reality began to creep over us. A moment I'd dreamt of was now being replaced by a moment I'd dreaded and I could already feel my heart start to pound twice as fast as it already had been, my chest tightening as I prepared for that cold, unwanted reality to hit.

'I had to come here,' he gasped, his breathing still heavy and ragged as he gently put me down. 'I had to see you, Lana. I had to…' He briefly bowed his head before looking back up at me. 'Everything I've done, I had to do it because I love you. Do you understand that? Everything I've done is because I love you. And because I'm fighting for it this time. I'm fighting fucking hard.'

I cocked my head slightly as I looked at him, searching his face for some kind of explanation because, if I was being completely honest, I was having trouble believing this wasn't some kind of weird and beautiful dream. He was here, but I still couldn't quite get my head around it. It didn't sound like him talking. Everything felt just a little too surreal.

'What have you done?' I whispered, running my fingers over his still-bearded chin. Although his beard wasn't quite as heavy as it had been when I'd last seen him, which told me he must have shaved it off at some point. But obviously not for very long. His hair was shorter than before, much shorter. It made him look tougher somehow, more edgy. Different. He really did seem different this time.

'I want us to start again, Lana. You and me…'

That blanket of reality had well and truly been thrown over me now. Had he really come all this way just to re-open old wounds? Go over old ground? Try and resolve a situation that couldn't *be* resolved?

'Adam, I…' And then I saw it. Saw that his hair wasn't the only thing that had changed. How the hell hadn't I seen it earlier? Four large letters twisted together in the most beautiful design, the black ink stark and bold as it spelled out my name on the underside of his forearm. I couldn't take my eyes off it because I couldn't quite believe it was there. 'Is that…?' I was asking an obviously rhetorical question because I could see it was real. I'd been around enough tattoos to know it was very real. And very new. Jesus, of course it was new! I'd only seen him a few weeks ago and he hadn't had it then.

'I needed you to see how committed I am, Lana. How committed I am to *you*. To us.'

'Did Finn…? Did *he* do this?'

Adam looked down at his left arm. 'He was the only one I trusted to do it.'

Finn hadn't said a thing to me about this. Hadn't mentioned seeing Adam at all. And I didn't know whether I was angry about that or not. I was too surprised, too stunned at what Adam had done to feel anything but utter confusion right now.

'Adam... Jesus. I... You hate tattoos so... so why... why do this to yourself?'

'I don't hate tattoos, Lana. I don't *hate* anything. Except the stupid, mindless crap that was tearing us apart. And I'm sick of it. Sick of the constant ache in my stomach because all I can think about is you. Sick of not being able to sleep at night because I need you there beside me. I miss you with a pain so raw it's wearing me down and I can't do it anymore. I lost you once and losing you a second time made me realise how empty and shallow I'd become. Those things I said to David... I am so sorry, darling. I am so, so sorry.'

I finally tore my eyes away from his arm to look at him, a strange feeling washing over me. One I really couldn't explain and I wasn't even sure I needed to. Just running with things seemed like a much better option right now, given how crazy and surreal everything was. 'I still don't understand...'

'When you walked out, Lana, I fell apart. I couldn't function, couldn't cope. I didn't want to. I... I tried pulling myself together, shaved off the beard, tried to go back to that man I'd been before, to see if that would help, but it all felt wrong. Nothing felt right. Everything was all jumbled up and disjointed and none of it... none of it was what I wanted. Not anymore. Then one morning, I walked into the office and I knew – I just knew I couldn't do it. It wasn't worth it. My heart wasn't in it.'

I pulled my robe back around myself and walked over to the bed, sitting down on the edge of it, looking up as he sat down beside me. 'What... what have you done, Adam?' Because he still hadn't answered that one. Oh, I could see he'd got that tattoo, that he'd cut his hair, but I was sure those things were only part of the 'everything' he was talking about.

He stared straight out ahead of him, his eyes focusing on nothing in particular. 'David's taking over the business because

I just don't want to be there now.' He turned his head to look at me, those beautiful blue eyes of his boring deep into mine. 'I want to be with *you*.'

None of this was sinking in. I was struggling to get my head around any of it.

He looked back down at his arm, tentatively touching his new ink. 'When I asked Finn to do this for me he spent about an hour quizzing me as to whether I was sure. And he... he tried to talk me out of getting your name tattooed on my arm because...' His eyes met mine again, '... because he said I needed to be certain that my feelings for you were going to be as permanent as the ink he was about to embed into my skin.'

'He should have told me what was happening. You two keeping secrets from me – I'm getting a feeling of déjà vu here.'

Adam shook his head, his gaze dipping again. 'I didn't want him to tell you. If you'd known I was coming, known what I was doing, it would have lessened the impact. It would have given you time to think about things and I didn't want that.' He looked back at me. 'I just wanted you to see how serious I am, about us. Because we're the only thing that matters, Lana. The only thing.'

'Oh, baby,' I whispered, resting my hand against his cheek, leaning over to kiss him gently, closing my eyes as his mouth moved slowly against mine. 'I love you so much, Adam.'

'I want to spend the rest of my life with you, Lana. A life I am changing because I need you more than I need business meetings and status and dinner parties that bore the crap out of me.'

Was this really my ex-husband saying those words? Or was this just some crazy, messed-up dream sent to raise my hopes to ridiculous levels, only to have them crash down around me in the cruellest of ways the second I woke up.

'Finn and I, we're going into business together.'

Okay. I'd heard those words come out of his mouth, but now I really was beginning to think I was about to wake up any second now. 'I'm... *sorry*? You and Finn? Going into business –*together*?'

He nodded. 'We got talking, while he did this…' He indicated his tattoo. 'We're going to set up another studio, in Durham, with a third one, in time, somewhere near the coast. He's getting snowed under at the Newcastle studio, and there isn't enough room to accommodate any more staff there, so opening up more studios is the only feasible option. And it's something Finn's wanted to do for a while, apparently. Expand the business. Have a chain of Black Inks right across the north-east. But he doesn't have the capital he needs to be able to do that just yet, so, that's where I come in. We've already checked out the perfect site in the centre of Durham, in an ideal location…'

'Whoa, okay. Slow down there.' I stood up, going over to the window, taking a minute to look out over a town that seemed to make people crazy the second they set foot in it. 'You're investing money in Finn's tattoo business?' I turned back around, barely able to believe I'd just uttered those words.

'I'm investing in his business, yes,' Adam replied, walking slowly over to me. 'Bobby's going to run the Durham studio, and, as for the next one we open – well, both Finn and I think that should be yours, Lana.'

I was completely speechless now. This couldn't be happening, surely. I mean, I was all for spontaneity, but this – this was crazy. This was everything being turned upside down in a way I could never have envisaged. 'Me?' My voice was little more than a whisper. 'But…'

'Once you're qualified, of course.'

I just stared at him. I was still too stunned to do anything else.

'You are being trained by one of the country's most acclaimed tattoo artists, Lana. And I know that, to you, Finn Black is just your brother, but, he really is exceptional at what he does. I know that now. I've spoken to people, looked at his work, seen how he runs that studio back home and – he's a very talented, very organised young man with a reputation I'm not even sure *he's* fully aware of. But the fact you are serving your apprenticeship under him, that will mean that *your* name as a tattoo artist will attract custom. Do you understand?'

I narrowed my eyes as I stared at him, still trying to process all the information he was telling me. But it was like a million things were all being thrown at me, all at once. He'd been here all of five minutes and suddenly everyone's lives were in the process of being changed beyond recognition. It was hard to take in. 'I... Jesus. I can't actually think straight right now.'

'Look, we can just have sex, if you like, and then see where we go from there? You know, fuck first, talk later, if this is too much to take in.' He never spoke like that. Who was this man? Whoever he was, it wasn't the old Adam I knew, but Jesus, he was HOT!

He smiled, moving closer to me, sliding a hand under my robe, the touch of his fingers on my skin taking my breath away. Those unfamiliar gasps were back, and there was nothing I could do to stop them. I wasn't even going to bother trying.

'I'm quite happy to fuck first,' I whispered, breathlessly. His body pressing lightly against mine was making me shiver, my heart picking up a heavy, fast rhythm as his fingers brushed over my naked breasts.

I ran my fingers through his now-shorter hair, messing it up as much as I could, his head lowering for a second, his mouth briefly brushing over my breasts, first one, then the other, before he raised his head back up, smiling at me. I'd never felt a wave of love and lust so strong as he pulled me against him, his mouth crashing down onto mine. It was almost as if he'd had some sort of personality change on the way over here. He was oozing a kind of confidence he'd once reserved only for the boardroom; displaying skills he'd never let loose before as far as sex was concerned. Something seemed to have happened to Adam between me leaving him and him turning up here. Unless, like me, everything he was doing now had been there inside of him all along, just waiting for the chance to be set free. I didn't care – where it had come from or where he'd learnt it, I didn't care. He was here and that was all that mattered. *We* were all that mattered. Was my happy-ever-after finally about to happen…?

37

'Okay, so, you're handing the business over to David. But you're still involved, right?' I asked, turning onto my stomach, my arm flung over Adam's chest, his hand holding mine.

'Yes, but, from now on, I'm going to be very much a silent partner. No more business meetings, no more dinner parties or networking evenings at country hotels… You disappointed?'

I smiled, kissing him quickly. 'Devastated.'

He laughed, a sound that made my heart dance, and I was determined never to let that feeling go. Ever. I'd learnt my lesson on that score.

'Adam?'

He looked at me, his hand squeezing mine ever so gently. 'Hmm?'

'All this change… I know you said you wanted to prove to me how committed you are, to us…' I hadn't really wanted to bring this up, but it needed to be said. I needed to know. Because if there was any chance he was going to regret this, there was still time for him to pull back. The handing over of the business to David was still in the hands of lawyers, nothing had been signed yet, as was the case with him and Finn. They weren't due to start putting any wheels in motion until we got back home. Even the tattoo could be removed, if he really didn't want it. He could turn it all around if he wasn't one hundred per cent sure. And that's what I needed to know – that he was one hundred per cent sure. Because, as far as he was concerned, he was making some huge personal sacrifices and he needed to be certain, really certain, that he was doing – that he'd done – the right thing. 'I don't want you to be unhappy, Adam. Because I know…'

'Hey, come on. Listen to me. Do you know what was making me unhappy? Not having you. All the success in the world, all the money and power and business awards, they mean fuck all in reality. We let life get in the way, Lana. We *both* let that happen. We lost *us*. And finding each other… I can't lose us again, so, I am willing to do anything – *anything* – I can to make sure that never happens. I would have had any number of tattoos, darling. I would have ridden a motorbike over burning flames, grown my hair if the beard wasn't enough… anything, as long as it meant we could be together.'

'The short hair's just fine. In fact, this shorter hair of yours makes you look even sexier.' I smiled, letting go of his hand to run my fingers over his beard. 'And, please, leave the fire-related motorbike stunts alone, but, we could *get* a bike… a big bike could be fun,' a cheeky, knowing smile spread across my face, 'and as far as the tattoos are concerned…' I closed my eyes as we kissed, allowing every second of his lips touching mine to embed themselves into my brain so I didn't, couldn't, forget how he felt. How he tasted. We'd known each other for so long, been together for almost two decades, but this was all brand new to me. To him. To us. 'Feel free to have as many of those as you like. You'll hear no complaints from me.'

He returned my smile, pulling me over on top of him, his arm circling my waist. 'Finn tells me you're planning another one.'

'Yeah. My hip and thigh are feeling particularly naked. They need some decoration.'

314

'Can I watch?' he asked, pulling himself up slightly, but keeping his arm tight around me.

I straddled him, sliding a hand around the back of his neck, kissing him slowly. 'You want to watch me get inked?'

'I want to be in your world, Lana,' he whispered, lifting me up just a touch, my body instantly relaxing the second I felt him slip inside me. 'I want to see what you do, how you live, how you work. I want to see it all.'

'Oh, baby…' I arched my back, pushing down onto him, pulling him in deeper, my mouth resting lightly on his as I spoke. 'You can watch whatever you like.'

'Good. That's good.' He clung onto my hips, keeping me in position, pushing me down harder against him. 'Because I've got a whole lot more to learn now.'

'You got that right, handsome,' I breathed, closing my eyes and throwing my head back, my fingers intertwining with his on my thighs as I felt the rush already begin, that delicious tingle that, for a few brief, beautiful seconds, pushed everything else aside and let me concentrate on nothing but him. Inside me. And this time, he wasn't going anywhere.

'Hiding any more secrets from me, hmm?'

'I was only doing what he asked me to do, Lana.'

'Again. You're becoming his bitch, Finn.'

'Fuck off, Saunders,' he laughed. 'Anyway, isn't that *your* job?'

'Oh, I'm a whole different kind of bitch for that man, believe me.'

'Okay… That's enough info right there, sis. So, it's going okay, then? You and Mister CEO?'

'Except, he's not Mister CEO anymore, is he? Or he won't be in a few weeks, anyway.'

'You gonna miss the bad-girl-in-the-boardroom role play or something?'

'I'm really not going there with you, Finn.'

'And for that I'm eternally grateful.'

I paused for a second or two, looking out at the view ahead of me – of the hotels and the crowds of people all making their way along the Strip. It was just another day in Vegas. But not for me.

'He's different, Finn. Adam, I mean. He really seems different this time.'

'Different?'

'Yeah… And it's not just that he *looks* different, it's the way he's acting, too. The way he talks, the things he does now…'

'Is that not a good thing?'

'Yeah, of course it is, it's just… He said you quizzed him over his certainty about the tattoo.'

'He was asking for something to be permanently etched into his skin, Lana, and this was coming from a man with a history of dislike for ink. So I just wanted to make sure he knew what he was doing. And he was asking for a name to be tattooed onto him, which is never a good idea, and you know why. But he was adamant it was what he wanted. I just needed to know that he was certain about you and him – about your future together – before I agreed to do it for him.'

'So he must have seemed pretty certain, then? For you to have done that tattoo.'

'I wouldn't have done it otherwise, Lana. You know that.'

I leant back against the wall, looking up at the clear, blue sky as the hustle of the busy Vegas Strip carried on around me. 'We're planning a Vegas wedding, Finn.'

'What? While you're over there?'

'No. No, we're not rushing back into marriage. We're taking our time, trying to remember what it was like when we first met. There's a lot we need to get back, Finn. A lot we have to get used to, and that's going to take time.'

'You're really sure this time, sis?'

'Well, Adam landed here with a shedload of surprises, some of which I'm still not sure I've got my head completely around, but we're working it out. One day at a time. There's gonna be a lot

to sort out once we arrive back home, but, him coming here…
We've both realised we want this, more than anything. We're
gonna be just fine.'

'And this new Adam? You getting used to him?'

I smiled to myself, picking at the frayed knee of my jeans. 'He's
not *that* different, really. He still looks as hot as hell; it's his way
of thinking that's changed the most.'

'And what's happening with Scotty? He still there in Vegas?'

'Yeah. He's still here. I'm meeting him in a few minutes, actually.'

'Why?'

'To tell him Adam's back. For good this time.'

'And will this stop him from bugging you about going to Los
Angeles?'

'He's not some infatuated sixteen-year-old kid, Finn. I think
he'll get the message. Look, Eddie's been good for me. He's given
me experiences I could never have found alone, given me a taste
of something I will never forget. But he also focused my mind,
made me realise that I can't love anyone but Adam. It's as simple
as that. I liked being around Eddie and for a brief time I thought
that was gonna be enough. But it wasn't. It never will be. I need
Adam. And I can deny that all I like, claim I'm stronger than that,
that I don't really need anyone, but I do. I need Adam, and without
Eddie I'm not sure I would have realised that.'

'And you're absolutely sure this time?'

'I'm absolutely sure.'

'Then I'd better be coming with you to Vegas when you tie the
knot – again – with my future business partner. You doing the
whole Elvis thing or what?'

I laughed, suddenly feeling like a weight had been lifted from
my shoulders. 'Don't know what we're doing yet. We just know
that we want it to be fun.'

'So, when are you two coming home, then?'

'Wednesday. We thought a couple more days here wouldn't do
us any harm.'

'You not sick of the place yet?'

'I don't think I'll ever be sick of this place,' I sighed. 'Not after everything that's happened here.'

'Jesus. You going soft on me, sis?'

I laughed again, aware of a figure walking towards me now. Eddie. 'I've got to go, Finn. Eddie's here.'

'Okay. You take care, you hear? And you tell that extremely generous man of yours that I'm grateful. More grateful than he'll ever know for the help he's giving me. And I mean that. So you tell him, alright?'

'Alright. Speak to you soon… Oh, and Finn?'

'Yeah?'

'Love you.'

'Love you back, kiddo.'

I ended the call, looking down as I felt Eddie approach.

'Hey there, gorgeous.'

'Hey.'

He stopped in front of me, reaching out to tilt my face up, lightly touching my cheek, his fingers stroking my skin, and it still felt good when he touched me. But he wasn't Adam. He never would be. In one respect Eddie was everything I'd ever dreamt of, but in another he was nothing I wanted.

'Was this deliberate?' he asked, indicating the spot we were standing in. The very same spot where he'd pushed me back against the wall I was leaning against now, and kissed me like I'd never been kissed before, on that very first night out together.

I looked up into those dark, almost black, eyes of his. 'This wall holds a lot of happy memories for me.'

He smiled, and I returned it, trying to push back a completely unexpected wave of sadness.

'Adam's here.' I needed to get straight to the point. No use dragging it out. 'In Vegas. He turned up yesterday, just after you'd left…'

'I know.'

I frowned, cocking my head in question. 'You do?'

'I saw him, down in the lobby. I was on my way out of the hotel, and… I spoke to him, Lana. I told him where you were, which room you were in because… The guy has a tattoo now, kid. Your name… Jesus!' He threw back his head and let out a low groan of frustration. And I felt another wave of sadness hit. 'And he did that because he loves you so fucking much.'

I laid my hand over his, our eyes locked together. 'I'm sorry, Eddie. I thought I could walk away, you know? I thought I *had* to walk away, that me and Adam – I thought we could never be together. That we were bad for each other, but I was wrong. Everything I thought…' I broke the stare, looking at our hands still joined down by our sides. 'We wasted so much time, me and Adam, and we need to make that up.'

'He really does love you enough, huh?'

I raised my gaze again, smiling slightly. 'You have no idea.'

Eddie squeezed my hand, a faint smile on his handsome face. A face that seemed just a little tired now. 'I played this all wrong, Lana.'

'No, Eddie, you didn't. Whatever you'd done, however we'd tried to make something work between us it… it was never gonna last. Because he was always there – Adam. He was always there, and I was never really gonna let him go. I can't. I can't do it.'

He bowed his head, his fingers tightening around mine. 'When you said I was always gonna be in your life…' He looked back up, our eyes locking once more, '… did you mean that?'

'Yeah. I meant it,' I whispered, my smile a little wider now. 'Look, Eddie…'

'Just start living that life now, Lana. You hear me?'

I nodded. 'I hear you.'

Neither of us said anything for a few seconds. Neither of us felt the need. We just looked at each other, his hand still holding tightly onto mine.

'One last time, Lana. Just one last time, darlin'…'

I leant in towards him, my forehead resting against his, closing my eyes as I breathed him in – that now-familiar smell of beer and engine oil and stale cigarettes that I'd found strangely comforting for so long. 'I've got to go,' I whispered, slowly pulling away from him.

'Aye,' he sighed, letting go of my hand and stepping back from me. 'Aye, you'd better get back to him.'

'Eddie, I... thank you. What we had, it's ... it's been an adventure.'

He smiled, and I allowed my stomach one last flip, sticking my hands in the back pockets of my jeans as I started to walk away.

'Lana?'

I turned back around.

'I would have had your name tattooed on me countless times, darlin'. And I mean that.'

38

'Did he stay over?'

I turned to look at Adam. He was standing there with his hands in the pockets of his jeans, his legs slightly apart, his dark-grey shirtsleeves rolled up to the elbows, exposing his brand-new tattoo that I still had trouble believing was there. He looked so beautiful, so handsome it took my breath away. It felt as though I was looking at him for the very first time, and it was the strangest feeling. But one I never wanted to lose.

'I saw him, down in the foyer the night I arrived here. Did he tell you that? When you saw him yesterday?'

I nodded, leaning back against the sideboard, my fingers gripping the edges behind me.

'So, *had* he stayed the night? In this room? With you?'

'You know he did, Adam.'

He looked down, pushing a hand backwards and forwards through his hair. 'You slept together?'

'Adam, please…'

'I'm sorry.' He threw his head back, sighing heavily, once more pushing both hands through his hair in an almost nervous fashion. 'I didn't mean to…'

'It's a mess, Adam, we can't deny that. But me and Eddie, it's finished, baby. I promise you. We are done.'

He walked over to me, untying my robe and sliding his hands underneath, resting them on my hips as he lifted me up onto the sideboard, stepping between my open legs. 'It's none of my business anyway, darling. We weren't together, so you sleeping with him…'

'We were never over, Adam. You and me, it was never over. But that's exactly *why* I knew it was over with Eddie. Because I couldn't get past *you*.'

He smiled, pulling me forward slightly and I wrapped my legs around him, closing my eyes as he kissed me long and deep. A new kind of Adam kiss. From a new kind of Adam. 'The thought of someone else…'

'And you were a saint all the time we were apart?'

'Almost.'

'Almost?' I laughed, running my fingers over his beard, safe in the knowledge he wasn't getting rid of it now. Not without my say so, anyway. 'Oh. Little Miss Socialite wear you down a bit too much, huh?'

He couldn't help laughing, too, turning his head away for a second before his eyes locked back on mine. 'Whatever we did in the past, it doesn't matter now.'

'No,' I whispered, gently stroking his cheek. 'No, it doesn't.'

'We should be going. We've got dinner reservations and…'

I reached down, loosening his jeans, unzipping him slowly. 'We can get dinner anywhere, Adam. We're in Vegas. We can get anything we want, any time we like. New life, remember? You don't have to play by the rules anymore, baby. You don't have to stick to regimes and timetables.' I kissed him, gently at first, building up to a much deeper, harder kiss, sliding my tongue inside his mouth, loving the taste of him. 'We can do whatever we want.' I took him in my hand, my fingers lightly stroking him. 'Whenever we want.'

'Jesus, Lana…' he groaned, pulling me closer still.

'It's too late now, handsome.' I smiled, wrapping my legs back around him. 'It's way too late.'

'You're a dangerous woman, Lana Saunders,' he whispered, holding onto my hips as I leant back slightly, angling myself so I could feel every inch of him pushing inside me.

'Believe me, Adam, you haven't even scratched the surface.'

We'd managed to find the perfect spot outside The Bellagio, both of us looking up into the darkness as those famous fountains shot their impressive jets high into the Las Vegas sky, the accompanying music loud and in perfect rhythm with the shots of water. I couldn't take my eyes off the show. I'd seen it over a dozen times now, yet every single time seemed to throw up something different. Something new.

I leant in against Adam, clinging onto his waist like the nineteen-year-old girl I'd been when we'd first met, his arm flung across my shoulders, his fingers absentmindedly playing with my hair as he looked up into the sky. I moved my gaze from the fountains to him, the lights from the show illuminating his strong profile. When had my husband got so beautiful? I really had been walking around with blinkers on for the best part of our marriage, and I could have kicked myself for letting that happen. For letting everything that had pulled us apart happen. I still got so angry sometimes, so frustrated that I – that *we'd* just stopped trying, that we hadn't even realised that's what we'd done, until it was too late. That we could have, maybe, saved us sooner. Without all the shit that had had to happen to get us here. But then, maybe… I shook all thoughts of Eddie and fate and all that stuff I still wasn't convinced by, looking back at Adam. He'd always been handsome, I knew that much. Always been someone that had turned heads with his once-smooth, clean-shaven face and those incredible ice-blue eyes that were so rare in dark-haired people. But now, with the beard and the tattoo and that edgier, slightly rougher, look, well – he was just heartbreaking to look at. And he was mine. I smiled a small smile as I wondered whether bondage was something I should seriously consider looking into. I mean, if he spent a lot of time tied up then it was going to be so much harder to lose him again, wasn't it?

'Lana?'

His voice shook me out of my *Fifty Shades* fantasy, although I'd made a mental note to pop into Ann Summers as soon as I was home and check out what kit I needed. That was a lunchtime shopping trip that was going to freak Finn out big time when I came back with *those* carrier bags.

'Something on your mind there?'

I looked at him, blinking a few times, trying desperately to focus on something other than the beer-fuelled bondage nights I was now planning. 'Hmm? Sorry? Did you say something?' Did they have Ann Summers over here in Vegas? What the hell was I saying? They had *anything* you needed over here. All I had to do was ask and someone would no doubt point me in the direction of the local chain and whip stockist. Oh, I really had to stop this now. I could feel that ache between my legs kicking up all over again. Time and place and all that.

'You looked miles away,' Adam went on. 'Is something wrong?'

I smiled at him, kissing him quickly, which did nothing to abate that ache. But what the hell. It wasn't going to go away in a hurry anyway. 'Nothing's wrong. I was just thinking about something, that's all.'

'Thinking about what?'

I moved my mouth closer to his, lowering my voice just enough so he could hear me above the noise going on all around us. 'About you and me and a whole new world of adventure that will rock your hot, hard body, Mr Saunders.'

He smiled, his hand running up and down my back, which really, *really* wasn't helping ease that ache between my legs. The probability of this night out being cut short was looking more and more likely. 'Are you about to drag me down further into your pit of degradation?'

I laughed quietly, my hands clutching his forearms. Such incredibly sexy forearms. Even sexier now they'd been inked. 'Oh, I am gonna drag you so far down you won't ever want to get back out.'

'Promises, promises,' he murmured, kissing me gently. 'So, my bad but incredibly beautiful angel, are you going to put this back on now?' He reached into his pocket, pulling out the black-diamond engagement ring he'd given me just a few weeks ago. 'It's for keeps this time, Lana. Okay?'

My stomach turned a million somersaults as he slipped the ring back onto my finger. I felt like a teenager who'd just been asked out by the best-looking boy in school. The excitement I felt right now, it was impossible to describe. 'For keeps,' I whispered. 'Jesus, Adam… What are you *doing* to me?'

He threw back his head and laughed, a sound I loved. Because I loved *him*. I always had done. Always. It had just taken me all this time to realise that.

'We're gonna be okay, baby. This time. I promise you.'

He rested his hand against my cheek, smiling the most beautiful smile. 'I know.'

I took his hand, pulling it away from my face and turning it around, staring down at the words etched in brand-new, jet-black ink on the underside of his wrist – *in omne tempus* – *forever (until all time)* in Latin. In turn he took my left hand, the exact same words tattooed there on the underside of my own wrist. And never had so few words meant so much, carried so much weight. Never.

'We're going to be just fine, Lana. This time.'

Did I believe in fate now? Yeah. Maybe I was starting to…